SHARE IN TH[E]
OF THE MOTHE[RS] DAY

No holiday is as special as Mother's Day, the occasion when we celebrate the joys of love and family. And these six stories of Regency England share in this happiness as they tell of the romance and drama of young mothers in love and the children who make their lives so very special.

From the tender sight of a newborn babe opening its eyes for the first time to a ragtag band of orphans with mischief on their minds, these stories will bring a smile to your lips and a warmth to your heart. Scraped knees, curious questions, rounded eyes . . . these are the things little children share with their mothers, as well as their affection and love.

So return to a time of dashing heroes and spirited heroines, and share in the Regency romance of a new marriage and passionate love. And let Julie Caille, Georgina Devon, Karla Hocker, Anthea Malcolm, Cynthia Richey, and Olivia Sumner take you to an age when romance was the order of the day and mothers were the order of the heart.

A Memorable Collection of Regency Romances

BY ANTHEA MALCOLM AND VALERIE KING

THE COUNTERFEIT HEART   (3425, $3.95/$4.95)
by Anthea Malcolm

Nicola Crawford was hardly surprised when her cousin's betrothed disappeared on some mysterious quest. Anyone engaged to such an unromantic, but handsome man was bound to run off sooner or later. Nicola could never entrust her heart to such a conventional, but so deucedly handsome man. . . .

THE COURTING OF PHILIPPA   (2714, $3.95/$4.95)
by Anthea Malcolm

Miss Philippa was a very successful author of romantic novels. Thus she was chagrined to be snubbed by the handsome writer Henry Ashton whose own books she admired. And when she learned he considered love stories completely beneath his notice, she vowed to teach him a thing or two about the subject of love. . . .

THE WIDOW'S GAMBIT   (2357, $3.50/$4.50)
by Anthea Malcolm

The eldest of the orphaned Neville sisters needed a chaperone for a London season. So the ever-resourceful Livia added several years to her age, invented a deceased husband, and became the respectable Widow Royce. She was certain she'd never regret abandoning her girlhood until she met dashing Nicholas Warwick. . . .

A DARING WAGER   (2558, $3.95/$4.95)
by Valerie King

Ellie Dearborne's penchant for gaming had finally led her to ruin. It seemed like such a lark, wagering her devious cousin George that she would obtain the snuffboxes of three of society's most dashing peers in one month's time. She could easily succeed, too, were it not for that exasperating Lord Ravenworth. . . .

THE WILLFUL WIDOW   (3323, $3.95/$4.95)
by Valerie King

The lovely young widow, Mrs. Henrietta Harte, was not all inclined to pursue the sort of romantic folly the persistent King Brandish had in mind. She had to concentrate on marrying off her penniless sisters and managing her spendthrift mama. Surely Mr. Brandish could fit in with her plans somehow . . .

A Mother's Heart

JULIE CAILLE   ANTHEA MALCOLM
GEORGINA DEVON   CYNTHIA RICHEY
KARLA HOCKER   OLIVIA SUMNER

ZEBRA BOOKS
KENSINGTON PUBLISHING CORP.

ZEBRA BOOKS

are published by

Kensington Publishing Corp.
475 Park Avenue South
New York, NY 10016

First printing: May, 1992

Printed in the United States of America

CONTENTS

Journey's End

The Marquess of Taunton fixed a critical eye on the sitting room of the house known as Rose Cottage. It was small and shabbily furnished, and if it also held a certain charm, he was in no mood to acknowledge it. Taking in the threadbare carpet and darned curtains with vague depression, he decided there couldn't be much that was rosy about living in such a place.

At the sound of light footsteps, he turned, curious to see what sort of woman Jonathan had married. As he waited, he comforted himself with the knowledge — conveyed to him only days before — that the woman was a vicar's daughter, a member of the local gentry. Yet he braced himself inwardly, knowing the sort of female his brother had usually preferred.

But the girl who stood in the doorway was not at all what he was expecting. Petite and slender, with a face as composed and dignified as a madonna's, she faced him with apparent intrepidity. "Lord Taunton?" she inquired, in a voice that was well-bred and musical.

"Miss—" Repressing the urge to stare, he cleared his throat, unwillingly forcing out the title. "Lady Jonathan Aubrey?"

She walked farther into the room, her luminous gray eyes examining him with equal frankness. "No, I am Miss Canfield. You refer to my sister."

Without conscious intent, the marquess noted the excellence of the lady's proportions. "Perhaps your servant misunderstood. I seek an interview with your sister, Miss Canfield." Seeing her frown, he added, "I have traveled no small distance

7

to meet with Lady Jonathan. If she is from home, might she be summoned? I am prepared to wait as long as necessary."

"Indeed." Miss Canfield's gaze was assessing. "I regret to say that is not possible, my lord. You will have to state your business to me."

Nettled by her tone, he injected coolness into his own. "I have no intention of disclosing my business to anyone other than Lady Jonathan."

"Then you may as well leave," she said, "for my sister is unavailable."

He walked closer and stared down at her. "Am I permitted to ask why?"

For a long instant their gazes locked, but at last her eyes fell, though only to the level of his neckcloth. "Because, Lord Taunton, my sister is dead."

"Dead." He considered her answer, surprised he had not been apprised of that fact. "When?"

"Not recently. It's been over four years." Yet her voice held the faintest tremble of grief.

Recalling the year and month of the marriage, he guessed, "Then she died in childbirth."

"Yes. How did you know?"

"Logic, Miss Canfield. My sources told me there was a daughter. The child, of course, is the reason I am here."

"What do you mean?" she said sharply. "What can you want with Gillie after all this time?"

"Gillie?" His brows rose.

"Gillianna. Caroline named her." Miss Canfield's fingers plucked at the skirt of her vastly unbecoming gown. "Perhaps, Lord Taunton, you had better state exactly what it is that you want." Her politeness had vanished; she was looking at him as though he were a vagrant who had wandered in from the street.

Offended, the marquess abandoned the tactful route he had meant to employ. "Why, the child, of course. What else?"

"No!" Sardonically, he watched the way her eyes widened, as though she had not known all along—which she surely must have, he assured himself complacently. "No, you can't have her! Why now? Where is her father, for pity's sake?"

8

Rather than answering, he allowed his gaze to roam the room, leisurely taking in its impoverished condition. "Tell me," he said brutally, "will any of these chairs support my weight?"

Quick color flooded her face. "Yes, of course. Try that one," she added with a gesture. "It's quite comfortable, really."

Bowing, he waited for her to sit before he did likewise. "So tell me, Miss Canfield, do you have any money to support this establishment?" Once more he cast his eyes around, this time noting a crack in the ceiling.

"That is none of your affair!" she said hotly.

"True, but Gillie is. Assuming she is really my brother's daughter —" He broke off as Miss Canfield sprang to her feet, magnificent despite her lack of height.

"How dare you suggest such a thing! I don't know what sort of women you are accustomed to, Lord Taunton, but my sister was a decent, respectable woman who was faithful to her husband, though a more shiftless ne'er-do-well I have yet to meet! However, that is nothing to the point and —"

"Spare me," he drawled, carefully concealing his detached appreciation for her blazing eyes and heaving bosom. "You need not enumerate my brother's faults, my dear. I'm well acquainted with 'em. You'll forgive me if I say that the women he usually associated with were far from virtuous."

"That doesn't surprise me at all," she muttered.

The marquess's mouth twisted. "Pray note that I am not leaping to my feet in my brother's defense. To put it bluntly, Jonathan was a wastrel with a weakness for women, but he was a satisfactory soldier. Yes, Miss Canfield, I said *was*. Jonathan is dead. I received word of it only last Tuesday. He was killed weeks ago in Spain, during the siege of Badajoz."

She sat down abruptly. "I . . . I'm sorry. How dreadful." Despite her aspersions of a moment before, she looked stricken by the news.

"Yes." He inclined his head. "However, the fact remains that he and your sister were bound in legal wedlock. That means that the product of their marriage is an Aubrey by birth, and as such deserves —"

"The *product!*" she flashed, her head jerking up. "We are

9

speaking of a child, my lord, not a head of cabbage."

"Forgive me," he said dryly. "I shall rephrase. The child of their union is an Aubrey—"

"*And* a Canfield," she struck in.

He reached for his quizzing glass and surveyed her through it. "May I continue?" he asked, very gently.

As he watched her cheeks tint a delicate pink, Anton Richard Charles Aubrey, eighth Marquess of Taunton, experienced an unwanted, almost dizzying surge of desire. He shifted restively. Why should this young woman, with her gold-brown hair and piquant features, evoke such a powerful response from him?

"I beg your pardon," she told him, her straight white teeth firmly clenched. "Pray go on, my lord."

"And as an Aubrey," he resumed, "Gillianna ought certainly to be raised in the ancestral home of her father's family."

"Never," pronounced Miss Canfield with uncompromising flatness. "I am sorry, my lord, but Gillie stays with me."

This time he leveled his quizzing glass with annoyance. "You cannot be serious. What can you give the girl? Look at this place. How the devil are you managing to live?"

"I manage," she shot back. "That is all that need concern you. What right have you or any other member of your family to come here after all this time? Why, after the first two months of her marriage, Caroline never set eyes on her husband again! I doubt he cared enough to take the trouble to find out about her . . . or the child or . . . oh blast. Thank you." Accepting his proffered handkerchief, she dabbed her eyes and blew her nose. "We never had an address," she went on gruffly. "I couldn't even write to tell him when . . . when Caroline . . ."

"Jonathan has been in Spain for most of the last four years," the marquess informed her in a tightly controlled voice. "Fighting with his regiment. Apparently it was not until after he was wounded that he wrote the letter which informed me of his marriage. There was another with it—from a comrade who was there with him . . . at the end."

"Are you saying that he never told his family about Caroline?" she said in astonishment.

10

"That's what I'm saying. Doubtless he had his reasons, but we will never know what they were. His letter requested that I locate and care for his wife. I imagine he would have included his progeny in that request, had he known he possessed any." Anton crossed his long legs. "In case you are wondering, I made certain the marriage was authentic before I came here."

He expected Miss Canfield to take offense, but she surprised him by smiling. "It was," she replied, her eyes soft with the memory. "I was there. Caroline was very much in love."

Again, it happened—that sweep of incomprehensible hunger for this woman with her sad, lovely face. Impatient with himself, he pushed the emotion away, saying, "I'll see the child now."

If he had shouted the words, she could not have looked more startled. "Why? What do you want with her?"

"The girl is my niece," he pointed out. "Surely I've a right to see her." He did not add that he fully intended to remove his niece from her care.

As if deliberating, Miss Canfield touched a finger to her mouth, drawing his attention to the sweet fullness of her lips. "I suppose you do," she said doubtfully. "You won't . . . do anything?"

"You mean tuck her under my arm and dash out the door?" he asked in an ironic tone. "I would do nothing so crude, Miss Canfield. I'm a civilized man." As relief flooded her face, old bitter memories stirred in his chest. In a hard voice, he added, "You may rest assured that when I take the girl, it will be with your full knowledge and consent."

Carissa Canfield hurried upstairs, her heart thumping with apprehension. Even if she had met Lord Taunton under less perturbing circumstances, he still would have made a tremendous impression. She had never met anyone like him in her life; he was so striking, so elegant, so overtly masculine. Had she ever encountered a man so tall and well-built? At once she suppressed the thought, telling herself it was irrelevant. No matter what sort of man he was, the Marquess of Taunton represented a threat to her happiness.

11

As she expected, Gillie was still napping, her favorite doll tucked under her arm, her dark curls spread across the pillow. Gazing down at the little girl, a lump formed in Carissa's throat. She would not let him take her, she thought fiercely. How could she bear to lose this child who was the focus of her whole life, the only family she had?

"Gillie," she said softly. "Wake up, sweetheart."

When Gillie didn't stir, Carissa gathered her up, wrapping the blanket around the thin, bare legs. Lost in sleep, Gillie cuddled into Carissa's warmth, sighing with pleasure when Carissa kissed her gently on the cheek.

When she reentered the sitting room, the marquess was standing with his back to the window. For a moment he was only a silhouette, a shadow looming against the brightness, then he stepped forward and became flesh and blood once more. Carissa stared up at him, hoping to see her own awe at the infinite perfection of this child mirrored in his eyes. Yet his face was still, betraying nothing.

"She looks like Jon," he remarked after a few moments of silent surveillance.

"Yes." Carissa looked down at the bundle in her arms. "But her eyes," she added without thinking, "they're like yours. Blue as a slice of summer sky."

As if on cue, Gillie's lids came up, and she gazed sleepily at their dark-haired visitor. "Who's he, Mama?" she asked.

"She calls you 'Mama'?" The marquess sounded disapproving.

"It's only natural," she defended. "For all intents and purposes I *am* her mother."

"She's too thin."

Carissa bristled. "She has never lacked food, Lord Taunton. Simply because I am not wealthy does not mean I lack the means to provide for my own. I have a small inheritance that is sufficient to provide—"

"She's not your own," he cut in.

"Well, she's certainly not yours," she fired back.

The marquess's pale eyes probed hers, their expression as fathomless as an icy sea. "I mean to take steps," he warned softly, "to see that I am named her legal guardian."

12

As Carissa's arms tightened, Gillie repeated her question more loudly. "Who's he, Mama?"

With effort, Carissa forced herself to speak calmly. "Darling, this is your uncle. You must say 'how do you do.'"

Gillie stared solemnly at the marquess. "What's an uncle?"

"He's your papa's brother, dear. He's come to . . . to meet you."

"You may call me Uncle Anton," the marquess suggested.

Gillie tried to pronounce the difficult syllables, then ducked her head into Carissa's shoulder. And then, to Carissa's dismay, Gillie peeped up and sent her uncle a radiant smile.

Out of courtesy, Carissa was forced to invite him to stay to tea. By this time she was shaking, not outwardly, but on the inside, all the way to the center of her being. Her stomach was a mass of quivers, her heart one solid ache. Over and over, she told herself that there must be a way to convince this man to leave Gillie in her care, but as she watched the marquess's dark, implacable face, she nearly despaired.

At the moment he seemed so enchanted by Gillie it was hard to remember the words he had uttered a half-hour before. His piercing blue gaze pinned on Gillie, he talked and joked and teased as though they had known one another for years. He hid a coin in one hand and let her guess which fist it was in, which had Gillie giggling with high-pitched delight. His effect on the little girl unsettled Carissa, for although Gillie was not a shy child, she didn't normally take to strangers so readily.

As soon as teatime was over, Carissa held out her hand. "Come, Gillie, I'm going to take you to Agnes now. Your uncle and I have things to discuss."

When Gillie was safely bestowed into the care of their only domestic, Carissa returned to the sitting room, squaring her shoulders aggressively. "There," she said, "you see how happy she is? Gillie is deprived of nothing, Lord Taunton. She has food, clothing, love —"

"And what happens to her if something happens to you?"

She blinked. "Nothing is going to happen to me."

"I trust not. But one can never say that for sure, can one?" His gaze was unnervingly direct, his expression as relentless as a storm cloud.

"I have friends, Lord Taunton," she said steadily, "people who care about Gillie and would see she was safe."

"She needs more than that. She needs to be educated. Would they see to that as well?"

"For pity's sake, Gillie is only four—"

"She'll grow older," he countered. "Nothing you can say, Miss Canfield, will persuade me to let this matter stand. My mind is quite made up, so there is no point in coming to cuffs about it."

Carissa walked over to stand before him, her fists planted firmly on her hips. "And so is mine. I don't care what you say or do, Lord Taunton. Gillie and I belong together."

The marquess's dark face was mocking and cynical. "I mean to persuade you otherwise. Would ten thousand suffice, do you think?"

"Ten thousand?" Carissa looked at him blankly.

"Ten thousand pounds. And the right to visit when you please."

Her head spun with a mixture of emotions. "You're offering to *buy* Gillie from me?"

A flicker of impatience crossed the marquess's face. "I'm simply trying to appease you. This place"—his hand swept out, just missing her midriff—"is surely not what you desire for yourself. You're a well-bred woman; you can't hide that from me. With ten thousand pounds you could be independent. You could go where you wished whenever you wished it." His expression grew strangely enigmatic as he added, "You could look where you wished for a husband."

Her temper simmering, Carissa clung desperately to the last remnants of her self-control. "Lord Taunton, you don't understand. No amount of money you could offer would ever induce me to give Gillie up. She is worth more to me than all the wealth in the world."

"I see." Those icy eyes linked with hers. "Then there is only one other solution to our problem, is there not?"

"And what is that?" she asked in trepidation.

14

"I'll have to take you both."

If she'd been older and plainer, he'd have suggested it at the outset, for it was, after all, the obvious solution. But given the fact that she *was* young and pretty, he'd fought against it, anticipating complications and headaches.

By the following day, however, he had managed to convince himself that it was all for the best. True, her presence in his household might give rise to gossip, but once it became known that she was his sister-in-law — or at least the sister of his sister-in-law — that ought to stifle the talk. And since he had never dallied with respectable women, why should anyone accuse him of starting now?

Anton sighed inwardly. The real root of the trouble was his increasing fascination with Miss Canfield's face — or to be more accurate, with every inch of her extremely delectable person. He'd spent torturous hours in the local inn last night, tossing and turning in an effort to dispel her from his mind. But then he'd dreamed of her, so that when they'd met again this morning, he'd found it more difficult than ever to tear his eyes away. And he didn't in the least wish that to be so, particularly since he didn't trust her at all.

No, he didn't trust this little maternal performance of hers. Oh, she did it convincingly — just the right touch of emotion in her voice, exactly the proper amount of anger and indignation at his suggestion that she hand over the child. Mrs. Siddons could not have done it better. And the way she'd held the girl in her arms . . . it had struck a chord deep inside him. All too clearly he remembered being held just so by a stepmother whose only motive had been to demonstrate what a loving, caring woman she was. It had been part of the facade she'd manufactured to control his father, but the veneer had been thin as a crust of bread, a deceit he had seen through as early as the age of five. And if he had not been fooled at that age, how much more discerning must he be now, at the age of one-and-thirty?

His one fleeting memory of his real mother was more tactile than visual, yet he'd kept it close to his heart all these years: a

15

brush of warmth, a soft sweet scent, a sense of complete security and unconditional love. She'd died when he was four, but he'd never forgotten her—though his father had done so easily enough. The thought brought a ripple of bitterness, and his mouth hardened. No one knew better than he that there was no substitute for one's true mother.

"We're ready, my lord."

He turned.

Miss Canfield stood in the doorway, drawing his eyes like a magnet. Despite her outmoded traveling dress and country bonnet, she managed to look so remarkably fetching that for the briefest of instants he was stunned by the strength of his attraction to her. "Where is Gillie?" he said curtly.

"She's bidding goodbye to Agnes. Agnes won't be coming with us. She has a family of her own, here in the village." As he sauntered forward, Miss Canfield quickly retreated into the tiny front foyer where their portmanteaux waited.

"I hope you and Gillie had a large breakfast," he remarked. "I'd like to go as far as Exeter before we stop for nuncheon."

Miss Canfield regarded him militantly. "I think I should warn you that Gillie does not travel well."

Anton studied her face, involuntarily comparing her clear skin with the rouged and painted complexion of his last mistress.

"How is that?" he said neutrally.

"Well, we have never gone any great distance, you understand, but the rocking of a coach makes her queasy."

Before he could answer, Gillie came flying down the hall to hurtle against her aunt's legs with such force that Miss Canfield nearly fell. Later, the marquess would remind himself that he had had no choice but to reach out. Yet he would also remember that his arms had closed around her with far more alacrity than was necessary. While it was happening, however, his mind shut down. All he could do was suck in his breath and savor the sweet feminine feel of her against him. To his discomfiture, it took Gillie's tugging at his coat to make him recall propriety . . . and his own mistrust of the woman in his arms.

"How many horses do you have?" Gillie was demanding.

16

"Shall they go very fast? Is your coach very big?"

Immediately he released Miss Canfield and smiled down at the eager four-year-old. "I suppose to you it will be." Reaching down, he swung Gillie up to his shoulder. "But from up there, I daresay it will look quite small. It's all relative, you see."

While Gillie giggled and knocked off his beaver hat, he cast her aunt a sidelong look and was pleased to see that Miss Canfield was looking extremely flustered. Why it should please him, he did not pause to analyze but carried his niece outside where his elegant coach-and-four stood waiting and ready for their departure. As the coachman loaded their baggage, he settled Gillie onto the squabs, maintaining a flow of nonsense that kept the little girl grinning.

Not long after they started off, Miss Canfield recovered from her bout of silence. "I don't know how far Gillie can go at a stretch," she said quietly, "but I trust you will bear in mind what I said."

He watched the way she pressed her lips together and wondered what she was thinking. "It is unfortunate that my country seat is on the other side of England, but I can do nothing to remedy that. We will simply have to travel slowly to accommodate Gillie." Indeed, his sprawling ancestral home was situated in Kent, far to the east, while Rose Cottage lay in the southernmost tip of Devonshire.

"Thank you. You are very good."

The remark startled him less than the low, vibrant sincerity with which it was uttered. "Am I?" he drawled, arching a brow. "I wonder you should think so. That was not the opinion you held yesterday."

"No," she admitted, "yet I know that Gillie likes you, and she is an excellent judge of character. Children usually are."

"So now you trust me?" he quizzed.

Those beautiful gray eyes surveyed him doubtfully. "Yes, I think so. You were born and bred a gentleman, and I think you are one in spirit as well . . . beneath your prickles," she added with a candidness that took him aback.

"I shall endeavor to live up to your image of me," he said dryly, "but I promise nothing. You elected to come with me of your own free will. No argument I put forth could sway you. I trust you will remember it and not repine at some future date."

Carissa sat uneasily, trying to ignore the physical presence of the first man who had ever made her heart beat faster. Had she made a mistake in agreeing to this scheme? Yet what else could she have done? If she'd crossed him he might have gone away, true, but he would have come back. She was not naive enough to believe he would not do as he'd said — and once he was Gillie's legal guardian there would have been no way for her to fight him.

Of course, he would probably take steps to become Gillie's guardian anyway, though she intended to try to persuade him to make it a joint guardianship. Failing that, perhaps he might allow her to stay on as the child's nanny. Perhaps he might pay her a wage, so she would feel she had a place other than as an unwanted guest. Sneaking a peek at his taciturn countenance, Carissa decided to save the subject for a more propitious moment.

Gillie, meanwhile, was on her knees at the window. "Look!" she cried, pointing to the view inland. Surmounted by a dramatic cloudbank, Dartmoor pressed against the sky; below the moor, the land fell away in colorful layers toward the South Hams and the sea. "Is that not pretty, Mama?"

"Yes, dear, it's wonderful. I shall miss it terribly." As emotion trembled her voice, Carissa could feel the marquess's eyes on her face.

"Have you lived in Devon all your life?" he inquired.

She forced herself to meet his piercing gaze. "Yes, I was raised in a vicarage just outside Salcombe. When my father died, my mother, Caroline, and I moved into Rose Cottage."

"And yet you're prepared to leave it behind."

Carissa's eyes flew to the dark-haired little girl at her side. "Of course," she answered simply. "For Gillie, I would do anything."

As she feared, by the time they reached Totnes, Gillie was looking pale. Carissa held the child on her lap, cradling Gillie's head against her breast. "We'll stop soon," she soothed,

18

sending the marquess a pleading look. "Your uncle under-stands that the motion bothers you."

Though Lord Taunton had not seen fit to inform her, the coachman must have had his instructions, for almost as she spoke the coach rolled into the yard of the first inn they passed. Inside, the marquess bespoke a private parlor, and they were given an opportunity to tidy themselves. After-ward, the landlord brought them cider and scones and clotted cream with treacle on top, of which Gillie partook with relish.

"Before we attempt any more traveling," put forth the mar-quess when they were through, "I think Gillie would benefit from some fresh air."

Since this was precisely what she had been about to suggest, Carissa was pleasantly surprised. Her heart lightened at the change in his lordship's behavior. As they walked out into the sunshine, she could not help musing that, beneath his prickles and arrogance, Gillie's uncle was proving himself a kind and honorable man. Hopefully, yesterday's conduct had been an aberration, based on his misunderstanding of the situation.

Totnes retained the walls of a medieval walled town, and as they turned their steps up the hill toward what was left of Judhel's castle, Gillie skipped along happily. Harmony reigned until at one point, Carissa stooped to kiss the little girl, admonishing her to be careful not to slip. From then on the marquess's expression grew more and more shuttered until at last Carissa determined to take the bull by the horns. "Lord Taunton," she ventured, "is there aught that disturbs you?"

"Yes, as a matter of fact there is." He paused. "You," he added, a hard edge to his voice.

"I?" Slightly affronted, she glanced up at him. "My good-ness, why?"

"You seem so fond of the child."

This fell so far short of an explanation that her brow fur-rowed with perplexity. "Well, of course I'm fond of her. As you must surely realize, I love Gillie as dearly as though she were my own child."

Tall and arrogant, Lord Taunton sauntered at her side, his mouth curling into what was almost a sneer. "Come now, my

19

dear. A little plain speaking will not come amiss."

"Plain speaking?" she said indignantly. "I do not take your meaning."

"Why play games? A pity a career as a play actress is not respectable, else I'd recommend you try your hand at it. She cannot possibly mean that much to you."

"How can you say something so odious?" she gasped. "Have you no heart? Even if you've no children of your own, you had a mother, didn't you?"

His sneer turned to frost. "Certainly I had a mother. I did not crawl out from under a rock."

"Well? Don't you remember what it felt like?" Desperately, she searched for words to make him see. "Gillie is the most precious of creatures to me, as any child is to its mother. As the only mother she has known, I am the mainstay of her existence —"

"Very pretty," he interrupted. "But you are not her mother. In plain English, Miss Canfield, you are pitching it too strong."

"And in equally plain English, Lord Taunton, you are talking like a nodcock. Why else would I be here, if not for Gillie's benefit?"

Drawing to a halt, the marquess's eyes drilled into hers. "One very simple reason comes to mind. Since you refused my offer of ten thousand pounds, you are obviously very ambitious. I can understand that. I can even sympathize. Your life in Rose Cottage has been difficult. You have no husband to care for you . . . I presume?"

"No, I have no husband," she acknowledged, "but —"

"Perhaps you hope to find one," he suggested. "I believe I explained yesterday that mine is a bachelor establishment."

Carissa went pale as his meaning sank in. "You think that I would . . . I cannot believe you would think . . . Lord Taunton you are . . . you are horrible!"

And since he was standing quite near, his face very close to her own, she took full advantage of that fact.

She slapped him as hard as she could.

As she stalked away, Anton quelled both his chagrin and his

20

impulse to dash after her and apologize. Her resentment meant nothing, he argued, for wouldn't his stepmother have behaved just so? The vain and beautiful Anastasia had been a consummate actress, always fussing and cooing over him when his father — or anyone she wished to impress — was around. Anton had hated her insincerity, loathed her false smiles and kisses. In reality, she'd cared less for him than for a curl of dust, but she had adored being hailed as the perfect mother. "Little brat," she'd called him when no one else could hear.

Pushing the memory aside, his attention returned to Gillie, who had run ahead to clamber over the earthworks. As he increased his pace, he saw her trip and fall, but there was nothing for him to do. Miss Canfield was already there, picking Gillie up and brushing her off, consoling with kisses and hugs that looked so sincere he was struck with a pang of doubt.

As he neared the woman and child, he could not help but notice the affecting picture they made. Gillie was an adorable elf, while as for Miss Canfield . . . for a stunning moment she seemed a beautiful blend of everything he had ever desired, a miracle of radiance in the darkness he called his life.

What fatuous idiocy, he taunted himself. Firmly quashing the fancy, he turned his gaze to Gillie, whose cheeks were smudged with dirt and tears. "Here," he said abruptly. "I'll take her."

From Miss Canfield's expression, he might as well have suggested they throw Gillie off a cliff.

"Thank you, but I can manage," she responded in chilling accents.

"Don't be absurd. She must be heavy for you." There, that would give her a face-saving way to yield; she could not possibly wish to hold the grubby, sobbing child against her clean dress.

"On the contrary, my arms are quite accustomed to Gillie's weight. I don't need your help, Lord Taunton."

"As you wish," he said tightly. "But it's a long walk back to the carriage."

As they started down the hill, the marquess did not repeat his offer, even when Miss Canfield found it necessary to shift

21

Gillie from one hip to the other. Instead, he kept a sharp look-out for anything that might cause her to trip, but rather to his annoyance she did indeed manage very nicely without him.

They soon set off once more in the direction of Exeter, but since Gillie did not take her customary afternoon nap, they were forced to continue their travels in short stages. Consequently, they did not reach their destination until nearly six o'clock, at which point Miss Canfield, with the air of a small Amazon prepared to do battle, informed him that Gillie could go no farther that day.

"I agree," he said.

"You do?" She scanned his face disbelievingly.

"Certainly. Did you think I would not?"

"Well." She moistened her lips. "Since you wished to reach Exeter by nuncheon, I assumed that—"

"You assumed I would be an ogre and insist on torturing the child," he cut in. "Well, you are mistaken, Miss Canfield. I am perfectly prepared to do whatever is best for my niece. We shall take rooms at the White Hart for the night."

Almost before his eyes, her hostility thawed. "Thank you, my lord, I—" She paused. "Gillie and I appreciate that."

As before, they took a private parlor, and the marquess bespoke dinner, which arrived in due course. While they ate, Gillie wished to hear more about their destination, so he described his estate, focusing on the nooks and crannies and secret places most likely to intrigue a child. "We won't be near the sea," he explained, "but we'll be near London. Speaking of which, I'll take you up to see Astley's Amphitheatre. You'll like that, and it won't be a long drive like this one."

"Will we take Mama?" the little girl asked.

He glanced at Miss Canfield. "Of course . . . if she wishes to go." After another few seconds he added, very gently, "She is not your real mother, Gillie. You do understand that, don't you?"

"I know." The child's tone was pragmatic. "She's really my Aunt Carissa. My own mama went up to Heaven."

"Carissa," he repeated. His eyes moved to Miss Canfield's face, taking in her indignant expression. "A pretty name," he added.

22

"My dolly's name is pretty, too," Gillie told him. "Her name is Maria." She reached behind her for the doll, which was sharing the chair. "Mama made Maria for me. Would you like to hold her on your lap?"

Mama or Maria? he thought humorlessly.

"If you'll sit there, too," he said aloud.

Full of trust, Gillie slid from her chair. "I like you," she confided as he lifted her up. "Mama says you're going to take care of us now, just like my papa would have done if God hadn't taken him up to Heaven to be with my other mama."

Despite his inherent cynicism, Anton was unaccountably moved by the prosaic little speech. "And I like you," he said honestly. "I'm glad you're coming to live with me." Chancing a glance at Miss Canfield, he surprised a hint of approval curving the corners of her lovely mouth.

Before he could evaluate its cause, Gillie began to squirm. "I can't eat any more. I want to get down."

"But you've scarcely eaten anything," he protested.

"She's tired," Carissa put in. "I think it best that Gillie and I retire for the night, my lord."

Regret jolted through him that the evening was to end so soon, but he rose to his feet, his expression impassive. Carissa stood also, her eyes a trifle brighter than they had been a moment before. "Thank you, Lord Taunton."

"For what, Miss Canfield?"

"For being . . . kind," she responded. "I think that you are —" With a slight frown, she broke off.

"Yes?" the devil inside him prompted.

"I think there is a great deal more to you than meets the eye."

His mouth took on a sardonic slant. "I hardly dare hope that is a compliment."

"Well, it is," she assured him quite seriously.

For a long moment, they looked at each other, then he cleared his throat. "Would it be too much to ask that you and I spend some time together after Gillie is asleep?" As her frown returned, he added, "No, Miss Canfield. That is not what I meant. You have my word that I shall conduct myself like a gentleman."

"You mistake," she said quickly. "That wasn't what I was thinking at all." Then she bit her lip. "But I cannot, my lord. I'm sorry, but Gillie is in a strange place and I'd feel uneasy leaving her alone."

"I understand," he said, after another pause. "Very well, then. I shall bid you good night."

As Carissa prepared Gillie for bed, she recalled the marquess's unkind accusations. Why in the world should he think so poorly of her? His assumptions had infuriated her, yet his kindness toward Gillie had tempered that fury, forcing her to acknowledge that he was not as heartless as he seemed. There had to be some reason for his behavior, she mused. And since they had only just met, it could not possibly have anything to do with her personally. Therefore, his prejudice had to be founded upon some distasteful experience from his past.

As she helped Gillie to brush her teeth, she found herself wishing she could have accepted his invitation. The notion of sitting with him for the evening, perhaps in chairs drawn companionably close before a fire, filled her with a yearning bordering on recklessness. One by one she'd lost her family — first Father, then Mother, and finally, most agonizingly, Caroline. Since then Carissa had spent more evenings than she cared to remember alone by her hearth. And during those long, lonely evenings, she'd imagined that eventually someone would come to bear her company — someone special and wonderful and loving. She had craved companionship, dreamed of strong arms holding her, of lips brushing hers and whispering endearments, yet she had never imagined anyone like the Marquess of Taunton.

His name was Anton. She tried to picture herself calling him that, tried to envision walking into his arms, slipping her own arms around his waist in an easy gesture of familiarity. What would it be like to be loved by him? The fantasy made her heart race. It was too mesmerizing, too beguiling — and probably very dangerous since she knew next to nothing about him. Yet she intuitively trusted him, though she was hard put to explain why.

24

Mulling this over, Carissa tucked the sleepy four-year-old between the sheets, then proceeded to ready herself for bed. As she drew on her nightdress and brushed out her hair, she wondered what Lord Taunton would find to do with himself for the evening. Surely he would not retire so early, she reflected. Ah well. It was better not to think about it.

Lifting the covers, she slid in beside Gillie and gathered the small body close, just as Gillie drew Maria close to her. But as Carissa stared into the darkness, she could not help wishing that there was someone large and solid for her to snuggle up against — someone who would want to draw her close as well.

Downstairs, Anton was restless. Normally, he was perfectly content to spend an evening in his own company, but tonight was proving the exception to the rule. After drinking whiskey for half an hour in solitude, he left the private parlor for the taproom, thinking to claim one of the tables so that the surrounding talk might distract him. However, the instant he sat down, all conversation ceased. The taproom was full of travelers — but they were common folk, not of the aristocracy. Feeling their curious eyes taking in his fine clothes and aristocratic appearance, he ignored them and ordered more whiskey, staring at nothing in particular until, one by one, the voices resumed.

And then, contrary to intent, he stopped listening and thought only of Carissa and the little girl. *Carissa.* He ought to have known her name would be something like that, something silky soft, evocative of passion. The name made him think of stroking her body, loving her, covering her with kisses and with himself . . .

Curse it. He closed his eyes and clenched his teeth. How the devil was he going to manage having her in his household?

It was a question that had been plaguing him all day. Last night it had seemed a simpler matter, but a mere twelve hours in her company had changed all that. Sipping his whiskey, he reflected that he was simply too attracted to her. If he had met her under other circumstances, he would probably have tried to seduce her, but he was not knave enough to take advantage

25

of her current vulnerable position. And yet, *was* she so vulnerable? His suspicious nature could not help but wonder whether she knew perfectly well what she was doing. He did not want that to be so. He prayed it was not so, but over the years he had learned that women were frequently more intelligent and subtle than men ever gave them credit for being. It was not inconceivable that she had planned this from their moment of meeting, nor was it inconceivable that, despite her show of outrage, she had every intention of using her position as Gillie's aunt to force him to make her an honorable offer.

Even if this were true, he was beginning to believe that her affection for Gillie was genuine. Oh, it might be a trifle exaggerated, but surely it was logical that she would bear some honest feeling for her sister's child. After all, they were blood relatives, and blood created a bond of sorts, even if it were not the stronger bond of a mother to a child born of her body. He could accept that.

He frowned slightly. She had referred to Gillie as the most precious of creatures, to herself as the mainstay of Gillie's existence. The phrase was so apt, so perfect, that he wondered if it had been rehearsed. Yet it had not seemed so, he mused.

As raucous laughter split the air, his attention transferred to a trio of burly men who had been drinking heavily for the past hour. If he were any judge of the matter — and he was — he would have said they were utterly castaway. Suddenly, he thought of Carissa.

Had she remembered to lock her door?

Even as concern shot through him, Anton sought to reassure himself. Surely she would have thought of it. Yet she was unused to staying in public inns.

After a few minutes, he knew he had to be sure. Cursing himself for a fool, he mounted the steep, narrow stairs, but when he reached her door, he reached unhesitantly for the knob.

It turned easily.

Anger drew him into the room like an invisible force. Damn the woman. He wanted to drag her from the bed and shake her until her teeth rattled, berate her for her carelessness of both Gillie's safety and her own. Yet instead he stood,

26

still and quiet, allowing his eyes to adjust to the dimness. She had left a single tallow candle burning by the bed, and this, combined with a slit of moonlight, was quite sufficient for him to see.

She was asleep on her side, her legs drawn up, her arm curled around Gillie, who lay tucked into the curve of her body. In a similar pose, the sleeping child clutched her doll to her thin chest, her lips slightly parted, her dark lashes flat against pale alabaster cheeks.

Approaching the bed, Anton fought the wave of emotion that threatened to engulf him. Vague currents of desire washed through him, but this was submerged by something purer and stronger, something infinitely more complex. He gazed down at the sleeping mother and child . . . nay, aunt and niece, he reminded himself.

Not mother and child.

He wanted to touch them both. They had something he didn't, something indefinable that he had always lacked. He wanted to enfold them, to absorb their warmth and softness, to steal some of their contentment for himself.

Sentimental fool, he thought mockingly. *Your brains are turning to mush.*

Yet his fingers went out to brush the brown-gold curls that cascaded like silk over Carissa's pillow. She had exquisite hair, he mused. Exquisite hair, delectable shape, kissable lips, kissable everything. . . . Annoyed by his body's response, his hand moved to her shoulder, gripping it firmly, feeling the supple bones and fine skin through the fabric of her nightdress.

She woke with a frightened start.

"Don't be afraid," he said swiftly. "It's only I, Taunton."

She sat up, the bedclothes falling to her waist. "Only you," she repeated in obvious bemusement. "What . . . do you want?" One slim hand pushed that glorious hair from her eyes.

Anton held himself rigidly, keeping his gaze well away from the tempting outline of her breasts. "Your door was unlocked."

"Was it?" Her brow furrowed; she looked adorably rumpled and confused. "Oh dear, I must have forgotten . . ."

27

"Obviously," he said more brusquely than he'd intended. "For a woman who thinks herself capable of protecting a child, you're certainly damned careless." He used the profanity like a shield, an effort to create distance between them — because right now he desperately needed that distance.

She bit her lip and glanced down at Gillie, a stricken expression on her face. "But surely no one would come in here."

"You don't know that. There are a number of drunken louts down in the taproom at the moment. And when a drunk staggers up to bed, who's to say he'll be able to count doors correctly?"

This time his goading did not bring the expected results, for instead of growing indignant, she said only, "Oh, I . . . see. And so you're angry with me."

"I'm not angry," he said in real exasperation. "Hang it, I'm concerned! You're traveling under my protection, and I mean to make good my responsibility."

Her eyes raised. "That's very sweet of you. And very chivalrous."

Something inside him snapped. "Don't deceive yourself, Carissa. I'm neither good, nor kind, nor sweet, and if you understood the least thing about me, you'd know that. And if you don't pull up that sheet, you're going to discover exactly how unchivalrous I can be."

She took his advice, saying breathlessly, "Keep your voice down if you please. You'll wake Gillie."

His own breathing was on the ragged side. "I'm going to leave now," he said carefully. "As soon as I'm gone, I want you to lock the door."

"Yes, my lord," she whispered.

"My name is Anton." He hadn't meant to say those words, hadn't even known they were in his mind.

"But I really shouldn't . . . call you that."

"Why not?" He stared down at her broodingly, willing himself not to bend down and take advantage of those enticing lips. "I don't intend to stand on ceremony with you, Carissa. You're going to be living in my home, eating my food, sleeping —" He broke off with a muttered oath.

"But it's not proper," she mumbled.

28

Deliberately misunderstanding, he said roughly, "It's a little late for regrets, my dear. You should have accepted my first offer." It was cruel and he knew it. He didn't even know why he said it, except that in some way he knew that by hurting her, he was hurting himself, which was, he thought ruefully, exactly what he deserved.

She flinched just a little, but again her reply surprised him. "I have no regrets. My heart tells me that my decision was the right one." To his vexation, she pushed back the covers and stood up, her expression free of the anxiety she ought to have felt. "You'd better go now. Don't worry. I promise I'll lock the door after you."

Anton's arms hung at his sides, his fingers curled into hard knots. *Count to ten,* he told himself firmly. *One, two, three* . . . He forced himself to walk toward the door, cursing her for following only an arm's length behind. Devil take her, didn't she realize what she was doing to him?

When her fingers grazed his arm, he spun around. "Don't touch me," he snarled.

She snatched back her hand as though he had slapped it. "I . . . I was only going to ask you what time you intended to leave in the morning," she stammered. This time he could see that he had really hurt her feelings.

He glared down at her, feeling like a dastard. "For lord's sake, don't look at me like that. I'm trying to be honorable, damn it." He saw her blink several times as though there were moisture in her eyes. "Oh, Carissa," he groaned as his resolution slipped.

Even as he crushed her against him, Anton fought his yearning to kiss her sweet, trembling mouth. "Oh, God, Carissa, you're so soft, so sweet. But what you've got to understand is that . . . I'm not soft at all." He pulled her hard against his body, his lips brushing her hair. "There, do you feel that? That's why you shouldn't come near me. That's why I didn't want to bring you along. It's why you should lock your door every night, as much from me as from anyone else."

"Oh . . . my," she said weakly.

He let several exquisite seconds pass before he set her firmly away from him. "Go back to bed," he said harshly.

"We'll leave whatever time you and Gillie can be ready. As for this incident . . . let's forget it ever happened, shall we?"

Two days later, Carissa sat staring out the window of the carriage, thankful that Gillie had fallen asleep after nuncheon in Blanford. As long as she napped, they would not have to stop except to change horses; already they were nearly to Salisbury.

With a small sigh, Carissa smoothed a curl from Gillie's brow. Life under the marquess's roof was destined to be even more difficult than she'd at first believed, yet the alternative — separation from Gillie — was not to be contemplated. No matter how stressful, she would and must endure her new life.

In the past forty-eight hours, she and Lord Taunton had discussed a number of topics, none of which had any bearing upon their personal situation. Currently, silence reigned; the sway of the carriage had apparently lulled the marquess into sleep, which gave Carissa an opportunity to look him over without reserve. Examining him closely, she decided he looked a good deal younger and less daunting when asleep. With his black hair and strong, regular features, he was definitely a handsome man, but what drew her to him was the complexity in his nature, the brilliance that occasionally managed to shine through the rust created by . . . by what? What event or person could have made him so cynical? How could he be so kind and considerate one moment and so insufferable the next?

While she was pondering, his eyes opened. "What is it?" he asked.

For a moment she hesitated. "Er, about Gillie," she said, desperately hoping she had caught him in a fair humor.

"What about her?"

His tone was not discouraging, so she plowed bravely onward. "Do you still mean to take steps to be named her legal guardian?"

"Yes, of course I do."

"Do you think . . . you might consider . . . a joint guardianship?"

"With you, you mean?" His expression betrayed nothing. She nodded, holding her breath.

"I might," he answered. "I'd have to think about it."

"Please do." Carissa could barely contain her delight.

The marquess was studying her face, just as she had studied his a moment before. "Do you resemble Lady Jonathan?" he said suddenly.

"Caroline?" Carissa was surprised by the change of subject. "No, she was tall and blond and . . . very beautiful. I am said to—" She halted abruptly.

"Yes?" Though he was still relaxed, his eyes had narrowed.

"I resemble my mother." Carissa looked down.

Lord Taunton straightened his posture. "You're holding something back."

How could he know? she wondered, her heart beating fast. "No, I'm not," she protested.

He startled her by reaching for her hand, pressing his thumb to her pulse point. "You're nervous," he stated. "Why?"

"No, I'm not."

"Under no circumstances do I intend to share Gillie's guardianship with a liar." His voice was unpleasantly soft.

"I'm not a liar."

"Is there something about Gillie that I should know?"

"No, truly. What I've not told you is only a small thing, quite trivial actually."

"Then it should not trouble you to tell me, should it?"

"I don't see why I should tell you anything," she replied with spirit. "Particularly since you have already insulted me in every conceivable way."

"Every conceivable way?" Immediately she knew that she had angered him. "I don't think that's quite true, do you?" When she did not answer, the grip on her wrist tightened.

"It's nothing to do with Gillie," she told him. "It has to do with me."

The marquess's eyes were icy blue slits of suspicion. "What about you, my dear?"

"It is nothing of import," she insisted. "I never even thought of it until you asked me about Caroline. Indeed, it hardly signifies. It is only that Caroline was not my sister."

"Not your sister," he repeated in a hard voice. "Explain."

She pulled her hand away. "Caroline was a distant cousin. My own parents died when I was three, and Caroline's parents took me in and raised me as their own. Caroline and I always *felt* that we were sisters in truth."

"So Gillie is not your niece," he said slowly.

"Not precisely, but as I told you before, Gillie means more to me than my life. I regard her as a daughter, just as Caroline's parents regarded me as—"

"Spare me," he said rudely. "It makes a pretty story, my sweet, but I don't believe in fairy tales."

Carissa's jaw dropped. "Fairy tales?" she uttered. "What the devil are you talking about?"

One black brow cocked at her language. "If you'll think about it, I think you know exactly what I mean."

Suffused with fury, she glared at him, yet as angry as she was, her heart stirred with compassion for this man who did not seem to be able to understand the simplest thing. In a clipped voice, she said, "You know, I feel sorry for you. In some ways you're quite needle-witted, but in others, you're a complete and utter cabbage-head."

"I beg your pardon," he said freezingly.

Carissa nodded. "You heard what I said."

"Your manners, Miss Canfield—"

"Are no worse than your own, Lord Taunton."

They glowered at each other.

"So," Carissa said as evenly as she was able, "because Gillie is not my daughter in the true sense of the word, it is your belief that I am incapable of loving her. Therefore, by deduction, what you are saying is that you, as a mere uncle, are also incapable of caring about her or loving her."

"You're twisting my words."

"Am I?"

"Naturally as her uncle it is my duty to protect and guide her, but"—he hesitated briefly—"I suppose it is quite true that I will never look upon her as a daughter."

"How do you know?" she said bluntly.

For once, he looked taken aback. "Because it is logical—"

"According to whose logic? Yours?"

"Yes, mine!" he snapped. "Mine is the opinion that counts in my house. I am master there, Miss Canfield, and if you mean to reside there as well, you had better learn that."

Before Carissa could retort, she felt Gillie stir.

"Mama? I'm thirsty."

Tears pricked Carissa's eyelids as she gazed down at the dear little face. "We will stop soon," she promised. "Uncle Anton will procure something for you to drink and eat." Ignoring the marquess as completely as if he did not exist, she drew her child onto her lap and hugged her close.

Gillie snuggled against her. "I love you, Mama."

"I love you, too, darling."

"I think I'm going to love Uncle Anton, too."

A single tear rolled down Carissa's cheek. "I'm glad."

She'd called him a cabbage-head. It was a far kinder term than Anton would have applied to himself at that moment. He didn't know whether it was Gillie's artless words or that blasted wet trail down Carissa's cheek that brought it home, but the revelation of his own obtuseness jolted him with the effectiveness of a blow to the jaw. In his own arrogant way, he thought, he'd been as blind and benighted as his father. He'd been worse than a fool; he'd been a swine and a cretin and a. . . . In a burst of self-loathing, he thought of several more colorful expressions that were totally unfit for polite company.

Despising himself, his eyes slid shut, closing out the sight of the two females across from him. To Anton, it was like locking out a light so bright it hurt his eyes with its intensity. Only it wasn't his eyes that were hurting, it was his essence, his heart and his soul.

He'd known them . . . how long? Three days? Nearly four? How could love come so quickly? This couldn't be love he was feeling, not this soon, not this fast. How could he possibly care about them so deeply? He felt as protective of them as if they were his own wife and child—the family he'd never intended to have. And he was overwhelmed by the strength of an emotion he didn't understand.

He hadn't felt anything in years.

33

That was what it amounted to, after all. Oh, to a degree he'd enjoyed the diversions his wealth and position permitted him to pursue. He'd had his discreet liaisons, his so-called friends, his superficial successes. As the years had passed, however, the hypocrisy around him had motivated him to keep himself — his true inner self — apart.

Separate. Aloof.

But he couldn't do that with Carissa and Gillie. He might as well try to hide from the sun in a flat, empty field.

He reopened his eyes and looked at them, dazzled by the sight. So this was what it felt like. Love wasn't about guilt or vanity or the desire to manipulate others. He thought of his stepmother, then of the stream of mistresses who had professed their undying affection for him and him alone. Lily, Faith, Harriet, Nancy . . . he couldn't remember the rest of the names. They all merged together in his mind, a single female body without a face.

He gazed at Carissa, savoring the beauty that was so much more than surface. From now on, he promised himself, he would do better. He would be polite, gallant, attentive, caring. He would show her that he was a reasonable human being, capable of understanding the relationship between her and her child.

Her child. The slip was unconscious, yet it was as though some inner part of him had recognized the truth all along. He had been clinging to a string that was old and frayed, knowing it was about to break.

As it had.

He cleared his throat. "We're almost to Salisbury," he said heartily. "We stop at the Rose and Crown to change horses. In about fifteen minutes, Gillie, you'll have your drink, then we'll take a stroll by the river." His gaze transferred to Carissa. "That'll give her a chance to romp a bit."

"We are obliged to you." Her expression told Anton she was puzzled by his *volte face* — which was hardly surprising, he thought wryly.

Searching for some way to make further amends, he saw Gillie wriggle restlessly. "Would you like to hear a story?" he asked.

34

At once Gillie's head came up, the blue eyes regarding him intently. "Do you know any?" For a four-year-old, she sounded amazingly skeptical.

Anton hesitated, searching his memory for the long-forgotten tales spun by some long-ago governess. "Well, I know the ones about Lady Tizzy."

"Who is Lady Tizzy?" Gillie sat up straighter.

"Lady Tizzy was a rabbit. A very prolific rabbit," he added as an afterthought.

Gillie's head tilted. "What's p'olific?"

He shot Carissa a look, but she was staring out the window, her lips tightly compressed. If he wanted to be forgiven, he obviously had his work cut out.

"It means she had a great many children," he explained. "Er, bunnies, I should say. I believe there were nineteen of them in all."

Gillie regarded him expectantly.

"I don't know what Lord Tizzy was doing," he went on. "Probably gadding about the Continent while his long-suffering wife cared for his offspring. At any rate, Lady Tizzy had some very close friends—"

Carissa's head turned. "Are you quite certain this is a children's story?" she interrupted.

"Absolutely," he replied, adopting an injured air. "Now where was I? Ah yes, Lady Tizzy's three friends. Their names were Lord Squirrel, Sir Henry Hedgehog, and, er, Mrs. Magpie."

Gillie giggled.

"When Lord Squirrel came to visit, he always took Lady Tizzy for a walk in the garden, so they could search the ground for nuts . . ." Inventing as he went, Anton rambled on, allowing himself the luxury of behaving like an uncle . . . or a father. He soon discovered that Gillie was most interested in the nineteen bunnies, so he switched his plot to encompass one particularly naughty young rabbit who had stolen Lord Squirrel's quizzing glass.

"Why did he want it?" Gillie asked.

Anton wiggled his eyebrows. "He wanted to spy on Mrs. Magpie."

Carissa cleared her throat meaningfully.

"Because," he added in a smooth voice, "he thought she was up to no good. He suspected she was a French spy."

When Carissa rolled her eyes, Anton could not repress his smile. And when, to his very great delight, her mouth finally relaxed into a gentle upward curve, it was as though a pure, golden shaft of sunlight had found its way into his heart.

Three hours later, Carissa leaned drowsily against the squabs, content to listen to the marquess's rich voice. Ever since Salisbury, Gillie had been sitting on his lap, enraptured by the never-ending adventures of Lady Tizzy. By now Mrs. Magpie had been exposed as a French agent named Madame Noir and been very properly disposed of. The marquess was now heavily into Lady Tizzy's complicated relationship with the dandified Sir Henry Hedgehog, occasionally working in a witticism that, since it was well over Gillie's head, was obviously directed at Carissa. He had an amazing knack for it, she thought with reluctant admiration.

She sighed, confused by the seeming paradox of the man. One moment he was almost cruel, and the next he was unbearably kind. One moment he was insufferable and infuriating, and the next he was charming and patient — at least with Gillie. Apparently it was only she who antagonized him, she reflected.

"Go on," urged Gillie, tugging the marquess's sleeve. "What happened next, Uncle Anton?"

Carissa watched the way the little girl's eyes remained pinned on her uncle's face — just as her own were prone to do, she thought ruefully. Indeed, the longer she spent in Lord Taunton's company, the more difficult it became to focus her attention on anything else.

It was madness to think that she could live in his household, madness to think that she could remain indifferent to him. She gazed out at the passing scenery, listening as he wove his tale for Gillie. Was she in love with him? No, it was nonsensical, impossible. She barely knew him. Yet something inside her responded to him in the most fundamental way. Like the

36

perfumed air of a summer's eve, his presence filled her with an indescribable ache, a craving for a mysterious something that was almost—but not quite—within reach.

Journeys end in lovers meeting.

The quote entered her head without warning, echoing like a litany to the clop-clop of the horses' hooves. *Journeys end in lovers meeting, lovers meeting, lovers meeting* . . .

Now she knew why she had thrust back those sheets and followed him to the door of the bedchamber. Her own action had nagged at her, for she had never done anything so brazen before. Now she realized that, beneath the surface of her mind, she had wanted him to touch her. Like a common hussy, she had been tempting him to do so, desiring proof of his attraction to her. It had been an ill-bred, disgraceful thing to have done, and she had gotten exactly what she deserved. For now that she'd had a taste of what it was like to be held by him against the hardness of his body like a lover . . . now she knew it was going to be impossible to live with him. But she couldn't bear to leave Gillie!

What in the world was she to do?

They put up for the night in Winchester, where, as usual, Carissa retired early. Yet as soon as Gillie was asleep, she found herself pacing the floor, restless with pent-up energy. On sudden impulse, she summoned a maid, but when the girl arrived, Carissa regarded her with distress.

"What is your name?" she asked gently.

"Betty, miss."

"How old are you, Betty? You look too young to be employed in this place."

Betty looked shocked. "Oh no, miss, I'm near thirteen! I been workin' 'ere since I was seven."

Carissa frowned. The girl was remarkably pretty but didn't look more than nine or ten at the most. "Where is your family?" she inquired.

Betty's thin shoulders rose in a prosaic shrug. "Me ma's dead. I never knew me pa."

"I see." Carissa sighed. "Well, Betty, I was wondering

whether you could help me. I'd like to go down to the private parlor to sit with my, er, brother-in-law for a while, but I don't like leaving my daughter alone. Do you think you could stay here with her?"

Betty cast an eye on the sleeping child. "Glad to, miss, but I dunno whether it'd be allowed. I been workin' in the kitchen, and the work ain't done yet."

The weariness in Betty's voice filled Carissa with determination. "You look like you could use a rest. I'll explain to them if you like. Naturally you will be paid for your services."

"Thank you, miss," said Betty gratefully.

Filled with a sense of purpose, Carissa descended to the parlor. Lord Taunton was standing, looking down at the fire, when she entered; immediately he swung around. "Carissa"—as always, her heart lurched at his use of her name—"what is it? Where's Gillie?"

"Nothing is wrong," she said awkwardly. "I merely . . . came down to join you for a while."

"You left Gillie alone?" he demanded.

"Of course not. One of the maids is with her, a young girl named Betty." Trying to sound composed, Carissa crossed over and sat down. "She is thirteen, though she looks younger, and has been working here since she was seven." She hesitated, then said bravely, "With your permission, I should like to engage her."

"Engage her? To do what?"

"To help with Gillie. I have a feeling she is just what we need. She would be close enough to Gillie's age to enjoy some of her childish pursuits, yet old enough to be given some responsibility in her care. And I think it would be good for Betty as well. She looks as though she hasn't had much childhood."

Taunton was studying her closely. "Very well," he said, his voice calm. "If that is what you wish. I would like to meet the girl, of course."

"Of course," she agreed. "One other thing. Would you be so good as to ask the landlord to excuse Betty from her duties this evening? I do not want her to receive a scold."

To her relief, the marquess attended to this without argument, though when he returned his expression was decidedly

38

wry. "The landlord rates the girl's services high. One evening of her time cost me a whole guinea."

"A guinea?" Carissa was horrified.

He pulled a chair close to hers and sank into it. "Of course the old codger thought I had something else in mind for the girl. That's why it cost so much."

"Something else in mind?" Carissa's eyes widened as comprehension dawned. "He could not have thought that! Why, Betty's only a child. She could not possibly—" She did not complete the sentence.

"Oh, I imagine she could," he said quietly. "And probably has. It's a harsh world, my dear. It's time you faced up to that."

"Well, we must do what we can to make it less harsh," she retorted. Then she bit her lip. "But I'm sorry it cost you so much."

Taunton leaned forward. "The money isn't important, Carissa. I'd pay a hundred times that for an evening in your company."

"We're in each other's company all day," she pointed out, a shade unsteadily.

"But it's not the same, is it? We're not alone during the day." His eyes searched hers. "Tell me, do you . . . despise me very greatly?"

Perplexed, she answered, "No, of course not." Which was the truth.

"Good." Rising, he began to pace. "When I believed you were Gillie's aunt, I thought you could reside in my household without causing gossip. But you're not, and if the truth got out—" He stopped in front of her chair, gazing down at her with a strange expression. "It's not going to work, Carissa."

Shocked, she said numbly, "But have you considered . . . I mean, suppose you hired me as Gillie's governess? I'm willing to earn my keep. No one could say anything then."

"Yes, they could," he said frankly, "and they would, because you're too pretty. And because where women are concerned, my reputation is not unblemished. Like it or not, the tongues will wag."

Carissa pondered this for a moment. "Well, let them," she said defiantly. "I'm sure I don't care."

"Well, I do," he shot back. "I have no intention of causing your ruin."

"Is this another attempt to separate me from Gillie? Am I supposed to abandon her out of some spineless fear for my reputation?" She surged to her feet. "So I am to leave Gillie to spare your conscience, is that it? Well, understand this, my lord. I'd rather lose my reputation than my daughter!"

She expected him to react, to berate her with some furious reply, but instead he came and took her by the hands. "No, I'm not trying to separate you from Gillie. I'm trying to explain to you why we must marry." To her astonishment, he lifted the fingers of her right hand and kissed them, one by one. "Will you, Carissa? Will you marry me?"

Journeys end in lovers meeting.

Her heart beat in slow, unnatural jerks. "You're asking me to marry you because people will gossip?"

"In part, yes, but also because . . . I think we will suit." He gazed down at her with an enigmatic expression.

"Oh." She stared at his sun-browned hand where it covered hers, feeling its warmth and texture. He believed they would suit. What did that mean?

"It would certainly relieve the awkwardness from our situation," he went on, "which would be best for Gillie."

Best for Gillie.

And didn't she always do what was best for Gillie? whispered a voice in her head. It was the perfect solution, so perfect she could only wonder why she hadn't thought of it. Ah, but she *had* thought of it, taunted that same voice. Secretly, fleetingly, it had danced through her mind more than once these past days.

"I suppose you are right," she whispered.

His clasp on her hand tightened. "Then you agree?"

"No." Bemused, Carissa pulled away and stepped back, shakily smoothing her hair. "No, I . . . I'm afraid I cannot answer yes or no. I need time to think."

The marquess favored her with a slight, formal bow. "I understand. Take all the time you need."

* * *

Lord Taunton was gentleman enough not to press her for an answer, but over the course of the next two days Carissa discovered just how personable he could be. It almost seemed as though he had set about to win her affection and approval; certainly he displayed a flattering interest in anything she had to say.

Despite Betty's presence (the girl had been delighted to accept their offer of employment) Carissa found herself responding to his charm, confiding things she had never told anyone, stupid little memories about her early life in the vicarage before they had gone to live in Rose Cottage. She told him about her adoptive parents—the sweet, absent-minded vicar and his warm, clever wife. And she told him about dearest Caroline, who had married and died giving birth to Gillie. Amazingly, Lord Taunton seemed to realize how hard it was for her to talk about Caroline—and how necessary—for he listened quietly, offering her the opportunity to talk without interruption, asking only the most necessary of questions.

While Gillie napped and Betty drowsed, Carissa told him about the first days after Caroline's death, about the midwife and the wet-nurse and, more importantly, about her own sorrow and how it had been tempered by Gillie's survival. The baby who had come into the world, the new link in the eternal chain of life, had given Carissa a sense of direction and purpose. Her soft eyes focused on images from the past as she related how she had raised Caroline's daughter as if she were her own, taught Gillie her letters, stimulated her mind with stories and creative activities. Gillie could even count to twenty in French, she added with pride.

Eventually embarrassed by the fact that she had done all the talking, Carissa tried to urge the marquess to speak of himself.

"There's not much to tell," he said. "I was born and bred at my estate in Kent. I grew up there, attended Eton and Oxford, then traveled a bit after that. My father died when I was twenty-six, so I came home and took over the reins of the estate."

"And your mother?"

"She died when I was four."

"I'm so sorry." She hesitated. "Did your father never re-marry?"

"Yes, almost immediately. He chose a woman of great beauty, charm, and wit." His voice took on a distinct chill.

Carissa studied him. "You didn't care for her?"

"You could say that," he answered shortly.

"Why not?" It was a brazen question, yet she felt it was a crucial one.

He crossed his arms over his broad chest. "Anastasia," he said, "was universally admired for her unswerving devotion to me, her stepchild. She was a model mother, always fussing over me, fondling me as though I were a dog. 'Darling little Anton' she would coo to anyone who would listen to her hypo-critical mewling. Not even my father realized that it was all an act, that she did it only when there was someone around to impress."

Absorbing this, Carissa was silent for a moment. "And Jonathan? He must have been her son."

"Yes. I don't think she cared much for him either." His dark head turned so she saw only his profile. "But she made it clear she resented the fact that it was I, not he, who would inherit."

Suddenly, Carissa longed to reach out to him, to touch him, to comfort. "She sounds an utter fool," she said firmly.

His blue eyes shifted to her face. "Don't worry," he replied. "She won't be living with us. I believe she's on her fourth hus-band now, but I never see her at all. Of course, I've let her know about Jonathan."

Carissa shivered. He spoke as though she had already ac-cepted his proposal — as deep inside she longed to do. Yes, she was willing to acknowledge that the idea of wedding him ap-pealed to her, and not only because she found him devastat-ingly attractive. Her heart was involved with the interior man, the man who made the effort to weave stories for Gillie, the man who had once been a hurt little boy. What a thought-less, wicked woman his stepmother must have been, she thought indignantly.

Again, the urge to love and protect and nurture flowed powerfully within her breast. She yearned to teach this man that all women were not heartless monsters, intent only upon using helpless children as a means to an end, yet there was also a tug of sadness because he had not offered his love. Still, to be fair, how could he? They scarcely knew one another. He had said they would suit, and it might well be true. Was it unreasonable to want more?

For the past two days she had been trying to persuade herself that it was perfectly permissible to accept a proposal from a man she had known less than a week, yet the longer she thought about it, the more uneasy she became. What if they married and love between them never evolved? Worse, what if she fell in love and he did not? What if he went to other women while she waited alone, yearning for him? Would she ever be happy or content? It alarmed her to think what their marriage might be like years down the line when Gillie was no longer there to serve as a link.

It was a chilling prospect.

Late in the afternoon, on the outskirts of Tunbridge Wells, they came upon a fair. Masses of people milled among brightly colored stalls spread out across a flat, grassy field. The soft May breeze carried laughter and music, as well as the smell of pig and oxen roasting on spits. Horses and cows grazed in roped-off areas of pasture, lending their own particular fragrance to the air.

On her knees at the window, Gillie pointed excitedly. "What is that?"

" 'Tis a fair!" Betty blurted the words, then rolled her eyes apprehensively toward the marquess, of whom she was clearly in awe.

"What's a fair?" Gillie pressed her face to the glass.

"Fairs are for merrymaking," Carissa answered, "and for trading, of course. Perhaps we could stop for a while, my lord?"

Anton hesitated, but when Gillie added her plea, he gave in. "Very well, for a short while. I suppose it can do no harm."

Leaving the marquess's beautifully sprung chaise amid a slew of gigs and farm wagons, they strolled toward a crowd comprised largely of the lower orders. "Stay close to me," he

43

warned them. "This sort of entertainment attracts the disreputable as well as the honest."

Indeed, there looked to be a wide variety of folk in attendance. Young and old, farm laborers and maidservants, shepherds, tinkers, potters and peddlers—some of them definitely of Romany heritage—all milled about among a sampling of freaks, tumblers, jugglers, and acrobats. There were stalls selling gingerbread, beer and gin, toys and trinkets, hot loaves, ribbons, pies, and more.

Lured by the mouth-watering aroma, Anton purchased gingerbread for them all, then led the way past a fortune-teller's tent to a sideshow labeled "Toby, the Learned Pig." The sign claimed that Toby could not only spell, read, and cast accounts, he could also name the age of any party present. Anton purchased tickets, reflecting that this harmless entertainment would likely appeal to Gillie and should not take long. If they resumed their journey within the hour, they could still reach Taunton Place that day.

As soon as the show was over, however, it became plain that Carissa had other ideas. "Oh, but we've not seen the tumblers yet," she objected, raising those lovely gray eyes to his face, "and I'm sure Gillie and Betty would enjoy the Punch and Judy show."

Without blinking, he acceded to her wishes. After all, he reminded himself, what was one more night in an inn compared with the need to please the woman he desired to marry?

They lingered on for another hour, pausing here and there so that Carissa could examine the items for sale. At one stall, she purchased a length of blue ribbon for Gillie and another, in red, for Betty. This made him frown, for Carissa had been treating Betty as Gillie's equal since the day she had joined them. This, he felt, was a mistake and might lead the girl to future disappointments.

"Are you certain you wish to do that?" he inquired quietly.

Carissa arched her brows. "Why not? Betty is a child, too. I daresay no one has ever bought her a gift in her life. Look at her face. She is positively radiant."

"True." He shrugged. He did not quite trust Betty but was not going to risk alienating Carissa by voicing an opinion based on his admittedly flawed intuition. On the other hand, he thought grimly, Carissa was undoubtedly an innocent of whom almost anyone might take advantage. He shot a sharp look at Betty. What was it he did not like about the girl? Unable to put his finger on it, Anton resolved to keep an eye on her.

When he felt they had seen everything there was to see, he tried once again to steer them back to the carriage, whereupon Gillie demanded to be taken to see the Learned Pig again.

"You've seen Toby," he pointed out with more patience than he was feeling.

In the manner of a tired child, Gillie started to whine, "But I want to see Toby *again*. Why can't I? I *want* to! Just one more time?"

He was about to refuse when Carissa laid a hand on his arm. "Indeed, what harm will it do?"

"You spoil the child," he said repressively.

"I don't think so. You forget how many hours she has been sitting. You are unused to children, my lord. I don't think you realize how splendidly Gillie has behaved. I think she deserves this reward. You don't have to watch it again," she added. "Betty can take Gillie inside the tent while you and I wait outside." Her eyes twinkled. "That way neither of us will have to endure the Learned Pig a second time."

He opened his mouth to object, then closed it again. What could he say? Betty had done nothing unexceptionable; in the past two days she had done much to assist in Gillie's care, and with efficiency and obedience.

Once more guiding them through the throng, he paid the two girls' admission fee, then looked down in time to witness Carissa's expression. "What is it?" he asked in concern.

"I did not think about it costing money. Perhaps I should have paid . . ." Her voice trailed off in obvious embarrassment.

"Nonsense," he said in surprise. "The money is nothing."

"That's not true. You've spent a great deal on us all. It puts me under a tremendous obligation to you." Her gray eyes were serious.

45

"Rubbish. That's ridiculous, Carissa."

"I beg your pardon," she corrected, "but it does not seem so to me. In fact, I think I should pay you back every penny you spent at this place."

"With interest?" he added dryly. Before she could answer, he drew her away from the tent, away from the eyes and ears of the curious. "Have you given any more thought to my proposal?" he said abruptly.

She lifted her chin, her lovely mouth set with stubbornness. "Yes, but I've not arrived at a decision. Are you suggesting that *that* is how I should repay you?"

"Of course not, but it would make things a great deal simpler," he said frankly. He started to pace, hesitant to demand she make her decision before they reached Taunton Place, but it was as though she read his mind.

"I shall try to give you my answer by tomorrow morning," she said with constraint. "Now, since we've at least fifteen minutes until the show ends, perhaps you could escort me to that stall where Gillie saw the little wooden monkey. I would very much like to purchase it for her birthday."

As they strolled along, her slender hand tucked in the crook of his elbow, the marquess had the leisure to observe (as he had done many times these past days) how the male eyes gravitated toward Carissa. Astonishingly, she seemed unaware of it and certainly did nothing whatever to encourage it. That pleased and humbled him, for not once since they had met had she behaved as he had expected. How had he ever thought to compare her to the heartless Anastasia? Carissa had more genuine heart than any person he had ever known. As he glanced down, possessiveness streaked through him, gripping him in its powerful fist. Carissa was the woman he'd never believed in, the woman he'd never dared to imagine. And he'd not give her up. Yet, he brooded, what would he do if she refused to wed him? How would he survive?

Despite his somber reflections, Anton smiled as he listened to her bargain with the wizened gypsy who had carved the monkey. The man, recognizing them as members of the upper class, was attempting to charge Carissa ten times what the monkey was worth, but Carissa, contrary to his former fear, was not too innocent to recognize it.

"That price is ridiculous," she declared, glaring at the man. "I refuse to be cheated in this way."

Coming to her rescue, Anton reached in his pocket and flipped a half-crown at the swarthy old fellow. "Take it or leave it," he advised.

The gypsy caught the coin and grinned, displaying a gap of missing teeth. He handed the monkey to Carissa, who, as soon as they were away from the stall, said evenly, "You must allow me to repay you for that."

"There's no need," he answered. "I wanted Gillie to have the monkey, and the old codger wasn't going to part with it for less. He could see we could pay."

"That's not the point. Now the gift will not be from me. It will be from you."

He stopped so suddenly, they almost collided. "If you marry me," he countered, "we won't have to worry about it, will we? It will be from both of us."

"And if I don't marry you?"

Her words sent a chill through his entire system. "That would be a mistake," he said.

She looked away, the brim of her bonnet casting its shadow over the top portion of her face. "Would it?" She sounded troubled, unsure.

"Yes." He gazed down at her intently, wishing with all his heart that he could sweep her into his arms and kiss her breath away. Instead he glanced at his pocket watch and said, "We'd better go back."

Dodging revelers of all ages and states of inebriation, they hurried along until they reached the tent of Toby, the Learned Pig. However, the crowd which had been gathered near the entrance had dispersed.

"Where is everyone?" Carissa said blankly.

Anton strode forward, but no one other than the pig and his disgruntled owner occupied the interior of the tent. There was no sign of either Gillie or Betty.

"What happened to the show?" he demanded of the only man still lingering about.

"Pig wouldn't perform. 'Is owner says 'e was tired like. The

47

animal's got feelings, 'e says." The man guffawed.

"Did you see two girls?" Carissa put in. "One is only four, with dark hair, and the other is older, a servant girl of thirteen."

The man scratched his head. "Well, I dunno, ma'am. Can't say as I did."

Further questioning of the man eliciting no information, Anton drew Carissa away from the tent. "Don't worry, we shall find them," he said, scanning the surrounding sea of bucolic country faces.

Carissa looked pale. "This is my fault," she said fearfully. "I should never have suggested we leave them."

"The mistake was in trusting Betty. The girl is irresponsible."

"What do you mean? How can you say that?"

He ignored the query, his mind sifting through various courses of action. "They can't have gone far," he pronounced. "Come on."

Scurrying to keep up with him, she protested, "But would it not make sense for me to go one way, and you another?"

"No. I'll not run the risk of losing you also."

"But I wouldn't—"

"Absolutely not, Carissa."

They moved in a spiral pattern, but there were literally hundreds of people milling about, shifting and laughing, blocking their path, obscuring their vision. While they searched, Anton angrily assessed the situation. Of course, the blame rested solely with him; if he had heeded his instincts, this would never have happened. He had failed in his responsibility toward his brother's child, the only surviving Aubrey on the face of this earth besides himself. And he had left her in the care of an unreliable serving wench. He deserved, Anton thought viciously, to be flogged for his own shocking lack of good judgment.

After almost thirty minutes, Carissa tugged on his arm. "This is useless, my lord. Perhaps we should go back to the point where we started."

"Perhaps," he acknowledged. Yet even as he spoke, something caught his eye. "But wait." He pointed toward the edge

48

of the field, near a straggling hedgerow. "That looks like Betty, does it not?"

Carissa squinted. "It could be. But what in the world would she be doing over there?"

"There's someone with her." Anton did not add that the second person appeared to be male. "We'd better investigate."

As they tramped across the grass, the couple disappeared behind the hedgerow. Anton was now fairly certain it was Betty, and in a deliberate attempt to spare Carissa's sensibilities, he lengthened his stride so that she could no longer keep up. Consequently, he reached the couple first, plunging around the hedge with the thundered words, "What the devil do you think you're doing?"

The couple sprang apart. "Milord!" Betty gasped, cowering with horror.

Betty's companion was most obviously a gypsy. The boy was dark, handsome, and very young, with sparkling brown eyes and gold rings in his ears. He had been kissing Betty, but now his face betrayed nothing except, perhaps, insolence.

Ignoring the gypsy, Anton hauled Betty to her feet. "Where is Gillie? Speak, girl! What have you done with her?"

Betty promptly burst into tears. "Oh, Miss Carissa, don't let 'im 'urt me! The little 'un's all right, truly she is!"

"Where is she?" Thoroughly vexed, he shook Betty again—impatiently but not with the intention to cause pain.

Yet she shrieked as though he had twisted her arm off. "Lor' save me, Miss Carissa! 'E's goin' ter murder me! Oh 'elp, oh 'elp!"

Carissa stepped forward. "Let go of her, for heaven's sake. Can't you see you are making her hysterical?"

Releasing Betty, Anton's temper flared. "If any harm has come to my niece," he said savagely, "she'll wish I *had* murdered her."

Since his threat only caused Betty to recommence wailing and sniveling, Carissa cast him an exasperated look. "Come here, Betty, and stop your crying. No one is going to harm you." She put her arm around Betty's shoulders, murmuring soothing, sympathetic assurances. "Now calm down and tell us where Gillie is. We have been very worried about you both,

49

my dear."

Betty gulped. "She's wi' Mander's ma, over in the fortune-teller's tent. Miss Gillie was tired an' thirsty, so I left 'er there whilst Mander and me . . . well, we *was* goin' ter look fer you, but we got ter . . . talkin'." Her head hung with shame.

"You left my niece with a thieving gypsy!" exploded Anton. His gaze clamped on the gypsy boy, who lifted his chin and glared boldly back.

To Anton's outrage, Carissa took Betty's part. "My lord, please! I must ask you to keep still. Betty obviously felt that Gillie was safe with Mander's mother or she would not have left her."

"Your defense of the girl does you no credit," he snapped. "As far as I am concerned, she has committed the unforgivable. It was her duty to look after my niece, and she failed." His cold gaze transferred to Betty's ashen face. "You will be returning to that inn in Winchester. I do not employ servants who cannot do their duty."

They found Gillie, exactly as Betty had said, sitting on a stool in the fortune-teller's tent, contentedly sipping a glass of warm cider. Her attention was riveted on the dark, swarthy gypsy woman who, for more than the past hour, had been relating tales of caravan life to entertain the four-year-old.

Weak with relief, Carissa hugged Gillie close. "Oh, Gillie, thank God!"

None the worse for her adventure, Gillie burst out, "Oh, Mama, I want to be a gypsy and wear rings in my ears!"

By the time Gillie finished her rambling summary of gypsy life, Carissa had reached the conclusion that Mander's mother, whose name was Dooriya, had taken excellent care of her small guest. As one mother to another, Carissa quietly expressed her gratitude, at the same time wishing Lord Taunton would echo her sentiments. Could he not understand that this was a good woman with maternal instincts as strong as her own?

As Carissa shepherded Gillie toward the door, Dooriya followed. "Let me see your palm."

Carissa held out her hand, and the gypsy woman touched it lightly, her eyes full of secrets.

"Two roads lie before you," Dooriya said slowly, "but only one leads to your true journey's end." Her eyes slid over to the marquess. "Choose wisely," she warned.

"We must go." Lord Taunton's stiff tone radiated disapproval of the proceedings.

They left and were soon back inside the marquess's carriage, but it was now far too late in the day to attempt to reach Taunton Place. Within the hour they stopped in a charming, timber-framed inn called Old Chequers, where Carissa spent a restless night contemplating her future.

Just before sunrise, she awoke with a start. She had been dreaming about Gillie, only Gillie hadn't been little anymore but a grown woman, grandly dressed, dancing at her first ball. And she, Carissa, had been watching from a balcony far above, where no one could see that she was garbed as a servant.

Shoving the hair from her face, Carissa stared into the dark, for the first time questioning her own judgment. Perhaps as Jonathan's brother, Lord Taunton *did* have a prior claim to Gillie. In her insistence that they remain together, Carissa had the uncomfortable suspicion that it had been her own needs she'd been defending, rather than Gillie's. Perhaps Gillie's life really would be better and fuller and more satisfying at his estate than it had been at Rose Cottage. And perhaps, when Gillie had settled into her new life, Carissa ought to return to Rose Cottage. After all, her lease would not be up until the end of the year. In a year, perhaps two, Gillie would have forgotten her completely . . .

That thought was as painful as a vice squeezing her heart. No, she couldn't do it, she told herself quickly. She needn't do it because there was an alternative: marriage with Lord Taunton.

But was it the only alternative? The marquess had indicated that unless she married him she could not remain under his roof, but suppose she found employment within the neighborhood?

At once, memories of her dream returned to flood her with

51

hopelessness. How could she expect Gillie to grow up an aristocratic young lady, knowing the woman she called Mother was employed by one of the families who were her social equals? No, it was unthinkable; she would only jeopardize Gillie's future, perhaps even make her a laughingstock.

So she must either wed the marquess or go back to Rose Cottage. But the notion of returning to Devon filled her with panic, not only because she would be leaving her beloved Gillie behind but because she would be leaving *him*. Then, without warning, she understood why.

Because somewhere along the journey, she had fallen madly, agonizingly, head over heels in love with Anton Aubrey, Marquess of Taunton.

And that only made her decision more difficult, for she was painfully aware that he might never return her love. Moreover, his harsh conduct toward Betty must be considered. Before retiring for the night, Carissa had tried to reason with him, to argue in Betty's defense, but there had been no swaying him. He had been cold and unforgiving. Betty had made a mistake, and Betty would pay—pay by being returned to her former life of hellish servitude. And what did that say about him? cried her heart. That he was unfeeling, even cruel? That he would never overcome his prejudice against women? That they would never deal well together or understand one another? That any hope of marital bliss was hopeless?

These were some of the fears that chased through her head during those early hours. What would it be like to be wed to a man who could mete out punishment in such a way? How could she love a man like that?

Two roads.

Which should she choose?

Self-doubt plagued Anton during that same long, restless night; it was nearly time to arise when it finally occurred to him why he had resisted Carissa's entreaties to retain Betty. Once again, it came back to Anastasia. His stepmother had employed a young serving girl, a sly wench named Effie who had spied and lied for her mistress. Anton had despised the girl nearly as much as his stepmother, but when Effie had caught a fever and died, he'd eventually forgotten her existence. Now he realized that his distaste for Betty stemmed from her strong physical resemblance to Effie. It would also account for his bullheaded refusal to give in to Carissa.

Unfortunately, this final idiocy had probably destroyed any chance he might have had that Carissa would accept his offer of marriage.

For no particular reason, his thoughts drifted back to the incident with the gypsy woman. What had she said to Carissa? Something about only one road leading to her true journey's end. What rubbish. It could mean anything or apply to anyone. Yet for some reason the words haunted him, niggled at the edge of his consciousness. Journey's end, journey's end, journey's end.

Shakespeare, he thought suddenly. *Twelfth Night*.

> *Journeys end in lovers meeting,*
> *Every wise man's son doth know.*

But he, a fool's son, had been the greatest fool of all. His journey had ended the day he'd met Carissa, and he had never realized it until this moment.

She and Gillie had been content in Rose Cottage. He realized that now. If he had not been such an arrogant fool, he would have recognized it from the start. If he had not been such a dolt he would not have spirited them away in such a high-handed fashion. He could as well have given them money and servants. He could have had their cottage enlarged, made more comfortable. Eventually, over time, he might have courted Carissa properly and earned a place in her heart. Instead, he had thought only of himself and what was expedient.

Hoisting himself from the bed, Anton went and studied his bloodshot eyes in the mirror. For once he was glad he had left his valet at home. What Pringle would have said about his appearance, he did not like to contemplate.

As though to echo his inner gloom, the morning's sky loomed gray and cheerless, and the air carried the heavy smell of rain. As they set out, the marquess noticed the tiny frown gathered between Carissa's delicate brows. She looked burnt to the socket, he thought. Was she still distressed about his attitude toward Betty? Or was the prospect of marriage with him so distasteful it made her ill? Or both?

His depression deepened as he turned to Gillie, who, as though sensing Carissa's mood, huddled close to her aunt. Normally Gillie's tongue ran on wheels this time of the morning, but today proved the exception. To his left, Betty shrank into the corner as though to put the greatest possible distance between him and herself.

He felt like a pariah in his own carriage.

About five miles from Taunton Place, it started to pour, yet the coachman urged the horses on since they were close to home. Very soon, the air inside the carriage grew close from the need to keep the windows up. To make matters worse, Gillie started to sob, "I want to go home. I'm tired of riding in a carriage. I liked our house. Why did we have to leave?"

"Shhh," Carissa soothed. She drew Gillie onto her lap, stroking the little girl's back. "Everything will be fine," she repeated, over and over.

Anton thought she sounded unconvinced.

When at last they rolled past the gatekeeper's cottage and up the long, graveled drive leading to the huge ancestral mansion that was his principal seat, Anton braced himself for what must be done.

They were inside. Betty had been sent to the kitchen, while the marquess's housekeeper, at his request, had taken Gillie in hand. Carissa had wished to follow, but his lordship had bidden her to attend him in a nearby saloon. She faced him now with inner trepidation, wondering what he meant to say.

He cleared his throat. "Since last night, I've decided I was wrong about Betty. She will be given a place in this household and the opportunity to prove herself as a member of my domestic staff."

Startled, Carissa opened her mouth to thank him, but he went on, speaking in a grave tone that set her nerves aquiver. "Miss Canfield, I owe you an apology. From the beginning my

54

behavior has been unconscionable. It has been obvious to me for some days that you are a splendid mother to Gillie."

"But—"

He held up a hand. "Please hear me out. I realize that my proposal of marriage is distasteful to you. It was wrong of me to try to use Gillie's needs to pressure you into it. It has been a long journey, and . . . I hope you will stay for some weeks."

Carissa's spirits plummeted. *He wanted her to go*.

"When you are ready, I will make arrangements for the two of you to return to Rose Cottage. I will see that you are amply provided for, that all your wants are met. If it meets with your approval, I will have the cottage enlarged. You will have what servants you require, along with free rein to raise my niece as you see fit. On one condition," he added.

She eyed him in stupefaction. "Which is?"

"That when she reaches the age of eighteen, you will permit that she be brought out into society. I would like her to be given the chance to make a marriage befitting her rank and station."

"You . . . you do not wish her to remain here?" Carissa stammered.

Something stirred in his eyes. "Of course I do," he said, his voice roughening. "I want you both to stay. But it is plain to me that you will never be happy here."

He loves Gillie, Carissa thought wonderingly. *If he did not, he could not have made such an offer.*

"Suppose," she said slowly, "I were to leave Gillie here and return to Rose Cottage?"

He frowned. "Why?"

"Because I think that to deprive Gillie of her birthright is wrong." Carissa's eyes swept the magnificent saloon. "You have stated time and again that I am not her mother. You are quite right; I am not. I am only a cousin, and a distant one at that. I believe you care about Gillie's happiness." A lump grew in her throat. "If I did not, I could not leave her, but as it is . . ." Her eyes squeezed shut with the effort to contain her pain.

Instantly her hands were seized in a strong grip. "I do care about Gillie," she heard him say fiercely, "but you are wrong about the other, just as I was wrong. You've raised and loved Gillie from the time she was a babe. That makes you Gillie's mother. And in my opinion, she could not have had a better one."

Carissa's eyes flew open during this incredible speech. "Anton?" His name left her lips of its own accord.

His grip tightened, drawing her closer. "Oh, Carissa, Carissa, would it be so dreadful to be married to me? Lord knows I have my faults, but if you'd help me, I'd do my best to change, to become the kind of man you'd want as your husband."

Love welled in her breast as she studied his face, saw the stark creases in his brow, the lines at the corners of his mouth where it had so often twisted with pain. "You are precisely the kind of man I want for my husband," she said tenderly. "And if you truly feel that you want me—"

She broke off as he hauled her against his chest, his eyes blazing with light and hope. "Not only do I want you, but I am madly in love with you. My little love, I want you in my life more than I have ever wanted anything! Say you'll marry me! Say it, I beg."

Carissa's lips trembled into a soft smile. "I shall be happy to become your wife, my dear, dear love . . . for I love you too, oh, so very much!"

For a long moment Anton simply gazed down at her, then his mouth lowered, claiming hers with a passion and need that found its echo deep within her soul. In answer, Carissa clung to him, her lips sweetly parted, accepting this new experience with a fearlessness born of love and trust.

When they finally came apart, reluctantly, bemusedly, they discovered Gillie lurking in the doorway.

"Mama?" she said mournfully. "Why are you kissing Uncle Anton?"

Carissa turned and held out her arms to Gillie, who ran into them. "Because I love him," she said, joyously swinging the child high, "and because we are to be married." Her eyes went to Anton, and as though she had spoken aloud, he gathered them both into his embrace.

"He's going to be my papa?" Gillie inquired with interest.

Carissa's eyes glistened with happy tears. "Yes, dear. Just as I have always been your mama."

"Will I have brothers and sisters?" Gillie pursued.

Carissa's future husband grinned. "Well, Gillie," he answered, "not at once, but your mama and I will give the matter some attention."

Gillie smiled and, with childlike impetuosity, leaned over to kiss her uncle's cheek. "Don't forget," she whispered.

"I won't," he promised.

Carissa laughed, her heart overflowing with love. No doubts or worries lingered.

Together, they had chosen the right road.

Midnight Lady

All she wanted from life was the gift of Tony's love, Annabelle Levy-Gower thought as she scowled at the couple dancing. Tony, dressed in fashionable black coat and pantaloons, his almost-white hair falling rakishly over his brow to hide the scar running from his temple to his right eyebrow, held Lady Harriet Treadle in his arms.

Why, Annabelle fumed, couldn't Tony have asked *her* to waltz instead of cavorting around with Harriet Treadle? It was a silly question, and Annabelle knew it. Harriet Treadle was Tony Crenshaw's mistress, and everyone at the Levy-Gower hunt party was privy to the liaison — even Lord Treadle.

Still, Annabelle decided, that was no reason for Tony to completely ignore her. But no, he wasn't ignoring her, he plainly wasn't even aware of her and hadn't been for the last fortnight. No matter how she had tried to engage his attention, Tony had treated her like the child she no longer was. She was twenty-one with three Seasons.

Her jaw firmed. This was the last night of the house party and her last chance to make Tony realize she was a grown woman. She had to make him notice her tonight. She had loved him for so long that her love was an ache that seemed rooted in her heart, reminding her of Tony every minute of every hour of every day of her life.

Pain and impotency shot through Annabelle in equal measures as Tony bent his head and surreptitiously nuzzled the neck of the woman in his arms. A small hurt laugh wrenched from Annabelle. How could she compete with a well-endowed woman like Lady Harriet Treadle? Obviously, she could *not* compete with the buxom matron. Hadn't she been trying?

Lady Treadle giggled at something Tony said, causing her ample bosom to jiggle against the fine lace of his dress shirt. Even at this distance Annabelle could see the smoldering look the older woman turned on him.

Turn away, you ninnyhammer, Annabelle ordered herself. *There's nothing but heartache in watching.*

But she could not. It was pure agony to see Tony making subtle love to his mistress to the strains of a waltz. And as much as she wanted to walk away from the sight and everything Tony had always meant to her, Annabelle could not.

Annabelle wanted to be in Tony's arms. She wanted his mouth a breath away from *her* lips, his hands discreetly kneading *her* waist.

The need to do something, anything, to win Tony's attention lent a martial air to Annabelle's step as she moved to the edge of the dance floor. She knew her next actions would be considered audacious by anyone's standards, but she no longer cared.

Plastering an artificial smile on her face, Annabelle waited impatiently until the musicians finished. Before another song could start, she walked up to the couple and laid a hand on Lady Treadle's shoulder. "Excuse me, but I believe this next dance is mine."

Eyebrows raised, Harriet Treadle turned to look at Annabelle then laughed. "Why, how quaint. This child is cutting in on us, Tony. I thought that was the gentleman's prerogative. But . . ." With one hand she caressed Tony's cheek even as she moved aside for Annabelle to take her place. "Never mind. Have fun, darling," she drawled, her eyelids lowering seductively.

Annabelle felt about as big as a child not yet out of leading strings. "Old biddy," she mumbled under her breath and looked up to see Tony's reaction.

Her hopes of establishing their old rapport faded. He

hadn't even heard her. His attention was riveted on Lady Treadle's voluptuous swaying hips.

Irritation at his preoccupation, combined with the painful knowledge that no matter what she did she wasn't capable of engaging his interest, made Annabelle's voice sharp. "Tony, the music has started."

His gaze finally rested on her, and he chucked her under the chin. "Minx! You're the only young lady of my acquaintance with the gumption to interfere as you did." He put his arm loosely around her waist and swung her into a twirl. "But then, you always were one step ahead of everyone else."

Annabelle wasn't sure his words were a compliment, but she intended to take them as such. They were the closest he'd come in two weeks to saying something besides platitudes to her. Dimpling up at him, she said as archly as she knew how, "And you were always right there with me."

He shook his head at her, making the light from the many-candled chandelier sparkle like diamonds off the white blond of his hair. "Don't come the coquette with me, Belle. You haven't the style for it."

"Unlike your Lady Treadle?" she asked, almost sulking but too full of spirit to sink quite so low.

His eyes narrowed, and he dipped her deeply, causing her to momentarily lose her footing. He smiled at her, but it didn't reach his eyes. "That is not a subject for you to discuss with anyone, let alone me."

She sniffed but turned her face, unable to meet the rebuke in his ice-blue eyes. Why did he have to love Harriet Treadle? Why couldn't he love her?

"Since when did you become so prim and proper?" she asked, unwilling to let the subject die until she had tried everything imaginable to win his interest. "You didn't used to look like you were eating a lemon all the time."

"Ah, Belle," he said on a long sigh. "Ever the confronter, but your stubborn determination to have your own way no longer has the blush of childhood to render it cute. You're no longer the ten-year-old tomboy who followed me around

61

when I was home from Eton. You're a young lady who has already made her curtsy to Polite Society a number of times. And turned down several very eligible *partis* if rumor is to be credited."

Annabelle flushed to the roots of her hair. Wasn't it enough that she had to watch him seducing his mistress at a Levy-Gower house party? Must he lecture her and berate her at the same time? His words would devastate her if she allowed them to. She could not.

"Pardon me," she said, her back stiff with pride to cover the wound he had inflicted. "I did not know my behavior was so distasteful to you."

Just then the music ended. Annabelle twisted from his hold and stalked off the dance floor as regally as one could when furious. No one, and especially not Sir Anthony Crenshaw, was going to realize the blow he had so cruelly dealt her.

Unconsciously, Tony rubbed the scar above his right eye as he watched Belle march off. The girl had grown almost beyond recognition. Gone was the pigtailed urchin who tagged along behind him like a faithful puppy. In her place was a young woman with long, straight black hair rolled and curled into the latest fashion and a body that was both slim and curvaceous. Only her eyes were the same. Large and lustrous, they were the color of light reflecting off polished silver and framed in lashes so thick they seemed to drag her eyelids down.

However, no matter what her outward trappings, she was still the same headstrong hoyden who had haunted his every visit home. He regretted having to speak so sharply to her, but her forward attitude would only get her in trouble if allowed to continue unchecked. As the older brother she didn't have, he felt it was his responsibility to nip her behavior before she landed in brambles she couldn't get herself out of.

"Tony, darling," Harriet cooed, interrupting his thoughts as she trailed one gold-painted fingernail over the knuckles of his hand, " 'tis time to put the chit out of your mind.

She's nothing but a child, and we both know how boring green girls can be."

Tony turned to his mistress who had come up while he was watching Belle's proud back. Harriet was alluring in a full-blown way that never failed to arouse him to a feverish desire that left them both winded and replete. From her chestnut hair and brown eyes to the ripe mounds of her breasts and the flowing roundness of her hips, Harriet was a very satisfying lover. Yet, for just a second, she appeared old and too well-used.

He blinked and looked at her again. She was once more the desirable woman she had always been. He must be tired. Perhaps he should make an early night of it.

"To . . . ny," she purred. Her fingers lightly caressed the lapels of his black coat. "Let's go to the conservatory."

He eyed her, considering, weighing, the pleasure to be gained with her amongst the hot-house plants versus a good night's sleep. For he had no doubt that what they started would have to be finished, and it would tire him for tomorrow's journey. Still. . . . Harriet Treadle was an extremely sensual woman and a very skilled lover.

A sardonic smile curved his lips. "That's an invitation I don't intend to pass up. I'll meet you there in ten minutes."

She gave him a wickedly alluring smile before moving away, her walk a long, slow glide of provocation. Tony found his interest increasing. However, he would make this a short bout and then insist that Harriet return to her husband. She was, after all, only his mistress.

Anger, pain, and despair rolled over Annabelle in waves she couldn't check as she watched the by-play from across the room. At least the two were separating. Still, her chest was so tight with unshed tears that it seemed she couldn't suck enough air into her lungs.

Yet, even now, her eyes blurring the picture of Tony and Lady Treadle together, it was impossible to uproot the love for Tony from her heart. It had been there too long. Eleven years too long.

All the pride and stubborn will that had held Annabelle's

shoulders erect for two weeks fled with this fresh hurt. There wasn't even a chance of her finding Tony alone one last time before he left tomorrow. All her dreams of Tony finally proposing, telling her he loved her, were about to be dashed on the rocks of his affair with Harriet Treadle.

Her hands clenched into fists as she fought for control. The delicate ivory sticks of her fan snapped.

Startled at the sound, Annabelle stared at the shattered accessory. When she lifted her gaze, Tony was disappearing into the conservatory.

Only then did she finally move. Stiffly, as though the blood had drained from her veins, or as though her heart had broken, like her fan.

Propelled forward by that deep core of herself that made Annabelle who she was, she went to the conservatory entrance. Several steps farther and she was in the world of moist, earthy tropical plants. Trees, vines, flowers so fragile that England's frigid winter would remorselessly kill them if they were exposed, surrounded her.

In her fancy, she thought of the plants as herself. If Tony left without her tomorrow, her heart would wilt as quickly as the rose blossoms in the outside garden did in the cold. Somehow, she must find a way to tell him she loved him.

She stopped for the first time that evening and consciously pondered what she was about to do. Tony was in here, somewhere, and she would find him. He already liked her; it was a small step to winning his love. She would make him see that she loved him and that they were meant for each other—had always been meant for each other.

Anxiety and uncertainty fell from her shoulders like a cape discarded. Now that she knew what she must do, there was no doubt in her mind that she would succeed. Her steps considerably lighter, Annabelle proceeded down the pathway made by containers of potted orange trees. Tony was around here someplace.

Voices stopped her.

Harriet Treadle's words dripped honey. "So tiring having Treadle here also. He's such a stick-in-the-mud. Anyone would think our being lovers is unusual."

"Considerate of you to remember your husband," Tony replied.

Tony's voice gave Annabelle pause. Never in all her twenty-one years could she remember hearing him sound so tired, so bored . . . so cynical. It was almost as though he didn't even care about the woman with whom he was trysting.

But that was wrong. Tony wasn't the kind of man to make love to a woman he cared nothing about. She knew Tony better than that. He was the boy who once carried her two miles home after she fell from a tree and broke her arm. He was the same young man who found time when he was home from Eton to make sure that a scrawny little ten-year-old was included in fishing.

"Darling," Lady Treadle's voice was closer now, "you know one doesn't care a fig for one's spouse. Not in our circles."

"There are exceptions," Tony replied.

With a start, Annabelle realized that they were moving closer. Twisting from side to side, she searched for a place to run. If she moved onto the path, they would see her. Then they would know she had overheard them. She felt herself blush to the roots of her hair. She might be a lot of things, many reprehensible, but she wasn't an eavesdropper. At least not when she could help it.

Lady Treadle's words, closer still, drawled, "You must be referring to that dreadfully boring Earl of Hunt and his countess, the horrid Lady Jewel."

Fascinated by a conversation about people her parents had forbidden her to discuss, Annabelle lingered.

Tony said, repressively, "They are in love."

"Bah! They both sowed their wild oats after marriage. They're just unfortunate enough to have fallen in love after the fact. Something, I assure you, I won't do with Treadle."

Annabelle thought that her ears were growing from curiosity, and as much as she wanted to stay and hear more, it was time to leave. Taking a step in the only direction that offered escape, she glanced to the side just in time to see the flaming gauze of Harriet Treadle's dress round the edge of a fern.

Drat! Annabelle scrunched back, wiggling her way into and behind the orange trees that grew several feet taller than she. Careful not to make any more noise than necessary, she positioned herself with her back against the wall that separated the conservatory from the ballroom.

There was nothing else to do unless she wanted to step forward and reveal herself. She couldn't do that. It was one thing to interrupt Tony and his *chère amie* on the dance floor in front of everyone; it was something altogether different to interrupt them during a clandestine meeting.

"So blasé, my dear," Tony said dryly, "but then that's one of your charms."

Lady Treadle didn't answer, but Annabelle could hear the hushed, moist sound of lips meeting lips. Small moans of pleasure wafted to her on the humid warmth of the air.

Tony was kissing his mistress, and Lady Treadle was obviously enjoying it . . . very, very much. Annabelle's throat tightened on the words she wanted to say to stop them. More than anything, she longed to break the couple apart. She couldn't. Neither could she escape. They stood in front of her only exit.

A soft, high-pitched giggle penetrated Annabelle's agony. "Tony, you devil, that tickles."

What was he doing to her? Annabelle's stomach twisted with anxiety. Their lovemaking, so obvious, was more than she could tolerate. Tony was hers. Had always been hers. She had to stop them.

Annabelle took a step forward, resolved to reveal herself and end their interlude.

"Ohhh, Tony," Harriet Treadle moaned. "That feels so good."

Annabelle froze. What was he doing? Was he . . . was he touching Lady Treadle somewhere special? He couldn't be kissing her if she could speak.

Annabelle's courage trickled away. She wasn't up to interrupting them. She stifled the sob rising to her lips at her own weakness. Because she wasn't strong enough to intervene, Tony might very well make love to his mistress as she listened.

"Ahhh, yes, Tony. Lower."

Harriet Treadle's voice was coming in little gasps, and curiosity bade Annabelle look and see just what was so wonderful that a woman with Harriet Treadle's reputation would be so moved. Leaning forward just the teeniest bit, Annabelle moved a leaf.

In the dim light, all she could see was Tony's back. The flash of a diamond on Lady Treadle's finger caught Annabelle's eye, and she noticed how the other woman's hands were threaded through Tony's thick hair. The two seemed to writhe, and Annabelle could stand to look no more.

Pulling back, she squeezed her eyes tightly shut and put her fingers in her ears to block out any sound. And yet . . . and yet, what if they said something she should know? Slowly, half eager, half fearful, Annabelle lowered her arms.

"Tony," Lady Treadle said in a voice as breathless as though she had just finished galloping through an entire hunt, "I want to feel you in me. I'll come to your room. At midnight."

Would he refuse? More than life itself, Annabelle hoped so.

Yet, in spite of her anxiety over Tony's answer, goosebumps peppered Annabelle's flesh at the blunt desire Lady Treadle made no effort to hide. Surely what the pair were doing must be magnificent.

Long minutes went by with no other sound, but Annabelle's imagination ran wild. What was he doing to Lady Treadle? Was it truly as pleasurable as Harriet Treadle's tone intimated?

Another soft, sibilant noise and Tony's husky voice said, "I'll be waiting."

Frozen to the spot, Annabelle felt the heat drain from her body. He had said the words she dreaded, but she felt no surprise. A pain so intense it was like to split her apart ripped through her.

She didn't think she could bear it. It was bad enough *knowing* about them, but being privy to specifics was worse than anything she might have imagined. And in her own home. His last night under her roof, and Tony was going to make love to his mistress instead of listening to her own protestations of love.

No, it was more than she could endure.

Squeezing her eyes shut, as though to deny the coupling she knew they were anticipating, Annabelle forced herself to take slow, deep breaths. There had to be a way to keep Tony from consummating what he had begun.

An idea began to form. An idea as outrageous and desperate as any she had ever concocted. An idea that her very future hinged upon.

The grandfather clock chimed midnight, its tinkling bells incongruent with its massive height, as Annabelle watched her cousin claim Lady Treadle for another dance. David had balked at making a cake of himself over an older woman, but when Annabelle offered to let him ride her Arabian-bred stallion he had quickly agreed with no further questions asked.

Satisfaction curved Annabelle's lips into a grim smile. Her plan just might work. All she needed to do was reach Tony's room before Harriet Treadle could free herself from David's importuning.

Spinning around on the balls of her feet, Annabelle sped to the servants' stairs. Skirts lifted high, she took the steps two at a time until she reached the floor where Tony's room was. Winded, she pulled in large gulps of air as she leaned against the wall to give herself time to regain her momentum.

So far so good. No servants were around yet, and the guests were still below dancing and talking. Soon a supper would be served, giving her even more time before anyone came upstairs.

A quick glance showed the wall sconces not lit. Good.

With luck, Tony would have his candle out when she entered. It wasn't part of her plan for Tony to know who his visitor was until after the fact.

Desperate times called for desperate measures. And she was embarking on the most desperate act any woman could envision.

Not knocking, Annabelle cracked open the oak door to Tony's room. Relief flooded her. No light showed. He didn't have a candle lit. And there was no fire going. She should have expected the fire to be out: Tony had always been the one who was too hot.

Slowly, careful not to make a sound, she entered. The room was pitch black. For long seconds she stood still, her back against the solid security of the door, and allowed her eyes to adjust.

In the center of the room stood a large, completely curtained bed. Things couldn't have worked better. This room had a bed to match the architecture of the house: both dated from Elizabethan times. With Tony in the bed and the curtains drawn, there wouldn't be any chance of a faint moonbeam or of eyes adjusted to the dark betraying her identity until it was too late.

Still, even though everything was going smoothly, Annabelle could not still the racing of her pulse or the pounding of her heart. She was risking everything on one act. Her whole life depended on Tony's response to having her in his bed. He had to love her after making love to her. He had to.

For the second time that night, her courage almost failed her. Her hands curled into balls, and she squeezed until her nails bit painfully into her palms. Coming to his room like this! She belonged in Bedlam.

"Harriet," Tony's sleep-roughened voice intruded on Annabelle's wavering thoughts, "is that you?"

Annabelle stood riveted. She couldn't have budged if her life depended on it, and in a very real sense, it did.

"Harriet," Tony said, impatience creeping into his tone, "come to bed. I haven't all night to play your little games. I have to leave early in the morning."

The irritation Annabelle detected in his voice gave her hope. Was he becoming unenamored of Lady Treadle? Could she convince him tonight that he no longer needed his mistress? Did she have a chance?

She swallowed the lump in her throat and turned the key in the lock. She would never know if she could lure Tony away if she left now. If she didn't go ahead as planned, he would ride out of her life again—perhaps for good.

"Harriet, my patience wears thin."

The dry indifference in his voice decided Annabelle. She would stay. And she would love him as no other woman ever had.

Slowly, as though totally immersed in water, Annabelle made her way to the side of the bed. Instead of the calm she always felt after making the decision to attempt a difficult jump, she found herself shaking. What lay ahead of her was totally beyond the realm of her experience. Only luck and love would see her through it.

She stopped at the edge, unable to go any farther. Her breathing was fast and shallow. Perspiration beaded her forehead. She stood there and grappled with her own fears.

"Harriet," Tony's voice came from behind the curtains a split second before Annabelle heard the rustling of heavy fabric and felt Tony's hand close around her arm. "Don't make me get out and fetch you. It's damnably cold in here and I haven't a stitch on. As I'm sure you're aware." .

Haven't a stitch on. Annabelle was immobilized. He was . . . naked. A moan of dread escaped her trembling lips.

"Come along, Harriet. You needn't play the eager lover with me. I know it takes more than the thought of me unclothed to heat your blood to a moaning fever." He chuckled, low and deep in his chest. "That comes much closer to your own ultimate pleasure, and well I know it."

The meaning of his words burned its way through Annabelle, turning to ash the fear and nervousness that held her in their grip. Tony, her Tony, was so intimate with another woman that he knew the exact moment their coupling could make the woman moan.

She would show him. When she finished with him, he wouldn't even remember Lady Treadle's name, let alone the moment during lovemaking when the woman moaned.

Quickly, before she lost her nerve, she pulled her arm from his grasp then slipped off her shoes and undid the buttons of her gown that she could reach. Wriggling out of the narrow opening of her dress, she stood in the dark, clothed only in her chemise, stockings, and corset. Tony would have to undo her corset before she could take off her chemise.

Behind Annabelle, the doorknob turned. Then someone knocked softly. Annabelle's stomach lodged in her throat. It was Lady Treadle!

"Shhh!" Annabelle hissed.

"Afraid it's your husband, sweet?" Tony whispered cynically.

Annabelle's heart bled at the tone of Tony's voice. He sounded disillusioned and uncaring. He wasn't the Tony she remembered. Somehow, some way, she would restore his faith to him. And tonight was the beginning.

Her decision made, she threw restraint to the wind. Shrugging, she crawled through the open curtain and into Tony's bed. She would enjoy his lovemaking and revel in the delight of having him completely to herself. Tomorrow, she would worry about the consequences.

Tremors rode her flesh as she slipped between the covers Tony held open for her. The fine cotton sheets were cool on her heated skin. Tentatively, she turned on her side, brushing Tony in the process. He was hot enough to burn her, and Annabelle bolted backward.

His hand descended on her hip, branding her with fire and making her buck. Shivers ran down Annabelle's spine and curled her toes.

"Easy," he soothed, his voice deep and soft as plush velvet.

The breath caught in Annabelle's throat as Tony ran his palm down her hip to her thigh, pleating the fine lawn of her chemise. His fingers dug gently into her sensitive curves and massaged her tensed muscles.

His voice laced with surprise, he said, "You're not

71

Harriet."

Then he chuckled deep in his chest, setting the bed to jiggling and rocking Annabelle toward him. Her breasts, thrust upwards by her corset and barely covered by her chemise, grazed his torso. Lightning flashed along Annabelle's nerves, tightening the already taut points of her nipples.

"Oh!" she gasped, surprised by the intense enjoyment that such an ephemeral touch incited.

Tony's chuckle deepened. "You liked that."

He moved his hand until his fingers closed around one tight nipple, then he began to tease it until, if possible, Annabelle felt her flesh harden more. Her hands, where they rested on his shoulders, fluttered.

His voice rough yet rich like clotted cream, Tony murmured, "You definitely aren't Harriet. You're much slimmer and your skin is silkier. But who are you?"

Unease stilled Annabelle's trembling. What would she do if he insisted on knowing? She hadn't thought of that.

"Not going to tell me?"

His words were muffled against her flesh. Tony's mouth, wet and hot, closed on her breast. He took her inside him and sucked. Shock made Annabelle rigid as sensations darted from his moist tongue and sharp teeth to her tensed belly. She told herself it was all right for him to do this to her. This was Tony. And it felt so good.

"Will you tell me now?"

Wildly, she shook her head.

"I can't see you," he said, but he was amused.

She always knew when Tony found something humorous. It showed by a little catch in his words.

"How about now?" he asked, bringing his mouth down on hers and one hand down on her breast.

His lips moved leisurely over hers, his tongue enticing her with flicking motions identical to the action of his fingers on her aching breast. Then, before she realized what was happening, his mouth slanted down and his tongue darted through her lips, plunging deeply into her. His hand tightened on her breast, squeezing and kneading in rhythm

72

to his tongue's questing.

The world spun out of focus for Annabelle.

Somehow, she didn't know quite how, she found herself divested of clothing. Vaguely she thought she might have helped him, remembering his hot mouth roving over her shoulders as his nimble fingers undid the strings that laced her corset. It didn't matter.

They lay side by side, their bodies pressed curve to hollow, his leg thrown over hers, pinning her to the mattress. He kissed her neck, moving lower until his mouth found her eager breasts.

"You smell of roses," he murmured against her flesh as his fingers pressed lightly into her ribs, moving downward.

The words meant nothing to Annabelle as her concentration centered on Tony and what he was doing to her body. Impressions as new as womanhood flowed over her, making her languorous and yet . . . restless. She began to writhe under his ministrations. The urge to speak, to ask him to help her became overwhelming. Just as she began to ask, his mouth covered hers again.

She sank into the bed, pulling him to her.

"Greedy little vixen," he murmured against her lips. "Is this what you want?"

Even before he finished the question, his hand was moving down her stomach, sending tendrils of fire spreading out to her limbs. Annabelle sucked his tongue into her mouth. It was the only thing that kept her from screaming when his fingers entered her.

Cold chills alternated with fiery need as she realized just what he was doing to her. He dipped deeper, moving with slick intensity, and her hips began to respond.

A small part of her mind rebelled at so invasive a touch, but this was Tony. Tony, whom she'd loved since he took her to see tadpoles in the lake. This was Tony making her feel like a wanton woman, hot for his caress.

Then just as she was relaxing and beginning to enjoy what his fingers were doing, her legs were spread and he was between them, his hand holding her open. One long surge and pain flashed through Annabelle. He'd hurt her.

"Oh, my God!" Tony ejaculated. "You're a virgin."

She almost cried. The pleasure was gone, leaving only the memory of tingling excitement in its wake. She felt invaded. But again, she reminded herself that this was Tony. Her beloved Tony. The only man she would ever love, the only man she would ever allow this intimacy.

He began to withdraw, saying, "I can't continue this . . . even. . . ." He inched out. "You feel so right. I can't." He withdrew a little more.

Desperation motivated Annabelle. She couldn't let him stop now. It wasn't enough. Her hands went to his hips and she pulled him back.

"Damn!" He sunk deeper and his breathing became labored as he held his body stiffly. "I shouldn't."

She exerted more pressure with her hands.

He gasped and chuckled, a deep ragged sound. "I was brought up never to deny a lady." Then his voice barely recognizable through his passion, he said softly, "It will never hurt again. I promise you." He surged forward.

She nodded, unable to speak even had she wanted to. There was nothing else she could do. She was impaled by him, and there was no going back. Instead, she sucked in air and began to move her hips.

"Ahh," he groaned, burying his head in her neck, his tongue and mouth seeking her skin. "You feel so good."

He filled her to exploding. Slowly the pain receded, and something else began to replace it. Long, slow undulations that stoked her inner fires raised Annabelle's pleasure. His lips moved from her neck to her mouth, and his tongue began to emulate his hips. His fingers tangled in her hair.

"Your hair is as silky as the rest of you," he moaned against her mouth. "Spread your legs wider, sweet. Take all of me in. I want you to enjoy this as much as I am."

She did as he bid her. And she thought her world would shatter with the intensity of her reaction.

Slowly, so exquisitely slowly, the tenseness that had settled in her womb began to expand outward. Tony's movements quickened. Annabelle's fingers clenched his shoulders, her nails biting into his muscles as he increased the friction until she could contain herself no longer.

Her body contracted and then shuddered in time to his thrusting hips. With a soft, sibilant cry, she felt herself explode into myriad little parts.

"Ahh, yes!" he shouted at last. Then lightly, like the wings of a butterfly, he kissed her lips. "Thank you."

Only later, as Tony lay sleeping beside her, one of his arms flung possessively across her stomach, did Annabelle allow reality to impinge on the magic they had shared for such a brief moment in time. Tony had made love to her, changed how she would forever view the world. But it had meant nothing to him.

Even knowing that he took her virginity had not kept him from falling asleep immediately after without another word. Without even asking who she was. He didn't care.

Forgetting the mystery of her identity in the pleasure of her body, he had made love to her. He would have made love to any woman who entered his bed — and thought nothing of it.

She had given him her innocence, but more importantly, she had given him her heart. Tony took both and never gave either a second thought. She could never tell him who she was now. He would hate her for coming to his bed and trapping him in marriage. She had been a fool to think she could make him love her by giving herself to him. That only happened in a young girl's dreams.

Tears began to seep from between her tightly shut lids. She had risked everything and lost.

May, 1817 — eight months later.

Dressed in an emerald green satin dressing gown, Tony Crenshaw flipped through his mail. With the Season in full swing, his collection of invitations grew daily. Near the middle of the pile, he came across a cream-colored envelope

75

with the scent of gardenias wafting from it.

This was the third *billet-doux* he'd received from Harriet Treadle in as many days. The lady did not take kindly to having the gentleman end the affair. As he'd done with the other notes, he threw this one in the grate where it would be burned when the fire was laid later in the day.

His mouth curved cynically at Harriet's persistence, and he absent-mindedly fingered the scar above his right eyebrow, rubbing the ridged skin with practiced ease. Ever since his night with the unknown woman at the Levy-Gowers', he'd been unable to enjoy Harriet's jaded expertise as he once had—or the allures of the experienced women who made it obvious that they would welcome his attentions.

The girl's innocence, so completely given, had ruined him for mere dalliance. Many times in the intervening months he'd been tempted to try and discover his mystery lover's identity, but in the end he respected her privacy. If she'd wanted him to know, she wouldn't have sneaked out like a thief in the middle of the night.

Perhaps she'd only been curious about his abilities as a lover. It often seemed to him that many women of the *ton* were more interested in him now than they were before Waterloo and his injuries: a scar over one eye and a left arm damaged enough that there were times, when he was particularly tired, that the arm wouldn't respond. But this wasn't a line of reflection he wanted to pursue. He refused to wallow in self-pity over physical ailments he couldn't change.

Taking a drink of the strong, black coffee sitting on the mahogany desk by his mail, he relaxed in the warm sunshine coming from the large French windows behind him. It was a beautiful spring day, and life was good to him.

With renewed vigor, he returned his attention to answering invitations. He enjoyed the social interaction of replying himself, even though his secretary often deplored this usurping of his job.

At the very bottom of the stack was a fine blue vellum envelope. The writing was definitely feminine and none that

Tony recognized. Raising the paper to his nose, he couldn't detect any scent. His curiosity piqued, he ripped the seal and immediately looked at the signature: Elizabeth Levy-Gower. Why was Belle's mother writing him?

The contents were brief and succinct: Belle was pregnant and wouldn't tell anyone who the father was. And Elizabeth wanted him to visit and try to get the father's name out of Belle.

"Bloody hell!" Tony slammed the letter onto the desk and surged up to pace the library floor. He'd known Belle would get herself into trouble sooner or later, but *never* had he imagined *this*.

He picked the letter back up and reread it. There was no mistaking the request.

"Bloody hell!" he reiterated as his pulse pounded in his temples.

He crushed the paper and threw it into the fire, then thought better of it and retrieved it. He wasn't taking any chance of a servant's prying eye seeing this. Deliberately, he smoothed the sheet out.

Belle was in trouble and very likely didn't even realize it. Only two choices were before her — ostracization from society for the rest of her life or marriage to the father of her child, and even then it would be a long time before she would be invited into polite company again.

Rubbing wearily at his scar with one hand, Tony tucked the crumpled sheet into the pocket of his dressing gown with the other hand and headed for his bedchamber. With luck, traveling alone on horseback, he would be at the Levy-Gowers' before three days were up.

His third night on the road, rain coming down in torrents that turned the roads into nearly impassable morasses, Tony ate his mutton pie in the common room of a country inn and cursed Belle's impetuosity. After exhausting every name imaginable for Belle, he started on her parents because they had raised her to flout convention.

He was still venting his spleen late on the fourth day when he turned into the gravel-paved drive that led to Winterwood, the Levy-Gowers' estate. Pulling up on the reins, Tony leapt from the lathered horse's back, threw the leads to a young boy hurrying from the stables, and ran up the steps to the front door.

Several quick raps on the massive oak door with no answer left Tony even less charitable than he already felt after four days on the road with minimal sleep and no valet. To make matters worse, his arm was a mass of knotted muscles that hurt more than usual.

Not waiting any longer, he turned the brass handle and stomped into the black-and-white tiled foyer. Throwing his riding crop onto an Egyptian side table, Tony glimpsed the butler speeding his way.

"Sir! Sir Anthony," the poor man blurted, coming to a skidding halt several feet from Tony's mud-encrusted boots. "I beg your pardon. I was in the kitchen. If you'll come this way, I'll announce you to Mrs. Levy-Gower."

Tony, his mouth a straight line and his jaw clenched so tightly he thought it would become permanently frozen in place, glared at the servant. "I didn't come here to see *Mrs.* Levy-Gower, Lewis. And I know the way."

With that, Tony bolted up the stairs. Behind him, Lewis sputtered but didn't attempt to follow. Almost Tony could find it in himself to feel sorry for the man, but the anger that had started as a simmer was now a full-blown inferno. There was no room left in him to feel anything else.

Turning right at the top of the stairs, Tony made straight for the second door. Without knocking, he banged the door open so that it hit the wall. The impact reverberated through the room.

Without asking permission, Tony strode into the center of the room before halting with his fists on his hips. The surprise on Belle's face was a small form of repayment for all his inconvenience. His satisfaction, however, was short-lived when he found himself nonplused by the picture she presented.

Belle had never looked so beautiful as she did now. Her skin was a translucent ivory, and her midnight tresses were pulled back in a soft chignon that allowed wisps to curve caressingly around her long neck. Even increasing, she was a desirable woman. She hadn't gained extra weight, only roundness that enhanced the aura of femininity surrounding her.

The scent of roses surrounded Tony, and he found himself inhaling deeply of the fragrance even as he tried to still his unreasonable response to Belle. He was here to find out who the father was and to arrange for Belle to marry that man.

When the door banged open, Annabelle's hands instinctively went to the swell of her stomach, and her concentration switched from the book in her lap to the man standing in front of her.

"Tony!"

She stared in disbelief at him, and hope, never long absent from her heart, blossomed like a rose where before there had been barren winter. Was he here because he loved her? Was there a chance for them?

His hair was disheveled, his clothes were disreputable, and his boots weren't fit for polite company. He wasn't the usually fastidious Tony. Then she noticed his scar. It stood out in stark white contrast to the tan of his skin. And his eyes, while stormy with an emotion she couldn't read, were creased with pain. Her heart went out to him. She could wait till later for him to tell her his reason for arriving like this.

"Tony," she rose and took a step toward him, her hand out to smooth his hair back, "your arm must be paining you. Why don't you let me show you to a room where you can rest."

"I am not an invalid."

The words were clipped, and his face was void of emotion, but the bleak, bitter look in his eyes told her how badly she'd hurt him. His pain pierced her as surely as a thorn. Choosing her words carefully, her eyes calmly meeting his, she said, "I never thought you were. But it is obvious that you rode instead of taking a carriage, and anyone

79

would be exhausted after such."

Drawing himself up stiffly, he said, "I didn't come here to discuss myself. I came because rumor has made its way to Town."

It was nothing she hadn't expected. In fact, she had anticipated its happening much quicker than this, but even expecting it did nothing to keep her from feeling as though impending doom now hung over her.

To combat the dread lurking just over her shoulder, she forced her voice to lightness and quipped, "You mean you didn't rush all the way here to see how I am doing?"

Even as she said the words, she realized that Tony was more angry than she had ever seen him before; his eyes sparked with it and his body vibrated with it. Had she known him less well, she might have been afraid. As it was, she felt only loss at the knowledge that he was not here because he loved her.

He took a step farther into the room and roared at her. "Damnation, Belle! Your condition is nothing to joke about. Name the bastard and I'll see that he pays for this if I have to hold a gun to him in the church."

Annabelle felt the blood drain from her face as though he had slapped her. For eight long months she'd thought only of Tony. Her dreams had been fevered panoplies of their one night together, and her days had played agonizing creations through her brain of him with Harriet Treadle. Now he was back, but only because he intended to see her married to another man.

Drawing herself up as straight as a young sapling, but feeling unwieldy because of her unaccustomed girth, she said haughtily, "There is no need for your heroics."

His eyes were the color of a frozen lake, and she could see the bunching of muscle under the snug fit of his blue superfine coat. His scar was a slash that throbbed with his anger. Never had she seen him this livid. Never. He leaned forward until she could see the golden hairs of his unshaven beard distinctly against the sun-bronzed color of his face.

Carefully enunciating every word, he said, "Someone

must do something to extricate you from this disaster you have gotten yourself into. And your mother wants me to be that person. She can't make you see reason, so she wants me to try and convince you to tell us the man's name."

Anger flared in Annabelle. How dare her mother ask Tony of all people for help.

She laughed, a trill which glided quickly up the scale and ended on a hiccup. Her anger died with a whimper.

Really, it was all too absurd. Her mother asked the father of her child to come and coerce out of her the name of the man who got her in the family way. It was a farce. It should be humorous, but moisture blurred her vision so that she had to blink several times.

Finally, she managed: "I didn't tell her to ask you, Tony. You've wasted your time. I have no intentions of telling you who the father is because I do not intend to marry him." *Because you do not love me.*

"Bloody hell, Belle!" He twisted on the heel of his boot, his right hand rubbing at the scar on his face. Then before she could speak, he faced her again. "Is the man so vile that you cannot abide him? I doubt that, otherwise you wouldn't have committed the act that got you this way. I insist that you tell me his name. I'll make him marry you."

All she had to do was say his name, tell Tony she was the woman who shared his bed that last night. Just one word: *you,* and he would be hers for eternity. Everything she had ever wanted in life was being offered to her by the only man who could provide it, and she couldn't say a word. She couldn't speak because he did not love her. She shut her eyes to block out the sight of him.

"Belle." He grabbed her shoulders and shook her. "This is not a game of charades. This is the rest of your life."

Sadly, she looked at him, her hair coming down from its pins to lie in waves against her neck. He pushed the heavy tendrils back, a look almost of tenderness momentarily softening the harsh line of his mouth. She trembled at his touch.

Denying her reaction, knowing it for the weakness it was,

81

she said wearily, "I never thought this wasn't real, Tony. Every morning I see myself in the mirror. I know that I am growing."

He mistook her sadness for regret. "Belle, we can right this. I won't let you live in shame. Tell me his name."

"Shame?" She latched onto the word to give her raw emotions something to focus on besides his closeness and the agony caused by the knowledge of what she was losing by refusing to tell him what he wanted to know. "I'm not ashamed of what I did. I would do it again today." How could she feel shame when she was carrying his child? Rather she gloried in her condition.

Shock held him like granite. His eyes narrowed to slits of ice. "You should be ashamed. No decent man will have you now, and your child will be born a bastard."

"How dare you," she hissed, her hand descending on his face.

The slap echoed in the silence as they stared at one another. How could she have hit him? She had never felt so horrible. She couldn't stand any more of this. With a sob, she buried her face in her hands.

"Please," she managed through the obstruction in her throat, "go away. Leave Winterwood."

He didn't say another word, but Annabelle knew when he was gone by the nearly silent closing of the door. No slamming this time, only controlled emotion that told her better than any act of violence just how far she had pushed him.

Raising her head, she stared at the closed door. All she had ever wanted was for him to say he loved her. But he hadn't. He didn't love her. It was hopeless, and she knew it.

Part of her longed to cry, to let out the anguish of the past eight months, to sob for all the dreams that had just been shattered. She couldn't. Too many tears had wet her pillow already. There were none left.

The baby chose that moment to kick.

A small smile of pleasure at her child's spirit curved her lips as Annabelle sank to the carpet. Part of her mind told her she would have trouble getting back up because her center of gravity would insist on pulling her forward, but she didn't care.

Leaning back against the window seat, she rubbed her hands over her swollen belly. Then gently she pressed where the babe had kicked. Another kick. Her child was active and healthy. It was enough. It had to be.

Several hours later, Annabelle crossed the hall to the dinning room. Raised voices coming from the cracked open door made her pause.

Tony's voice, implacable in its quietness asked, "Why have you let her get away with not naming the father?"

"Tony," Mr. Levy-Gower said firmly, "we have asked. Annabelle is a stubborn chit."

Her mother spoke next. "That's why I wrote you the letter, Tony. I hoped you would be able to convince her that she should tell us—for her baby's good if not her own."

Annabelle could stand no more. She had learned her lesson eight months ago. Never would she eavesdrop again. Taking a deep breath, she pulled her shoulders back and marched into the room.

Tony stood on the opposite side of the room, the distance of the mahogany Queen Anne table between them. His blond hair was brushed in the Brutus, and he had on a dark gray coat, black pantaloons, and a white waistcoat that emphasized his lean physique, not formal dress as she was accustomed to seeing him wear at dinner. For the first time she realized how quickly and sparely he must have traveled. It brought a warm glow to her heart that he cared enough to do so. She tried to deny the feeling by concentrating on her parents.

Beside him stood her parents, her father with his balding gray head and rotund silhouette, and her mother with her still black hair and tall, spare figure. They were both dressed formally: her father in a black satin coat and pantaloons, and her mother in a lemon yellow muslin evening gown and gold spangled shawl.

Annabelle apprehended that her parents were still getting short shrift from Tony. She would quickly end that.

"Tony," she said, her words ringing forth in the large, high-ceilinged room, "my parents are not the cause of my plight, and I take it unkindly of you to berate them so." She moved around the table until she was within arm's distance of Tony before stopping.

His piercing look descended deliberately to the rounded swell of her stomach that her formal evening wear didn't hide. As coldly as a winter's wind, he said, "Perhaps your mother and father aren't directly responsible for your condition, but they allowed you too much freedom."

Mrs. Levy-Gower forestalled Annabelle's vehement retort with one of her own. "That will be quite enough, Anthony. I have endured your reprimands, for they are deserved. I *have* allowed Annabelle far too much freedom. However, you will not scold Annabelle for her upbringing. She had nothing to do with it."

"Mama," Annabelle said, pleased by her mother's support, but still determined to fight her own battles, "I can handle Tony."

"Daughter," Mrs. Levy-Gower replied, obviously enjoying herself in spite of her harsh words, "you didn't appear to be doing so, and I have had quite enough of this young man's impertinence." Turning her gray eyes on Tony, she stared him down. "I asked you to help, not stand in judgment, an attitude that has never corrected any wrong that I know of. And I dare say you have done your share to get young women in the same predicament Annabelle now finds herself in."

How could her mother say that? Annabelle tried desperately to suppress a gasp as her blood ran cold. Surreptitiously, Annabelle wiped her moist palms against the folds of her ample skirts. Then noticing the fire in her parents' eyes, she realized her mama was only voicing her liberal views, nothing more.

Undaunted by her child's gasp, Mrs. Levy-Gower continued, "I know it is unseemly and that Hannah More would be scandalized as would the Queen and every other lady of society, but we do not move in the *haut ton*. And I will not let one mistake ruin the rest of Annabelle's life. If she loved the father of her babe and wished to marry him, that would be one thing. But that is not the case. I will not force the issue. Although," she added wistfully, "I would like to know the father of my grandchild. But enough of this."

Tony made the matron a curt bow that did nothing to hide his disapproval. "As you wish. But I repeat that you have coddled and spoiled Belle too much. No young woman with a conventional upbringing would have allowed herself to get into this condition."

Tested beyond her endurance, Annabelle flushed pink with irritation. She could *not* allow Tony to disparage her parents so. "Tony, unless you have something nice to say, be quiet. How I behave is none of your affair."

For a brief moment, she thought he would say something further. Emotions warred across his face, but he turned aside to ask her father about the year's yield on wool.

Shortly they were seated at dinner, just the four of them. Annabelle did nothing to hide a small ironic smile as they all diligently attempted to steer the table conversation away from her controversial condition. And it was with a sigh of relief that she rose with her mother to leave the gentlemen to their port.

Standing in the hall several minutes later, Annabelle decided to retire early. The day had been long and emotionally exhausting for her. Both she and her unborn child needed rest.

"Annabelle," Tony said from the dining-room doorway, "I wish to speak with you."

Annabelle stopped with one foot on the first step of the stairs and looked back over her shoulder at Tony. He approached her until he was close enough to touch her before stopping. Their eyes met, and she was again shocked at the suppressed wrath she saw in the cold blue depths of his irises.

It shouldn't have surprised her. Whenever he called her

Annabelle, she knew he was furious.

She clenched the banister so tightly that her knuckles turned white. Wishing she could tell him to leave her alone and yet not able to deny him anything—even now—she asked, with a resigned sigh, "What is it, Tony?"

He spoke stiffly. "I want to apologize for the things I said to your mother this evening. I know they upset you, and she raised you the best that she knew how."

Annabelle raised her eyebrows and blurted, "That's very nice of you, Tony. But why don't you tell her yourself. After all, she's the one you insulted."

He turned a dull red at her sarcasm, and his shoulders tensed in their close-fitting black jacket. "I intend to do so but wanted to tell you first since you took such exception to my words before dinner."

Now it was her turn to blush. She should have realized that he would also apologize to her mother. Tony had always shouldered the responsibility for his actions. Even when he had been a young boy and gotten the cook in trouble by sneaking tarts so that there weren't enough for dinner, Tony had come forth and admitted his actions to clear the servant's name.

"Of course," she said, "I should have known." She half-turned, intending to mount the stairs. "If that's all, I'll see you tomorrow." His hand descended on her shoulder, a fiery brand against her bare skin that sent tendrils of warmth radiating down her arm and spine.

"No, Belle, that isn't all."

She looked back at him. A lock of hair hung over the scar on his forehead, almost hiding it. And there were lines of tiredness bracketing his eyes and mouth. "Tony, you are exhausted and will have to stay with us tonight instead of traveling on to your estate. Surely whatever you have to say to me can wait until tomorrow."

The fingers on her shoulder tightened, and she looked pointedly down at his touch. When he didn't release her, she looked back up at him and lifted one eyebrow in query.

"Your mother has invited me to stay here several days,

Belle." Weariness entered his voice. "And while I'm here, I intend to learn the name of the man who did this to you. You're too young to realize what having this baby out of wedlock can do to the rest of your life."

"Tony," she said pointedly, "I'm no longer a child, and you are not my older brother."

His eyes flashed and his voice hardened. "It's obvious your body isn't that of a child's, but it's equally obvious that your emotions haven't caught up with the rest of you."

"Oh!" Her chest tightened until she thought a vise was inexorably squeezing every emotion except fury out of her. "How dare you! How dare you denigrate me. At least I didn't cuckold anyone. *You* openly slept with your mistress the last time you were here — and she was a married woman. Whose action was worse, Tony? Answer me that."

His mouth whitened around the edges, and his grip on her shoulders tightened. "The very direction this conversation has taken speaks loudly of your immaturity, Annabelle. Young ladies of breeding do not discuss mistresses with men."

"You hypocrite," she hissed.

Twisting out of his hold, she took the stairs as rapidly as her condition would allow her. When she reached the landing, she glanced back down. He stood where she had left him, his hands clenched at his sides, his face raised so that his eyes blazed at her.

Her chest heaved with suppressed tears and rapid breathing. Even now, after what he had said, the sight of him pulled at her heart. She loved him and always would.

Why must it hurt so?

The grandfather clock struck ten o'clock, jolting Tony's attention from Belle's ruched lavender skirts as she turned at the top of the stairs. He hadn't realized how late it was, and he was tired. Better to continue this discussion with Belle on the morrow.

Later, in the same room where he'd stayed during the

hunt party, Tony paced the floor. Memories of his last night in this room and the innocent whose charms he'd thoroughly enjoyed flooded his senses. Making love to the girl had spoiled him for Harriet Treadle. A soft laugh began in his chest even as his loins tightened. Part of him hoped the woman would come again. No other woman had been able to erase from his nerves the intense pleasure she'd given him.

Desire shuddered through him. It had been an experience he would gladly repeat, only the next time he wouldn't let the girl escape without finding out who she was.

But right now he needed a good night's sleep in order to battle with Belle in the morning, for he had no illusions that he would have to fight her for every scrap of information he received. He crossed the room and opened his portmanteau to get his nightshirt.

On top of his belongings rested a small velvet box. He'd forgotten about packing it. He picked it up and crossed to the brace of candles resting on an Elizabethan oak chest positioned at the foot of the bed. Falling to his knees, he opened the box.

A cameo of Belle as she'd looked at eighteen shimmered in the flickering light. She'd had it commissioned for him just before he left for Waterloo.

He studied it. She'd been a child with the exuberant joy of youth, and the artist had caught that exuberance. Her eyes twinkled with mischief and her chin jutted with determination. Both were traits he would always associate with her.

Where had the young girl gone? For the first time since arriving, he faced the knowledge that the child Belle had been was gone forever. Pain shot through him at the realization that Belle wasn't the same girl whose likeness he'd taken to Waterloo. The innocence that had helped him keep his sanity was gone forever from her face and mind. An unknown man had taken that from her.

Had Belle given herself to her lover as generously as the mysterious girl had given herself to him that night? It was a stupid question and irrelevant to Belle's situation.

Irritated with himself for such maudlin thinking and angrier at Belle for changing, Tony snapped the box closed, his fingers squeezing until his whole arm ached with the tension. He rose and returned to his portmanteau where he carefully positioned the box at the bottom, under his clothes, where he wouldn't see it and be tempted to open it again.

The Belle of his childhood was gone.

Dressed in a lightweight muslin morning dress to combat the heat of early spring that seemed worse than normal because of her additional burden, Annabelle entered the breakfast room. Sunshine poured in the bay window and glinted off Tony's bowed head as he examined the contents of one of the chafing dishes on the sideboard.

She wanted to remain upset with him over yesterday, but her pleasure at seeing him up this early overcame her ill will. As children they had always been the first ones up and at the breakfast table. This encounter was reaffirmation that the two of them hadn't changed so much that they had no common ground. Her silly hope reasserted itself.

Grinning, she told him, "It's probably kidneys."

He turned around and looked at her warily before breaking into a smile. "Have you decided to forgive me for my inexcusable words last night?"

She had always been more prone to dwell on wrongs than Tony, and relief flooded her as she realized he hadn't changed in this aspect either. Laughter bubbled up in her, but she managed to speak coherently. "I said some rather horrible things myself."

"True," he replied, shrugging.

Annabelle knew that with the gesture he was letting go of the incident. Perhaps it would be easier between them today.

She was just eating the last of her toast and smiling at something Tony had said, when she noticed that he no longer looked amused. His eyes were somber and his hands were folded in front of him on the table.

"Belle," he began, "I don't like badgering you on this subject, but it's too important for me not to."

When he paused to let her absorb his meaning, she felt tension begin to build in her shoulders. She should have known that he wouldn't rest until he got the information he came for.

"Tell me his name, Belle. It's the only way."

"I can't, Tony." It was so hard to deny him, and the darkening of his eyes at her refusal only made it more difficult. "Please, Tony, don't ruin this morning by insisting."

But he was implacable. "Can't tell me, Belle? Or won't?"

"You always were as stubborn as I, Tony." Her gaze slid away, and she stared out the window at the fluffy white clouds that skittered across the blue sky. She didn't want to tell him more, didn't want to reveal her innermost hurt to him, but she knew he wouldn't settle for a superficial answer. "Tony, I don't want to tell you." It was impossible for her to continue. The final words were so painful, she didn't know if she could speak them out loud, and especially not to him.

"Why not, Belle?" he asked gently. "You know I'll do everything in my power to help you."

She knew it. He would even marry her if she asked him: she saw the determination in his eyes, the way his fingers clenched around each other as he tried to remain calm and reasonable.

"I can't tell you his name because he doesn't love me." There, she'd said the truth, hurtful as it was. Her vision blurred and she quickly looked down at her own hands, clasped so tightly in her lap that her bones were sharp outlines under the skin.

He laughed. Surprised, she immediately raised her head. His hands were no longer fisted on the table and the lines of anxiety around his eyes were gone.

"Is that all?" He reached out and lifted her face so that he gazed directly into her eyes. "That's nothing, Belle. People in our class don't marry for love. The man who did this to you understands that, and he'll marry you if only you tell him he's the father."

She stared blindly at him. When she spoke at last, the words were torn from her heart. "I don't want a marriage of convenience."

He frowned and released her chin to rise and pace once across the room. Returning to her, he clasped her elbows and raised her so that they stood inches apart, her swollen belly grazing his waistcoat.

Gently, he shook her. "Belle, no one marries for love. They marry for money and social position." He moved his palm to her stomach and rested it on the distended mound. "And this child is a more potent reason for marriage than either of those. You may want a love match, but you owe it to your unborn baby to marry its father—whether the man loves you or not."

He was right in his logic, but her heart had never been practical. "I love him."

His hand fell away from her, leaving searing cold where his warm flesh had been. Unwilling to see the shock and distaste she knew Tony felt, Annabelle pulled from his clasp and rushed from the room.

Tears flowed freely down her face to land in dark blotches on the muslin of her bodice.

The next day, Annabelle sat in the rose garden. She had skipped breakfast because she didn't want to hear Tony announce his plans to leave. After the way she had broken down yesterday, he must realize that his reasons for coming were fruitless. So he would go.

Once more he would walk out of her life. She had thought it unbearable when he left her after making love to her, how much more agonizing would it be to have him leave when she was heavy with his child? She couldn't even begin to imagine it.

She sighed deeply, determined to put the thought aside

91

and not mar the beautiful day. Tipping her head back, she enjoyed the warmth of the midmorning sun on her face. Her baby shifted, and she put her hands on her stomach to feel its movements. It was becoming more and more active. Soon it would be time.

"Belle," Tony's deep voice intruded on her reverie, "so this is where you've been hiding."

The moment she'd been dreading had arrived. She had to be strong.

Opening her eyes, she watched him cover the remaining distance separating them. He moved with smooth grace that accentuated his long legs and lean hips. In one hand, his fingers carefully grasping its long stem, he held a red rose. Her gaze flew to his face.

"This is for you," he said, handing her the flower. "I saw it as I was coming out the library doors and thought you might like it. You always did like the smell of roses."

"Thank you," she murmured, taking the proffered gift. She inhaled deeply of its delicate scent and then snapped the stem off so that the flower itself could be nestled in her hair.

"Let me," Tony said, taking it from her suddenly nerveless fingers.

He sat down beside her and proceeded to place the flower. Warmth from his body radiated to her, making her tingle in remembered awareness of his touch during their lovemaking. Her breasts, already swollen from pregnancy, ached with the need for his caress. She loved him so much, why couldn't he love her just a little?

A small moan escaped her.

His fingers stopped. "Did I hurt you, Belle?"

She shook her head, a sharp, small movement.

He lifted her chin to study her face. His eyes lingered on every feature, and Annabelle didn't know what to do. Almost he looked at her as a lover might, as she had so very frequently dreamed he might.

But when he spoke, it was mundane. "Would you care to go into the village with me? I promised your mother that I would collect some books she's ordered from London for her school." He chuckled and released her from his hold. "I gather Elizabeth doesn't trust the coachman to deliver the books safely."

The spell broken, her emotions plummeting from the heights of anticipation to the depths of reality, Annabelle barely managed to smile at him. "Mama knows John Coachman doesn't care for the idea of a school. He's more than vocal in his opinion that lack of schooling didn't hurt him, so it won't hurt these kids either. He argues with her, and she loves it."

Tony's chuckle turned into a full-fledged, deep laugh. When he regained his breath, he said, "Your mother is a rule unto herself. No one else of my acquaintance would allow the coachman to speak so boldly."

"Yes," Annabelle agreed, "Mama is an Original."

"Most certainly. But come, Belle, we are wasting time that could be better spent fetching and carrying for your mother." Grinning, he rose and offered her a helping hand up.

She wished she could blithely ignore his gesture, but she'd been sitting for some time, and she knew it would be difficult to rise. Embarrassed by her clumsiness, but knowing that to refuse would be even more embarrassing, she allowed him to help her.

"Thank you," she mumbled, not looking at him. But her skin turned a fiery red.

"Belle," he said in surprise, "you're blushing. Whatever is the matter?"

"Nothing," she muttered, skirting around him. Without a backward glance she hurried to the house.

She could hear his footsteps on the crushed gravel path as he tried to catch up with her. At the door he drew even with her, and his hand reached out and grabbed her upper arm. Even that impersonal contact made her skin ripple with sensual awareness of him as a man. She was so weak. Disgusted with herself, she gritted her teeth to keep another moan from escaping her lips.

"Belle," he persisted, "something is the matter. I know you too well to be fobbed off."

"Oh, all right," she finally answered, feeling coerced but knowing he would continue until she told him something. "I am not used to being helped up from a seat."

His eyebrows rose incredulously. "Is that the reason for your thunderous expression and the blush?"

"Yes." She averted her face from his intense scrutiny before she reddened again.

"Belle, look at me."

When she didn't do his bidding, he reached forward and cupped her face in his palms, forcing her to turn toward him. Then gently, firmly, he said, "Belle, your body isn't ugly, and you're not awkward. You are rounded in all the right places, a veritable goddess of fertility." He paused, and a look of wonder moved over his countenance. "You're beautiful, Belle."

Confused by his unexpected words, all she could do was stare at him. What was he telling her? Did it mean more than just a list of what she looked like? Could he be attracted to her?

No, most certainly not. She was ungainly and ponderous. And he didn't love her.

"So," Elizabeth Levy-Gower intruded, "this is where you two have gotten yourselves off to. Well, walking in the gardens won't get my books." But she smiled to soften the implied demand of her words.

Annabelle and Tony jumped apart, and Tony was the first to speak. "You're quite right. I was just convincing Belle to come with me."

But it was two hours later before they arrived in the small village near Winterwood. Leaving the carriage at the only pub with a stable, Tony and Annabelle walked the short distance to the solicitor's office where they gave the clerk directions for taking the books to the carriage. Next they went to the milliner's. Once inside, Annabelle moved away from Tony's side to finger several of the ribbons on display near the window.

94

Tony leaned against the counter and watched her. Even eight months gone, she still managed to move gracefully, her swollen belly held as proudly as her head. She bent over so that the summer sunshine coming through the paned glass burnished her profiled cheek. A wave of tenderness washed over Tony, taking him by surprise. Disconcerted, he turned his back on her and the picture she presented.

"I never!" A woman's indignant voice intruded on Tony's thoughts.

"Flaunting herself in public, and her unwed. Ain't decent, I says," a different female voice added.

Tony looked around the small store, immediately spying the two speakers. By the looks of them, they were merchants' wives, and by the direction of their gaze, they were discussing Belle — although even without their obvious stares he would never have been in doubt as to the subject of their conversation.

Glancing quickly at Belle to make sure she hadn't heard their criticism, Tony strolled in their direction. Stopping in front of the two women, he doffed his curly-brimmed beaver, but the polite gesture wasn't mirrored in the sparkling hardness of his eyes.

"Good morning," he said, his gaze carefully moving over each one in turn, taking in their matronly curves and self-righteous expressions.

Both recognized him. "Sir Anthony," each said simultaneously.

He smiled thinly. "I see that you *ladies* have found a topic of conversation." Blood suffused both the women's faces, turning their countenances into splotched purple maps. "I suggest that you keep your opinions to yourself in the future." He waited for the meaning of his words to sink in, only mildly interested in the further mottling of their complexions as understanding dawned on them.

The first woman's lips tightened as though to keep in hasty words. The second matron's eyes flashed with suppressed anger. Both women nodded briefly.

Tony once again tipped his hat to them before moving

away. Approaching Belle, he murmured, "Are you through yet?"

She lifted her head and smiled at him. "Almost."

He was taken aback by the softness of her skin and the look of contentment so evident in the curve of her mouth and the warmth in her silver-gray eyes. "Good. I want you to show me the school your mother has started for the laborers' children."

Momentarily she looked surprised, then her smile widened. "I'd be delighted to do so, Tony. All I need are a few more minutes here."

Her attention returned to the ribbons she'd been examining, giving Tony a view of the nape of her neck. Tendrils of black hair, having escaped her chignon, lay in gossamer curls against the creamy ivory of her skin. It was an effort for him not to run his finger down the soft line of her neck to the lace-trimmed collar of her gown. It was even more of an effort for him to walk away until she was through.

Shortly after, Annabelle paid for her purchases. Tony offered her his arm as they left the store. Exiting, Tony cast one last glance at the two women who were still huddled together near the counter. Both tried to stare him down but failed. He smiled grimly at them. They looked guiltily away.

Outside, Tony signaled to the Levy-Gower coachman to bring the cabriolet to the curb. Tony helped Belle into the open carriage then arranged a throw over her knees to keep the spring breeze from chilling her.

The carriage proceeded at a brisk clip to the old cottage on the edge of Levy-Gower land where Annabelle's mother had started the small school. Rounding a corner, the building came into sight.

Tony saw several children outside eating bread and cheese for lunch. Nearby an older woman sat with several young girls around her.

"Your mother is to be commended for this work," Tony said to Belle, meaning it.

She looked at him skeptically. "You weren't singing Mama's praises several days ago."

He stiffened at her criticism, but he knew it was deserved. "Yes, but several days ago I was angry at what her liberal beliefs had led you to do. My feelings had nothing to do with the rightness of her charitable efforts."

The coachman pulled up in front of the door, and Tony got out and helped Belle down the steps. Her condition made her clumsy, and she lost her balance on the last step.

With a start, Annabelle fell into Tony.

"Damnation!" Tony grabbed for her, catching her before she could fall into the dirt of the road and possibly hurt herself.

For several minutes, Annabelle lay in Tony's arms, breathing rapidly to regain her composure after the fright of feeling her feet meet nothing but air. If he hadn't been so quick, she might have hurt herself and her babe. She looked up to thank him, and the words stuck in her throat.

He was looking at her with such intensity that heat radiated from her skin. Where his arms circled her, it felt as though she were being burned. Not even the bulk of her distended stomach could lessen the magnitude of the embrace. If anything, her roundness increased the intimacy of their closeness—for Tony was the father of her babe.

His eyes darkened, taking on the hue of a stormy sky, and his pupils dilated until she could see herself reflected in their depths. His lips softened, their fullness becoming sensual. Was he going to kiss her?

Tony studied Belle's features one by one. Her eyes were smoldering coals that beckoned to him, and her lips were ripe red berries begging for his kiss. His head lowered and his gaze traveled downward. Her bosom swelled against his coat with the full curves of a woman preparing to nurse her young. A spasm of desire shot through him.

He closed his eyes momentarily to shut out the alluring sight of her. Never had he reacted to any woman this strongly, not even his mystery lover. He wanted Belle with a desire so strong it made his whole body ache.

Unconsciously, his left hand moved around her waist to rest on the evidence that she carried another man's child.

The result of her love for that man. He hoped the bastard knew how lucky he was.

The baby kicked against his palm, and Tony murmured, "He's a feisty little thing. Just like his mother."

She wanted to say, *Just like his father.* Instead her hand covered Tony's and she smiled.

"Miss Levy-Gower." A woman's voice intruded on their preoccupation with each other.

Tony's head snapped up and simultaneously he released Belle. How could he have so forgotten himself? And in front of a group of people?

Disappointment so intense it felt like a many-thorned rose bush tortured Annabelle as Tony set her aside. They had been so close . . . so very close.

A quick glance at Tony's averted face told Annabelle that he had not felt the same emotions as she. His jaw was hard and his brows were drawn in a straight blond arrow across his eyes. She sighed as she released her momentary fantasy that Tony was beginning to care for her.

Turning to the newcomer, Annabelle said graciously, "Louise, how are things going?"

Louise, her gray hair pulled sharply back from a narrow face with a protruding chin and prominent nose, replied, "Very well, Miss Levy-Gower. We're just taking a break from reading to eat our lunch. The children get a mite restless if they don't get time away to stretch their legs, so to speak."

Annabelle laughed. She always felt happy and hopeful whenever she came to this school and saw how eagerly these children of farmers learned their lessons. "Louise, I've brought Sir Anthony Crenshaw with me this afternoon." Quickly, she introduced them before taking Tony's hand and pulling him into the one-room building.

Sweeping her arm to encompass the entire area, Annabelle beamed. "Mama has done this all by herself. Of course, Hannah More set the guidelines, but Mama has gone one step further and instructed that the children be taught how to write."

Tony took in the well-equipped room with its desks, slate boards, and chalk. "Why shouldn't they be taught to write if they're being taught to read? It only makes sense."

"It makes sense to you, Tony, because you haven't thought it through as thoroughly as Miss More. Her hypothesis is that if they are taught to write, then they may become political radicals."

"Ridiculous," Tony said. "Hannah More is an Evangelist. That much even I know."

"True, and I agree with most of her writing, but Mama and I have decided that Miss More missed the mark on this." Then she sighed. "However, it remains to be seen just how long we can keep this school going. Many of the parents don't like this. It keeps the children from doing as much around the house and in the fields. When there are many mouths to feed and little money, every hand helps. Still," she forced herself to brighten up, "we are doing something."

Tony found that his admiration for Belle increased a thousandfold as she pulled herself up by the bootstraps instead of allowing herself to sink into melancholia. "You are doing more than *something*, Belle. You're starting these children on a new path in their lives and helping to break them out of the mold that keeps so many of their families hungry."

She searched his eyes for the truth of his words. "Do you really think so? I so long that it may be true."

Tony looked at her, absorbing the worry she didn't try to hide. "I think that you are one of the most extraordinary women of my acquaintance." Then, disconcerted by the emotions she evoked in him, he let her go and stepped away. A safe distance from her disturbing influence, he cleared his throat. "I never realized before, but you're no longer the little brat who used to dog my every step."

She frowned, then fumed, then giggled. "You, Tony Crenshaw, are infuriating." Then she sobered up. "But you were right, Tony. I was a child. I've done a lot of growing up in the last eight months."

His eyes held hers. "You had to."

She was the first to look away.

Soon the children were coming in for the remainder of their lessons. Tony leaned against the doorjamb and watched, fascinated by the trust the children exhibited for Belle. And Belle seemed equally contented around them. It was a facet of her personality he would have never believed possible if he weren't seeing it.

When Belle finally indicated her desire to leave, he took her hand and threaded it through the crook in his arm. "Come along and walk with me for a distance. John Coachman can pick us up by the big apple tree. Remember it?"

Amazed, Annabelle looked at him. "How could I forget? We used to meet there when I was ten and you were seventeen and home from Eton." For the first time, the disparity in their ages struck her, and she wrinkled her nose in puzzlement. "Why *did* you meet me there? I was only a child, and you were already away at school and doing goodness only knows what."

He looked thoughtful as they strolled slowly down the path. "I don't really know. I remember wondering at the time what sort of fascination a skinny, pigtailed little girl could hold, and each time I decided not to meet you, in the end I was there before you." He rubbed absent-mindedly at his scar then shrugged. "I still don't know."

She saw him finger the healed wound and part of her heart went out to him. "Does it still hurt?"

"What?" he asked, his eyes reflecting bewilderment at her question.

"Your scar. Does it still hurt?" She wanted to reach up and smooth the puckered skin; she wanted to cover it with kisses.

His voice turned brusque. "No. And that's not why I wanted to walk with you."

Momentarily taken aback by his abrupt change from openness to cold withdrawal, she pulled her hand from him. Just as suddenly, it dawned on her why he'd changed. For some reason, he felt uncomfortable about his wound. Did he think she pitied him? That would irritate him, and she knew it.

"Tony," she said, continuing on in spite of his sardonically raised eyebrows, "I don't pity you for your scars. I think they are very dashing and debonair. They give you an air of reckless danger — very intriguing. However, when you seem to be pained by them, I do want to comfort you. I can't help it and I won't apologize for it."

He stopped in his tracks, forcing her to stop with him. Astonishment writ plainly on his face, he said, "Belle you *are* extraordinary. No one has said such a thing to me since I returned from Waterloo."

"Well," she said, "someone should have. It might have kept you from being so defensive about it."

He laughed out loud, his voice echoing through the quiet countryside surrounding them. It was a sound full of release.

"Belle," he finally said, "you are a rare woman." At her look of scoffing disbelief, he added, "Yes, Belle, I said 'woman,' for that's what you've become."

Uncertain about what she felt now that he'd finally conceded she was no longer a child, she resorted to her childhood methods of dealing with his teasing. She made him a mock curtsy.

"And I have a proposal to make you," he said.

Her heart skipped a beat. Surely he couldn't mean what his words implied. Could he? She held her breath and clasped her hands together to stop their shaking.

"Belle," he said earnestly, "marry me."

The blood pounded in her ears, and her eyes sought his for confirmation of the love he must feel to ask her this. She saw entreaty, even longing in his eyes. Hope, more intense than any emotion she had ever felt, blossomed in her heart. Perhaps there was a chance for them.

He took her hands and carefully pried them apart so that he held one in each of his. "Belle, I know you love the father of your baby, and I know you want love in your marriage."

He paused and she searched his face for what he truly felt and thought. By his frown and the tenseness of his jaw, she knew that what he was saying wasn't easy for him.

He continued in a deep, thoughtful voice. "I wish I could give you everything in life that you deserve, but I can't. Therefore, I'm offering you my name and myself as a father for your babe. I promise to raise the child as though it were my own, and I promise to cherish you and care for you."

But he hadn't said he loved her. The rose that had begun to unfurl in her heart died. Carefully neutral, she said, "But you don't love me."

"I like you and admire you, Belle."

But you don't love me. Her vision blurred, and she looked away from him as she got control of her reactions. He'd called her a woman, now she had to act like one.

Pulling her hands from his clasp, she threaded her fingers tightly together and rested them on the swell of her stomach. "I like and admire you, too, Tony, but that isn't enough for me. Thank you for your very considerate offer, but I must decline."

She didn't wait for his reply but turned and walked to where the carriage was parked. Reaching the vehicle, she said, "John, Sir Anthony has decided to walk. Please take me home."

Only once did she glance back. He was standing in the shade of the apple tree. Funny, she thought numbly, she hadn't realized they had reached it.

Annabelle surreptitiously watched Tony as she knitted booties, her feet propped up to combat the swelling in her ankles. He sat across from her on the other side of the fire, a brace of candles on the table beside him and in his lap a copy of *Waverley* by an unknown author many thought to be Walter Scott.

His long, fine-boned hands lay restfully, one on his thigh and the other on the book. He appeared totally absorbed.

It seemed an eternity ago that Tony had proposed to her under the apple tree instead of just two days. His offer had plunged her to the depths of hell, but he'd acted as though nothing had occurred. And now this.

Here they sat, the perfect domestic couple that anyone not knowing the truth would think happily married and eagerly anticipating the birth of their first child. She knew that if she said something to him, he would look up from his book and reply courteously and then ask how she felt. And he would only be exercising his impeccable manners and his genuine concern for her well-being. There would be no love.

Her mouth twisted in emotional pain, and she had to look away. She stared at the dancing flames, seeing visions of impossible futures: her with a golden-haired baby boy, Tony by her side; both of them beaming happily down on a black-haired girl while a blond young boy stood between them.

"A penny for your thoughts," Tony asked, sending her dreams spinning away like smoke up a chimney.

The knitting needles stopped their clicking as her fingers stilled. Thoughtfully, she gazed at him, noting the relaxed smile that curved his lips and the lock of silver-blond hair that fell over his scar.

When she finally answered, she told him only part of the truth. She knew him well enough to understand that he wouldn't want to hear all of her fancies. "I was wondering what color hair my baby would have."

The angles of his cheeks became even harsher and the hollows even more pronounced. "What color should your child have?"

Annabelle's eyes narrowed. Even though he spoke softly, she could detect underlying steel in the words. Without even trying, she had angered him, and she was so tired of being constantly at odds with him. So, she would tell him only part of the truth. He wouldn't take kindly to more.

"Probably black, since mine is."

To change the subject, she levered herself from the chintz-covered chair and walked to the French windows. She opened one and stood looking out on the rose garden where the sun turned the sky into a multicolored frame for the lush flowers. She knew when he came up behind her even though she hadn't heard his tread on the thick carpet.

Without turning, she said, "I think I'll go for a walk."

"I'll come with you."

Together they moved outside, and bittersweet happiness took her at his intention to accompany her. He didn't love her, but he stayed by her side constantly. It was more than most husbands did. Perhaps she was a fool not to accept his proposal.

She pushed the weak thought aside. His favorable regard would quickly turn to complacent acceptance if she married him without love.

"It's beautiful here," she said, taking a deep breath of the fragrant scent of roses. "Some of the flowers are new hybrids and some have been grown from seeds."

"So many years of time and work," he said.

"Yes. Constant nurturing."

"Like a child," he ended her thought for her. "Belle," he said, his voice so soft she had to strain to hear it. "I'll only ask this last time. Will you marry me?"

She paused and gazed sadly at him. "I can't, Tony. I would never be happy in a loveless marriage." *In a marriage where only I loved.*

He bowed his head in acknowledgment. "I was afraid you would say that." He took a deep breath. "Then I think it best that I leave tomorrow. It's patently obvious that you will never tell who your lover was, and that was really my only reason for being here. I wanted you respectably and safely married. I've failed in that."

Her heart ached, and every beat was a painful constriction of her chest. To be given a glimpse of heaven and then to have to turn it down. How could life be so cruel?

The words were hard for her to say, but she managed. "That's probably for the best."

This time she didn't run from him: their time left together was too short and she wanted to cherish every remaining second. Silently they continued to walk through the garden, her hand in the crook of his elbow, his hand covering hers in a warm caress.

Annabelle didn't see the broken tree limb lying in the path. She stumbled and would have fallen had it not been for Tony's support. As it was, she found herself held securely in his embrace. Warmth as insidious and all pervasive as the time he'd made love to her flowed through her body, and turned her insides to thick cream.

"Oh," she said breathlessly, attempting to free herself from his arms.

"Easy," he said, his arms refusing to release her.

More than anything in the world, Annabelle wanted to stay near him. But she was only increasing her own agony. Pushing against his chest, she murmured, "Thank you."

When he released her, she almost stumbled from the shock of returning cold. Will power alone moved her feet away from him.

A sharp pain shot through her belly. "Oh," she moaned, squeezing her eyes shut and clutching her stomach against the pain that quickly repeated itself.

The third time the spasms shuddered through her body, she swayed and would have fallen if Tony hadn't grabbed her shoulders and pulled her against him. This time she didn't resist him. She needed his support.

"Oh my," she gasped and smiled in spite of another contraction. "I didn't know they would become this bad."

"What?" he said. "You mean this isn't the first time?"

"No," she managed to say around another spasm. "They've been going on most of the day, but only now have they been truly hurtful."

"Bloody hell!" Tony swept her into his arms, ignoring her protests. "You haven't sense to come in out of the rain."

Hastily he retraced their footsteps through the garden. Reaching the French doors, he kicked them open with his foot and moved into the room where Mrs. Levy-Gower had just entered.

"Annabelle is in labor," he said without preamble.

"Oh, dear," her mother said, coming up to them. "You really should have said something, Annabelle. Now we will have to send someone for the doctor and hope they can find him this late at night."

"Now, now, m'dear," Mr. Levy-Gower said, joining them. "I'll send Tom. He's a responsible lad, and I'm sure Dr. Smithfield will be home. Not too many pregnant women right now. Most be dropping later."

"Papa," Annabelle grinned even as she gritted her teeth, "you are nothing if not blunt spoken."

Patting her affectionately on the cheek, Mr. Levy-Gower replied, "I'm only making a practical assessment of the situation. There's nothing to worry about."

Another spasm shot through Annabelle, and her eyes unfocused momentarily. When the pain was past, she said tightly, "I know. This is a normal occurrence."

Brows creased from worry, Tony strode past the other two and up the stairs to Annabelle's room. Shoving open the door, he went through and deposited her on the bed. Once she was settled, he got a chair from near the fireplace and placed it next to the bed. Then he sat down.

Annabelle watched him in astonishment. "Tony, you can't stay here. It isn't proper."

His face pulled tight and his hands clenched on his thighs, he said, "The hell I can't. If you can be pregnant out of wedlock, I can stay here."

"To — oh!" she gasped as another contraction took her. "Please go." She didn't want him to see her like this, as fat as a cow and her face undoubtedly red from her ordeal.

"No."

Mrs. Levy-Gower entered as the two stared each other down. "Tony," she said, coming to his side, "Annabelle is right. This is no place for you. Nor any other man."

Tony looked at her, his mouth a thin obstinate line. "I won't leave until I am sure Belle is going to be all right."

Mrs. Levy-Gower studied him, then slowly said, "I could have a servant throw you out."

He met her scrutiny squarely. "You could try."

Into their confrontation entered a maid. "Ma'am," the girl said deferentially, "I brought the water, and Cook be heatin' up more for the birthin'." Her sight took in Tony's rigid posture, and her eyes popped. Under her breath she muttered, "A birthin' be no place fer a man."

Almost Tony smiled. He was behaving as unconventionally by insisting on remaining as Belle had behaved by getting in the family way. Almost it was a comedy of farces. Almost, but not quite.

The hours dragged by for Tony as he alternately wiped Belle's brow and held her hand. Whenever Mrs. Levy-Gower tried to replace him, he growled at her.

Belle's face contorted as her stomach contracted, and a soft moan escaped her lips. It was as close to release as she had come, and Tony's heart contracted with fear and sympathy.

Turning away from her suffering, he demanded, "How much longer before the doctor gets here? She can't stand much more of this."

Mrs. Levy-Gower shook her head and said soothingly, "Tony, this is not unusual. All women have a long labor with their first."

He stared at her in disbelief before returning his attention to Belle. She was sweating, and her hands were holding onto the covers so tightly her knuckles were white. The blue of her veins stood out in stark contrast.

He didn't know how to help her. Impotence shot through him, bitter as bile. Women died all the time in childbirth. What if Belle died?

His shoulders hunched and his stomach churned. Belle was a part of his life, always had been. When he'd been lonely, she'd been there. When he went away to school, he'd known she would be here when he returned. When he went to fight Napoleon, her likeness had reassured him that there was goodness in the world. He couldn't lose her now.

"Tony," Belle said softly, "you're hurting my hand."

Dazed, he looked at her. She was right. His fingers were clasping hers so tightly that his forearm was corded from strain. He released her and mumbled, "I'm sorry."

The door opened and a loud voice rang through the

room. "Nothing to fret about, Mrs. Levy-Gower. I'll shortly have everything in hand."

Tony twisted around to see a short, rotund man with a balding pate approach the bed. The doctor was here at last. Relief rolled like a tidal wave over Tony.

The doctor took one expert appraisal of Annabelle and pronounced, "Nothing to worry about." Then he transferred his attention to Tony. "Sir Anthony Crenshaw?"

Tony nodded.

"Well, Sir Anthony, this is no place for you. You aren't even the father. Be gone so this lady and I can be about our business."

Tony stood transfixed as the doctor's words penetrated his fear for Belle. No, he wasn't the father. But, he finally realized, he would like to be. He loved Belle. He felt as though he'd been landed a right to the solar plexus.

"Sir Anthony," the doctor prompted.

Dazed, Tony took in the doctor's implacable attitude. It took him several minutes to realize that he was out-gunned. With a curt nod, Tony left but halted right outside of the room. Immediately he fell to pacing the hallway. He didn't want to be far in case Belle needed him.

It wasn't long before Belle's father joined him.

After what seemed an eternity to Tony, Mr. Levy-Gower said, "Let's go to the library and have some brandy."

Tony shook his head no.

Mr. Levy-Gower put a hand on Tony's shoulder to stop him pacing and said, "Son, you can't help her, and the library is close enough to get back here within seconds. Come."

Ensconced in two large leather chairs, the brass studs holding the leather together glinting in the flickering light coming from a small fire, the men sipped their drink. Tony held his glass so that he could stare into the amber depths of the liquid. "Nice to be able to get brandy without having to deal with smugglers. That's one good thing about Waterloo. We beat the frogs."

Mr. Levy-Gower grunted his agreement.

Still concentrating on the liquor in his hand, Tony continued, "You know, I must be slow. I must have loved her all the time. When I was in the Peninsula and later at Waterloo, it was her miniature that helped me keep my sanity — and I didn't even realize it. Not really."

He fished the cameo from his watch pocket where he'd put it for safekeeping that morning after packing his portmanteau. Raising it so the firelight illuminated it, he studied every nuance of Belle's face. "Tonight, when I thought I might lose her forever, her importance in my life hit me like a team of runaway horses."

Tony looked away from the miniature to Mr. Levy-Gower. The older man was watching him with an intensity that made Tony think of a parent willing a stumbling child to succeed. Realization dawned on Tony, and he said, "You knew all the time."

Mr. Levy-Gower nodded. "That's why Elizabeth wrote you. You're the only person who could save Annabelle from this folly she's pursuing."

Tony laughed harshly. "I haven't done a very good job." His features contorted with the magnitude of his failure. "I asked her to marry me and she refused."

"Did you tell her that you love her?"

Surprise raised Tony's brows. "Of course not. I'm not that crass. Belle loves another man. I would never burden her with love that she couldn't reciprocate. And, besides," he looked away from Mr. Levy-Gower's penetrating gaze, wishing he could gloss over the truth, but knowing that now was the time for honesty, "I didn't know I loved her then."

"Then tell her."

The statement was calm and matter-of-fact, but goose bumps rose on Tony's arms making the hairs stand on end, and his palms were cold and clammy. He was being told to submit his whole being to Belle's care. It was a big step to take.

The library door opened, and the doctor entered, grinning from ear to ear. "Gentlemen, Annabelle is the proud mother of a bouncing baby boy with hair the color of sunshine." He shook his head. "Don't know where a black-haired woman could get a blond baby from, but 'tis a fact."

Tony jumped up and sped out the room and up the stairs. He didn't pause until he reached Belle's door. Catching his breath, he stood still and carefully planned what he would say.

But mingled with his consideration were memories: the scent of roses, the feel of silken flesh as a young woman gave herself completely to him, the passage of almost eight months. Belle's baby was a blond . . .

Pushing open the door, Tony entered, his gaze drawn like a magnet to the bed where Belle lay. Her hair was spread over the pillow like strands of silk, and her skin was smooth and white like fine cream. On her lips was a smile so gentle and happy that his chest constricted with longing to see it directed at himself.

He approached her, knowing that only the truth held any hope for him to gain the future he now realized was all that mattered. But would she have him? Could he make her see that his love was honest and deep? Was the strength of his love enough to make her realize that he couldn't live without her and the child she'd given him?

He had to try.

Annabelle felt his presence like a warm summer breeze that encompassed all it touched. She wanted to share with him the joy of their son, but resisted the urge to tell Tony that.

Tucking the baby deeper into the curve of her arm, she looked at Tony for the first time. The words of welcome died on her lips. Attuned to Tony's every emotional nuance, a change in his face — the curve of his lips, the tenderness in his eyes — told her that something momentous had taken place in him.

Hope flared in her heart, but she beat it down all in an instant. She was a woman now; she must put her girlish fancies to rest once and for all.

Tony took her hand and kissed it. "May I hold him?" he asked diffidently.

Nodding, Annabelle released the baby from her clasp so that Tony could take him. Tony took the tiny bundle and cradled the child as though he were porcelain. On Tony's face was such a look of wonder and delight, that it was all Annabelle could do not to cry at the magnitude of the emotions Tony made no effort to hide.

Softly, gently rocking the baby, Tony asked, "What will you name him?"

"David," she replied as quietly.

Tony looked from the child to her, and his eyes glowed with an emotion Annabelle had given up all hope of seeing.

"My father's name," Tony said. "Thank you."

His humbled acceptance of her decision made a lump form in Annabelle's throat as she tried desperately not to cry. She didn't think she could endure much more of this without breaking down and telling him of her love, the love that had sustained her through the years he was at war and through the months of bearing his child alone.

"Don't thank me, Tony. Please."

In one lithe movement, Tony was beside her on the bed, his arms still protecting his child. Tenderly he laid the precious bundle down beside Annabelle.

Taking both her hands, he said, "I can't thank you enough, Belle. And I can't ask your forgiveness enough."

"Tony, don't," she said around the tightness in her throat.

He squeezed her hands and slowly brought them to his lips and kissed the tip of each finger, then lingeringly her palms. "You've been through so much because of me, Belle, and you never complained or repudiated me."

She searched his countenance, taking in the agony he made no effort to hide or the moisture he didn't deign to wipe from his eyes. And she understood.

"I love you, Tony. I always have and I always will. That's all that matters to me."

"I know," he said, wonder making his voice crack. "I finally realize so many things I was too blind to see before. I'm the man who dishonored you. All this time I've been ranting and raving at you, demanding the name of the man

111

who disgraced you, and I was the bastard."

He paused, and Annabelle could see his throat working. Her heart ached for him and the agony he was putting himself through. "Tony, it doesn't matter. It never did. Please don't torture yourself."

He smoothed the hair back from her forehead. "It matters to me, Belle. Don't you see? I was so incredibly ignorant. I didn't even realize that I love you until I almost lost you." He pulled her into his embrace and held her tightly as though his very life depended on her being near him.

Gently, she untangled her arms from him and put them around his neck. "It's over now, Tony."

He gazed at her, his eyes brimming with the intensity of his love. "And we have David—my son—our son. I want to share him with you, the joys and the disappointments of raising him until we're both old and gray. I want to lie down each night with you by my side and tell you all the little things of my day and hear yours in turn." He took a deep shuddering breath. "God, Belle, I love you."

She knew him too well to doubt his sincerity. Her dream was coming true. The rose of happiness unfurled, sending tendrils out to every inch of her body and soul.

All Annabelle Levy-Gower ever wanted from life, the gift of Tony's love, was finally hers.

Matters of The Heart

Since first I saw your face, I resolved to honour
   and renown ye;
If now I be disdained, I wish my heart had
   never known ye.
What? I that loved and you that liked, shall
   we begin to wrangle?
No, no, no, my heart is fast, and cannot
   disentangle.

> *Anonymous. Songs set by Thomas Ford,*
> *ii. Oxford Book of 16th Century*
> *Verse (Music of Sundry Kinds, 1607)*

The newfangled gas lighting had not yet reached Upper Brook Street, and the postilion astride the near leader peered intently at the shadowy facades of the houses they passed. Giving a shout to his colleague on the wheeler, he reined in and brought the post chaise to a stop.

Inside the dark, stuffy chaise, Caroline Hartford stretched her stiff, travel-weary body as best she could in the cramped space. She had arrived.

Heart pounding, she groped for her hat on the seat beside her. Her fingers shook, and she was still fumbling to tie the ribbons beneath her chin when the door opened.

"Number 'leven, Upper Brook Street, ma'am," the postilion said cheerfully. "Made it in good time. Ain't ten o' the clock yet, but it don't look like anyone's expectin' ye."

Caroline touched the reticule dangling from her wrist. Augusta's letter crackled reassuringly.

"If you'll just wait," she said. "I hope it won't be necessary, but we may have to go on to Curzon Street."

She clasped her bandbox and alighted. Oblivious to a blustering wind that felt more like April than May, she stood in front of the imposing two-story building with its wide portico and proud columns. She scanned the tall, arched windows for a sign of light. There was none. Not even the lantern above the front door was lit.

Bleak. Dark. Inhospitable.

That was how she had thought of Hartford House when Sir Joshua and Lady Hartford lived here. Sir Joshua had passed away ten years ago; Lady Hartford had been dead three years. Yet nothing, it seemed, had changed. The same parsimonious spirit that had ruled the household in Lady Hartford's day still reigned supreme.

Unless the house was closed up.

Behind Caroline, the horses snorted and stomped restlessly. The postilions, undoubtedly, were just as impatient to be on their way.

She started up the wide, shallow steps to the double-winged front door. Five days had passed since Augusta wrote the urgent plea and sent a courier from London to remote northern Wales.

Five days. Much could have happened in that time. Alex could have removed Melissa from Town. He might have decided to travel. Perhaps he had taken Melissa to Brussels, where all the world was gathering along with the allied forces in anticipation of a final confrontation with Napoleon Bonaparte.

But, in that case, the knocker would have been taken off the door.

Caroline was reaching for the brass lion's head when the right wing of the door opened a crack. Her hand dropped, and she took an involuntary step aside into the shadow of the firmly closed second wing.

Slowly, stealthily, the door opened wider, wide enough to allow a slender female to slip outside. Caroline's eyes were well-adjusted to the dark. She had no trouble identifying the female as a young girl, hatless, and wearing not so much as a spencer over her short-sleeved gown.

She heard a soft thud and a stifled exclamation. The girl was struggling with or, rather, tugging at something. The something turned out to be a bandbox that had gotten stuck in the door. When, finally, it was free, the girl firmly pulled the door shut. Taking a deep breath, she faced the street—and caught sight of the chaise-and-four.

Caroline could see only the girl's profile, the high forehead, the straight little nose, and firm chin. It was dark. The outline was vague. But Caroline never doubted that this was Melissa, the girl she had come to see.

"Arthur?" Melissa called softly, peering at the chaise.

"No, dear."

Melissa swung around as Caroline stepped forward. They faced each other on the topmost of the wide stone steps—two ladies, each with a bandbox clutched in her hand.

Melissa's eyes widened. "Who are you?"

"Caroline Hartford."

"Caroline? How strange. I've never heard of a Caroline Hartford, except for my mother. And she's been dead sixteen years."

Above the pounding of her heart and the stomping of the post horses, Caroline heard the clatter of hooves and the rattle of wheels as a vehicle approached at a fast clip from the direction of Grosvenor Square.

"Melissa, I am your mother."

When Arthur Pemberton did not show up as ordered at White's, Alex Hartford had been seized by a premonition of disaster. He had given the young whelp a half-hour, but at nine-thirty Alex's famed self-control snapped, and he had stormed from the club.

Racing his curricle through the dark streets, Alex had cursed himself for believing he could talk man to man with the jackanapes who was the object of his daughter's first passionate infatuation. He had cursed Arthur Pemberton for being a coward as well as a damned fool.

As Alex approached his home, he saw the waiting post chaise. Anger such as he had not known in years heated his blood. While he had striven for a reasonable understanding with young Pemberton, the cad had arranged an elopement with Melissa. The deuce! He'd skin Arthur Pemberton alive.

He thrust the reins into the hands of his tiger and vaulted from the curricle before it had come to a stop. He saw the postilions, standing at ease, in no apparent hurry to be gone. Melissa—bless the little scatterbrain— must have forgotten something.

Alex rounded the chaise. He heard Melissa's voice, unusually high and shrill, from the steps of Hartford House.

"That's impossible! You lie!"

He leaped up the steps. Two shadowy figures stood on the dark stoop. He had eyes only for his daughter, a bandbox clutched to her breast as if someone were about to snatch it from her. Which he did immediately.

"Inside, Melissa!"

He pushed open the door and propelled his daughter into the dark foyer.

"And you, Pemberton!" he said sharply to the second figure. "We had an appointment at White's. But this will do as well."

"Father!" Melissa's voice was shriller than before. "She says she is—"

"Why the devil is there no light?"

Alex dropped the bandbox and groped for flint and tinder on the foyer table. He found the articles and, in seconds, had lit a candelabrum.

"Melissa, go upstairs. I'll have a word with Pemberton,

116

and when I'm through, I swear he'll never propose an elopement to anyone again."

"*Father!*"

"Go."

He swung to confront Melissa's swain.

His breath caught at the sight of the woman standing in the doorway.

Caroline.

She closed the door.

Alex forgot Melissa. Forgot Arthur Pemberton. He remembered only the night seventeen years ago when he had fetched Caroline from her father's house.

She had met him at the door, a riot of long, dark brown curls cascading from beneath the hat that was hopelessly askew and whose ribbons were only half-tied. She had dropped her bandbox and rushed into his arms, her eyes alight with love and laughter, her mouth curved in a smile as seductive as it was mischievous.

"Alex, we must talk."

The words jarred, and the voice, cool, distant, was not the voice of the girl who had greeted him seventeen years ago. With a jolt, Alex returned to the present.

He had been stunned, for she still looked like the girl in his past. The girl who had captured his heart and soul, then had betrayed him and their infant daughter. But the numbness was wearing off.

"How dare you show your face in this house!"

She flinched.

"Father!" White-faced, Melissa tugged at his arm. "Is it true what she said? Is she my mother?"

"Your mother is dead."

He took a step toward Caroline and saw that she had changed after all. The face was thinner, the mouth tighter. The eyes—He quickly looked away from her eyes and the pain he saw there.

"Madam, you can only do harm if you remain in Town. My daughter has embarked on her first Season—"

"*My* daughter, too. And if I don't mistake the matter, I

117

arrived just in time to prevent a piece of foolishness she'd regret for the rest of her life."

Tonelessly, Melissa said, "You are my mother."

"Yes, I am."

Caroline wanted to say more, but even while she searched for the right words, Melissa turned away.

She rounded on her father. "You lied."

"It was meant for the best."

He looked at his daughter's closed face and knew he had said the wrong thing.

He opened his arms. "Come here, little one."

Melissa backed away.

"You lied. I'll never, *ever* again believe anything you say."

Picking up her skirts, she fled across the foyer and up the stairs. On the dim half landing she stopped and turned, looking down at Caroline.

"They said you died when I was five months old. But you did not die. You left." Her voice rose. "How could you leave your baby? *How could you?* Don't you know all children want a mother?"

Suddenly alone in the far too quiet foyer, they faced each other — Caroline wary, Alex uncertain, thrown off stride by Melissa's outburst.

"I must go after her," he said. "A daunting prospect, having to justify my actions to a volatile sixteen-year-old. Remind me to thank you for putting me in this position."

Caroline ignored the injustice of the remark. "Give her time. Speak to her in the morning."

"What if she's gone in the morning?"

She took a step backward. If only he did not stand so close.

"She won't be. It is obvious that Arthur let her down. Else he would have shown up by now."

"It is not at all obvious," he said irritably. "The coward probably wanted her to meet him in Grosvenor Square or at some coaching inn. And how, if I may ask, do you know about Arthur?"

"Melissa called his name when she saw the chaise, and you mentioned an elopement. Also—" She hesitated. But only frankness could serve her now. "Augusta wrote."

"The devil fly away with her!" Grimly he contemplated wringing his sister's neck. "What else did she tell you?"

"That you forbade an engagement and that Melissa hinted at an elopement to her cousins."

"Why the deuce didn't she tell me?"

"You had best ask Augusta."

Caroline tried to take another step backward, but her heel hit the door. If only he were using a different shaving soap. The faint scent of sandalwood set her mind spinning along the path of memories. But there was no time for memories. Not now.

She clasped the door handle, an anchor for her whirling thoughts. "If you'll excuse me? I must not keep the horses standing any longer."

His hand shot past her to press firmly against the door.

"Believe me, I want nothing more than to see you gone. And if I'd had my wits about me when I first saw you, you'd be halfway back to Wales by now."

Her temper flared, but she had not fought and struggled in vain these past years to master that most destructive of her many faults.

"There's no need to be so scathing, Alex. We are no longer the children we were when we married, and I should hope—"

"I was one-and-twenty," he cut in. "Hardly a child."

"A youth, then. And I was three months older than Melissa is now."

He frowned. Melissa was a babe. Caroline, when he met her, was—

Sharply, he reined in the thoughts that wanted once more to delve into the past.

"Now that Melissa knows about you, I cannot let you

119

leave. She must learn the truth. From both of us."

"I agree. I have no intention of leaving Town. I'm merely going to Curzon Street."

"Augusta. I should have known." He removed his hand from the door. "But I think you had better do as you planned originally. Stay here."

Again, he seemed too close, the scent of sandalwood hauntingly familiar.

With an effort, she said, "You're mistaken, Alex. I never planned to stay here."

He looked at the bandbox she still carried. "Didn't you, Caroline?"

Following his gaze, she blushed.

Once again, she reminded him of the Caroline he had courted. A Caroline who was vivacious, impetuous, shy and passionate, whose mood and temper switched capriciously.

A Caroline quite different from the poised, dignified woman who had this evening entered his house and quietly turned his life upside down.

"I never was very subtle. Was I, Alex? I fear it is an art I cannot learn."

He made no reply. None was required. The silence between them spoke volumes.

"Let me show you to a chamber."

"The postilions . . . my trunk . . ."

He grew impatient. "You may leave everything to me."

He removed the strap of the bandbox from her unresisting fingers and started for the stairs, picking up and lighting a bedroom candle on the candelabrum as he passed the table.

Tonight of all nights, the house must be steeped in darkness—undoubtedly Melissa's doing. She must have given the staff leave to retire and had doused the lamps in the belief that it would make things easier for an elopement. Unfortunately, the dark stairs and hallways stirred memories he would just as soon keep buried.

He lighted the way up the stairs. As if to mock him,

the tall-case clock at the back of the foyer struck the half-hour past ten. A clock had struck half past ten when he returned home that March night sixteen years ago, the night his ill-fated marriage took yet another turn for the worse.

At the time, he and Caroline did not live here at Hartford House but had their own small place just off Harley Street . . .

Quietly, Alex had let himself into the house. He did not want to be quiet. He wanted to shout for Caroline, wanted to break open a bottle of the finest champagne and celebrate. It was his twenty-second birthday, and his father had made him a full partner in the bank.

Hartford and Son, Bankers. The new sign had gone up that afternoon.

But Caroline no longer wanted to share his life. She had turned from him during her pregnancy, banishing him from her bedchamber before the fact that he was about to become a father had properly sunk in. She had been irritable, constantly picking quarrels, and during the last months made it clear that she would just as soon not see him at all.

Perhaps he should have gone to his mother for advice or to Caroline's mother, but the two ladies had made it clear that they wanted nothing to do with a marriage contracted against their express wishes. Of the two families only Augusta, his older sister, occasionally called on the young couple.

"Give her time," Augusta had replied to Alex's troubled questions. "For some women childbirth is as easy as shelling peas. But not for your Caroline. Be patient with her. She'll snap out of the doldrums as suddenly as she sank into them."

He had relied on her judgment. After all, Augusta knew everything there was about increasing; she had just presented her husband with a third daughter.

121

Alex had done his best, had showered his young wife with gifts and attention—only to be rebuffed. Now the baby was four weeks old, and Caroline was still as skittish as a colt. He hardly saw her, for she retired early, slept late in the mornings, and lay down for a nap after lunch. She said she must make up for the many nights she had been unable to rest during the nine miserable months of pregnancy.

Alex removed his shoes and tiptoed up the dark stairs. He stubbed a toe against the pedestal table on the first-floor landing. But he did not curse. The baby always woke at the slightest noise, and so did Caroline.

And then he saw the sliver of light under one of the doors. For a moment, he was alarmed. The baby! Melissa was sick.

But it was the sitting-room door. The light could mean only that Caroline was awake. She was waiting up for him.

His pulse quickened. Dare he hope that Caroline had snapped out of the doldrums at last?

The sliver of light became a beacon, a signal of hope, as he approached the door.

He walked slowly. Knowing that Caroline was waiting for the first time in many a month, he felt as shy as he had been on his wedding night. And as eager. After months of uncertainty, of doubt, even regret and growing resentment, he felt very much in love.

He pushed open the door. She was sitting on the hearth rug, a book in her lap. But she was not reading. She was staring at the grate as if fascinated by the faintly glowing embers.

"Caroline."

The book went flying as she scrambled to her feet. She did not, as he half-expected, come running to him but stood there, a barefoot nymph with her long, dark hair streaming down the white silk robe he had bought her in Edinburgh the day before their fathers caught up with them.

"Alex, where have you been?"

Eagerness switched abruptly to wariness. He stopped halfway into the room, which was small enough that he could not miss the dangerous glint in her eyes or the splash of angry color high on her cheekbones. Not a nymph after all. More likely an angry goddess. But why?

"Father invited me to take dinner with him at his club."

"Your father?" Her eyes narrowed. "He has never before invited you to dinner."

"He made me a partner today."

What should have been joyous news must suddenly serve as an excuse — for what he did not even know. Alex gritted his teeth as disappointment and resentment started nagging again.

Caroline still watched him through suspiciously narrowed eyes.

"Your father always leaves the bank at four o'clock. If you had dinner with him, surely you would have been home by eight?"

"What are you saying, Caroline? Are you accusing me of lying?"

"Yes!" Her voice was shrill. "Yes, you are lying. You've lied to me for months. You've been with your mistress, Alex. And don't try to deny it!"

A pugilist could not have landed a harder blow. It took his breath away. Guilt and shame made his face flame.

"You cannot deny it, can you? Not when everyone in Town knows about your mistress. Only I didn't know — until today."

Anger flared, hot and unbridled. He refused to feel guilty for something he could not help.

"If I took a mistress, you have only to blame yourself. Or did you think a man could live celibate for nine months and more?"

She blanched.

"But for your information, madam, I was *not* with my mistress tonight. I was celebrating the partnership and my birthday with my father."

"It is true, then. You do have a mistress."

He caught the glint of tears in her eyes, and hurt and kindling wrath.

"Alex Hartford, I hate you! I am seventeen years old and already a discarded wife!"

"Alex! Are you ill?"

The note of alarm in Caroline's voice tore the shroud of memories. Unfinished memories.

He realized in some embarrassment that he was standing motionless on the second-floor landing of his Upper Brook Street home. His brow was perspiring and the candle in his hand tilted precariously.

Devil a bit! Surely he did not still feel guilty over some lightskirt to whom only sheer necessity had driven him. Whereas Caroline, the deceitful little wretch—

"Of course I'm not ill," he said curtly, annoyed that his mind persistently wanted to explore the past. "I merely wish Augusta hadn't meddled."

"I am grateful to her."

Caroline reached out and took the dripping candle from him. Her eyes met his above the dancing flame.

Softly, she said, "If nothing else can stop Melissa from an elopement, her parents' sorry tale surely will."

"*I* could have told her."

"But would you have done it, Alex? You told our daughter that I was dead."

"It was better so."

"Only for you." Caroline's gaze held his. "While I was dead, you did not have to think about me. You did not have to wonder if, perhaps, you were wrong when you accused me of betraying you."

Her words hung between them—a challenge. But he did not pick up the gauntlet. If he did, he couldn't be certain he'd be able to keep the bitterness from spilling over.

He turned down the left-hand branch of the corridor. "You've had a long journey, Caroline. We'll talk in the morning."

Sunlight streamed through the windows and danced across the priceless Persian carpet when Caroline entered the breakfast parlor. What a contrast to the gloominess that had marked the house when she stayed here as a young bride while she and Alex looked for a place of their own.

She saw Alex watching her from the sideboard, where an array of silver chafing dishes was set out. He wore riding dress, buckskin breeches and a corduroy coat, perfectly tailored to his broad shoulders and narrow waist. At eight-and-thirty, he looked every bit as trim and athletic as he had at one-and-twenty.

But this morning, in daylight, she noticed the wings of gray in his raven hair.

Her throat felt dry, and the distance to the table suddenly seemed more than she could handle. She must have been mad to think that seeing him again would not affect her, that only Melissa could touch her heart.

To cover her confusion, she said, pointing to the windows, "Your mother will be turning in her grave. She never allowed the drapes opened in this room until afternoon."

Alex shrugged. His features were as stern, his eyes as chilling as they had been the night before.

"Do you still like kedgeree for breakfast?"

"Neither for breakfast nor for dinner." Stiffly she seated herself. The rice dish had been the only fare her stomach would tolerate while she was increasing, and she had not touched it since Melissa was born. "I'll have toast."

Alex set his own plate, filled with beef and eggs, back onto the sideboard and joined her at the table.

"How long will you stay?"

"As long as it takes to bring Melissa to her senses."

"I was thinking you might take her to Wales."

Caroline sat in stunned silence.

"Just for a visit, of course."

"Of course," she murmured, the softness of her voice contrasting with the quick flash of anger in her eyes. "I wouldn't presume otherwise."

"Your Aunt Selina—"

"Great-aunt Serena."

"Your Great-aunt Serena would not mind having Melissa?"

"She'd be thrilled. But what makes you think Melissa would want to exchange a Season in Town for a visit to a remote Welsh village?"

"Melissa is sixteen," he said curtly. "She'll do as she's bid."

"Just as she did your bidding when you told her she mustn't see Arthur again."

"I never forbade her to see Arthur."

"I beg your pardon. You merely told her she couldn't be engaged for another two years."

"Damn Augusta and her tattling! I daresay she also told you that I tried to bribe Melissa with a visit to Paris once we've recaptured the Corsican monster."

"But Melissa was not interested in your offer."

"She wasn't. But Wales. . . . She'll be curious about you. She'll want to know where and how you live. She'll want to see the great-great-aunt who defied family and convention and became a—"

"Alex," Caroline interrupted. "Is my presence in your house so intolerable that you would sacrifice common sense? You must know as well as I do that Melissa won't be interested in anything but Arthur Pemberton and parties and balls until the Season is over."

He rose abruptly. "I don't know what's the matter with the staff. Someone should have brought fresh toast and tea."

"I don't want fresh toast. There's plenty left in the rack."

Hiding her trembling hands beneath the damask cloth of the breakfast table, she watched him stop halfway to the bellpull by the door.

"But I'd like an answer to my question, if you please. Is my presence intolerable? If so, I wonder that you offered your home in the first place."

Slowly, he turned. He was pale. A vein throbbed at his temple where the streak of gray began.

"Since you seem to consider Wales a foolish notion, stay here by all means. Your presence does not bother me. I was merely trying to give Melissa a chance to forget young Pemberton."

"Out of sight, out of mind? It wouldn't work, Alex."

"It worked well enough for you."

"And how would you know?" She rose and walked toward him. "In sixteen years you did not once inquire about me. Your solicitors made it quite clear that you wished to know nothing but that I received the allowance you so generously provided."

"I need only look at you to understand that you've long forgotten your husband and daughter. How calm you are. Detached. Not even memories haunt you. Do they, Caroline?"

She trembled in the effort to remain as calm as he perceived her. "If I have forgotten, why would I travel night and day to stop Melissa from making the same foolish mistake I made?"

"What mistake? That you trysted with a lover where your husband could find you? Since Melissa is not married, she can hardly follow in your footsteps."

She believed she had overcome bitterness and anger. But, hearing the ugly accusation once more from Alex's mouth, she could not help herself. She slapped him.

The sight of Alex, proud, unmoving, pursued her as she ran from the breakfast room. The imprint of her hand on his face—

Caroline's mouth tightened. So much for the self-control she believed she had learned under Serena's wise tutelage.

If only Alex had betrayed emotion of some kind. His silence, the inscrutable look in his eyes, had unnerved her more than an outburst of anger could have done.

Her mind in turmoil, she fled to her chamber. She should be looking for Melissa, but she needed a moment to herself. Her behavior had been outrageous. Unpardonable. A lady did not resort to physical aggression.

And yet, perhaps the slap had been overdue. She had been foolish sixteen years ago, but she had not betrayed her husband.

It should not matter what Alex believed. She had come to help Melissa. Yet somehow his accusations, one old, the other new but equally unjust, could not be banished. She had placed two floors between them but still heard his voice.

You trysted with a lover . . .

You've long forgotten your husband and daughter. Not even memories haunt you . . .

She had never forgotten her husband and daughter. She had not tried. How could she when the one had meant so much, and the other was growing more important to her with every passing year.

Neither had she fought memories, only the bitterness those memories carried.

Standing at the window of Alex's guest chamber, Caroline stared blindly into the sun-dappled garden below. Would that she could forget those painful weeks after she learned of Alex's mistress.

She had still been weak from a difficult pregnancy and the nightmare of a breech birth. And she had been so damnably naive.

Aunt Serena, when she heard the tale, had called her green, which, for Serena, was mild. She had called Farmer Dillan's young wife daft when the pregnant fifteen-year-old turned a cold shoulder on her husband.

128

Then Serena, who had never been married, explained to the two ignorant wives about a man's needs.

If Serena had been in London during Caroline's pregnancy and recuperation . . .

But Caroline, a wife at sixteen, a mother at seventeen, had been alone. While she fought nausea, migraines, backaches, and a loneliness that could be assuaged only through the companionship of a trusted female, she had bluntly told Alex to go to the devil. She had never dreamed he would turn to an opera dancer.

And when she found out, she had punished him. She had ruthlessly suppressed a reawakening desire for his lovemaking by reminding herself of the lightskirt under his protection. As soon as the Season opened, she ignored fatigue and immersed herself in a whirlpool of gaiety. She danced and laughed and gambled. And she flirted outrageously.

Predictably, Alex reacted strongly—but not as anticipated. She had expected the quarrels and heated scenes that followed her tempestuous emergence upon the social scene. She had even welcomed them with the same grim determination she had welcomed that last burst of pain when Melissa finally slid from her body. But she had not expected total devastation.

Pressing her forehead against the window glass, Caroline struggled with her emotions. She did not want to delve too deeply into the past. And yet, how could she face Melissa, how could she be frank and truthful if she blocked those last weeks with Alex from her mind?

She gripped the cord that tied back the drapes. Her fingers tightened on the silken strands as slowly, deliberately, she forced herself back into another time.

"Dammit, Caroline!" Alex stormed into her bedchamber shortly after she returned from the May Dance at Vauxhall Gardens. "I will not be made a laughingstock!"

She had already scolded herself for possibly having

overstepped the bounds of propriety but instantly po-
kered up under the wrathful look he bestowed upon her.
He had no reason to be angry! *She* was not the one who
had taken a lover.

"Pray keep your voice down," she said coldly. "You'll
waken Melissa."

"And what do *you* care about Melissa?" He slammed
the door, extinguishing one of the candles on the dresser
with the surging draft. "Whitly says she's croupy. But *you*
went to the May Dance!"

Touched on the raw, Caroline pushed back the dressing stool and jumped to her feet.

"How dare you! It was you who accepted not only a
wet nurse but also the formidable Mrs. Whitlaker your
mother sent over. It was you who said the nurse knows
best and I must bow to her rules about when I may or
may not see my baby!"

He had the grace to blush. "Whitly does know best,"
he muttered. "She raised Augusta and me."

"Your *Whitly* allows me half an hour in the afternoon
with Melissa. As if I were a schoolgirl, granted permission to play with her doll!"

"That's neither here nor there," he said in the lofty
tone he assumed when he felt out of his depth. "We were
talking about the May Dance and your outrageous behavior."

She gave him a look, partly expectant, partly defiant.
Perhaps, finally, her scheme of revenge would bring the
desired results.

"*You* were talking about it. And as usual you're way off
the mark. I did nothing the other married ladies did not
do."

"They did not dance all night with Justin St. Clair."

"I'm not a girl just out. I'm a married woman, and I
may dance as often as I like with the same man."

"The deuce you may!"

He covered the distance between them in two long
strides.

"Especially when my husband does not care to accompany me and shows up only to spy on me!"

Which was exactly why she had danced and flirted with such shameless abandon. She had to prove something. To herself and to him. She wanted to make him so jealous that he would give his mistress the *congé* and beg his wife to take him back.

He gripped her arms, his fingers biting into the tender flesh.

"I asked you to keep away from St. Clair. He's a rake, a—"

"You did not ask. You commanded." She tossed her head, meeting his furious look with what she hoped was a very cool one. "I will not be ordered around as if I were a slave. And pray let go of my arms. You're hurting me."

He snatched his hands away as if they had been burned.

"My wife will behave with decorum. My wife will not dance around the Maypole like some unprincipled hoyden. And, most importantly, my wife will kiss no man but her husband."

The confrontation was not going the way she had envisioned. She had *not* kissed Justin St. Clair. He had taken her by surprise and snatched a kiss, but in view of Alex's unreasonable demeanor, she'd bite her tongue rather than plead innocence.

She stomped a bare foot. *"Your wife* is following the example set by you."

"I do not flirt with every Tom, Dick, and Harry."

"And a fine thing *that* would be!"

"Dammit, Caroline! How vulgar—"

"Don't swear! I am not the brazen hussy with whom you've been cavorting these past months. I am a lady."

He said nothing, only looked at her.

Suddenly self-conscious, she took her hands off her hips where they had been planted when anger displaced scheming. She pushed back her long hair and wished

131

she'd had time to braid it before he arrived. It was disconcerting to know that the unruly mane was tumbling around her shoulders.

Alex's expression softened.

"My lady wife," he said, a husky note creeping into his voice, "who looks like a combination of hoyden and wood nymph."

She gathered her dignity and the thin white silk of her robe—the first gift Alex had purchased as a husband—and retreated a few steps. She did not fear him, but she feared that certain look in his eyes and the familiar, unsettling effect it had on her, the arousal of sensations she had believed conquered.

She retreated another few steps.

Slowly, Alex followed.

For the first time since he entered her room, she noticed that he was coatless and had removed his cravat. His shirt was open at the neck, and she saw the strong beat of his pulse.

Her own pulse quickened.

"Don't come near me." Maddeningly, her voice was low and breathless. "You're still seeing that lightskirt, that opera dancer."

"I am not." The warm light in his eyes deepened. "Caroline, pray stand still. Allow me to explain."

"I don't want to hear about her."

Another step backward brought her in contact with the fourposter bed.

"Allow me, then, to tell you how much I've missed you."

He reached out, once more gripping her upper arms. His hold was firm and at the same time tender. It was the tenderness that burned through the thin silk of her sleeves.

I hate him, she reminded herself while her bones turned to jelly and her blood changed to fire racing through her veins.

"Alex," she whispered. "Don't—"

He stopped her with a kiss, and she was lost.

She breathed the sandalwood scent of his shaving soap and the scent that was Alex himself. When his hands caressed her back and hips, her arms wound around his neck. Her mouth opened, responding to the demand of his tongue.

I love him, she thought while he expertly dealt with the hooks of her robe and the tapes of his shirt.

Eagerly, her hands explored. It had been so long . . . his shoulders seemed wider, his arms more muscular. But nothing had changed in the way his kisses and his touch ignited desire and passion.

She sank down upon the bed, drawing him with her. She pulled him close, arching against him, and reveled in the feel of his heated flesh against her nakedness. Readily, she opened herself to him, inviting his entry.

And then pain. Searing, rasping, totally unexpected. Discomfort worse than the first time, when he had broken through her maidenhead. She could not suppress a moan or stop the instinctive thrust of her arms that pushed him away. Tried to push him away.

Alex clutched her shoulders. "Caroline, for heaven's sake! Don't play coy now."

"Alex, stop!"

She was not being coy. The burning inside her made her eyes water. She squeezed them shut.

She heard a muffled oath. The weight of his body shifted. The mattress rocked as he rolled to the side of the bed.

"I'm sorry, Alex." Pushing herself up on one elbow, she opened her eyes. "I don't understand what happened."

He had donned his breeches. Shirt and stockings in one hand, shoes in the other, he stood by the bed.

"I apologize," he said woodenly. "I give you my word, it shall not happen again."

"I'm sure the next time—"

"*Next* time?" He drew himself up in a way that reminded her of his father, the proud, stiff-necked Sir

133

Joshua Hartford. "Rest assured, you won't have to suffer my attentions again."

She could only stare at him.

Turning away, he said, "I shall take my pleasure where I know it's gladly given."

"Alex!"

He strode to the door, his step firm, his bare back straight and rigid.

"Alex!" Her voice rose. "Where are you going?"

The ominously quiet click of the closing door was the answer to her cry. She scrambled off the bed and started after him, only to realize that she was naked. By the time she had struggled into her robe and ran into the corridor, she heard the front door close.

Still, she hurried downstairs. He wouldn't leave, clad only in breeches. He had merely opened and shut the door to punish her, to make her think he had left the house, because he believed she had rejected him.

But she had not. She did not know why she had hurt, but she would make him understand. Somehow.

The tiny foyer was dark, yet she knew immediately that he wasn't there. She would have sensed his presence if he were waiting for her.

With trembling hands, she lit the candle on the hall table. The feeble light fell on the open closet beneath the stairs.

Alex's caped driving coat was missing from its peg.

A part of her died at that moment, and it did not take the sight of Alex and his opera dancer in the park the following day to confirm where he had gone.

However, seeing him with the tawny-haired beauty, whose hand rested on his arm in a distinctly proprietary manner, gave her the necessary pluck to show herself in society that night and on the following nights. And Justin St. Clair was only too glad to stand in for the husband who had deserted her.

Unlike most young ladies, who just about swooned when they caught sight of Justin St. Clair, Caroline was not infatuated with the blond giant. But something about his raffish air, his boldness, appealed to the reckless streak in her.

When St. Clair flirted with her, she felt once again like the high-spirited girl she had been before her marriage. His admiration made her the envy of every young woman. And in her state of hurt, Caroline needed to be envied, needed to be admired.

She hardly saw Alex. The partnership placed new responsibilities on his shoulders, and the evenings he spent at his club or, as solicitous matrons did not hesitate to inform her, in the company of his mistress. The few times they did meet at the dinner table, they quarreled about her friendship with Justin St. Clair and about Melissa.

Mrs. Whitlaker continued to rule the nursery, and aside from the allotted half-hour in the afternoon, Caroline had no contact with her daughter. It was the way things were done. Caroline was well-aware of it. She and her siblings had been raised by nurses, by governesses, and tutors. And yet she chafed under Mrs. Whitlaker's restrictions.

She tried to assert herself and demanded more time with Melissa, but Mrs. Whitlaker, like the footman and the three maids, had come from Hartford House and would not permit changes in the household routine unless sanctioned by Alex. And Alex still insisted that Whitly knew best.

With time hanging heavily on her hands, it was no wonder that Caroline drew closer to St. Clair and his raffish set, which included several very dashing and fast young matrons. Rumors began to spread about her relationship with St. Clair, but she only tossed her head and flirted more outrageously.

Wagers were offered and entered in the betting books at the clubs as to the date she would present Alex with a bastard child. She burned with resentment. *One* kiss, and that not even freely given but snatched from her, yet the

135

gentlemen of the *ton* judged her an adulteress.

But Caroline made no change in her way of life. She wanted to punish Alex, and, apparently, she was succeeding. They quarrelled more violently than ever. Alex forbade her to see St. Clair and, when she ignored the command, started to accompany her on the social rounds.

It was to quench the rumors and to protect his name, he told her harshly, not because he enjoyed her company. And she was glad that every minute spent with her deprived him of the pleasure of being with his mistress.

The end of Caroline's campaign of revenge came quickly, before the Season had drawn to a close. She went to watch a balloon ascension in Hyde Park with Justin St. Clair. The great event was set for two o'clock, a time when Alex was at the bank.

But this afternoon Alex decided to play truant and invited his mistress to share the excitement of the aeronautic spectacle. He steered his phaeton toward the open space near the ranger's house just a few minutes after Justin St. Clair had pulled up his curricle in a spot where Caroline would have an unimpeded view of the balloon dancing on its mooring ropes and of the coming and going of the curious.

Caroline, perhaps because she always unconsciously looked for Alex, saw the phaeton first. The pang of guilt at getting caught with St. Clair was quickly superceded by anger and resentment when she recognized the curvaceous woman in the cherry-striped gown beside Alex.

"St. Clair, take me home."

He had seen the phaeton, too. His deep-blue eyes glinted.

"Afraid, my sweet?"

"Not at all," she snapped. "I refuse to be seen at the same event with that woman."

The glint intensified, but without further ado he backed the curricle out of the spot he had so carefully selected. To reach the carriageway, they had to pass Alex and his companion. Caroline stonily looked straight ahead and yet was aware of every long second that Alex's burning gaze was fixed on her.

"Alex, look! Isn't that your wife?"

The two carriages passed each other, and Caroline never heard her husband's reply to his mistress.

I don't care, she assured herself. But she could not stop thinking about Alex and how empty and horrid life was without him. She was seventeen, a wife without a husband, a mother without a child.

Lost in dark thoughts, she paid no heed to the route St. Clair was taking, and he said nothing to draw her attention. When he reined in, she looked in astonishment at the large mansion with its imposing front of Corinthian columns, quite a contrast to her modest house off Harley Street.

"Devil a bit," she said crossly, "I asked you to take me home."

"I did. This is *my* home."

Before she could utter a retort, he said, "I think you deserve something for having to miss the balloon ascension. Offering you a glass of champagne is the least I can do."

A glass of champagne sounded like heaven. She'd had her first sip on her wedding night and had not enjoyed it as much as she thought she would. But when she immersed herself in the whirl of balls and routs this past Season, she had acquired a taste for the bubbly wine.

St. Clair was right. She did deserve compensation for having her outing spoiled by Alex and his mistress. But alone, in a bachelor's house?

She met St. Clair's quizzing look and recklessly dismissed a small, niggling doubt. He would not try to take liberties. At the May Dance she had made it quite clear that she did not appreciate having a kiss snatched, and he had since behaved impeccably.

"Very well. One glass of champagne. Then you'll take me straight home."

"If that is what you want."

"It is what I want."

He tossed a coin to one of the loitering urchins tumbling over each other for the privilege of holding the horses. Before she had time to reconsider, he had ushered her into the house, told the footman in the hall to fetch a bottle of champagne, and led her upstairs.

Her slippered feet sank into luxurious carpeting. She caught glimpses of paintings and tapestries in the stairwell and corridors but was too distracted to admire them when she realized that St. Clair was taking her to the second floor — the floor where, in a large, fashionable town house, the bedrooms were located.

"St. Clair—"

"Here we are. Welcome, Caroline."

He opened a door, and she noted with relief that it led into a sitting room, although, most likely, adjoining a bedchamber.

The footman, as though his master's demand for champagne in the afternoon was an everyday occurrence, appeared promptly with a tray of glasses and a bottle resting in a bowl of ice. He departed, closing the door behind him, as soon as he had deposited the tray on the marquetry top of a large square table.

While St. Clair poured, Caroline settled herself on one of four brocade-covered chaise longues flanking the table and pulled off her gloves.

Handing her a brimming glass, St. Clair raised his own.

"May our dreams come true."

Her eyes fell under his intent look. Suddenly, she had no desire for champagne.

"Don't you have dreams?" he asked softly.

She thought of Alex. "Oh, yes."

"That is good."

Sitting down beside her, he draped an arm over the back of the chaise longue.

"Lean back, little Caroline. There's no need to sit

poker stiff when you're with me. No need to deny your dreams."

The champagne glass shook in her hand as the implication of his words sank in. He took the glass and set it on the table along with his own.

Smiling, he turned to her. "Why are you afraid, my sweet?"

"St. Clair, you are laboring under a misapprehension. I am—"

"You are adorable." Possessing himself of her hands, he said huskily, "I have waited a long time for this moment. Kiss me, Caroline."

His deep-blue eyes held her spellbound. She wanted to tell him no but seemed incapable of speech. In her mind, she saw Alex in his mistress's plump arms, saw him kiss her, saw him in her bed . . .

As suddenly as it had appeared, the image was dispelled by an imperative knock on the door.

A knock?

Still clutching the silk drapery cord at the window of Alex's guest chamber, Caroline blinked in confusion. Much had happened after St. Clair demanded the kiss. Disturbing, oversetting things. But there had been no knock.

And Alex, when he burst into St. Clair's sitting room a scant fifteen minutes later, certainly had not announced his arrival.

"Caroline!" The rapping grew more demanding. "Must I break down the door?"

She gave a cry, half laughter, half sob, and ran across the room to wrench open the door.

"Augusta!" She hugged her sister-in-law. "You cannot know how awfully glad I am to see you."

"I should hope you're glad," Augusta said dryly. "After all, I just returned your runaway daughter."

Melissa was confined to the house for this second at-

tempt to elope. Augusta warned Caroline to be on the
alert for a third try, but Caroline felt certain Melissa was
cured of her infatuation. Even the most romantic young
miss must lose interest in the swain who stands her up
on the night of the proposed elopement. A swain who
asks his mother to receive her in his stead when his beloved has him roused on the following morning by the
maid scrubbing the front steps.

Arthur Pemberton's mother, as was to be expected,
had immediately called for her carriage to convey Melissa home. However, she succumbed to the girl's entreaties and took her to Augusta instead.

Augusta had listened to her niece's tearful explana-
tions, made her eat a fortifying breakfast, then promptly
marched her off to Upper Brook Street.

And now Melissa, pale and listless, moped about the
house.

Augusta's two youngest daughters, seventeen-year-old
Mary and fifteen-year-old Eliza, stopped by on the second afternoon of Melissa's confinement. Chaperoned by
Eliza's governess, they planned to visit Gunter's for one
of the Italian ices advertised by the confectioner and offered to plead with their Uncle Alex for leniency on Melissa's behalf so she might accompany them.

"Don't bother." Selecting a strand of peacock blue embroidery silk from the workbasket at her side, Melissa
threaded a needle. "I don't care for an ice today."

Mary gave her a shrewd look. "You're afraid there's
gossip about you, that people will stare and whisper."

"I'm not afraid of anything," said Melissa, working her
sampler.

The lofty tone reminded Caroline of Alex sixteen years
ago, when he wanted to hide uncertainty. Melissa also
resembled her father physically. Her features, except for
the eyes, which were wide set and gray like Caroline's,
were Alex's features. Softer, of course, and more
rounded, but definitely Alex's. The hair, too, was raven
colored like Alex's but showed the curliness of Caroline's

hair.

Pride swelled Caroline's breast. Her daughter was a very pretty girl.

Eliza's high young voice caught her attention.

"I heard Mama tell Lady Jersey this morning that Arthur Pemberton has gone to Brighton. Melissa, does that mean you're no longer betrothed to him?"

Melissa gave her youngest cousin a fierce look. "Arthur is a callow youth, and I do not wish to hear his name ever again."

"Oh," breathed Eliza, her eyes as big as saucers. "But—"

"Hush!" said Mary. "Not another word, or I'll have to tell Mama that you eavesdrop when she is receiving."

"Tattletale!"

Miss Richards, the governess, gave Caroline an apologetic look. She rose. "Miss Mary, Miss Eliza, if you still want an ice, we had best be going."

When the little party had left, silence, deep and heavy, spread in the garden room where Caroline and Melissa were sitting near the open terrace door. Caroline watched for a moment as her daughter, head bent over the sampler, set stitch after stitch on the colorful cloth.

They had sat thus, silent and distant, before Mary and Eliza arrived. And they had sat thus on the previous day, after Caroline's every attempt at conversation had been rebuffed with monosyllabic replies or silence.

Caroline took up the sewing she had earlier put aside and thought about the quirk of fate that had robbed Alex of a governess's services, while Augusta, who was perfectly able of looking after her two youngest daughters, still had Miss Richards. But perhaps Miss Richards did not have a mother who might fall and break a hip.

It was her mother's unfortunate accident that had forced Melissa's governess to tender her resignation. Alex had immediately advertised for a new governess but, according to Augusta, had stopped the interviews when the candidates showed more interest in their prospective em-

141

ployer than in the pupil.

Harassed, Alex had begged his sister to bring out Melissa this Season with Mary rather than the following year with Eliza. And at the come-out ball, Melissa had met Arthur Pemberton, a nineteen-year-old poet, aspiring to become the next Lord Byron.

Keeping her eyes on the work, Caroline said, "I planned to tell you my story as an example of how tragic the end of a marriage by elopement can be. But, I believe, you no longer need to be warned?"

Melissa's head came up. "You and Father *eloped?*"

"Indeed. Did he never tell you? It was a true runaway match. We were married in Gretna Green. We wanted to tour the Highlands on our honeymoon but got no farther than Edinburgh before our fathers caught up with us."

Melissa turned back to her embroidery.

For several minutes, which, for Caroline, stretched like hours, they worked in silence. She was beginning to despair of ever having a conversation with her daughter.

"Melissa, I cannot believe that you're not at all curious. Surely you want to know what happened?"

The question, when it came, was almost inaudible.

"Why did you leave?"

Caroline stifled a sigh. So much for her plan to lead up gradually to the final destruction of an ill-advised marriage.

"I had no choice. The Church granted your father the separation he requested."

"A *divorce?*"

The word with all its implications of disgrace and scandal hung between them.

"A divorce a mensa et thoro, which is granted by an ecclesiastical court. It is not an absolute divorce. Neither of us is at liberty to marry someone else."

"So that's it." Melissa appeared to be addressing her embroidery. "And I always believed—when I still thought Father was a widower—that he had loved you too deeply to remarry."

Caroline wanted to ask if there had been someone Alex might have wished to marry, but she said nothing.

She caught a sidelong look from her daughter. The hostility in those gray eyes made her want to cry.

"Melissa, what else do you want to know? I'll answer any question as best I can."

"After the separation," Melissa said gruffly, "what did you do?"

"I was a minor. I was sent back to my parents in disgrace."

"I visited Leigh House often. I never saw you." Melissa looked up from her stitching. She frowned. "Or did I, when I was very young? At times you look familiar."

"You did not see me at Leigh House."

But you saw me. More than once. Caroline gripped her sewing tightly to hide the trembling of her hands. There was so much to tell Melissa, it was difficult to know what to relate first.

She said, "My parents had not forgiven me for the elopement, and now I had caused another, worse scandal. So my father shipped me off to his aunt in Wales. Your Great-great-aunt Serena."

Again silence fell. Caroline was reluctant to break it. She knew that Serena, wise in matters of heart, soul, and body, would counsel her to let Melissa ask the questions that concerned her most.

And Melissa did ask.

"Why did Father want the divo—the separation?"

"He believed I betrayed him."

"Did you?"

"No."

Melissa sighed. Caroline had no way of knowing whether it was a sigh of relief or a sigh denoting doubt.

"Why, then, would Father believe ill of you?"

"I have wondered if it was because I agreed to elope with him. In retrospect, he must have judged me fast and unprincipled."

"That doesn't make sense. Didn't you love each other

143

when you eloped?"

"Indeed, we loved each other very much. But love alone is not sufficient to sustain a marriage. You also need trust. And that, I believe, was something we both lacked. Then, when Alex discovered that I had done something imprudent—"

"What did you do?"

"I visited a gentleman in his house."

Melissa gave her a quick, hard-to-read look. But, to Caroline's relief, she asked no further questions about the incident leading up to the divorce.

"Why did you elope? Did my grandparents Leigh forbid you to marry Father?"

"Naturally they did. And your grandparents Hartford also opposed the marriage. I was sixteen, Alex one-and-twenty. He had just left Oxford and was supposed to learn the banking trade."

"I wager Grandmother Hartford did not want Father to marry one of the extravagant Leighs. And Grandmother Leigh believed you were marrying beneath your station."

Caroline laughed softly. "You knew your grandmothers well. Lady Hartford had her heart set on an heiress for your father, and my mother—" She slipped into an imitation of her mother's proud, clipped tones. "Viscountess Eversleigh, daughter of an earl, granddaughter of a duke, could never countenance a marriage between her daughter and the son of a mere baronet in the *banking trade.*"

"You did that very well. The imitation, I mean."

"Hmm." Caroline snipped off a length of thread. "My father caught me once when I was doing my imitation and punished me with three days of bread and water."

"So did my father."

Two pairs of gray eyes met over the piecrust table separating them. Melissa was not exactly smiling, but the closed, hostile look was gone, replaced by one of pure curiosity.

144

"When Grandfather caught you in Edinburgh and found that you were married, did he disown you?"

"No, he took me home. He and Sir Joshua immediately started the process for an annulment."

The sampler forgotten, Melissa leaned forward in her chair. Elbows propped on her knees, chin on clasped hands, she stared at Caroline.

"But didn't you—hadn't you and Father . . . ?" Blushing, Melissa let her voice trail.

"Yes, we had consummated the marriage. But your grandfathers were willing to overlook such a minor detail."

"Only it wasn't minor, was it?"

Something, a flutter of a movement or a breath of a sound, made Caroline glance to her left, toward the hall door. Alex stood there, motionless, arms crossed over his chest, shoulders propped against the wall. She had no notion how long he had been listening.

He did not speak and made no move to join them.

Quickly, heart pounding irrationally, Caroline returned her attention to Melissa, whose intent gaze had not wavered from her mother's face.

"No, Melissa. A pregnancy is never a minor detail."

"Mary says it is indelicate to use the word *pregnancy*."

"I daresay. But since I've lived with our Aunt Serena and assisted her in her work, I've learned to call a spade a spade."

"I never heard of Aunt Serena until now."

"I'm not surprised." Caroline shot a quick look in Alex's direction but did not wish to turn her head and caught only a glimpse of a stern profile. "Like mine, Serena's name is never mentioned in the family. She, too, is in disgrace."

"Whatever she did, it must have been a long time ago. You said she's my great-great-aunt. How old is she?"

"Serena is seventy-two."

"Did she also elope?"

"No, she never married. As a young woman she

caused an uproar by attending lectures at the Royal College of Physicians."

Melissa's jaw dropped. "How daring! Is she a physician then? A lady physician?"

"She's more than qualified, I'm sure. But, of course, she may not call herself a physician or surgeon even though she does the work of both and acts as midwife as well. She has established an infirmary for miners struck with the black lung disease and has set up an orphanage. Coal-mining country has many orphans."

Melissa looked at the tiny garment Caroline was hemming. "Is that for the orphanage?"

"For the orphanage or for Serena's Cradle Shoppe."

"A store? I'd have thought that miners are too poor to buy anything."

"The women who come there don't buy. They pick out what they need for their infants and children and, later, return the items if they're not worn out."

"It seems to me the Leighs should be proud of Serena."

"Indeed, they should be. The people of Caernarvon call her Saint Serena. Not to her face. They know she wouldn't appreciate it, and they don't care to provoke a scolding."

"She must be quite a character."

"If you like, I'll take you to see her."

Immediately, Melissa's face took on a closed look. "Are you going back to Wales?"

"Eventually."

"Why?"

Very much aware of Alex listening in silence, Caroline fixed her gaze on the sampler, which had slipped off Melissa's lap. Why, indeed? She was no longer a minor who must bow to a parent's or guardian's decree.

Serena had wanted her to move back to London when she came of age, but pain and humiliation had still been raw. She had believed it beyond her fortitude to live where she must come face-to-face with Alex.

146

Now, she was three-and-thirty years old. From an impetuous, high-spirited, foolishly romantic girl she had changed into a wise, dignified matron. She *had* come face-to-face with Alex—and had seen wisdom and dignity go to the dickens.

Melissa's voice, low, intense, broke into her thoughts. "Why didn't you just stay in Wales, then?"

"I wanted to see you."

"Bah!" Eyes sparkling with angry tears, Melissa stood up. "Almost sixteen years you showed no interest in me. You forgot you had a daughter! And now you expect me to believe that, in the twinkling of a bedpost, you developed a burning desire to see me?"

"You are wrong, Lissa. I never forgot you."

The girl's dark brows knitted. "What did you call me?"

"Lissa."

Deliberately closing her mind to Alex's disturbing presence, Caroline rose also. This moment with her daughter was all-important.

"It is what I used to call you when we played at your Aunt Augusta's. And you used to call me—"

"Fairy," whispered Melissa, her eyes widening as childhood memories came tumbling back.

Caroline hardly dared breathe while she watched her daughter's expressive face. Hope soared at a softened look and was dashed to the ground when hurt and bitterness sharpened the vulnerable young features.

"I *loved* my Fairy. I told her so over and over again the few times she visited. But she never came back after I turned four."

Caroline ached to take Melissa into her arms, to kiss the hurt away. She wanted to tell her how much she loved her but was afraid even to reach out and touch her daughter's hand.

"Augusta said that you were talking about me all the time. I feared that—Oh, I don't know what I feared." Caroline started to tremble. "You kept saying you wished I were your mother."

147

"You left me *twice*."

"But I did not forget you. I watched you from afar whenever I came to London. I watched you run and play in the park with Mary and Eliza. I watched you ride your pony."

And how much it had hurt, knowing that the occasional glimpse of her daughter's life was all she could ever have, that she could never share the joys, the childish sorrows, would never again hold her in her arms.

"I wish you had never come here!" Melissa cried. "I hate you!"

Kicking the sampler out of the way, she ran from the room.

"Lissa!"

Caroline started after her. Tears blurred her vision, and she did not see Alex until he blocked her path.

"Leave her be, Caroline."

Her control snapped. "Damn you, Alex! I'm not going to hurt her! It was *you* who took the child away from me. *You* are the one who caused her pain."

"I'm not afraid you'll hurt Melissa. Only that she'll hurt you if you try to speak with her now. Give her time. Talk to her again tomorrow."

The tears fell unchecked. "I knew it would be difficult, that she'd be resentful. But I didn't think she'd hate me."

"Hate and love," he murmured. "Two sides of the same coin."

Their eyes met and held for just an instant before Alex reached into his coat pocket and pulled out a handkerchief. He handed it to Caroline.

She wiped her face, old tears and a fresh stream . . . because she foolishly remembered a time long ago, when Alex had kissed away her tears after some trifling incident overset her.

What a watering pot she had been during the early days of pregnancy. Alex had been very patient then, very gallant, even though she was perfectly horrid to him.

And now she was turning into a watering pot again

148

because she wanted her daughter's love . . . and because she now understood that the indiscretion with Justin St. Clair had not been the only mistake she made during the course of her brief marriage.

"Pray excuse me, Alex."

Clutching his handkerchief, she started past him to seek the sanctuary of her room — a guest chamber in her husband's house. But she was not to be granted solitude. Alex accompanied her.

"Caroline, will you join me in the study? I believe it is time we had a talk."

The study was located on the first floor. Like the other rooms Caroline had seen so far, it had undergone a change. The dark maroon window hangings she remembered had been replaced with bright gold drapes. The heavy walnut desk, behind which. Sir Joshua had spent his evenings pouring over bank ledgers, had been routed by a smaller, more elegant desk in the Louis XIV style.

Two armchairs stood vis-à-vis in front of the fireplace, each with its own lamp table at the side. One table supported a stack of ledgers, the other held copies of Maria Edgeworth's Gothic novel, *Castle Rackrent*, and Mary Wollstonecraft's *A Vindication of the Rights of Women*.

Caroline's heart ached at the sight. Alex and his daughter — *their* daughter. In her mind she saw them, seated in companionable silence, soft lamplight spilling on the dark heads bent over the pages of a book or a ledger.

"Won't you sit down?" Alex motioned to a chair.

Melissa's chair. Feeling like an intruder, Caroline leaned against the cool green and gold-striped satin of the chair back.

Alex elected to remain standing. With his shoulders resting against the wide mantel shelf and one hand in his coat pocket, he appeared totally at ease. Then he started to speak, and his voice betrayed the tension he concealed so well.

"It seems the families should not only be proud of Serena but of you, too."

She did not miss the use of the plural *families* and shot him a look of astonishment. Did *he* feel proud of her?

"I assist Serena. That's all. And I'm sure at first I was more hindrance than help. But Serena knew how important it was for me to keep busy. She immediately put me to work in the orphanage nursery to help look after the infants and toddlers."

"I hope," he said quietly, "the children softened the pain of losing Melissa."

Nothing had softened the pain, but there was no point in dwelling on past hurts. The present still held more than she wished to face.

Tartly, she said, "Working with the children showed me how much I did not know. Nurse Whitlaker had never even permitted me to bathe Melissa."

Alex stirred, as though uncomfortable with the inadvertent reminder of past quarrels.

"What did you wish to discuss, Alex? I'm sure it wasn't my life in Wales."

"No." He met her gaze squarely. "I want to talk about you and Melissa."

Her breath caught. "You'll allow me more time with her, won't you? I couldn't bear leaving before—"

"I'm not asking you to leave."

"Then . . . what about Melissa and me?"

"When she was small and talked about her Fairy, I refused to believe it was you."

"Why? So you would not have to confront me?"

"I did not want to have to acknowledge that I might have been wrong in denying you the right to visit our daughter. I permitted myself to believe that you were content in Wales, that you had no desire to see Melissa. A belief conveniently confirmed when she stopped talking of her Fairy."

Caroline gripped the armrests of the chair. What if she

150

had confronted Alex? What if she had demanded the right to see Melissa? She might have spared herself sixteen years of longing.

"You still have the most expressive face," said Alex. "Pray don't torture yourself. I doubt I would have changed my mind had you challenged me then. Only recently has pride succumbed to wisdom."

Breathlessly, she asked, "Are you saying you have changed your mind now? That I may see Melissa—if she is agreeable—anytime I wish?"

"I am saying more than that."

Pushing away from the mantel, he came to stand directly in front of her.

"I am admitting that I committed a grave error in separating mother and child. I should have allowed Melissa to visit you in Wales. She needed you, your love, as much as you needed her. Caroline, I am sorry."

The apology threw Caroline into confusion, but it also sustained her during the following days. Melissa did not avoid her, but neither did she initiate contact or conversation. Once more Caroline had to hack away at the barrier of indifference Melissa erected between them. Until Alex took a hand.

He went to the bank in the mornings but started to spend the afternoons at home. In Melissa's presence, but always addressing Caroline, he initiated conversations revolving around Melissa's childhood days and Caroline's life in Wales.

Thus, without having to participate or betray curiosity, Melissa learned of the long days her mother worked at the orphanage and the infirmary, the evenings spent studying Serena's medical books. She learned of Caroline's trepidation when Serena had first sent her out on her own to attend a birthing, the pride of accomplishment when Caroline heard the babe's lusty cry.

Melissa witnessed the eagerness, the joy tinged with

151

sadness, as Caroline learned about her daughter's first word, the first wobbly step, the first pony, the summers spent in Margate with Alex.

They talked all afternoon, but in the evenings after dinner, Alex retired to his study. And Melissa, muttering an almost inaudible excuse, followed him after a few minutes, leaving Caroline in the drawing room to enjoy the dubitable pleasure of her own company.

Invariably, Alex's butler entered the drawing room at ten o'clock. "Will you be joining Sir Alex and Miss Melissa, my lady?"

The first time it happened, she had looked at him in confusion. Sir Alex? My lady? But, of course, on Sir Joshua's death Alex had inherited the baronetcy and had become *Sir* Alex. And she was Lady Hartford. Or was she? Caroline had no notion whether or not a woman acceded to the husband's rank after a divorce.

The question had not been worth puzzling. More immediate was the concern that she might betray sadness when she shook her head and, night after night, gave the same answer to the butler's question.

"I'll take tea here, Baxter."

And as she sipped her tea and pictured the study with its two chairs in front of the fireplace, she told herself that tomorrow was another day. Another afternoon to be spent as a threesome.

On the fourth afternoon rain drove them from the terrace into the garden room. Alex lit a fire, and when the flames danced brightly, Melissa knelt on the hearth rug to toast muffin halves on a long-handled fork.

Handing a muffin to Alex for buttering, she suddenly looked at Caroline. "Did you truly still come to London to see me after you stopped visiting Aunt Augusta's house?"

"Twice a year." Caroline spoke calmly, but she had to set down her teacup for fear of spilling. Ridiculous to be shaking because her daughter had addressed her! "If travel was possible, I came for your birthday. Otherwise in March. The second visit I made in the autumn . . . except this past autumn and spring."

"What happened?"

"A mine shaft collapsed. And in February influenza struck."

Caroline did not add that when in late March the last patient recovered, she had succumbed to the infection. She had been worn out, and the attack was a severe one. When it finally passed, she was as weak as a newborn kitten and had only just regained strength and vigor when Augusta's letter arrived.

"Where did you stay when you visited London?"

"At Grillon's. The hotel was Serena's choice. She usually traveled with me to take in a lecture or two."

Spearing another muffin, Melissa nodded. "At the Royal College of Physicians."

"There's also the Royal College of Surgeons now," said Alex.

"Yes, Serena attended both. And she visited the bookstores. She always bought a trunkful of books."

"Medical textbooks, I wager," said Melissa and with those words once more withdrew into the role of silent observer.

But it did not matter, Caroline assured herself. If the silence was broken once, it could be broken again.

Gradually, over the next few days, Alex introduced the topic of their long-ago marriage into the conversations. Caroline was startled at first and hesitant to discuss that dark side of the past. But reluctance waned as she realized that she and Alex could talk quite rationally about incidents that had caused major quarrels sixteen years ago.

Indeed, the conversations were an excellent tool to teach Melissa about the inadvisability of an elopement. Unfortunately, delving into the past, it was easy for Alex and Caroline to forget that Melissa was listening. But, perhaps, forgetting Melissa's presence was for the best. Only if they addressed each other without regard for an audience could they speak without reserve.

Melissa watched Alex and Caroline closely. She knew her father to be a fair, just, and scrupulously honest man. Yet he had let her grow up in the belief that her mother was dead. And he had divorced her mother, even though Caroline said that she had not betrayed him.

Had her father been wrong? Or had Caroline lied?

Caroline . . . her mother.

Melissa listened intently as over the next days the story of her parents' brief marriage unwound. She was torn this way and that, feeling first with one, then with the other.

Arthur Pemberton—and she could not help thinking about him occasionally and drawing a comparison between herself and Caroline—shrank to insignificance. If Arthur had truly loved her, he would not have been such a coward and escaped to Brighton without speaking to her. He would have either told her that they must wait the two years her father stipulated, or he would have found a way, as her father had found the way and means, to marry in the face of opposition.

And if she had truly loved Arthur, wouldn't she feel the hurt and misery that was so often mirrored in Caroline's eyes?

Always truthful, Melissa admitted that, although she did cry herself to sleep, Arthur's defection had hurt her pride more than her heart.

But it had been different with her father and Caroline. They had loved each other deeply—even when they fought most bitterly. The hurts they inflicted on each other had always found their target in the heart.

They might have lacked trust, as Caroline believed. But, watching and listening, Melissa understood that the lack had been more fundamental. Her parents, she realized in some shock, had lacked wisdom. Like children fighting over a butterfly they were lucky to have caught,

Alex and Caroline had pummeled each other, not seeing that in the process the butterfly must get crushed.

Another dinner was over, and Alex rose to go to the study.

"Wait, Father."

Pushing back her chair, Melissa looked at Caroline. "Won't you join us? It cannot be much fun sitting alone in the drawing room."

"No." Caroline's voice was unsteady. "I cannot say that it is fun."

"I'll fetch your sewing, shall I?" Melissa twirled from the room in quite an unladylike manner.

Alex stepped around the table to draw back Caroline's chair. She did not look at him. He had been relaxed, even friendly, these past days, and she did not want to witness a recurrence of the former stiffness if Melissa's invitation had met with disapproval.

"Why so hesitant, Caroline? I promise you, I did not bribe or coerce her."

Rising, she turned to face him. "And you, Alex? How do you feel about my joining you?"

"I'll let you judge for yourself. Come along."

Silently she went with him to the first floor. He opened the study door and motioned her into the room.

She saw it immediately. The third armchair in front of the fireplace.

Her eyes filled with tears, but she blinked them back. She would *not* be a watering pot on this happy occasion.

"The chair has been here these past three nights," Alex said. "But I wanted the invitation to come from Melissa."

"She did not disappoint you."

Lightly touching her elbow, he ushered her across the room. "Will you sit between Melissa and me?"

She nodded but did not immediately sit down.

"How did you know, Alex?"

He raised a quizzing brow. "Know what?"

"How I felt about the chairs."

"I told you. Your face—it's still as expressive as it was when I first met you."

"But I've worked so hard to master my emotions!"

"With admirable results. I congratulate you."

She gave him a sidelong look. Was that laughter underlying the gravity of his voice?

"Neither of us is as explosive as we were sixteen, seventeen years ago," he said. "But that does not mean we are without feelings. And *your* feelings are still mirrored in your eyes—as they were all those years ago."

He smiled at her—a smile that softened and transformed the stern features, and she saw Alex as she first saw him that night long ago . . . when she had fallen in love.

"Caroline—" His grip on her elbow tightened. "Do you remember?"

Their eyes locked.

"The *bal masqué* at Vauxhall," she said, feeling as giddy and breathless as she had felt as a young girl, pitchforked from the schoolroom straight into society. "My first grown-up party."

"You were a wood nymph in floating white, with garlands of some greenery draped over your bosom and one shoulder. You looked happy, excited, eager to embrace the world." His voice low, warm, he added, "And you looked ravishing."

"You were a Corsair, carefree, daring and dashing with your sword. And with a patch over one eye."

"I was a silly braggart, wearing a real sword in a heavy, jewel-encrusted scabbard that hit and poked everyone careless enough to get too close."

She laughed softly. "It was a marvelous sword. If it had been papier-mâché, it might not have torn the velvet garlands on my gown."

"And we might never have exchanged a word that night."

Engrossed in each other and their memories, they did

not hear Melissa enter the study or see when she retreated a few steps. Motionless, a sewing basket clutched in each hand, Melissa stood just inside the doorway.

She could see them only in profile, but there was something about Caroline's upturned face and the way her father looked at Caroline that made her feel shut out. Her heart thumped, as if she were a Peeping Tom about to be caught.

She wanted to leave, and yet she wanted to stay. She wanted to hear what they said, and yet she was reluctant to listen for fear of what she might hear.

Once or twice these past days, she had wondered what it would be like if Caroline stayed forever. And she had asked herself whether she would want her to stay. She did not remember what had brought these questions on. They had suddenly been there when she was trying to gage her father's feelings, for she had begun to suspect that Caroline's betrayal—if there had been one—no longer mattered to him.

She had learned much about that brief, stormy marriage of her parents. She had heard about her father's mistress, which should perhaps have shocked her since it had so terribly upset Caroline at the time. But she had only been curious whether the woman was the same one her father visited occasionally in St. John's Wood now. Aunt Augusta had explained all about gentlemen and their need for female companionship.

Her parents had also talked about Caroline's friendship with a gentleman named Justin St. Clair. But so far her father had not touched upon the day he found Caroline in the gentleman's house. This silence about something so important, Melissa could not understand. Whatever her father had seen that day had been the climax of his quarrels with Caroline. It had ended the marriage. But Caroline said she had not betrayed him.

Caroline . . . her mother.

She had never yet called Caroline "Mother." Perhaps the omission was an unconscious answer to the question

157

whether she wanted Caroline to stay.

Fascinated, Melissa watched the couple by the fireplace. They looked different. Younger. Happier?

The occasion was no different from all the previous times when she had listened to their reminiscences. And yet it was. Because *they* were different.

They were talking about the time they met at Vauxhall, about escaping from Caroline's chaperon and walking, hands entwined, down the dark, secluded paths where only lovers walked.

She saw tenderness in Caroline's smile, tenderness in the way Alex leaned toward her. He had one hand on Caroline's elbow. The other hand went up to touch her cheek.

Slowly Melissa backed into the corridor. Her throat and mouth were dry. She felt lost, thrust by some unknown force into an unknown territory.

Dropping the workbaskets, she fled along the hallway, up the stairs to her room, where everything was constant and familiar.

"What did we say?" Caroline frowned at the baskets, which Alex had set on the chair usually occupied by Melissa. "What could she possibly have heard to make her run off?"

"I'd say it was something she saw." Alex took up his favorite stance, shoulders resting against the fireplace mantel, one hand in his coat pocket. "That I was about to kiss you."

Caroline sat down rather quickly. He *had* wanted to kiss her. She had wondered and wished when he released her after the thud in the hallway but had not expected confirmation. With difficulty, she kept her mind on Melissa.

"Alex, you don't suppose she'll pack her bandbox again?"

"And run off to Brighton in search of young Arthur?"

He shook his head. "Hardly. She may have inherited the Leigh recklessness, but she also received a goodly portion of Hartford pride."

"A Leigh has pride, too."

A hush fell over the study, a silence thick with memories of the past and awareness of the present.

"Caroline."

Her name, spoken in deep, husky tones, hung in the air like a cloud of frozen breath.

Alex stepped away from the mantel.

She was unaware of rising, of moving toward him, knowing only that she must have done so when he caught her in his arms and his mouth claimed hers in a kiss that left her breathless and shaken. One kiss, one embrace, and she was once again the giddy, reckless, and foolishly romantic girl of her youth who dreamed of love everlasting.

Relaxing his tight hold, Alex looked into the upturned face with the soft, luscious mouth and bewitching eyes. His Caroline, his love, the way she had been during their whirlwind courtship and the first days of marriage.

His pulse quickened, and he bent to taste her mouth again, to kiss her eyelids, nose, temples. Her hair was like silk in his hands, just the way he remembered it. And she clung to him, kissed him with the uninhibited eagerness that had enchanted him when he kissed her the first time.

She had always felt good, but over the years her body had acquired a suppleness and softness even more alluring than her sylphlike slenderness during their honeymoon days. He felt himself drowning in the scent and feel that was Caroline, and he made no attempt to save himself.

But, relaxing his hold once more, he offered her the opportunity to draw back.

"Alex," she whispered, her eyes dark and mysterious.

He needed no other invitation. As eagerly as the day the blacksmith at Gretna proclaimed their marriage, he scooped her up in his arms. She seemed as light as this-tledown, and a heady sensation of strength and power lent wings to his feet as he carried her upstairs to the bedchamber adjoining his own.

The chamber that should have been his wife's.

The aroma of sandalwood tickled Caroline's nose. Raising her arms above her head, she stretched lan-guidly. She could not remember waking up so happy, so content, since—

Since the early days of her marriage.

Her eyes flew open—and met Alex's quizzical gaze.

"Good morning, Caroline." Freshly shaven and dressed in champagne-colored pantaloons and a coat of blue su-perfine, he stood by the bed.

"Good morning," she muttered, aware of the warmth stealing into her face.

She pushed her arms back under the covers, a defen-sive gesture which brought a glint of amusement to his eyes.

"I took the liberty of acting as lady's maid." He mo-tioned to a small table and chair at the foot end of the bed. "There's a cup of chocolate for my lady, and your robe. And if you care to step through the connecting door, there's also a bath waiting."

Clutching the sheet to cover her nakedness, she sat up and looked about her at the dark wall paneling, the dark, heavy furniture, the dull brown draperies on bed and windows. Not surprisingly, she had noticed none of it the previous night in the glow of a single candle.

"This is madness, Alex! Why the dickens did you choose your mother's chamber?"

"It is the chamber where Hartford brides have slept since the house was built."

"I am not a Hartford bride." Her eyes widened. "Devil a bit! It was bad enough when I was a divorced woman. Now what am I? A *fallen* woman?"

Handing her the cup of chocolate, he sat down on the edge of the bed. There was warmth in his look but also a certain measure of sternness.

"You are Lady Hartford. So what's this nonsense about a fallen woman?"

"We are divorced, yet we made love."

"Regrets?"

"No, Alex." She smiled, savoring the warm glow that still lingered inside her.

"Good." He caught her in a crushing embrace, sending cup and chocolate flying to the floor. "I'm on my way to the bishop now. He'll be pleased, for the Church is always preaching reconciliation."

Caroline's head was spinning. "The Church, perhaps. But what about Melissa? And what about *you?* Don't you still believe that I betrayed you with Justin St. Clair?"

Slowly he let go of her.

"Caroline, I cannot answer for Melissa. But I know what I want. I want you for my wife."

"Even if I betrayed you?"

"Even then."

"But, Alex, don't you see that I want you to believe me? I told you I did not make love with St. Clair. He tried to. And for a moment, when I pictured you with your mistress, I was tempted to let him make love to me. But I couldn't."

"Caroline . . ." His voice was ragged, the hand that raked his dark hair unsteady. "Are you saying—Damn! I was a fool, wasn't I?"

"We were both young and foolish."

"When I walked in and saw you in his arms, all I could think was that there had been more than enough time. You see, I had wasted a precious half-hour driving home. When you weren't there, I knew you must be at St. Clair's."

She shuddered. "You were so angry. I feared you'd kill him."

"I wanted to. He was lucky to get off with a bloodied

161

nose."

"You never believed me when I told you that nothing had happened."

Alex took both her hands in his. "Caroline, if you weren't having an affair with St. Clair, why did you not let *me* make love to you?"

"You tried only once."

"A man has his pride."

"And so does a woman. Lud, how ignorant we were! I asked you to stop that time because it hurt. I didn't know why—Serena said it isn't uncommon after bearing a child, that it gets better after a while. But you left the house so quickly, and then I saw you with *her*."

His eyes never left her face. Slowly he drew her hands to his lips and kissed first one wrist, then the other.

"Caroline, I love you."

A lump in her throat made speech impossible. She swallowed painfully.

"I love you, Alex. No matter how hard I tried, I never stopped loving you."

"Melissa and her cousins sang an old sixteenth-century song once—a year ago or even two—but the words have stayed with me. Now I know why."

"Why?"

"The song could have been written for us." Softly he quoted, " 'Since first I saw your face, I resolved to honour and renown ye; If now I be disdained, I wish my heart had never known ye. What? I that loved—' "

He faltered, and Caroline finished the verse for him.

" '—and you that liked, shall we begin to wrangle? No, no, no, my heart is fast, and cannot disentangle.' "

"Those are the lines," he said, his voice rough with emotion. "And I wish I had known sixteen years ago that my heart cannot disentangle. Caroline, will you give us another chance?"

"Yes." Her smile was shaky. "If you will give *me* another chance. If I had been wiser in matters of the heart—"

He cut in. "If *we* had been wiser. Caroline, we lost sixteen years. Let us not lose even a precious minute looking back. Promise?"

"I promise."

"Good." He kissed her, his mouth hard, possessive. He rose. "I'm off to see the bishop. Annulment of the divorce, remarriage, whatever it takes, we'll have it done by tonight."

"But what about Melissa?" she called after him.

"I don't doubt that you'll handle her."

Opening the door, he looked at her over his shoulder. His grin reminded her of the carefree days of their brief honeymoon.

"My concern is that by tonight you're no longer a *fallen* woman."

"Alex, wait!"

But he was gone.

She remembered the previous occasion when she had tried to call him back and was hampered by her state of dishabille. But the reason for wanting to stop him this time was quite different.

Facing Melissa an hour later in the garden room, Caroline wished *she* had gone to see the bishop. She did want to be married to Alex again—but not in the pell-mell fashion he proposed, not without first giving their daughter a chance to get used to the notion. Logically, therefore, someone had to tell Melissa that her parents wished a reconciliation. Since Alex had left the house, that someone, perforce, must be Caroline.

And she feared very much that Melissa would refuse to accept her.

Seated in a chair by the open terrace door, she watched her daughter's nimble fingers featherstitching a border around the finished sampler. Her own work lay idle in her lap. It was a piece of knitting, a child's sock, waiting for a heel. But Caroline knew she would only have to unravel again if she attempted to knit while searching for words to convince Melissa of—

She gave a start when the girl suddenly flung down her embroidery.

"I cannot work when I'm being stared at. If you're angry with me, very well, I apologize! I behaved childishly last night. It shall not happen again."

"I am not angry, Melissa. But if I knew what made you run off, perhaps I could explain."

Melissa jumped to her feet. Hand on hip, she demanded, "Confess! You're trying to make my father fall in love with you again. That's why you came to London, didn't you? Not because you wanted to see me or warn me off an elopement."

Caroline's hands clenched on the cuff of the small sock. Why the dickens wasn't Alex here when she needed him!

"I came here because I wanted to stop you from making a tragic mistake. Your Aunt Augusta wrote that you were contemplating an elopement if—"

"Mary!" Melissa said in disgust. "She has always been a tattletale. But I *saw* you and father last night. You were about to kiss, weren't you? And you want me to believe that your elopement was a tragic mistake?"

"It was an act that had tragic consequences. Or do you consider a divorce and sixteen years of separation from husband and child fortuitous events?"

Melissa's dark brows knitted in a scowl. "Did you miss us?"

"Horribly."

Two pairs of gray eyes met and held. Melissa's expressive little face softened.

"You and Father were terribly immature."

Caroline shot her a surprised look but said meekly, "We were."

"Especially you. But Father, since he was an older man—"

"A *what?*"

164

"An older man. An experienced man. He was one-and-twenty when you married, wasn't he? That's two years more in his dish than Arthur has."

Thinking back, Caroline had to admit that she, too, had regarded Alex as an experienced man of the world when they met. Which proved that the judgment of a sixteen-year-old could not be trusted. But, of course, she did not say so to her sixteen-year-old daughter.

Melissa started to pace. She had twice covered the distance between the terrace door and the hall door when she stopped to face Caroline.

"If you want my advice on how to win Father back, tell him you'll chaperon me for the next year or two, and that way he won't have to look for another governess. Tell him you'll keep me out of mischief."

"Lissa—" Unmindful of the ball of yarn and the half-knitted sock in her lap, Caroline rose. "Do you *want* me to stay?"

"You're my mother, aren't you?"

Melissa's tone was belligerent, but Caroline had known her share of young people and under Serena's tutelage had learned to recognize a plea beneath a show of fierceness.

"Yes, I am your mother. And I would very much like to stay with you and Alex. Because I love you both."

Melissa gave her a guarded look. "You don't know me. How can you love me?"

"You forget, I have an unfair advantage over you. I know you through your Aunt Augusta's letters. And I secretly saw you twice a year."

They were still measuring each other—Caroline with hope and fear warring in her breast and Melissa's expressive face alternately showing skepticism and longing—when a man's firm steps approached from the hall.

Like a conqueror, Alex strode into the garden room.

"My two favorite ladies! Listen. The bishop was over-joyed to hear of the reconciliation. There are some formalities to be observed, but everything can be taken care

165

of this afternoon. Caroline, be ready—"

He broke off when he encountered her fierce look. Directing a frown first at one of his favorite ladies, then at the other, he said, "Lud! Haven't you two settled the matter yet?"

Neither Caroline nor Melissa deigned to reply, but after an endless moment, Melissa walked toward Caroline.

"Mother, you may not need my advice on how to win Father back, but you clearly need me to show you a trick or two that will keep him in line."

Mother. Melissa had called her "Mother."

Opening her arms to her daughter, Caroline looked at Alex. Her husband.

Truly, there could never be a happier occasion in her life than this precious moment of love—a moment she would make to last forever. For she had finally gained wisdom in matters of the heart.

The Perfect Mother

A fragment of sound, not a gull's cry, was blown back on the wind. Melloney slowed her steps, the vague anxiety she always felt when the children were out of sight giving way to relief. They had gone to the cove, safe enough when the tide, as now, was low. But not safe enough for her to return to the house and leave them on their own. The Cornish coast was treacherous on the mildest of days, and Miles, in most things an indulgent father, had forbidden them to go to the beach without adult company.

But the children did not want her company. They had begun their walk together, but a quarter-mile from the house the children had run ahead, making it clear that she must amuse herself as she pleased.

Melloney paused by a clump of furze, golden in the August sun, and looked out at the bay below. It was calm this morning, the sea rolling with gentle, incessant movement toward the shore. The sky, striated with clouds, bare wisps of white against a timeless blue, was gentle, too, and the air, not quite warm and with the faintest stirring of wind, was like a balm. Strange then that her eyes should sting with tears and she should feel an intense moment of longing for her own childhood.

Melloney knew this part of Cornwall well. Her father's house stood a few miles to the west, near St. Agnes. She had summered there when she was young, in her father's lifetime and later, when her father was only a dim memory. Her brother Derrick had the house now, though he came here but seldom, and it had been years since she had visited Cornwall at all.

Till this summer, when she had returned as Miles Pengarrick's bride, mistress of Ennis Court and mother to his two young daughters.

Melloney moved on, more slowly now, reluctant to invade the children's privacy. The path narrowed, then ceased altogether. The cove was reached by clambering down the slaty rocks, an easy descent when they were dry, more treacherous when they turned slippery with rain. When she was nearly at the cove, Melloney sat down and placed her paint box by her side. She had brought it to assure the children that she would not intrude on their games, though for once she had no desire to paint. She wrapped her arms about her knees and looked out at the sea. A few steps more and she would see them, running on the sand or kneeling by a rockpool, reaching for the strange creatures the receding tide had left behind. But for now she wanted only to feel the sun-warmed rocks through the thin muslin of her dress and listen to the lonely cry of the gulls wheeling overhead.

It had seemed so simple at the start. Her marriage was not a love match; Miles had made that clear and Melloney had expected nothing else. There was Celia, dead little more than a year, and still a presence in her husband's and children's lives. Then there was the matter of the difference in age between Miles and herself—twelve full years—and the fact that he had known her most of her life. Miles had been her mother's friend. Melloney had been a child to him, not a woman. It was a wonder he had learned to think of her in that way at all. He would not, had she not been left at home to look after her two half sisters when her mother went off on a wedding journey with her third husband. Miles, ever kind, came by the house to see how she did. It must have been the sight of her playing with her young sisters that led him to propose. His own children were in need of a mother.

Melloney closed her eyes for a moment, seeing again Miles's kind eyes and rueful smile, recalling her own shock and exhilaration. Who would have thought such a prosaic proposal could send one into such transports of joy. Of course she had not admitted her feelings to Miles, not then or at any time since. To do so would only cause them both embarrassment. Miles must not know that the young woman he had offered for, for the most sensible of reasons, had loved him as long as she could remember.

Melloney sighed, pulled the pins from her hair, and placed them carefully in her pocket. She would put her hair up again when she got back to the house, but now she gave it to the wind, feeling her spirits lighten with the loosening of each long strand. In truth, she had no cause for complaint. Miles was fond of her. He was often occupied with his own affairs, for he sat in the Commons and took his work there seriously, but when they were together he treated her as a companion and friend. There were even moments when she felt there was some real feeling between them, though there were others when he retreated behind a mask of reserve and she knew she could not reach him.

A vagrant breeze blew her hair across her face, and she pushed her locks behind her ears. Miles was a complicated man. He could return late from the House, tired and harassed, stay up until the small hours working on notes for a speech, and then rise early to breakfast with the children. He had been passionately in love with his first wife, yet when she was forced to go abroad for her health, he had remained in England and had not once visited her. Melloney frowned. This last would never cease to puzzle her, but she doubted that Miles would ever confide in her about Celia or anything else.

Melloney lifted her hair from her neck and let it drift through her fingers. The action brought a memory of Miles's hands doing the same. If he denied her the intimacy of shared feelings that she had hoped would come with marriage, he had shown her another kind of intimacy, a world of the senses that she was only beginning to explore. For that she would always be grateful.

As for the children, they could not avoid her forever. At

five, Audrey still followed her sister's lead, but she was disposed to be friendly. Even Diana, eight years old and grave beyond her years, might be coaxed out of her discontent. It was unreasonable to think that these past few weeks at Ennis Court, with their governess on holiday and their new stepmother to look after them, would be enough to bring the children to embrace her as part of their family.

The breeze shifted, and Melloney again heard the faint sound of voices. She stood, stretched her arms above her head, and drew a long breath, savoring the faint tang of salt in the air. Reluctant to leave this small island of comfort, she stepped slowly down the rocks and looked about for the children.

They were nowhere in sight. Stifling a vague feeling of unease, Melloney sat down again, removed her shoes and stockings, and moved out onto the sand. It was warmer here, the air almost still. She stopped and listened but heard only the gentle movement of the sea. A fishing boat came into sight from the direction of Polly Joke. Nothing else was to be seen, on the water or in the cove. Then she heard the voices again, somewhere to her left. Of course. They were in one of the smaller coves formed by the rocks where they spilled down onto the sand, exploring a pool left by the ebbing tide or perhaps merely seeking isolation to share secrets that must be kept from their unwelcome stepmother.

There was a fine line between respecting the children's privacy and abandoning her responsibilities altogether. Melloney walked up the beach toward the voices, following along the base of the rocks. Her feet left faint imprints in the still damp sand, as faint as her impact on the lives of her husband and stepchildren. *I won't be ignored,* Melloney told herself, fighting off a feeling that she was drifting without an anchor in an uncaring sea.

The voices were closer now, though the words were indistinguishable. Melloney realized where the children had gone. A little farther on there was a deeper cove where the sea had worn the rock away, leaving it overhanging the sand to form a cave, small enough in fact but vast enough for a child's imagination. Melloney smiled. Were she still a child, it would be her favorite retreat.

She moved on more slowly, wondering how to make her presence known. The voices were louder now and over the distant murmur of the sea she heard Audrey's raised in shrill complaint. "I don't *want* to be the mother."

"You have to, it's your turn." It was Diana, her voice filled with exasperation. Then, more cajoling, "You can have the flowers."

Audrey continued her protest. "But I don't want to be dead."

"You won't be dead, silly. I'm going to make you well."

"Melloney will come. She'll hear us."

"She'll never find us here." Diana's voice was tinged with scorn. "She's painting or something. She's probably forgot all about us. Come on. Help me."

There was a mumbled reply and after that Melloney heard nothing but fragments of words and the sounds of movement in the cave, as though objects were being dragged into place. The children never talked about their mother, but here they were, playing out some drama of her death. At least that's what it sounded like. Melloney stopped, then moved on, knowing she should not intrude, telling herself she had a right to know. Celia's death stood between them. If Diana and Audrey could not let her go, what chance did a stepmother have to create their family anew.

"Close your eyes," Diana said.

Intent on what was happening in the cave, Melloney tripped on the rocks and fell, scraping her hands and knees. Biting back a cry of pain and railing against her stupidity, she crept forward till she could see round the edge of the cave. Audrey was stretched out on a flat rock at the far end of the cave, hands folded on her chest, eyes obediently closed. A lace scarf, soiled and torn, covered her hair. Behind her, set on a narrow ledge in the wall, the stubs of two candles were burning, and between these stood a chipped cup crammed with a handful of thrift, its pink and white

171

blooms rising on naked stems from a tuft of narrow stiff leaves.

Melloney held her breath. She could not see Diana till she appeared suddenly from the near side of the cave, a napkin-covered basket on her arm. Oblivious of Melloney's presence, Diana walked toward her sister and knelt beside her rocky pallet. "Hullo, Mama," she said. Then, in a long-suffering tone, "Open your eyes."

"Oh." Audrey looked at her sister. "Can I get up now?"

"Not yet, you're too sick." With a practiced gesture Diana lifted the napkin off the basket and brought out a small vial. Then she turned sharply to Audrey. "You're supposed to be glad to see me."

Audrey looked puzzled. Then with sudden recollection she said, "I remember." She reached out her arms. "Oh, Diana, it really is you. I'm so happy you've come."

"It took a long time," Diana said, unstoppering the vial. "I had to go on a big ship, and the sea was rough, and the captain thought we would all be drowned, and then we were attacked by pirates —"

"You never had pirates before." Audrey's voice was indignant.

"There could be pirates. But the brave captain fought them off and brought me all the way to Italy, and here I am, come to save you. Drink this."

She held out the vial. Audrey turned her head away. "You have to," Diana said. "It's the medicine." Then, as Audrey continued to balk, "Don't be a goose, it's only barley water."

Audrey took a sip, shuddered, then set down the vial. "Oh, my child," she said in dramatic tones, flinging her arms wide, "you've saved me. I'm well, I can come home." She leaped off her pallet and seized her sister's hands. As the two girls began to dance about the cave, Melloney hastily retreated. She had stayed too long and heard too much, though even the first words would have told her what she had long suspected. The children would never accept her. They wanted their mother back.

Conscious of the stinging in palms and knees, Melloney

got to her feet and brushed the gravel from her hands. She felt unbearably sad, for the children's loss as well as her own. She might come to some sort of accommodation with Diana and Audrey, as a kind of superior governess, but she would never take their mother's place.

Melloney walked back a hundred feet or more, then turned and called the children's names. Their game was over, and the interruption would not come amiss. She waited, wondering if they had heard, and then Audrey's face appeared around the edge of the cave and as quickly disappeared. A moment more and both girls came into sight, as innocent as if they had indeed been exploring one of the rock pools.

"We didn't know where you were," Diana said as they came toward her.

There was no sign of the basket or the other accompaniments of their drama. Melloney trusted they had snuffed the candles. "I was sitting on the rocks farther down," she said. "It's so beautiful today. I lost track of the time."

Audrey looked at her critically. "Your dress is torn."

"So it is," Melloney said, looking down at the garment. "What a dreadful nuisance that will be to mend. I fell down," she explained. "It was the stupidest thing; I was looking at some gulls and didn't watch where I was going." She held out her hand which was studiously ignored. She let it drop. "I think it's time we started back."

It took them a while to get sorted out. The children could not remember where they had left their shoes and stockings, and when these were recovered, they had to stop to allow Melloney to retrieve hers, and then they had to find her paint box. They climbed the rocks in silence and came out onto the gorse-lined path that wound inland to Ennis Court. The children seemed in no mood for conversation, and Melloney did not try to force it. Diana walked on ahead, her eyes on the path, while Audrey ran from side to side, humming tunelessly to herself, picking flowers as she went. At one point she thrust a stiff little blossom of lavender-blue scabious into her stepmother's hand, a gesture that

173

gave Melloney heart and enabled her to approach the house with at least an appearance of having enjoyed their morning outing.

As they topped a small rise, the pleasantly wayward character of the countryside gave way to well-tended grass, and the dirt of the path became the sweeping gravel drive that led up to Ennis Court. Melloney had always liked this sudden view. The small Elizabethan house, its symmetry marred by a blank-faced wing containing the offices and kitchen quarters, stood golden in the sun, light glinting off the tiers of mullioned windows. The door could not be seen, only its stone lintel visible above a large traveling chaise which had pulled up before it.

Diana, who had been walking ahead, stopped abruptly, forcing the others to stop as well. "Who is it?" she said, a note of suspicion in her voice. They were not used to such conveyances at Ennis Court. Melloney supposed that Celia had entertained lavishly when she had been in residence here, but Miles showed no taste for company.

"I can't imagine," Melloney began, but even as she spoke she knew who it must be. "Of course, it's Mama." A week early, with no notice at all, and none of the rooms made ready. Melloney felt the familiar mixture of pleasure and exasperation that her mother's presence always aroused.

Two young girls appeared at the far side of the carriage, caught sight of the others, and began running toward them. "Melloney!" the younger one called. Her name was echoed by the other, and then they were upon her, wrapping her in a confused embrace punctuated by cries and descriptions of the journey and assertions that they did not know how they had ever managed without her.

Melloney drew away at last and regarded her half sisters with delight. "I swear you've both grown, and it hasn't been much above a month." They were wearing identical dresses of white muslin sashed in cornflower blue, the exact shade of their eyes. Juliana's pale gold hair streamed down her back, and Melloney was struck once more by her resemblance to their mother. But Juliana, who was not yet twelve,

174

had neither their mother's good manners nor her considerable charm. Nor did Jennifer, whose arm was still around Melloney's waist and who seemed to have forgot that she was a guest and owed something to the children of the house.

Melloney gently disentangled her arm and turned to her stepchildren. Audrey was looking at her with surprise and something that might have been envy. Diana had retreated behind a mask of indifference and disapproval which fell quickly before the onslaught of Jennifer's high spirits. She and Jennifer were of an age and had been friends from nursery days, for when Miles's daughters were in London they frequently played with Melloney's sisters.

Jennifer and Diana started toward the house. Juliana picked up her skirt and ran after them. Melloney was about to follow when she saw Audrey staring pointedly at the flower which lay on the ground near Melloney's feet, dropped during that exuberant reunion. Melloney stooped to pick it up, then rose and smoothed out the bruised petals. Audrey watched her without expression, but as they moved to follow the others she reached out to take her stepmother's hand.

It was in this manner that they rounded the carriage and went in the open front door to find Pamela Mulgrave (Pamela Duffield at the time of Juliana and Jennifer's birth, Pamela Kilmarth at the time of Melloney's), attended by McBride, her maid for the past thirty years, and assorted members of the Pengarrick staff. McBride appeared to be giving instructions to the housekeeper, Mrs. Quin, about the disposition of a large number of trunks and boxes strewn about the hall. Mrs. Quin appeared affronted. "We did not expect you for a week, your ladyship," she was saying to Pamela who shrugged her shoulders and smiled helplessly at the other woman.

Melloney walked forward briskly, determined to ignore her torn dress and windblown hair. "No, Mama, we did not expect you, and you have put us all out of sorts. The rooms haven't been aired and the beds are not yet made up, so if

175

you want to lie down you must use my bedroom. But I'd much prefer that you come into the small saloon and talk to me. I'll have tea sent in. Luncheon is at one, so we'll have time for a good coze." Then, before her mother could reply, she had a hurried consultation with Mrs. Quin, told the housemaid she was to assist with the preparation of the rooms, gave instructions to the footman for the disposal of the luggage, and satisfied herself that the groom, who was helping carry in the boxes, would see to the comfort of the coachman and horses.

They scattered. McBride followed the footman up the stairs, Pamela's jewel case under her arm. The children were nowhere in sight. Melloney turned back to her mother who was staring up at the portrait of Celia Pengarrick and her daughters which hung on the wall opposite the great stone staircase. Aware of her daughter's scrutiny, Pamela quickly looked away. "You're so efficient," she said, making it sound at once a compliment and an accusation. "I'm not efficient at all." She held out her arms. "Come here and kiss me. I do miss you so. These last weeks have been a nightmare."

Melloney returned her mother's embrace, but her eyes strayed to the portrait. She saw it every day. She could not escape it. Dressed in a pale pink frock, Celia sat in a grotto of the painter's imagination, her fair hair in loose ringlets, her face glowing with joy and satisfaction. Audrey, who must have been barely two, clung to her mother's skirt. Diana, tall for her five years, stood on Celia's other side, holding her hand. The dark-haired children, in coloring and features far more like their father than like Celia, looked up with wonder at their radiant mother.

Melloney had been only fifteen when she had had her first glimpse of the lovely Celia Pengarrick. She could still remember the occasion. Pamela had taken her driving and had stopped the carriage to have a few words with Miles and his wife. Celia was wearing a loose gown of rose and white-striped silk and a bonnet with ribbons of the same shade of rose. Her hair, a darker shade of gold than

Pamela's, seemed to burn with life, and her eyes, of a changeable blue-green, were bright with laughter. Melloney had been unable to say one word, but Celia was very kind and told Pamela that her daughter was charming. Charming indeed. No one had ever called Melloney that before, but she treasured the compliment nonetheless. Pamela told her later that Celia was beginning to increase with her first child. No wonder she had looked so happy. No wonder Miles had been filled with love and pride, unable to take his eyes off his beautiful young wife.

Melloney tore her eyes from the portrait and led her mother to the small saloon, a low-ceilinged sunny room with windows facing the lawns and shrubbery bordering the gravel drive, and they were soon settled with a tea tray and a comforting number of cushions at Pamela's back. "We've been on the road since seven. We had to break the journey at Launceston, for it was growing much too late to push on last night." Pamela finished her tea and held her cup out to be refilled. "Not that you would have welcomed us arriving somewhere close to midnight."

"Mama, you're welcome at any time, but the household staff would have preferred a few hours warning. Why did you change your plans? I had counted on you for next week."

"Oh, it was much too sudden a decision," Pamela said, rearranging a handsome paisley shawl. "A letter would scarce have arrived before I did. And I was at my wit's end seeing John off to Scotland and trying to think what I must pack for the visit—"

"Lord Mulgrave?" Melloney scarcely knew her second stepfather and could not speak of him other than formally. "Did he leave earlier than expected?"

"But of course he left early," Pamela said with a faint note of asperity. "Didn't I tell you? No," she added, suddenly contrite. "That's why I put up my own visit. I didn't intend to, you understand. I was looking forward to some time alone with the girls, but Melloney, oh my dear, it was just too much." Pamela threw up her hands and sank back into the

177

cushions. "However did you manage?"

Melloney laughed and set down her teacup. "Mama, you exaggerate."

"I do not," Pamela said firmly. "They scarce listen to a thing I say, they're bored to tears when I take them into company, and they—" She shook her head in incomprehension. "They move about so. They're never still. Not that they've been behaving badly, you understand. Jennifer has the happiest disposition, but I'm beginning to despair of Juliana. On the morning that John left she went out her bedroom window and climbed all the way down the big oak that stands outside it. The gardener's boy saw her. Six o'clock in the morning. Bare feet and in her nightdress. She couldn't give me a reason. She woke early, she told me when I learned about it later. It promised to be a beautiful day and she wanted to feel the grass between her toes before the dew had dried. And that's all she had to say for herself. I don't understand her, Melloney, I don't understand her at all. I never had such trouble with Morwenna. By the time she was twelve she knew very well how to go on."

Morwenna, Pamela's first child, had been the image of perfection as long as Melloney could remember. A flirtatious, laughing girl who loved to be in company, she had had a wildly successful first Season and had married to suit both her heart and her family's expectations. Melloney was used to being compared unfavorably with her older sister. She was a drab little mouse beside Morwenna, pale of skin, with hair and eyes of a nondescript light brown. That would not have bothered her mother, who believed that charm of manner could compensate for an undistinguished appearance. No, it was Melloney's unwillingness to put herself forward that drove Pamela to distraction. Girls had no business, she said, preferring books to parties.

Nor, Melloney thought with an echo of the old resentment, climbing trees and feeling wet grass under their feet. Poor Juliana.

"Mama," she said for the thousandth time, "we can't all be Morwennas. You fret too much. Juliana is only eleven.

She'll grow up at her own pace if you leave her be."

"Yes, but *how* will she grow up? Melloney, the world is not at all kind to girls who climb trees."

Her mother was right, but saying it would do Juliana little good. "You can't make her other than she is," Melloney said. "And she'll learn to cope with the world's unkindness." Better yet, she would learn not to care. That was the lesson Melloney had learned five long years ago when she had been thrust into the maelstrom of the London Season and found it not at all to her liking. When the first humiliations were over, she was able to find mild enjoyment in the foolishness of it all, but in the end she had found it merely tedious.

She had tried to explain this to her mother, but Pamela, unable to hide her disappointment in her second daughter, had insisted that she try. So Melloney did, dutifully accompanying her mother on her engagements till even Pamela agreed that she might be allowed to stay at home when she chose. And Melloney chose to do so with increasing frequency. She had long since taken over the running of the house, and as her half sisters emerged from the nursery, she spent more and more time with them. It was an arrangement to her liking, and Pamela had found it useful as well. She had never been a bad mother, but she had never been a particularly good one either. She meant well, but she could only tolerate motherhood in very small doses.

After Melloney's last remarks Pamela turned pensive, her fingers playing idly with her shawl. "I daresay you're right," she said at last without conviction. "I know I haven't been the best of mothers, but I love John to distraction, and I want us to be a real family. Poor Melloney, you never had a chance, did you? Kilmarth was the most forbidding man, and he never really forgave me for Owen."

Melloney thought that her father had been quite forbearing about the business. Owen was Pamela's second child, the product of a youthful indiscretion with an equally youthful John Mulgrave. Kilmarth had not accepted the boy, but he had taken Pamela back, for she had yet to bear

179

him a proper heir. Melloney had known Owen, who had been raised by one of Pamela's cousins, all her life, but it was only last winter, when Pamela had met Mulgrave again and agreed to be his wife, that Melloney had learned Owen was her brother.

"I never got a chance to be a proper mother to Owen," Pamela went on, "and then after he was born things were so muddled that I didn't do very well with you and Morwenna and Derrick. We were scarcely a family at all. And it was no better when I married Duffield, though I was as much to blame as he. We'd agreed from the beginning to go our separate ways." She paused, perhaps to review her other indiscretions. "But I mean to go on far differently now. Only I'm so dreadfully inept."

Melloney looked at her mother, startled by her candor and by the note of regret in her voice. "I daresay it will come easier with time," she said, aware of the inadequacy of her words. She was in much the same position as Pamela and was not prepared to take such counsel herself.

There seemed to be no more to say. Both women turned their gaze to the windows, as though in want of occupation, and it was thus that they saw the lone horseman cantering up the drive. "Why, it's Miles," Pamela said with sudden animation. She moved toward the window to watch the black-haired, black-coated figure on the superb black mount. "He seats a horse admirably. Come, let's go and meet him."

Melloney followed Pamela to the door, feeling unreasonably jealous. Her mother knew Miles far better than she did herself, and she would set herself to charm him throughout a visit of what was likely to prove several weeks' duration. *It's not Mama's fault,* Melloney told herself. *She can't help it. It's as natural to her as breathing.* And with this bracing thought Melloney crossed the hall and went outside to greet her husband.

She felt a familiar rush of delight. Miles was impossibly handsome, and though some claimed his face was forbidding, Melloney had seen nothing but kindness there. He was leaning down from his horse, a welcoming smile on his face, Pamela's small hand clasped in one of his own. "We didn't expect you so early," he said.

"I have not been expected by a great many people, but Melloney at least has forgiven me." Pamela turned and drew her daughter into the group formed by Miles and herself. The gesture was meant kindly, but it left Melloney feeling that it was she who was the unexpected guest.

Miles swung down from the horse, patted its sweat-drenched flank, and gave instructions to the stable boy who had appeared around the corner of the house. "Walk him till he's cool," he said, turning the reins over to the lad. "I rode him hard today." Then he put his arms about the two women and led them toward the house. Pamela, who was built on delicate lines, came barely to his chest. Melloney reached his shoulder, a dubious distinction, for her height was another of those things that had given her mother cause for despair. Melloney longed for a look from her husband, a pressure of the hand, that would tell her Miles set her apart from her mother, but his embrace was general and made no division between them.

As they entered the hall, the children clattered down the stairs and flung themselves upon him. Miles had long been a favorite with Juliana and Jennifer. They called him "Uncle," which they considered entitled them to quite as much attention as he was bestowing on his own daughters. For a moment Melloney saw the reflection of her own jealousy in Diana's eyes. Miles must have seen it, too, for he turned his attention to his daughter and soon had her laughing. The ease of it filled Melloney with admiration and left her puzzled. How could such a man have kept his daughters from their mother in her final illness? Celia had died alone, with neither husband nor children at her side. How could Miles have abandoned that lovely creature? How could he have denied her a last meeting with her children? In the wake of what she had overheard this morning at the cove, Melloney's questions about Celia were more pressing than ever.

Luncheon was announced. It was a noisy meal, leaving

181

Melloney no time to think of the problem of her husband and his first wife. Afterwards, Miles proposed a walk to the abandoned mill that stood on the edge of a small wood about a mile from the house. The children were enthusiastic. Next to the cove, it was Diana and Audrey's favorite excursion, and Juliana and Jennifer were eager for activity. "Do come," Miles said to Pamela who was seated beside him. "It's an easy stroll and will leave you plenty of time to rest before dinner."

To Melloney's surprise, her mother agreed, stipulating only that she be allowed to change her shoes, and in less than a quarter of an hour the seven of them had rounded the house and were making for the path that led inland to Ennis Wood. They stayed together for a time, but Pamela found the pace too strenuous and was forced to lag behind. Melloney stayed beside her and watched her husband and the children grow smaller in the distance. Diana and Jennifer walked by his side, matching his long steps. Audrey ran as often as not, and Juliana followed her example.

"You see?" Pamela said, as though Melloney had not taken her complaints seriously.

Melloney laughed. "Mama, you must get Juliana a horse."

Pamela looked at her in surprise. "I'm not objecting, but why? We have plenty of horses in the stable."

"The only ones she's allowed to ride are far too slow. She needs something lively, so she can go for a proper gallop. She should have a horse of her own, and she should learn to care for it herself." Melloney saw the doubt in her mother's eyes. "Mama, she must do something with all that energy. Wouldn't you rather see her grooming a horse than climbing a tree?"

Pamela laughed, a light sweet-voiced sound that had always reconciled Melloney to her mother's faults. "Then a horse it shall be. I'll try anything. You may not credit it, but I am trying very hard to be a good mother." They walked in silence for a time, then Pamela said, "John is trying to be a good father, but he hasn't Miles's touch." She

182

watched Miles, his head bent to the girls by his side, disappear around a bend in the path. "Whatever do you suppose he finds to talk about?"

At this moment Miles was not talking at all. The girls had kept up a companionable chatter from the moment they left the house, but now, as they approached the small stand of elms known as Ennis Wood, they demanded that he tell them the story of the old man who had kept the mill and met an untimely end.

Diana knew the story well, but she never tired of hearing it, particularly here, in the shadow of the trees twisted by the north wind, sitting on the stone wall that bordered the roofless mill, listening to the water splashing on the rocks in the stream bed. The mill was old. Miles had said it was nothing but a ruin when he was a boy, and he had the tale of it from his grandfather. They gathered round him now while he told it again, how the miller had tried to keep his young daughter from other folk, lest she run off and leave him, and how in spite she had done just that, running after a handsome tinker who chanced to pass by the mill, and how he had left her, and the girl had come home with her babe to make her peace with her father. And how it was too late, for the old man, grieving for what he had lost, had flung himself into the stream at its flood, and the girl took her babe and walked away, and no one ever saw her again.

Diana shivered as her father's voice died away. He had made them all come to life, the stubborn old man who could not understand his daughter's wish for a bit of fun and the company of her own kind, the whimsical tinker who told her tales about the world, and the girl herself, her red hair shining in the sun, walking after him with laughter in her eyes. Everyone said hair that shade was not to be trusted, but she was a brave lass as well as a foolish one. That's what Miles said. She left the mill for the last time, leaving all that had been hers, and with a proud eye turned her back on the neighbors of Ennis Wood who had nothing good to say about her and went out to make her way in the world carrying her child in her arms.

Juliana and Jennifer had not heard the tale before. Juliana shivered. Audrey looked at her critically and said, "It's only a story."

"It's a true one," Diana insisted. Audrey did not yet understand how quickly everything could change, how happiness could turn to sorrow and no one know why it should be so.

Audrey ignored her sister. "I want to go into the mill." She looked at her father with pleading eyes, for she knew he wouldn't let her go without him.

"All right," he said, leaping to his feet as though exploring the mill was what he wanted to do more than anything in the world.

"I'll go, too," said Juliana who did not like to think about things very long.

Jennifer was different. She hadn't said anything at all while Miles was telling the story, and she hadn't said a word after he stopped. She and Diana stayed where they were, sliding to the ground on the inner side of the wall so their backs were against the warm stone and their voices wouldn't carry when they talked. Diana was sure Jennifer wanted to talk.

But Jennifer didn't say anything for a while. She had found a stick and was writing on the dirt between them, *Jennifer Duffield,* and then *Jennifer Mulgrave.* "You can't be Mulgrave," Diana said. "He's not your father."

"He is now," she said. "Or he's trying to be."

Diana was curious. "Do you like him?"

"I think so." Jennifer's voice was uncertain. Then with more enthusiasm, "I like Uncle Miles. He knows how to talk to us."

Diana could not have agreed more. Even when he was busy or angry or upset, her father always had time to talk. She felt a moment of pity for her friend. "Doesn't Mr. Mulgrave?"

"Lord Mulgrave. He's a lord. Papa was a sir. Mama had to change her name, so she's Lady Mulgrave now. Melloney was Kilmarth and now she's Pengarrick. We're still Duffield.

184

It's very confusing."

"Do you miss him? I mean, your real father."

Jennifer was silent for so long that Diana thought she wasn't going to answer. "I don't remember him very well," she said at last. Then, after another pause, "He was always cheerful. He'd come to see us when he was home, but he never stayed long. Sometimes he'd take us up on his horse. But we didn't see him very often. I suppose I miss him, but not like I miss Melloney. She was always there."

It was Diana's turn to be quiet. She had not missed the warmth and affection Jennifer and Juliana had shown her stepmother on their arrival. Nor had she missed the sudden glow in Melloney's face when she saw her sisters running toward her. For a moment she hadn't looked like Melloney at all, not the Melloney Diana had grown used to. Oh, she was cheerful enough, but there was an undercurrent of sadness beneath her gaiety, as though she mourned the loss of something she had loved.

That was it: she loved her sisters and she wanted to be with them, not here in Cornwall playing mother to Diana and Audrey Pengarrick. *She doesn't like us,* Diana thought, but even as she thought it she knew it was untrue. Melloney had tried very hard to like them, and Diana had pushed her away, pushed as hard as she could, and when Audrey showed signs of weakening, she had made Audrey push her away, too. Melloney had no right to interfere in their lives.

Jennifer must have sensed some of her friend's confusion, for she said, "Do you like Melloney?"

"Of course I like Melloney." It was almost true. Under other circumstances Diana might have enjoyed her company.

"I mean, do you like having her for a mother?"

Diana couldn't tell her friend that she did not. Not that her own mother had been perfect — she'd gone away and died, leaving an uncomfortable hole, and Diana did not want Melloney nor anyone else to fill it. She saw Jennifer watching her with critical eyes and said, "I don't really want a mother."

"But you have to have one," Jennifer said reasonably. "You have to have someone, even if it's only a governess or a housekeeper. We were lucky. We have Mama, but she goes about a lot, at least she did until she got married again, and we also had Melloney. I think you'd want to have her. She doesn't have to be your mother. She can be your friend."

"She can't be my friend; she's my stepmother." But as she thought about it, Diana wondered if this were really true.

They sat there in a companionable silence until Melloney and Lady Mulgrave came upon them. Diana heard the voices and raised her eyes to see two faces looking down at them over the wall, Lady Mulgrave, no longer young but still soft and pretty, and Melloney, tall and pale, a host of emotions warring in her eyes. Two mothers, who were mother and daughter in their turn. It was very confusing. If one thought about what it meant one would get the headache. Diana sprang up to elude their scrutiny and informed them that Miles had taken Juliana and Audrey into the mill.

Lady Mulgrave looked at the rotted structure that was sometimes described as picturesque. "Is it safe?" she asked with a trace of alarm.

As if in answer, there was a shout from the direction of the mill. Melloney led her mother through an opening in the wall. Diana and Jennifer, their curiosity aroused, followed the women. Juliana, her skirt hiked well above her knees, was standing high above them on the remnant of the loft floor. "Hullo!" she called, waving with such vigor that she nearly lost her balance.

Lady Mulgrave gasped. "Juliana! Juliana, come down at once."

Mothers were always apprehensive. Then Diana saw that Melloney was smiling and waving back at Juliana, and for a moment she felt sorry for Jennifer. It seemed that she and Audrey might have got the best of the bargain.

Of course it was not nearly as dangerous as it looked. Miles appeared and crossed to the fragments of ladder that led up to the loft, stepping carefully over the places where

186

there were no planks in the floor. He waited till Juliana had got down by herself, then went back for Audrey, who was leaning out of an opening that must have once been a window, and swung her to his shoulders. "Home," he shouted, "I've work to do. You'll have to amuse yourselves for a while."

For some reason this struck Diana as very funny. Talking about mothers could hardly be classed as amusement, but she felt suddenly light-hearted. She looked at Jennifer who giggled, and with one accord they followed the others to the path that led back to the house, keeping well behind them so they could continue their conversation. How had it been for Melloney, Diana wondered aloud, when she had been a little girl and Lady Mulgrave had been her mother. Then it occurred to her that Lady Mulgrave was still Melloney's mother as much as she was mother to Jennifer and Juliana, and that Melloney was as much a daughter as she was stepmother to Diana and Audrey.

"Of course she's a daughter," Jennifer said. "She's my sister, even if she *is* years older. What's strange is her turning into a mother."

"What's strange is her being like us," Diana countered, "and being a mother, too. Do you suppose she has trouble remembering which she is?"

Jennifer considered this. "Maybe now, when Mama's here. I wonder if it's hard for Mama, too."

Diana could not answer this, and the girls remained silent till they reached the house and joined the others in the hall. Miles went straight to his study. Lady Mulgrave, who looked tired after the walk, started up the stairs, then turned and asked Melloney to come to her room. Melloney followed her without question, though she did not seem eager to do so. Diana concluded that her unexpectedly meek stepmother had remembered that she was a daughter.

As Melloney climbed the stairs, listening to the shouts of the four girls who had run back outside, she was feeling anything but meek. In truth, she was annoyed with her mother who had talked about nothing but her problems

187

with Juliana and Jennifer. Not only in that brief interview in the saloon, but all the way to the mill. Not once had she said, "How is your marriage?" Not once had she said, "Are you happy?" Melloney did not think she could answer these questions, but she would like to be asked. And she had questions of her own, questions about Celia Pengarrick that her morning at the cove had made it imperative to answer.

But it was hard to stay annoyed with Pamela for long. When they reached her bedroom and the door was shut behind them, Pamela turned to her daughter with a remorseful smile. "You must think me a monster of selfishness," she said. "I have talked of nothing but the girls and have not asked you a thing about yourself. I fear I did not quite know how to do it. Melloney, my dear girl, how do you go on?"

There was a world of meaning in that question. Are you glad or sorry you came to Cornwall? Do you mind very much having such a prosaic marriage? What lies between you and Miles? Do you like the girls, and do they like you? Does Celia cast a very large shadow?

If she could only tell her mother how she felt. She was glad and sorry to be in Ennis Court. She minded bitterly that Miles did not love her. There was friendship between them and perhaps something more at night, but it was not enough. She liked the girls, but they did not like her. And Celia's shadow threatened to destroy the whole. Instead she said, "As you see, I go on very well. I love the house and the sea air is good for me."

"Oh, Melloney, you'll have to do better than that." Pamela sank down into a small chair upholstered in a pale blue satin that intensified the blue of her eyes. With the light behind her she looked both young and fragile, reminding Melloney that she was no match for the Pamelas and Celias of this world. "You look well, I'll grant you that, but there's something worried behind it." Pamela busied herself removing her shoes, and when that was done and she had stretched her small feet in relief, she looked up and met her daughter's eyes. "You'd much better tell me, you know. I'll

188

fret it out of you in the end."

Melloney was not sure how to respond. To gain time she pulled up a footstool and sat down by her mother. She folded her hands upon her knees and stared at the narrow band on her finger that had made her at once a wife and a mother.

"Is it Miles?" Pamela asked.

"No," Melloney said quickly. "No, not at all. Miles is kind and considerate, and he's wonderful with the children."

Pamela gave her a shrewd look. "He's busy and preoccupied. I know. You mustn't mind that, it's in the nature of men. He's not a stripling besotted with having a woman all to himself and unable to think of anyone but her."

"I don't expect him to be," Melloney retorted. And then, to make sure that her mother understood that her daughter was not wholly undesirable, she added, "Miles can be quite ardent."

Pamela looked at her thoughtfully but made no comment. Perhaps she did not believe her, or perhaps she thought that Miles's ardent nature could be expressed with anyone. It was a lowering thought which Melloney did not wish to pursue, so she turned to her more immediate problem. "Mama, tell me about Celia."

"You've met her." Pamela's tone was dry. "You can judge as well as anyone."

"She was very beautiful." Melloney's image of the portrait in the hall blurred with her memories of Celia in the flesh.

"Yes," Pamela acknowledged with what might have been the faintest shade of reluctance, "she was a beautiful woman."

Melloney put her mother's tone down to jealousy. Small wonder, she was wildly jealous herself. "I didn't really know her," she said, "and I didn't know her at all when she and Miles were first married. They must have been very much in love."

Pamela smiled. "He was disgustingly oblivious of anyone else for months."

Melloney felt a stab of pain. "She was charming with the

189

children," she said, pushing away the thought of Miles and his wife. "I remember a night you took me to dine with them. The girls were brought down to the drawing room after dinner. Audrey was in her nurse's arms, but Celia insisted on holding her. And Diana stood by her side, looking as though she could never bear to leave her. I thought then that they were the most perfect family I'd ever seen." Melloney paused, remembering the morning at the cove. "The children think about her still. They're obsessed with her. They play out her death and pretend they can save her from it and bring her back home. She's all they want, Mama. Miles married me to give them another mother and they won't have me." She stopped, aware that she had said more than she intended, that she had in fact told her mother nearly the whole.

"Time—" Pamela began, echoing her daughter's words.

Melloney could not hide her impatience. "Time will do no good. I see Celia's face every time I enter the hall, and I know. I can never take her place, not with Miles, not with Diana and Audrey. They won't talk about her in front of me, but she's always there. I'm a shadow at the feast, belonging nowhere, belonging to no one."

"Oh, my dear—"

"Don't pity me, Mama, pity won't help." But the anger did. It forestalled the tears that were gathering in her eyes and the appalling self-pity to which she was about to give way. Melloney unclenched her hands and relaxed her rigid body. "I don't mean to complain," she said with the ghost of a smile. "I have a life far better than I ever hoped to have. I have a home I'm loath to leave, and a husband I admire and respect, and children I could learn to love. I can't be what Miles wants, but I can make a place for myself here. But I need to know what happened. Why did Celia go to Italy? Why didn't Miles follow her there? He knew she was ill. How could he bear to be separated from her? He let her die alone. He kept the children from her. It's unnatural, Mama, it's not like him. You have to tell me why he treated her so badly."

190

Pamela took a deep breath which was almost a sigh, and a furrow appeared between her brows. "I think you worry too much about Celia. She's in the past. You must live your life in the present."

"Oh, Mama." Unable to contain her exasperation, Melloney jumped up, kicked the stool out of the way, took a few long strides across the room, then turned to face her mother. "Don't you understand? Celia *is* the present. Diana is taking her death very hard. She doesn't understand what happened to her mother and she doesn't understand why her father behaved as he did. If I'm to be her friend—and that's all I can ever hope to be—I must know why."

Melloney held her mother's eyes, willing her to respond. "They were eight years married," Pamela said with obvious reluctance. "That brings problems in its wake."

Problems? Melloney remembered Celia and Miles as she had first seen them together in the park. She had never thought that anything could be wrong in that perfect marriage. And then she chided herself for her naiveté. Every marriage had its problems, but with love and goodwill people worked them out. Something must have gone terribly wrong for Miles to abandon his wife. "Did he stop loving her?" she asked, wondering how that could be possible.

"You mustn't think harshly of Miles. He did no more than other men do when they're bored or unhappy. It won't happen with you, Melloney, and even if it does, it won't mean anything."

Pamela was always evasive when there was anything unpleasant to say, but Melloney had no trouble understanding her meaning. She stared at her mother in dismay. "He had a mistress, is that what you're saying? Miles was married to the most beautiful woman in London, and she was not enough for him?"

Pamela shrugged as though this were not a great matter for surprise.

"How long, Mama? All through their marriage? After she went away? While she lay dying? Is that why he stayed in England, because he couldn't bear to leave his latest flirt?"

Pamela rose abruptly to confront her daughter, her face pale with anger. "Stop it. You know nothing about it. You don't understand."

"You're right, I don't understand. I don't understand any of it. Mama, you know. Don't keep it from me. The truth can't be worse than my imagining."

"My dear child." Pamela lifted her shoulders in a gesture of helplessness. "I've told you all that I can. If you want to know about Celia, you must ask Miles. It's his story, not mine."

That was all her mother would say. Melloney knew that neither pleading nor anger would move her. But to go to Miles and ask him directly, to open wounds that must be inexpressibly painful, was more than she dared do. And yet she must, for Diana's sake if not her own. With this resolution, Melloney apologized to her mother for her outburst and left the room, intent on confronting her husband at once.

But as she reached the landing, she realized she could not go to Miles now. He was occupied and would be impatient of interruption. And even if he was willing to hear her, what she had to say required the privacy of the night. Very well. She would seek him out after the children had gone to bed, after Pamela had retired. And then she would insist that he tell her what her mother had refused to say.

Melloney sat alone in her bedchamber, one eye on the mantel clock. She wanted to wait long enough for Miles to have dismissed his valet, but not so long that her husband would have retired. The tall double doors looked particularly daunting just now, and Melloney had a vivid recollection of her wedding night. They had been in London then, but there, too, she had sat watching the doors to her husband's chamber. Only then she had waited for Miles to join her. He had knocked at the door and sat on the edge of the bed and looked at her with concern and a tenderness she hadn't expected.

We don't have to do anything until you're ready.

Melloney could still remember the confusion she had felt at Miles's words. Such consideration for her feelings was of course admirable, but it was hardly the ardor one hoped for from a bridegroom on his wedding night. Not that she had had any right to expect ardor from Miles, but if she had had qualms about her marriage, it was not because she had not been ready for intimacy with her husband. Melloney felt her face grow warm as she recalled her awkward attempt to explain this to him. As it turned out, her wedding night had not been so lacking in ardor after all. In bed, at least, Miles's reserve vanished, and if Melloney suspected that in this, as in other things, she would never be Celia's equal, Miles had a delightful way of banishing such thoughts. But though Melloney had learned that she need not fear to express passion, it would never have occurred to her to initiate their nights together. She always waited for Miles to visit her chamber, and afterwards he always vanished behind those intimidating doors and left her to sleep alone.

But tonight was different. Tonight she needed to talk to her husband about the welfare of his daughters. Melloney moved to the doors and for the first time knocked on the gleaming dark wood. After a pause which was sufficiently long for her to wonder about the wisdom of her decision, the doors were pulled open and her husband stood before her.

Miles had changed from his evening clothes to a loose dressing gown of dark blue wool, and he did not appear to be wearing anything beneath it. Melloney, who hesitated to meet his gaze, found herself staring at the dark hair on his chest. She had seen him so before, óf course, but as always the sight sent a tremor through her. She looked up quickly and found Miles regarding her with a bemused expression in his dark eyes. It occurred to her that he could well misconstrue her reasons for visiting him late at night. For a fleeting moment she wondered what would happen if she stepped forward and put her arms around him and lifted her face for his kiss. It would be so easy. They were scarcely more than a foot apart. But such an action would alter the unspoken rules of their marriage, and if what they had between them was not everything she wanted, it was too precious to jeopardize.

"It's the girls," Melloney said. "I mean, I need to talk to you about the girls. May I come in for a few minutes?"

"Of course." It seemed to Melloney that some of the light went out of Miles's eyes, but perhaps she had only imagined it. He stepped aside, and Melloney moved past him into the room. She had only seen it once before, when Miles gave her a tour of the house. Then the sunlight streaming through the mullioned windows had lightened the dark wainscoting and wine-colored drapery. Now the only light came from a lamp on the writing table at the foot of the bed and a single candle on the nightstand. It was impossible to avoid looking at the bed, a massive fourposter of carved oak which could well have been part of the original furnishings of the house. Had Miles ever shared it with Celia? Or with anyone else, Melloney wondered, recalling her mother's disclosures. No, surely not here, under the same roof as his daughters.

Miles had closed the doors and was watching her with those disconcerting eyes which always seemed to see too much. Melloney folded her hands in front of her and met his gaze. "I need to know about Celia."

Miles's brows contracted, and for a moment he looked quite unlike the man to whom she was accustomed. "Did your mother say something to you?"

"No," Melloney said, "it's Diana and Audrey. They seem to—they seem to feel responsible in some way."

A shadow of pain crossed Miles's face, but when he spoke, his voice was level. "For their mother's death?"

"Because they weren't with her when she died," Melloney said.

Miles expelled his breath very slowly. "And you want to know why I was such a monster as to keep them from her."

His expression was composed, but there was a challenge

194

in his gaze, and Melloney sensed that she was treading on dangerous ground. "I know you," she said. "I know you would never do anything to hurt them. But I need to understand."

Miles regarded her in silence for the space of several heartbeats. Then he gave a curt nod and gestured toward a high-backed upholstered armchair which stood beside the bed. "You'd best sit down." He drew up another chair and, when they were both settled, leaned toward her, meeting her gaze and compelling her to meet his own. "I'd have taken the girls to see Celia if she'd wished it."

Melloney frowned. "Celia didn't want to see Diana and Audrey?"

"Not in the end, no. She felt it would be too painful for all of them."

"And she didn't—" Melloney broke off, feeling herself color.

"Want to see me either? No, she made it plain that she did not."

The note of bitterness in his voice was faint but unmistakable. Melloney studied her husband's face. Her childhood image of his first marriage was crumbling to bits, but there was no new picture to take its place. She could understand Celia not wanting her children to see her ravaged by illness, though on the whole she felt it would have been easier for Diana and Audrey if they had. But what could have been so wrong between Miles and Celia that she did not want the comfort of his presence in her illness? And no matter what the state of his marriage, Melloney found it hard to imagine Miles neglecting his wife at such a time.

Something of her confusion must have shown in her face, for Miles gave an ironic smile and leaned back in his chair. "You wonder why I didn't rush to her side anyway, whatever her wishes? Believe me, I considered it, but I don't think it would have been wise." He hesitated a moment, then leaned forward again and possessed himself of her hands. "There was a great deal wrong with my first marriage, Melloney. But that doesn't have anything to do with us."

195

His clasp was warm and strong and distracting. Melloney looked at her husband's face, at his familiar, winning smile, and felt a sudden welling of anger. "But it does, don't you see?" she said, snatching her hands away and springing to her feet. "Everything I do, I do in Celia's shadow. I'm sure the servants compare me to her, and God knows the girls do, and you—"

Melloney broke off, conscious that her voice had risen and that she was breathing hard and not in the least in control of what she might say next. Miles got to his feet and faced her. "I would never compare you to Celia, Melloney. You're nothing like her."

It was a dubious compliment. Melloney turned her head away, aware of the pressure of tears behind her eyes.

"I know the girls have been difficult," Miles continued. "But we both knew it wouldn't be easy. You've done wonders. I'm sure with time—"

"No," Melloney said with a vehemence which surprised her. She turned back to look at Miles. "They may accept me. I may be a sort of glorified governess or, if I'm very lucky, an aunt. But they'll never think of me as their mother. Not that there's any reason they should," she added quickly. "It was silly of me to expect more." There was a bitterness in her voice which she had not intended, and Melloney knew that she spoke of her relationship with her husband as well. "If I can't be their mother, I can at least try to be their friend," she continued in a more moderate tone. "I think they need a friend very much. But I can't even be that until I understand the past. What did Celia say to them before she left England?"

Miles had been watching her with concern, but at her question a guarded look appeared in his eyes. "Celia's health worsened very suddenly. She was obliged to leave directly for the Continent from London. The doctors didn't think it would be wise for her to return to Cornwall."

Melloney stared at him as the import of his words sank in. "Celia didn't say goodbye to the girls at all?"

"She wrote to them. Every month."

Melloney shook her head, trying to make sense of the fragments of information she had acquired in the past few hours. She could not fit them into a coherent picture. Something was missing. She drew a breath and fixed her husband with a firm gaze. "I think you should tell me the truth, Miles."

Miles's eyes seemed to bore into her own. Melloney was acutely conscious of the faint sound of the sea in the suddenly still room. "Everything I've told you tonight is the truth," Miles said at last. "My word on it."

"But not the whole truth. Dear God, Miles," Melloney said with a desperation which had to do with far more than her need to understand about Celia, "I'm your wife. Don't you know you can trust me?"

"Trust you?" Miles said with sudden violence. "I'd trust you with my life, Melloney. In God's name, can't you trust me enough to believe I've told you all I can?"

He had never used such a tone with her before. For a moment Melloney was too startled to respond. She heard Miles draw in his breath, a quick, harsh sound, and then, with a suddenness that took her quite by surprise, he strode across the room and pulled her closely into his arms. "I'm sorry," he said, his voice at once rough and tender, his chin resting on her hair. "So very sorry. I never meant for you to be hurt. Perhaps it was a mistake—but no matter." He took her face between his hands and looked down into her eyes. "We all have secrets, my darling. Every one of us. Is that so hard to accept?"

The unexpected endearment sent a shock of delight through her, as did his touch. She could feel his fingers trembling, and his eyes seemed to be pleading for something she did not understand. Yet he had just very nearly said it had been a mistake to marry her. Thrown into confusion, Melloney spoke the first words that came into her head. "Does my mother know your secrets?"

The sudden stillness of his fingers and the wariness in his eyes answered her question more plainly than any words. Feeling more desolated than she had at any time since her

197

marriage, Melloney pulled away from her husband and fled to the sanctuary of her own room.

Diana leaned back against her white-painted bedstead, listening to the water dripping off the eaves and the wind rattling the windowpanes. The rain had begun early this morning, frustrating plans for a visit to the cove. Rainy summer days were far from unusual in Cornwall, and Diana's father had a seemingly inexhaustible fund of amusements to while away the hours, but after lunch he had had to go and speak with the estate agent. By that time the rain had slackened to a drizzle, so Juliana and Audrey had ventured outside. Less restless than their sisters, Diana and Jennifer had instead sought refuge in Diana's room. Lady Mulgrave had gone to her own room to lie down, and Melloney . . .

Diana frowned. She wasn't sure where her stepmother had got to. Melloney had been quiet this morning. And she'd scarcely spoken to Miles. Could they have quarreled? Diana felt a sick feeling in the pit of her stomach at this last thought. Not, she reminded herself, that it was any concern of hers if they had quarreled. It wasn't as though Melloney was her mother.

Diana looked at Jennifer who was seated crosswise from her on the bed, engrossed in a handsomely illustrated book which had been a gift from Miles on Diana's last birthday. Jennifer had been her friend for years and was the best friend she had. Diana needed to talk to her, but she wasn't sure how to begin.

"Does your mother ever write to you?" Diana asked, deciding she had better speak before she lost her nerve. "Letters, I mean."

Jennifer looked up from the book, apparently not surprised by the question. One way or another, they had been talking about their mothers a great deal in the past twenty-four hours. "Not very often," she said. "I mean, usually we aren't that far away. But she wrote to us when she was on her wedding journey. Twice, from Paris and from Rome."

"What were the letters like? I mean, did they sound like the way she talks?"

Jennifer considered for a moment. "I suppose so. I never thought about it much." She leaned back against the footboard, drawing her legs up and wrapping her arms about her knees. "Your mother wrote to you all the time, didn't she? When she was—I mean—"

"When she was sick," Diana concluded, keeping her voice without expression. "Yes, she did, every month."

Jennifer studied her friend. Diana knew what she was thinking. Jennifer might be something of a chatterbox, but she'd always been careful not to ask Diana about her mother, even two years ago when Celia had gone away and they were only six. "Didn't your mother's letters sound like the way she talked?" Jennifer asked at last.

Diana hesitated. It felt horribly like betraying a confidence. Not that anyone had ever told her not to discuss it. No one had ever admitted there was anything to discuss. Perhaps the problem was that she had a vague sense that she was setting out to discover something she didn't want to know. "Not really," she said. "But perhaps it's just that I don't remember her well enough." Even as she spoke, Diana knew that this last was a cowardly excuse. Nearly every tantalizingly brief moment she had spent in her mother's company was indelibly etched in her memory.

"You must remember," Jennifer objected. "I was six when my father died, and I remember how he talked. Not that he ever talked to me very much."

With sudden decision, Diana jumped off the bed and crossed to the little rosewood writing table Miles had bought for her when she was starting to learn her letters. She hesitated a moment, then pulled open the central drawer and took out an ebony-inlaid box. From the velvet-lined interior she took a packet of letters, neatly tied up with pink ribbon. She hesitated again, the letters held in both hands. But she had already made her decision before she spoke to Jennifer. Diana returned to the bed, set the packet down beside her,

199

and untied the ribbon. "There," she said. And then, when Jennifer looked at her in puzzlement, "Go ahead, read them. I want to know what you think."

Cautiously Jennifer picked up the first of the letters. Diana watched her closely. She couldn't say exactly what it was she wanted from her friend. It didn't seem likely that Jennifer would be able to make any more sense of the letters than she had. Perhaps she wanted reassurance that the vague fears which she had never put into words, even to herself, were groundless. Yet Diana knew that even if Jennifer told her as much, she would not believe it.

Whatever Diana had expected, it was not the reaction she got. "That's funny," Jennifer exclaimed midway through the first letter.

"What is?" Diana asked sharply.

"Your mama makes her *i*'s just like mine does, with little circles on the top instead of dots."

Diana felt something twisting deep inside her, something she would even now not admit to. "Perhaps that's how grown-up ladies write," she said casually.

Jennifer shook her head. "Melloney doesn't. And that isn't how our governess taught us. She ought to know. She's supposed to be teaching us to be grown-up ladies."

"Do our mothers write any other letters the same way?" Diana asked in a carefully detached voice.

"Oh, most of them, I suppose," Jennifer said, her attention back on the letter. "But the *i* is the most obvious."

Diana felt her nails digging into her palms. She would have to admit it, that deep dark fear that had been lurking at the back of her mind ever since the first letter arrived. Then the fear had been buried beneath grief and confusion, but it had remained, constant and nagging, surfacing whenever the letters arrived, continuing even after Mama died and the letters stopped. It had never occurred to Diana that Jennifer's mother had anything to do with it, but she began to see how Lady Mulgrave might have been involved. "Jennifer," Diana said, trying to speak as if she were asking a perfectly commonplace question, "do you think it's possible

200

that your mother wrote those letters?"

Jennifer stared at her friend in utter bewilderment. "My mother wasn't in Italy. Not two years ago, anyway. And the letters are written to you. This one says 'My dearest Diana and Audrey' at the top."

Diana drew a breath. "I know. But perhaps—suppose my mother couldn't write to us for some reason. Daddy might have asked your mother to write to us instead, so we wouldn't feel bad."

Jennifer frowned. "Why wouldn't your mother have written to you? Even if she were sick, she could have told somebody else what to write, couldn't she? My father dictated letters to his secretary when he was sick."

"I don't know," Diana said in an expressionless voice. "I don't know why she wouldn't have written. But I think that letter sounds more like your mother than mine. Don't you?"

"I suppose so," Jennifer said after a long moment of consideration. "But I didn't know your mother very well. Didn't you ever see her handwriting?"

Diana shook her head. "She never wrote to us when she was in England." She had also not liked to have the children bothering her when she was busy with her correspondence, but Diana did not see any need to tell her friend that.

Jennifer looked back at the letter, weighing it in her hand. "It certainly looks like my mama's writing. It's too bad I didn't bring one of her letters with me. We could compare them." She frowned, apparently caught up in the puzzle now that her first surprise was over. "I know," she said, swinging her legs to the floor. "Melloney must have letters from Mama in her room."

Diana hesitated, reluctant to invade Melloney's apartments. "That would be stealing."

"No, it wouldn't," Jennifer assured her, jumping up and tossing back the long blond hair that Diana had always envied. "We're not going to take them anywhere. We'll look at them in Melloney's room." She studied her friend gravely. "Don't you want to know?"

That settled it. Diana wasn't at all sure she *wanted* to

know, but she knew she *had* to know. Without further protest, she led the way down the corridor. Oddly enough, while Diana had rarely been in her mother's apartments, she had spent a good deal of time in Melloney's. They were the same rooms Celia had occupied, but Miles had had them redone when he and Melloney became betrothed. Diana pushed open the door of the sitting room, recalling it as it had been in her mother's time, with its fragile pink silk curtains and damask-covered furniture. She had a sudden image of her mother reclining on the rose-colored chaise longue, her golden hair falling in silky waves over the shoulders of an elaborate lacy dressing gown. It had been a great treat to be allowed to go in and sit with her for a time, but it had been nerve-wracking, too, for at any moment Celia might ring for the nurse, and when her mother did so, Diana always felt she herself was somehow at fault.

Now the walls were pale cream, and the curtains and upholstery were patterned in dark green and ivory. The room was perfumed not by the scent Celia had always worn, but by the fresh flowers Melloney arranged every week. Diana hadn't liked it at first, for it didn't seem like the fairy-tale bower her mother's chamber had been, but now she had to admit there was something restful and soothing about the room.

In place of Celia's gilded escritoire, Melloney had a writing table very like Diana's own. It stood against the windows which overlooked the back garden, with ink and paper ready for use. Diana crossed the room and stared down at a half-finished watercolor which lay on the table top. It was a view of the cove with the sea in the distance — a wonderful blend of blues and greens that brought the water vividly to life — and two small figures in white on the sand. She and Audrey, Diana realized, and found herself wondering if Melloney would allow her to have the picture to hang in her room. Then, firmly ordering her thoughts, she drew a breath and pulled open one of the drawers.

Jennifer was already investigating a second drawer. "Ink, sealing wax . . . these look like letters. Only that's not Mama's hand."

Jennifer was holding up a packet of letters, very like Diana's, save that there were fewer and the ribbon was green, not pink. Diana recognized the decisive scrawl at once. "Those are from Daddy."

"Really?" Jennifer's eyes lit with mischief. "Do you suppose they're love letters?"

Diana was taken aback. "I shouldn't think so. I mean, he and Melloney are a bit old for that, aren't they?"

"Not necessarily. Mama and Uncle John are always holding hands and things, and they're even older."

"Daddy and Melloney don't hold hands," Diana said firmly. "They're probably just letters about Ennis Court. Daddy came down here to see to the remodeling while they were betrothed."

"But she kept them. Tied up with ribbon, too."

Diana felt a moment of curiosity, followed by an attack of conscience. "All the same, we shouldn't look at them," she said, absently toying with a stack of writing paper in the open drawer. "They haven't anything to do with—" She broke off, for beneath the writing paper lay a half-folded sheet covered with a flowing hand which was all too familiar. Subduing an impulse to push the letter to the back of the drawer and pretend she had not seen it, Diana picked it up and turned it over to look at the inscription. It was signed "Fondest love, M." rather than "Your loving Mama," but otherwise it appeared identical to the letters she and Audrey had received from their mother. Wordlessly, Diana handed the letter to Jennifer, but as she did so, she was arrested by a voice from the doorway.

"I was wondering where the two of you had got to. Did you want to see me about something?"

Diana turned and met her stepmother's gaze. There was no censure in Melloney's expression. She was giving Diana the benefit of the doubt, waiting for an explanation before she passed judgment. Without stopping to think, Diana took both letters from Jennifer, walked across the room, and held them out to her stepmother.

203

Melloney looked at her sister and stepdaughter in surprise. They appeared to have been going through her writing table, but she knew both girls well enough to be sure they would not do so without a reason. Jennifer held a ribbon-wrapped bundle of papers which Melloney recognized at once. Those maddeningly prosaic letters Miles had written to her during their betrothal (beginning "My dear Melloney" and ending "Yours, M.P.") which she had treasured as if they had been the most passionate avowals of love. Now Diana was holding two letters out to her. Miles's letters? There was, loweringly, nothing in them which she would not wish the girls to see.

Schooling her face to betray nothing more than curiosity, Melloney took the letters and saw that they were both from her mother. She searched her memory, wondering what Pamela might have said to cause the girls concern and what had prompted them to look for the letters in the first place. She recognized the first letter at once. It was the one Pamela had written announcing her planned arrival at Ennis Court. The second was not familiar. Melloney turned the paper over, searching for the date, and looked at it in puzzlement. "Perugia, November, 1814." And, just below, in her mother's unmistakable hand: "My dearest Diana and Audrey."

It made no sense. Pamela could well have written to Diana and Audrey, but Melloney knew her mother had not been in Perugia in 1814. There must be some explanation, some harmless, perfectly logical explanation. Melloney turned the letter over again and looked at the signature. "Your loving Mama." Despite Pamela's handwriting, the words were unmistakable, but Melloney's brain refused to acknowledge what they implied. The familiar, flowery hand blurred before her eyes. Then, with the suddenness of a thunderclap, the truth forced itself upon her. Melloney drew a breath, released it slowly, and tried to impose some order on her thoughts. Then she raised her eyes and met Diana's steady gaze.

"I'm not surprised you're puzzled," Melloney told her

stepdaughter. "I'm puzzled myself."

Diana nodded. Her face was without expression, but her lips trembled slightly. Melloney started to reach out to her, then checked herself. She ached for the child, the more so as she could not offer comfort as she would to Juliana or Jennifer. Then it occurred to her that while Diana looked shaken and hurt, she did not appear nearly as shocked as might have been expected. Could she possibly have guessed?

"I'll speak to my mother and to your father," Melloney said. "I think it will be best if I talk to them alone, but I promise to tell you what I learn. May I take the letters with me?"

Diana, who had not taken her eyes from Melloney's face, nodded slowly. Jennifer, who had come up to stand beside her friend, regarded Melloney with concern. Melloney smiled and ruffled her sister's hair. Diana continued to stand very still. Melloney hesitated a moment, then touched her lightly on the cheek. Diana's expression remained unchanged, but as her stepmother turned to leave the room she said suddenly, "Melloney?"

Melloney turned back at the door. "Yes?"

Some of the tension left Diana's face. "Thank you."

Throughout the scene with the girls, Melloney had been too shocked to feel much beyond sympathy and bewilderment. But as she walked down the corridor to her mother's room, anger lanced through her, sharp and white-hot. The guilt and confusion Diana had been living with were intolerable. Whatever this charade—she still did not understand it—it was going to end today. Melloney knocked once at her mother's door and then, without waiting for an answer, walked into the room.

Pamela was reclining on the cushioned window seat, her golden hair and azure dress vivid against the gray of the sky. "Darling," she said with a smile, looking up from the book she was reading. "Have you come to keep me company? It's such a dreary day and this novel is not at all interesting." Then she noted Melloney's expression and her own changed. "What's the matter?" she said. "Is it the girls?"

"The girls," Melloney said with deliberation, "would like to know the truth. So would I." She walked quickly across the room and held out the two pieces of paper.

The color drained from Pamela's face, a bitter confirmation of all of Melloney's worst suspicions. Pamela stretched out her hand for the letters, then let it fall, as if she had no need to look at them.

"How could you, Mama?" Melloney said, her voice shaking with anger. "You told me I'd have to ask Miles about Celia, and all the time you knew—"

She broke off, for she still did not know what her mother had known, save that it must be far more complicated than anything she had hitherto imagined. Pamela placed her book on the window seat beside her and sat up very straight. She was still pale, but despite her loosened hair and simple jaconet frock, she looked almost regal. "What I knew was not my secret to tell," she said. "I told Miles you should know the truth, but short of betraying his confidence, I could not compel him."

So it was Miles who had insisted she be kept in the dark. Melloney's throat tightened. "I see," she said in a flat voice. "Miles didn't think I could be trusted with a confidence."

"I don't think you see at all," Pamela said with some asperity. "You must know Miles is an honorable man. His own code wouldn't let him betray Celia. Besides, he doesn't confide easily in others."

"He confided in you."

"The circumstances were entirely different. He was in great distress and had to talk to someone. Miles has known me since he was a little boy. He—"

"Trusts you," Melloney concluded. "Perhaps you should have married him."

"That's nonsense," Pamela said sharply. She regarded her daughter with concern. "I first met Miles when your father brought me to Cornwall. Miles's parents were his friends, but I must confess they bored me to tears. As did your father, there's no sense pretending otherwise. Miles was five years old then and quite starved for affection — his parents have a great deal to answer for — and I found him far more interesting than any of the adults in the vicinity. We've been friends ever since. But you must know Miles has never been in love with me."

"Then we're even. He's never been in love with me either." Melloney retreated to a nearby chair, arms wrapped tightly around her to ward off further pain. The mournful wail of the wind sounded louder, and the damp and chill seemed to have intensified.

"You have every right to be angry, Melloney," Pamela said quietly. "I think perhaps it's as well this has come to light, though I could have wished — " She frowned. "You say the girls know?"

"Jennifer and Diana do. I found them going through my papers, looking for a letter of yours to compare with one of Celia's." The memory of the girls' confusion brought Melloney's anger back to the fore. "Dear God, Mama, didn't it occur to you that they might guess the truth?"

Pamela's eyes clouded. "They're so young. I didn't realize — "

"That children think?"

In the gray light from the window, Pamela's face appeared drawn, and for once she very nearly looked her age. "It seemed best at the time. And once we had begun, there was no turning back."

The use of the word *we* hurt Melloney as much as anything. "Why?" she said. "Why was it necessary at all? I don't understand."

Pamela adjusted a lace frill on her sleeve with care. "Yesterday I told you to ask Miles."

"I did. Last night. He said Celia didn't want to see the girls after she went abroad."

"That's certainly true," Pamela agreed.

"And then he said we all have secrets and he couldn't tell me any more. He admitted Celia hadn't even said a proper goodbye to the girls, but he insisted that she had written every month. Why didn't she? Or did Miles keep her letters

207

from the children and substitute yours instead?"

Pamela's eyes darkened with something approaching anger. "Surely you don't believe that of him."

Melloney did not know what to believe of her husband, save that she loved him and was convinced he was incapable of cruelty. "No," she said in a low voice, looking down at the plain gold of her wedding band, "no, God help me, I don't."

She raised her eyes to find her mother regarding her with the air of one who has just made a discovery. "I have been a great fool," Pamela said softly. "I didn't realize."

"Realize what?" Melloney demanded.

"How long have you been in love with him?"

Had Melloney been less shaken, the question would have startled her more. "Since I was twelve. At least that's when I first admitted it to myself. Does it matter?"

Pamela's mouth curved in the faintest of smiles. "Oh, yes, I think it matters a great deal. And I think you had better talk to Miles again, Melloney. Only this time I wouldn't ask. I'd insist."

"I have every intention of doing so," Melloney said, getting to her feet and shaking out her cambric skirt. Whatever role her mother had played in the drama, Pamela was right. This was something Melloney would have to settle with her husband. Without another word she turned and walked from the room.

Melloney made her way down the stairs to Miles's study and knocked briskly on the door. If Miles were still with the estate agent, she would say she had to see him as soon as he was free. But when Miles bade her come in, she found him alone, staring out one of the tall narrow windows which faced the back garden. His hands were braced on the window sill and tension was evident in the set of his shoulders. He turned round as she closed the door behind her. There were lines in his face which had not been noticeable that morning when he played with the children. For a moment Melloney felt an intense desire to smooth the lines away.

Oddly enough, Miles's face seemed to lighten when he looked at her. "You're a welcome sight on a gloomy afternoon," he said with a smile. And then, in a more serious tone, "I've been wanting to apologize for last night. I didn't handle it very well."

"Nor did I," Melloney said. "I should have insisted that you give me an explanation." She expected Miles to protest, but he merely stood watching her, waiting for her to continue. Melloney drew a breath. "I know, Miles. About Celia's letters. So do Diana and Jennifer. They came to me with the story, and I promised them an explanation."

Melloney had seen her husband in many moods. She had seem him grave and preoccupied and laughing and tender. Last night she had seen him in a fury. But never had she seen him as he looked now, stunned and shaken to the core, as if he had no defenses left to call on. She had the sense that she had made an unpardonable intrusion into a part of him that he had never wished her to see. "Oh, God," he said, pressing his hands over his eyes, "I thought I could spare them this."

Melloney longed to offer comfort, but she did not think he would accept it, anymore than Diana would. And how could she offer comfort for something she did not understand? "Spare them what?" she said. "The knowledge that their father lied to them?"

Miles stared at her, as if only then recalling that he was not alone. His mouth twisted in a mockery of a smile. "That's the least of it."

A flash of anger cut through Melloney's compassion. "If your clever little charade was meant to comfort the girls, it's been a miserable failure. I think Diana knew something was wrong from the first. She's been torturing herself because she doesn't understand, and she thinks she's at fault. Nothing could be worse than that."

"Nothing?" Miles gave a bitter laugh. "Oh, my sweet Melloney, how little you know."

"At least I know one of the worst sins a parent can commit is to lie."

Miles had fallen to staring at the floor, but at that his head jerked up. "What would you have had me do?" he de-

209

manded with sudden fury. "Tell my children that their mother didn't want to see them? That she couldn't bother to write and found it more convenient to pretend they didn't exist? Oh no, Melloney, I may be a number of things, but that much of a monster I'm not."

Melloney stared at him. "But . . . Celia loved the children," she protested, feeling very stupid. "I saw her with them. She was devoted."

"Devoted?" Miles gave another bark of laughter. "Oh, yes, Celia could be devoted enough. There was practically nothing my dear wife couldn't be when it suited her. I have made a number of mistakes in my life, Melloney, but the most criminally stupid of all was to think Celia and I had the remotest chance of being happy together."

Melloney's shock must have shown in her expression, for Miles looked away and ran his hands through his hair, as if in an effort to regain his self-control. "God. I didn't mean you to think—" He took an uncertain step toward her, then stopped and gestured toward the sofa which faced the windows. "It seems I had best begin at the beginning. It's not a pretty tale, but I can at least endeavor to tell it with some moderation."

At last she had what she wanted. Yet how could she feel triumph or relief when Miles was in such obvious torment? Melloney sank down on the sofa, conscious that her mouth was dry and her hands were trembling. As she leaned back against the soft brown velvet, she realized that what she felt was fear. Fear that when Miles finally told her the truth, it would only show her how wide the gulf between them really was.

Miles moved to a leather-covered chair opposite her. He had recovered his self-command, but Melloney sensed that his anger had merely been leashed, not extinguished. Just beneath the controlled surface of the husband to whom she was accustomed lay the angry, bitter stranger of a few moments before. Miles tented his hands and stared at her. "You met my parents," he said abruptly. "Do you remember them?"

It was wholly unexpected. Miles's father had been dead seventeen years and his mother six, both long before Celia's illness. Then Melloney remembered her mother's words a short while before. *His parents have a great deal to answer for.* Melloney had not known either of them well. Mr. Pengarrick, a stern, rather frightening man, had been a friend of her father's, but Mrs. Pengarrick and Pamela had never got on well. Like Melloney's mother, Mrs. Pengarrick had been a great beauty, but she had been ten years Pamela's senior. Melloney suspected she had been jealous of the younger woman. "A little," Melloney said. "I never saw a great deal of them."

Miles gave an ironic smile. "Nor did my sisters and brother and I. Father had little but criticism for Ned and me, and little interest whatsoever in Barbara and Helen. And Mother—I'm not sure Mother ever forgave any of us."

"For what?" Melloney felt rather as if she had stepped into a Renaissance painting, far more detailed and complex than it at first appeared.

"For being constant reminders of her dwindling youth. In any case, she hated Cornwall. She spent her summers in Bath whenever possible, and her Christmases at amusing house parties. We once went a whole year without seeing her at all. When she was about, she and Father were generally quarreling. We were confined to the nursery most of the time, but we couldn't help but notice. If she had any feeling for us, I think Father's coldness managed to kill it."

His measured, level voice could not hide his pain. Melloney thought back to her own childhood. Whatever her inadequacies, Pamela had generally kept her children with her. And, Melloney realized, she had never doubted that her mother loved her. Melloney studied her husband, thinking of his younger brother and sisters. They were a close family, and all three looked up to Miles, almost as though he were a parent rather than an elder brother. "So you tried to take your parents' place?" she asked.

"I suppose so, though I don't know that I'd have put it that way at the time. I was hardly an effective substitute."

"I doubt Ned and Barbara and Helen would agree. Perhaps it's because of them that you're so good with Diana and Audrey."

Miles shook his head. "We all survived. We had a more comfortable childhood than nine-tenths of the children in England. But I swore that when I had a family of my own it would be different." He fell silent, staring at his hands. "I was twenty-five when I met Celia, but what with standing for Parliament and coping with Father's death and seeing to the girls' dowries and Ned's education, I hadn't found time for falling in love. I suppose I was an accident waiting to happen. God knows Celia was beautiful. Or perhaps ravishingly pretty would be more accurate. In those days my tastes were sadly conventional."

He stared at her for a long moment, as if about to say more. Made oddly uncomfortable by his regard, Melloney looked away. "I remember meeting you in the park before Diana was born. You looked—I thought you looked so very happy."

"Happy?" said Miles, as if his thoughts had been elsewhere. "I suppose we were, for the first year or so. It took that long for us to discover that we hadn't a thought in common." He pushed himself out of his chair abruptly and moved to the windows. "I think Celia thought she loved me as much as I thought I loved her," he said, looking out at the misty, rain-drenched garden. "At least, she liked the idea of being in love. Life to her was a drama with herself as the central character. She could believe passionately in whatever role she was playing at the time, but she got bored quickly. And I was scarcely an ideal husband." He turned and gave Melloney a sudden grin. "Believe it or not, I think I was even more preoccupied then than I am now. You at least had fair warning that you weren't getting a particular bargain for a husband. Celia had none."

Melloney thought of Miles's consideration, of the moments of laughter they had shared, of his skillful, eloquent lovemaking, and decided that whatever else Celia Pengarrick had been, she had been a great fool. Then Melloney

212

considered the rest of what Miles had said and began to have a glimmering of understanding. "When the children came, Celia played at being a mother the way she played at everything else?"

The ghost of a smile crossed Miles's face. "You always were abominably perceptive, my sweet, even as a child. Celia could be charming with the children for a few hours at a time, but she had little patience when they made too much noise or demanded too much attention. If I'd been different, if there'd been something real between us . . ." His face grew bleak. "As it was, the more impatient she got with me, the more impatient she got with Diana and Audrey. A few months after Audrey's birth, I realized I'd managed to marry a woman strikingly like my mother. And I feared I was turning into a man like my father."

"You aren't a bit like your father," Melloney said indignantly. "He was the most forbidding man imaginable, and there's nothing forbidding about you—at least not with the children. Or with me."

"A touching vote of confidence," Miles said. "At any event, I was determined that Diana and Audrey would at least have the security of believing that their mother loved them."

"In other words, you began to lie to cover up Celia's deficiencies."

"The odd present with Celia's name attached to it, the excuse that Mama had to stay in Town because I needed her with me—yes, I suppose you could call them lies. I liked to have the children in London with us, but Celia complained that they were always underfoot. We took to leaving them at Ennis Court more and more. I got down whenever I could, and Celia always spent summers there, and the Christmas holidays. I insisted on that. That, and that she behave with reasonable discretion."

Melloney drew in her breath. "So that was why you—" She broke off, aware that she had almost made an unpardonable statement.

Miles's eyes told her she had already betrayed herself. He

213

regarded her for a moment, as if debating whether or not to put it into words. "Why I failed to honor my own marriage vows?" he said in a surprisingly mild voice. "I hadn't realized there'd been gossip."

Melloney felt the blood rush to her face. "It wasn't gossip," she assured him. "It was—"

"Pamela," Miles concluded. "What the devil was she thinking of?"

"You mustn't blame Mama," Melloney said, feeling oddly protective of her mother. "I was pestering her about what went wrong between you and Celia, and she said I shouldn't think harshly of you, that you did no more than other men who are unhappy with their marriages, and—" Melloney bit her lip, recalling the rest of her mother's words.

"And?" Miles prompted.

Melloney met his gaze. "And that it wouldn't happen with me, and even if it did, it wouldn't mean anything."

"Your mother is a woman of great charm and intelligence," Miles said grimly, "but even she can behave like a fool." His brows drew together. "Did you believe her?"

Melloney felt a stab of pain. "I'm Pamela's daughter, Miles. I'm hardly ignorant of the way the world works."

Miles drew a sharp breath and stepped forward, then checked himself. "No, perhaps that had better wait, or you'll never get your explanation. I stopped sharing Celia's bed not long after Audrey was born. I found I preferred uncomplicated passion to a pretense of love. There hasn't been another woman since I asked you to be my wife."

Melloney wondered if he would describe what was between them as uncomplicated passion. It could, she supposed, have been worse.

"At all events," Miles continued, his voice suddenly brisk, "Celia was discreet and so, I trust, was I, and we managed to rub along tolerably well until the summer of '14." He began to pace the length of the room, speaking rapidly. "You remember, Bonaparte was defeated, at least temporarily, and the *ton* flocked to Paris. Celia was determined to go, and I must confess I found it more comfortable in London without her. It was in Paris that she met him."

"Him?" Melloney asked.

Miles stopped pacing and scowled at a small seascape on the opposite wall. "Count Umberto Cortona. Younger than I, handsome, quite damnably charming. And not at all a bad man, though it took me some time to admit it. When Celia returned to London, Cortona followed her. She was in love, she said, but she'd said it before, so I didn't pay much attention. But this was different, at least in its intensity. Celia began to grow reckless. I comforted myself with the thought that the Season was almost over. But the night before we were to leave for Ennis Court, Celia announced that she wasn't going with me. She couldn't bear to be separated from her lover."

Miles paused, his hands tightly clenched, and drew a shuddering breath. Then he strode to the fireplace and stood with his arm on the pine mantel and his foot on the brass fender, staring into the cold, unlit depths. "If you think I lost my temper last night, it was nothing compared to the scene I had with Celia two years ago. I reminded her of our agreement. I told her I'd see her in hell before I'd let her disappoint the children. She said if I was a more entertaining husband I wouldn't have to bully her into going home. If I took her there by force, she'd run away. We both of us said a lot of things we'd managed to avoid saying for years. Celia was right, of course. I couldn't force her. The next morning I left for Cornwall on my own. I told Diana and Audrey their mother wasn't feeling well and had to stay in Town."

"But she wasn't really ill yet?" Melloney asked.

"Her health had never been strong, but no, she wasn't ill." Miles continued to stare fixedly into the fireplace. "A few days after I arrived in Cornwall, I received a letter from her. She hated me and had known nothing but misery since our marriage began. She couldn't bear to look at the girls because they reminded her of me. She was going to Italy with Cortona, who was the only man she had ever loved, and I could tell the world and our children whatever

215

I liked."

Melloney felt a cold sick chill which had nothing to do with the rain and damp. She couldn't speak. After a moment, Miles lifted his head and looked at her. "She was furious," he said quietly, "and she wanted to hurt me. I don't think she really meant it about the girls, not in that way. But it's true that once she'd decided to run off with Cortona she couldn't be bothered with them."

"Then she wasn't ill at all?" It was the first question that came into Melloney's head, and it seemed a wholly inadequate response.

"Not then, no. I wrote and asked if she wanted me to divorce her, but Cortona had a wife of his own, so there was no question of marriage. Celia's second letter was a little more temperate. She agreed to subscribe to the fiction that she'd gone abroad for her health. That at least stopped the gossips from saying anything to my face. But the girls wanted to know when she'd write to them. That's when I went to Pamela." He turned to face Melloney, hands clasped behind his back. "So now you know. Why my wife wouldn't write to the children and why I found it necessary to lie to them. It may have been cruel, Melloney, but it seemed less cruel than the truth."

"Perhaps it was," Melloney said quietly. "The trouble is, it's difficult to conceal the truth forever." She frowned, arrested by a sudden thought. Had Diana guessed the truth about her mother even before Celia left? In which case, did her hostility to Melloney stem not from the fact that Melloney could never measure up to her mother, but from a fear that Melloney's love would prove as elusive and transitory as Celia's? "What happened?" she asked. "I mean, how did she—"

"She caught a chill which settled on her lungs and turned into a fever. She was dead within a fortnight. Cortona wrote to tell me of it. He seemed quite devastated, poor devil. I think his feelings for Celia were genuine. More genuine than mine." Miles passed his hand over his face. "But God help me, I wouldn't have wished that upon her."

216

He sounded unutterably weary, and there was more than a trace of guilt in his voice. "You can hardly blame yourself for something that happened hundreds of miles away," Melloney said firmly.

"No," Miles agreed. "But if it weren't for me, perhaps she wouldn't have been hundreds of miles away."

Melloney was on her feet without realizing how she had got there. "It takes more than one quarrel for a person to decide to abandon home and family. You didn't drive her away, Miles."

"No?" Miles gave a twisted smile. His disarranged dark hair fell over his forehead, and he looked younger and more vulnerable than she had ever seen him. "Perhaps not. But we'll never know, will we? Melloney—" He stretched out a hand to her again, then let it fall. "I must see the girls," he said brusquely. The vulnerability was gone from his face, and the time for confidences was plainly over. "I only hope they take it as well as you have." He strode to the door, then turned back to look at her, frowning. "Are you all right?"

Melloney summoned up a smile. "I'm fine, Miles. It's the children who need you."

The door closed behind him with a quiet click. Melloney walked to the windows, hugging her arms around her. A shaft of sunlight had escaped from behind the clouds, and the raindrops clinging to the grass and shrubbery sparkled with light. Normally Melloney felt a thrill at such a sight and an instant desire to fetch her paint box. Now it only served to emphasize her dismal humor. She had a sudden image of Morwenna's radiant face at her wedding; of Owen, who had been married only a few months ago, grinning as his bride walked down the aisle; of her mother and Mulgrave when they returned from their wedding journey. Such happiness seemed so simple and so far out of reach. She had thought Miles could never love her as much as he had loved Celia. What she knew now was worse. After Celia she doubted if Miles would trust himself to love anyone at all.

Melloney left the study wanting nothing so much as to shut herself up with her thoughts and have a good cry. But she had barely taken half a dozen steps down the hall when one of the footmen intercepted her with the news that McBride and Mrs. Quin had come to blows again. After a half-hour of strenuous diplomacy, Melloney escaped to the small saloon. The time for tears had passed, so she busied herself with lists of the tenants who might need assistance to make it through the winter. The recent poor harvests and the number of husbands and sons who had returned less than whole from the Peninsula and Waterloo had put a strain on many families. Here at least she could do some good as mistress of Ennis Court.

When a knock sounded on the door, Melloney looked up, expecting her mother or sisters. Instead she found herself looking into her stepdaughters' grave faces.

"Daddy talked to us," Diana said into the silence. "About the letters and everything."

"I'm glad." Melloney got to her feet, aware that this scene was crucial to her future relationship with her stepdaughters, uncertain how to proceed. She moved to a sofa which was comfortably strewn with cushions and gestured for the girls to join her. After a moment of hesitation, Diana sat on a nearby stool. Audrey looked from her sister to Melloney, then marched over to the sofa and perched beside her stepmother. "Mama didn't go away because she was sick," she said, looking up at Melloney with wide eyes. "She went away because she didn't want to be our mother."

Melloney felt a wave of pain and helplessness. *Oh, Miles, were you right after all? Would anything be better than this?* And yet, for all the words, Audrey sounded surprisingly matter-of-fact.

"I don't think that's true," Melloney said, wondering how much Miles had told them. "I think she went away because she didn't want to be your father's wife."

"Oh." Audrey digested this in frowning concentration. Then she looked back at Melloney, her eyes filled with concern. "Are you going to go away, too?"

Dear God, no wonder both girls had been so terrified of growing attached to someone new. Melloney checked an impulse to gather the little girl into her arms. She should let Audrey make the first move. "No," she said, looking from Audrey to Diana, who was staring at the carpet. Sincerity was the only weapon she had to convince them. "I'll never leave your father. And I'll never leave you either."

Audrey studied her stepmother for a long moment. Then, still solemn-faced, she slipped her hand into Melloney's own. "I don't remember Mama very well."

Diana looked up from the carpet. "She wasn't a very good mother." It was a flat, unemotional statement. Then, with sudden vehemence, "Sometimes I didn't like her very much."

Anger, Melloney decided, was infinitely preferable to guilt. "That's understandable," she said. "There've been times when I haven't liked my mother very much."

Diana looked at her in surprise. Then she scowled. "Your mother didn't go away." She stared at Melloney, daring her to claim that their two cases were similar.

"No," Melloney agreed. "You have far more reason to be angry than I ever did."

Diana's scowl deepened. "It wasn't *fair*."

"There's no reason you should think it was," Melloney said quietly.

There was a long pause while Diana mulled this over. Then, with an air of great indifference, she stood, walked to the sofa, and seated herself on Melloney's other side. She was silent several moments longer, as if considering possible responses. At last she said, "I'm glad Jennifer and I found the letters. I'm glad we know." She hesitated, then added, "The picture on your writing table. Could I have it to hang in my room when it's finished?"

The worst was over. The future might not be easy, but when she and the girls left the saloon, Melloney had a confidence she had not felt since the day Miles brought her into his house. Audrey was still holding her hand, and Diana was walking quite close on her other side. "I wonder where Jennifer's got to," Diana said. "Someone should tell her the story. I mean, she already knows about the letters."

"I imagine my mother talked to her," Melloney said, wondering how Pamela had managed.

They found Pamela and the girls in the drawing room along with Miles. He looked, Melloney thought, a good deal more relaxed, but he did not meet her eyes, and Melloney sensed that he did not want to. Perhaps he was embarrassed by how much he had revealed in their previous encounter. Perhaps that moment of honesty between them was only going to lead to more constraint.

Juliana wanted to visit the stables to see the foal which had been born less than a fortnight ago. Before Melloney quite realized what was happening, they were all trooping across the soggy ground toward the stable block. Diana, who was in suddenly boisterous spirits, led the way, chattering to Jennifer. Audrey tagged along behind them, and Juliana, to Melloney's surprise, walked beside Pamela, leaving Melloney and Miles to follow.

Quite suddenly, Miles turned his searching gaze upon her. "Did they talk to you?" he asked softly.

Melloney nodded. "I'd say they took it remarkably well. One forgets how resilient children are."

They walked on in silence for a few moments. Diana and Jennifer were running into the stable with Audrey and Juliana close behind, but as Pamela followed, Miles caught Melloney by the arm and detained her. "I owe you my thanks," he said. "And an apology. I should have told you the truth before we were married. You had a right to know."

Miles's touch was disconcerting, impersonal though it might have been. "You warned me it wouldn't be easy," Melloney said in a determined voice. "I didn't expect it to be. But I'm glad I may be able to be a mother to the girls after all. It was rather lowering to find myself a failure at the very thing you married me for."

Miles's response took her quite by surprise. "Damn it, Melloney," he blurted out, seizing her by the shoulders, "stop saying that."

Melloney looked up into her husband's angry eyes. At

220

least there was nothing impersonal about his touch now. For some reason her heart began to beat absurdly fast. "Why not?" she asked, struggling for composure. "You made that quite clear when you asked me to be your wife."

"I—" Miles broke off and stared at her for a moment, then shook his head and gave a smile which was at once rueful and despairing. "I've made a mull of this from the start, haven't I?"

Melloney had loved Miles for half her life, yet never had she felt such tenderness for him. "It's all right." He was still holding her by the shoulders, and she reached up a hand and laid it over one of his own. "I understand, now more than ever. I never expected you to love me. At first I thought it was because of Celia, and I suppose I was right, though not in the way I thought. After Celia, I don't suppose you ever wanted to love anyone again."

Miles was watching her, his face still, but his eyes filled with turbulence. He started to speak, then looked away, as if overcome by some emotion. "No, I didn't want to. And I was sure I was immune." He dragged his gaze back to her face. "Until I found myself falling head over ears in love with my own wife."

"But—" Melloney stared at him, searching for some meaning to his words beyond the obvious, which was unthinkable. For a moment she was aware of nothing but the pounding of her heart and the pressure of his hands on her shoulders. Then reality reasserted itself, and she tried to pull back. "No, Miles, don't. I'm too old for courtly lies, and there's been enough pretending already."

"Pretending?" Miles thundered. "Do you call what's between us at night pretense?"

Melloney lifted her chin. "I thought it was just 'uncomplicated passion.'"

"Uncomplicated? Oh, no, my sweet, there's nothing remotely uncomplicated about it. Melloney—" He hesitated and looked away again, struggling for the right words. "Look, my darling, I didn't mean to place any sort of demand on you. I've been too bloody terrified of my feelings

221

to admit them to myself, let alone anyone else. Then today when we talked about Celia it seemed—But I won't speak of it again if you'd rather I did not."

Melloney's heart, which had been hammering so wildly, seemed to have ceased beating altogether. She was either very cold or very hot, she could not be sure which. "Miles?" she said, in a small voice. "Miles, I fell in love with you when I was twelve years old. You'd called on Mama, and I was painting in the morning room, and you sat and talked to me, and the sun was streaming through the windows and I thought—"

She broke off, for Miles was looking at her again, and there was a quality in his gaze which made speech quite impossible. He lifted one hand and brushed his fingers against her cheek, his eyes filled with wonder and disbelief. Then his arms closed around her in a fierce embrace, and he sought her mouth with his own. He had kissed her before with passion, but never with such desperate need. This was not the skillful lover she had known on her wedding night, but a man seeking something for which he had been starved. Something for which she ached every bit as much and which miraculously they seemed to have found. Melloney parted her mouth beneath his and returned his embrace with an urgency equal to his own.

At last Miles raised his head and looked down at her with a smile of extraordinary sweetness. "What a setting for a declaration," he said, smoothing the loosened hair back from her face.

Melloney laughed. The air was damp, the ground muddy beneath her feet, the scent of the stables unmistakable, but the most elegant bower could not be more romantic. The thought of bowers turned her mind in another direction. Perhaps it was too soon to ask, but she was ready to throw caution to the wind. "Miles?" she said, staring fixedly at the top button on his waistcoat.

Miles tilted her chin up. "What is it, heart's delight?"

"Will you spend the night with me—the whole night?"

The light in Miles's eyes was answer enough. The kiss

that followed was added reassurance. At last some sort of sanity prevailed, and, after an attempt to smooth their clothes and repin Melloney's hair, they followed the others into the stable. Melloney feared she was blushing, but the stable was dark, and the girls were too interested in Juno's new foal to pay much heed to a mere human.

"Come and look at Tristram, Daddy," said Audrey, who was hanging on the stall gate. "He gets bigger every day."

Miles gave Melloney a rueful smile and walked over to the children. Melloney didn't mind. They had found happiness, and the children were part of it. She went to join Pamela who was sitting on a wooden bench against the wall, her skirt pulled indecently high to avoid the stable straw. Pamela cast her daughter a glance which seemed to see entirely too much, but when she spoke it was not of Miles. "Diana and Audrey seem to be coping very well."

Melloney nodded. Then, impulsively, she said, "Mama, I'm sorry if I spoke harshly this afternoon. I was very angry."

"With good reason. I made a dreadful mistake, though goodness knows it wasn't my first." Pamela toyed with the fringe on her shawl. "I explained it to Jennifer and Juliana this afternoon. It was surprisingly easy to talk to them. I quite forgot that they were children."

Melloney laughed. "Perhaps that's the secret."

Pamela smiled and put an arm around her daughter. "Perhaps it is."

They sat watching the children in companionable silence until Jennifer and Diana ran over to join them. "Uncle Miles says we can have a picnic at the cove if it's sunny tomorrow," Jennifer said, plopping down on the bench beside her mother. She looked up at Pamela with a faint frown. "You'll come, won't you?"

Melloney glanced at her mother. She had heard Pamela complain more than once about the horrors of getting sand in her hair. "Of course I will," Pamela said. "It sounds delightful."

"We can go wading and build sandcastles," Diana said.

223

Then she paused and looked at Melloney. "Audrey and I want to show you our cave."

Melloney drew in her breath. She hadn't dreamed Diana would offer such trust so quickly. She looked across the stable at Miles, who was trying to persuade Audrey not to climb on the stall gate, and met his eyes for a moment. Then she held out her hand to Diana. "I can't imagine anything I'd like more."

A Breath of Scandal

Somewhere in the house someone had set up a persistent pounding that grew more relentless as time wore on. If Lacey hadn't counted the children chanting times tables in unison at the tops of their lungs, she might have thought one of them — one of the younger ones, of course — was pounding the floor in a furious display of temper.

But all her charges were present and accounted for, from fourteen-year-old Gordie down to three-year-old Cassie, who if the truth be told was reciting the times tables with as much understanding as her oldest sibling was, and with far better humor. He was growling the equations in an unreliable and surly voice as he cast lowering glances outside, where, Lacey suspected, he longed for more cooperative weather than the watery overcast that darkened the budding ornamental garden. He was far happier ambushing the gardener or slipping toads down Katelin's dress than reciting sums.

Her heart swelling with motherly affection, Lacey smiled and gave thanks for her noisy brood. One and all, the children had wrapped her heart around their grimy fingers. Their love had covered her, smothering everything except their need for a mother, and allowed her to hope that, like a fire denied fuel, the ungrounded gossip that concerned her would die out.

And so it had.

Until the gentleman whose name had been linked with hers decided to take a wife. Then the rumors had again assumed the characteristics of a wildfire.

The rapid-fire tattoo seemed to echo Society's unwarranted condemnation, *Unwed Mother, Unwed Mother,* within her head until Lacey feared the children could hear it, too. Casting a worried look among her oblivious offspring, she compelled herself to stop dwelling on the controversy and think of the peace they had enjoyed since leaving the depravity and gossip of London. Scandal was the very breath of Town life. And Lacey Fremont's sudden and repeated forays into motherhood without benefit of marriage were the stuff of scandal's breath. Never mind that she had wrested the children from the clutches of chimney masters and procuresses or received them from tearful parents in debtor's prison. Gossip cared nothing for truth.

She tried to tell herself she cared nothing for gossip or that inopportune uproar. But it was giving her the headache. Why, she wondered, passing a hand over her temples, did someone not do something about the noise?

Just as suddenly as it had begun, the annoying pounding suddenly ceased.

Ending the chant at eight times seven, so as to rub muscles gone tense with the effort to remain calm under fire, Lacey asked of no one in particular, "Have the roofers begun work on the nursery wing?"

Her answer came not from one of the children but from a deep voice in the doorway. "No, ma'am, they have not."

Lacey's startled gaze swept from her fidgeting children toward the irresistible baritone that excited tremors of recognition and alarm. The handsome gentleman to whom the attractive voice belonged looked familiar but anything but approachable at the moment. His dark brows were drawn together in an angry knot over pale eyes that sparked with white heat, the corners of his full mouth turned down in disdain, and his broad shoulders hunched over arrogantly crossed arms. He looked as if he were keeping his temper under a rigid control that might snap at any moment.

Her wide-open blue eyes captured in his furious gaze, Lacey felt a frisson of fear shake her. Crossing the birch rod before her as if parrying an expected thrust, she attempted with a flutter of her eyelashes to break the spell under which her visitor had placed her.

But he apparently enjoyed the power with which he held her

mesmerized. Baring his teeth in what might have been a smile except that it did not warm the arctic light in the depths of his silver, wolflike eyes, he said, "I doubt very much whether you'd have heard if the roof had tumbled around your ears."

The sound of his voice rippled over her like the frigid surge of a trout stream. To quell another shiver that made her feel alternately as if she were freezing and melting, Lacey gripped the rod so tightly her fingers whitened. She felt as if she were coming down with a fever, and could not help touching her fingers to her brow. To her surprise, it was no warmer than usual and could not account for her fluttering pulse or the feeling of bewilderment that only increased when her handsome visitor grinned sardonically as if he realized he was the cause of her sudden self-consciousness.

Suddenly, in what seemed to her a volte-face of concern, he enquired, "Does the nursery need reroofing?"

Though he should care about the physical state of the nursery at Woods Hole, he had not come at her request, nor had he ever when she had needed his support. Her angry visitor was her landlord, Charlton Trent, the lofty Marquess of Helverton. But she also knew the condition of his roof would not have caused him to travel to his estate in Wiltshire, nor would it have fueled his temper. His engagement, reigniting the gossip which had forced her to leave London, brought him here posthaste and in a fury. This time, she hoped they would do something about the scandal.

But not in front of the children. Now they would deal with material issues. She moistened her lips anxiously. "Only a few slates," she replied, biting her lower lip anxiously and wiping her chalk-dusted hand down the side of an elegant green day dress. Lacey, an acknowledged beauty with a cloud of auburn hair surrounding a sweet heart-shaped face and a figure that had tempted several gentlemen to consider altering their blessed single state, looked as if she were the center of attention at an elegant soiree rather than an unwed mother surrounded by her scandalous brood.

Swallowing her anxiety, she added, "Your solicitor said you had approved the repair."

"If he said so I must have," Helverton said, negligently leaning a shoulder against the doorjamb as if considering when he could have taken time to make such a mundane decision. He did not appear at all happy with the expense. Or, Lacey thought, perhaps it was the presence of the children whom he seemed to be counting.

To forestall the questions she knew would be forthcoming, she dismissed them to the garden, telling them not to wander too far away as she would call them in for tea shortly. In their custom, they scrambled toward the French doors in a noisy celebration of freedom, the elder ones shoving the doors open and barreling past their younger brothers and sisters as if determined to embarrass their mother and give their illustrious visitor a further disgust of childish manners.

Hoping to smooth over the children's ragged departure, Lacey reached forth a dusty hand. "Welcome to Woods Hole, my lord," she said, as if the property to which she was ushering him was not his own.

Helverton regarded the chalk-smutched fingers with undisguised horror, then shouldered past the schoolmistress to inspect the shreds of what had been his mother's morning room in Woods Hole's previous life. He did not even try to mask the pained expression that seemed to settle over his handsome face as he inspected the room.

Sums and essays executed in childish scrawls on crumpled scraps of paper were tacked on the walls without regard to the cream-colored watered silk paper underneath. A mishmash of unmatched tables and chairs had scarred Lady Helverton's parquet floor. The only sensible thing Miss Lacey Fremont had done was roll up the marchioness's priceless Persian carpet, but Lord Helverton rather suspected she might have forgotten to treat it for moths before storing it away.

Turning toward his unsuspecting hostess, he pulled another sarcastic grin and said, "I love what you've done to the old place."

"It is rather horrible," she agreed, scuffing a toe along a particularly deep scratch in the wood so as to avoid his cynical stare. It was too mocking, as if he fully believed the scurrilous tales being bandied about Town at her expense. She was suddenly possessed of the awful feeling that he meant finally to avail himself of the benefits of the affair which supposedly linked them. Her heart pounding in fear, she said, "But floors can be refinished, and . . ."

"Walls can be rehung?" he completed in an arch tone. He directed a searching gaze at her, wondering if she were hoping one's reputation could be repaired as easily. What on earth had persuaded her to become the woman in a shoe with too many children? And what had possessed him to encourage such a misguided mission as she professed?

Lombard fever? Boredom was his only excuse. Now he was tired of the scandal. One way or other, he would have an end to it.

Lowering her head before his frowning stare like a child caught in malicious mischief, she said she wished he had told her he wanted to visit, so they could have set things straight beforehand.

He raised one eyebrow in a quelling manner. "Why? In my experience, 'tis better for a patron to make a surprise inspection of facilities. Reveals flaws in operation . . . staff deficiencies. . . ." He glanced around the room. "Do you not employ a tutor for the children?"

Fearing he should think her unfit for the charge she had taken on, Lacey shook her head nervously. "The last one quit when Paul and Ernie put a garden snake in his bed."

To her surprise, Helverton began to chuckle. "Did they?" he said at last, giving rise to the hope that he might be human after all. However, such optimism was premature as he cast another frowning look at her. She swallowed a nervous giggle in a hiccup as he demanded, "What other damage have you inflicted on the house?"

"Not every room has been so altered since we came here," she assured him. "Would you care for a tour?"

"Of my own house?" he enquired loftily. "No, thank you."

Lacey was of the opinion that he longed to see how well she had kept the place but was loath to see it in her company. His low opinion of her was depressing.

Of all people in the World, he was the one in a position to know the truth of their relationship and not despise her for it. It was plain he did despise her, and his contempt hurt.

229

In an attempt to raise herself in his estimation, she said, "Your chambers are in perfect order in the event you decide to stay overnight," blushing as it occurred to her that he would probably think, in light of the gossip, she had invited him to spend the night with her.

"No!" he said, rather too sharply, retreating a step. "I mean, I have lodgings at the Swan and Bell."

He gazed out the window upon what looked to be a mill. A small boy was throwing wild punches at a bigger boy who was holding him off with one hand as a crowd of children noisily egged them on. Another satirical smile creased his handsome face as he directed a scornful look toward his hostess. "I would not want to disrupt your happy . . . home any more than necessary."

"But you won't disrupt us in the least, my lord. After all, we are a family."

He seemed to choke at her gentle remonstrance, then sneered, "Family, ma'am? I want no part of your 'family.' "

Seeing the end of her dreams for her children in his abhorrent declaration, Lacey sank to a cushioned chair and clung to the back for support. She turned huge blue eyes on him, enquiring in a shaking voice, "You wish to cry off?"

"Cry off?" he repeated, stunned by an unexpected reaction to her frail desperation. For the first time in his life, he felt a protective impulse. Fighting it down, he demanded, "From what?"

"Providing a home for my children," she said, recklessly defending her brood. "I have never troubled you on their behalf in the past, my lord, only do not abandon them."

"Your children?" he demanded. He tossed his curly-brimmed beaver atop a table strewn with schoolwork. Advancing on her, he spat out, "Gossip aside, I was under the impression they were mine."

"Well, I must confess," she stammered. "Not every gentleman is as generous with his . . ."

"Good name," he finished curtly, shocking her into silence for several seconds.

"I do appreciate your standing in as male guardian to the children, my lord," she said at last.

"I'm sure you do," he said in tones that expressed his complete disregard for whatever Miss Lacey Fremont might think. Raking her with an appraising stare that was fully appreciative of her slender curves, he added, "You've certainly managed to take advantage of my . . . charitable nature."

Unused to such open appraisal, she nervously twitched a fallen curl off her shoulder in a graceful movement that unconsciously displayed to advantage the arch of her throat and swell of her bosom, saying, "I do count on it."

Stunned by the enticing lure she threw out, Lord Helverton was sorely tempted to shake some sense of propriety into her, but he controlled the impulse for the moment. He leaned a hip on the worktable and cursed her for turning his life upside down. He wanted—no, she owed him a full accounting. Clearing his throat and sweeping to his feet in a motion that drew her attention, he captured her blue eyes in a piercing stare and was struck that she did not avert them as would most other women with whom disgrace had caught up. She was regarding him steadily as if she were incapable of committing a shameful act.

But that was an absurd illusion. Shaking off the illogical response, he told himself that an innocent act was part of a female's bag of tricks meant to ensnare a husband, and asked, "I have heard several versions of this affair, but I want to know the truth. From your lips. How many of the children are mine?"

Relieved that the marquess wished to acknowledge her brood at last, she replied without hesitation, "All of them, my lord."

He seemed to stagger at the knowledge and took a moment to look at the rowdy bunch climbing his ornamental trees and throwing stones into the Italian fountain in his garden. Finally he gasped, "All?"

"Yes," Lacey replied. "Would you like to see Baby?"

He bestowed a horrified look upon her as if she were requesting whether he would like to make a baby. Lacey blushed at the indelicate idea, then rang a silver bell on her desk. "We've asked several times to have the bellpulls repaired, only . . ."

"I've been busy," Helverton ground out. Then, irritated, he came to the purpose of his visit. "Do you know what people, my fiancee in particular, are saying?"

"How is Edwina?" Lacey asked as if she had not heard his stiff enquiry. A maid entering, she was distracted from the marquess's reply as she requested a nursery tea set up in the conservatory. "Oh, and Mattie, will you send Nonnie with Baby down, too? And don't forget Cookie."

"Do you take tea with servants?" Helverton asked.

"Oh, they aren't servants," Lacey assured him. To keep from looking at him, she straightened the stacks of paper on her desk as she spoke. "They're part of the family. My aunts." Then, turning toward him, she asked again, "Speaking of Family, how is Edwina?"

He was possessed of the absurd vision of their extended "family." If Edwina knew that Miss Fremont considered her part of the family, she would waste no more time in planning a wedding with him, but give him short shrift. With a humorless grin twisting his face, he replied, "Nearly ready to cry off."

A rush of gladness filled Lacey's heart, but she thought better of congratulating him. For all that she knew the Honorable Edwina Carstairs was a spoiled daughter of the *ton,* it was possible that the Marquess of Helverton loved her. She ought to be happy he had found a wife to please his elevated notions of nobility, not rejoice that his choice was ready to call off the match.

Whatever her feelings, she did not wish him unhappy. But she realized from the marquess's visit that, just as she feared, Edwina was going to make trouble for the children. They must be her first concern.

And the marquess was glaring at her as if she were the cause of all his trouble. "But that's absurd," she blurted out.

"So I told her," Helverton said. "Which only got me in deeper trouble." He grinned candidly for the first time, as if amused by the upheaval in his life. Lacey's heart seemed to skip a beat as he ventured, "One is not supposed to call a betrothed's fits 'absurd.' "

"No, it is dangerous to do so," she laughed, reverting to her usual good humor. She began to move toward the conservatory.

The sound of her laughter was musical, and Helverton, despite his irritation, was drawn to it. He followed Lacey down a wide hallway to the glass-walled conservatory. It was warm, even on this cool spring afternoon, and bright with flowering plants. Lacey looked like a bird fluttering from pot to pot, pinching back overgrown stems and praising early blossoms in lilting tones. Helverton felt an inexplicable surge of appreciation for her. If Miss Lacey Fremont could coax unwanted children and hot-house flowers to thrive in an otherwise inhospitable environment, she could not be as evil as Society claimed. Deciding he'd like to know her better, he strode toward her.

"Would you like to take an orchid to Edwina?" she suggested, proffering an exquisite blossom of lavender and white on a spidery stem.

"No," he said, halting his progress to sweep aside the tail of his coat as he took a seat next to the indoor fountain. "She would think I was begging pardon."

Replacing the plant and seating herself, Lacey said, "That is one way of looking at it, I suppose. I would think you madly in love with me." He gave her a look that immediately depressed such a claim. She returned his regard levelly, without coyness, then asked, "Do you wish to cry off?"

"Of course not." He responded too quickly to sound convincing. "Edwina is everything nice — genteel, fashionable, just the right height of manner —" implying by association that Lacey in her chalk-smudged morning dress and gossip-smeared reputation was not nice. "Make me a perfect wife," he finished.

She heard the lack of conviction in his tone and prompted, "Only . . ."

"She misunderstands our," he waved a sun-bronzed hand back and forth between Lacey and himself, "relationship. Thinks we're . . ." His voice trailed off, and he looked self-consciously as if he had not tried very hard to discourage his fiancee's misapprehension.

"She thinks I'm your mistress," Lacey explained. Despite her assertion, she did not blush. She had seen too much in her

233

young life to turn missish over the scandal. As far as she was concerned, it was a tempest in a teapot. "I hope you told her the truth."

"She did not believe me," Helverton said, not feeling bound to defend Edwina's sensibility. In her lack of trust, she had revealed a side he found surprising and more than a little repulsive. Of all the parties involved, Miss Fremont was the one he felt the most need to protect, and that surprised him. Nevertheless, he confessed, "Miss Fremont, I have no wish to embroil you in another scandal."

"Nor I you, my lord," Lacey said. "But it seems we have been caught up in one."

"Yes, and I think the only way out is for you to find another guardian for your charges."

"Children, my lord," she reminded. His request crushed her. It was as if he half-believed the charges Society dared level at her. She wondered if anything could hurt as much, when a sudden premonition of disaster sent a cold chill down her spine. Stiffening her posture against the fear, she decided the only way to deal with it was to know. Placing a confiding hand on his sleeve, she enquired, "Do you also wish us to remove from Woods Hole?"

Helverton lowered his gaze to the hand that rested on his arm. Fighting the impulse to cover it with a protective hand, he confessed, "Edwina suggested that she'd . . . said she'd . . . like to refurbish the hall." He didn't tell her his betrothed had said she meant to rid Woods Hole of every trace of "that whore and her bastards." Such vituperation would only hurt Miss Fremont. He'd done enough of that in the last six years.

He had come to save Edwina the pain and embarrassment of hearing any more gossip. Now, recalling how she had managed to drag Miss Fremont over the coals in the weeks since their engagement had been announced, Helverton was not so sure his betrothed was the offended party.

Why had he put up with the "Honorable" Edwina's bullying ways? Had it seemed easier somehow to go along with her, their betrothal having been announced and all? But she would discover, if she shared any more of her vicious suspicions over scandal broth, that she had pushed him far enough. A man

234

could ignore only so much gossip about people he cared about.

Wherever would they go?

Releasing the marquess's arm, Lacey covered her lips to keep from voicing the desperate query. Woods Hole did belong to Lord Helverton, after all. It was only that the children had grown comfortable in the manor. There were fond memories in every room and along every pathway of the garden and in the home woods.

"Whatever happened to that little sweep?" Helverton asked, as if he had been stirred by remembrances as well. When she turned a distracted gaze upon him, he said, "You know, the one we saved from that chimney master."

"Oh, Ghillie," she said, on a note of distress. "He died not long ago. Weak lungs." The little boy they had championed six years ago, whose growth had been stunted by bad air, was buried on the grounds. She wondered whether the marquess's betrothed would demand the child's body be removed from— But no, even Edwina Carstairs could not be that cruel.

Could she?

Something of her torment must have shown on her face, for Helverton said, "Too bad. He was an excellent little chap." Actually, if he remembered correctly, Ghillie had kicked him in the shins and demanded he take his dirty hands off . . . well, one did not speak ill of the dead.

"You didn't know him very well, my lord," Lacey said with a half smile quirking up one corner of her mouth. "Oh, his heart was as good as gold, but we couldn't trust him around fobs and seals or snuffboxes. Said he had to snabble 'em." She laughed at the marquess's raised eyebrow. "Don't look so shocked, my lord. You would have known if he had taken something of yours. Ghillie always returned his ill-gotten gains. And living out in the country, he had very little chance to pick anyone's pockets, except the vicar's, which he gave up on. Said there was nothing in 'em to tempt him." Sighing, with the weight of accumulated troubles, she added, "He tried to be a good boy."

Helverton could not suppress the sudden vision of a consumptive Ghillie picking the pockets of the heavenly host or snabbling the key to the Pearly Gates. Saint Peter would have his hands full with that one, he thought. It was better for Miss Lacey Fremont to have lost him in a quiet death than to a public hanging.

He wondered what would happen to the other children after they moved away from Woods Hole. Frowning, because he felt responsible for turning them out on the road, he said, "I have another estate, farther from Town . . ."

"Farther from gossip, my lord?" she prompted, flashing a brief smile that made Helverton feel as if he'd been struck by lightning. Just as suddenly she waxed serious. He felt that with the passing of her bright smile, the sun had gone behind a cloud. "No," she said, sighing, "we cannot impose on your charitable nature much longer. But I hope you will give us some time."

"For what?" he queried in a rather sharp tone. As far as he was concerned, she could have anything she needed. She could even have Woods Hole.

"To find another property, one that I might purchase this time. Few people are willing to rent to a family with so many children," she explained. "And to be perfectly frank, I'm not sure whether anyone will sell to me."

"Here now," he said uncomfortably. "If you are going to cast me in the role of villain, I insist you take the estate in Cornwall. Edwina need never know about—"

Lacey shook her head. "No, my lord. I cannot come between you and your betrothed again. I think you are right: it would be best if we found another . . . sponsor for the children."

Before he could assure Miss Fremont that he would be master in his own home and she need not fear what the future Marchioness of Helverton might say against her, the children rattled into the conservatory on the wheels of the tea tray.

Lacey made introductions all around, beginning with her aunts Nonnie and Cookie—the Misses Yolanthe and Circe Bennet, Helverton was to discover. The elderly ladies, who must have known of Helverton's role in the "family," treated him more like a god than the bearer of bad tidings. Feeling unworthy of their adulation, Helverton cut short their speeches of greeting and moved onto the children.

Upon meeting the marquess, Gordie ducked his head more in the manner of a groom than a budding gentleman. Missie and Katelin giggled obnoxiously and posed as if they were opera dancers casting out lures. Helverton cast a horrified glance toward Lacey as she told the girls to remember their manners and act like "ladies."

After shaking his hand, Ernie and Paul stared daggers at the person they seemed to think of as an intruder. Helverton was glad he had made other sleeping arrangements. He had the uncomfortable feeling that they were contemplating dropping a snake in his bed.

Sitting apprehensively on the wrought-iron settee, he turned his attention to what he hoped was the end of the parade. Cassie toddled in on the heels of the maid carrying Baby. Oblivious of the marquess's fine buckskin trousers, the youngest Fremont climbed onto his lap and lisped, "Papa?"

Helverton stared ominously at the infant who was plucking at his meticulously tied cravat in an attempt to slobber on his chin. Holding him . . . her . . . whatever it was at arm's length, he returned Baby to his . . . her . . . its laughing mother. "I don't see anything funny in the brat's mistake," he said uncharitably.

"Not funny," Lacey said, cuddling the baby's cheek to hers, then placing a kiss on its open mouth. "Wonderful. Did you not hear, Nonnie, Cookie? Baby said —"

"We all heard," Helverton said repressively as the aunts cooed over the child's accomplishment. "I'd rather you didn't repeat it."

"Oh, never mind what he said," Lacey scolded, passing the child around to the aunts. "Only we think it wonderful he said anything."

"Why is that?" Helverton demanded, attempting to retie his spoiled cravat. Giving up, he tucked the loose ends within his shirt front.

"He hasn't said a word up till now," Lacey assured him. "Not a word. Only think. He called you 'Papa.' "

"Only think," Helverton said with an ironic lift of his eyebrows as he considered what the World would make of his assertion that Baby had been an immaculate conception. He didn't think much of it himself.

Lacey broke into his troubled thoughts, saying, "I couldn't be happier had he said 'Mama.' "

"I could," he said in a dry tone. "Have you been coaching her—him?"

"No, of course not," Lacey said, receiving her giggling infant from Cookie who almost dropped the squirming bundle on his head. "We did not know you were coming. Yes, you are a smart boy," she said, jiggling the baby in her arms. "Your first word . . . 'Papa.' Nonnie, we must write it down in Baby's book."

The white-haired aunt scurried away to do just that. Her gray-haired sister looked as if she were offended by Lacey's inadvertent slight. "Oh, Cookie," Lacey said, setting Baby on Helverton's knee once more and placing in his hand a pewter cup on which was attached a leather nipple, "pray do not be angry. You did fetch the book when Baby took his first step. And wrote it down so well." As he unwillingly fed Baby, Lacey began to pour chocolate for the children who were lined up impatiently for their afternoon treats. "I hardly had to note anything, except the date."

Thus appeased, the roly-poly Cookie preened herself and allowed that she had not taken the least offense, only she was so proud of Baby, she could not wish to give up that privilege. Then she turned a beatific smile upon the marquess and said, "You will understand when you set up your own nursery. Unless," she enquired hopefully, "you wish to claim these darlings?"

The marquess choked on a reply. Lacey popped a cherry tartlet into her aunt's mouth and shoved a cup of tea into her hands.

Helverton suspected he had entered a madhouse with babbling women plotting his eventual commitment.

He was not about to step into their snare, however. His betrothed had quite soured him on female entanglements and had further settled his intention to have as little to do with the female of the species as was absolutely necessary for begetting proper heirs. As for that obligation, he was certain the only

238

way to proceed was to marry Edwina Carstairs and promptly get her with child.

The prospect of making love to that harpie made him shudder. But as he accepted a cup of tea from his hostess, who thankfully seemed unable to read his mind, he saw no way out of doing his duty.

"Now, Baby," she said, holding out her arms to the infant, "do come to Mama and leave Lord Helverton to take his tea in peace."

The baby clung obstinately to the marquess's lapels. "Pa-papa Papa," he cried, turning his downy head from side to side as he prattled.

If only Edwina could see me now, Helverton thought, ruefully spilling hot liquid on his buckskins to keep from scalding the infant. *That lofty lady would cry off as soon as she had turned the teapot over my head.*

Grinning to himself, he allowed as how there might be a way to extricate himself from both the engagement and Miss Lacey's unwitting coil. Setting the teacup aside and plucking the infant's fingers from his coat, he turned an innocent gaze upon Lacey and asked, "Have you a copy of the agreement we forged to protect Ghillie and the rest of your brood?"

Looking at him over the rim of her teacup, Lacey nodded. "Yes, in my room." She set the cup on the teacart, quelling the apprehension that rolled like a stone into the pit of her stomach, and arose from her cushion. "If you would be so good as to hear the children recite for a few moments, my lord, I'll fetch it."

She had a little trouble getting her brood to attend to her wishes as they preferred to decimate the sandwiches on the tea table than show off their education, but she finally left them grudgingly chanting the eight times table, which allowed Helverton to deduce the surest route to freedom: the Primrose Path.

When the children completed displaying the sum of their mathematical knowledge before Miss Fremont returned, Helverton sent them outside, except for Cassie and Baby who were too young to be entrusted to the care of their older siblings for long. For a few moments, he listened to Nonnie and

Cookie relate the children's various accomplishments while Cassie mashed shortbread into the toes of his once-polished Hessians. Baby had begun to wriggle on his thigh, but he managed to keep a benevolent look on his face while Cookie corrected Nonnie's memory regarding the loss of Katelin's first tooth. "It was four years ago in 1811," she was saying in a voice that brooked no argument.

Drat. Where had Miss Fremont taken herself to?

Helverton was toying with the idea of going in search of his troublesome tenant when he felt an uncomfortable wetness anoint him and spread down one leg of his buckskins. "Miss Bennet!" he called out, effectively silencing the sisters' foolish debate. "Will one of you kindly remove this encumbrance from my knee?" The ladies outdid themselves vying for the honor until he confessed, "He has wet himself." Then, as one, they collapsed on benches, as if they had not the slightest intention of soiling their dresses with a waterlogged infant. Left in soaked nappies and a damp dress, Baby began to cry.

Helverton propelled himself from the settee. "Kindly tell Miss Fremont I have taken Baby to the nursery."

Lacey met him on the stairs. Flustered, she attempted to remove the fidgety infant from the marquess's grip, for he was carrying it under his arm like a bundle of dirty shirts, and she feared he might drop it.

"Nonsense," he protested. "Though I must admit the sight must be an appealing one, there is no use damping your dress when I have already been baptized. Come with me," he urged, leading the way toward the nursery at the far end of the third story. "We can talk while you change . . . Baby."

When he laid the bundle on a padded table and she had divested Baby of all his wet clothing, Helverton enquired, "Has he no other name?"

"Baby?" she asked, washing the infant down and dusting him with a sweet-smelling powder. "Oh yes, his . . . he was named Justice. His mother died in prison. Doesn't seem quite appropriate somehow, but I can't bring myself to change his real mama's will."

"And you cannot keep calling him 'Baby,'" Helverton said, watching as she drew a frilly dress over the boy's big head.

"He's bound to grow up. Why not call him Justus." When she frowned in confusion, he spelled the name. Then she pulled a face that conveyed her aversion even to the sound of the name, which led him to suggest, "How about Justin?"

Baby directed a level stare toward his sponsor. Grinning, Helverton asked, "Justin?" in an indulgent tone that made Lacey's heart sing for joy. "Do you like Justin?"

The baby smiled a two-toothed grin at him. Reaching chubby hands past Lacey, he babbled, "Papapa," followed by a string of nonsense syllables that led both adults to believe he was voicing his wholehearted approval of the name.

"Well, Justin it is," Lacey said, picking him up and passing him into the marquess's hands for the return down the stairs.

Instead of leaving the comfortable nursery, he set the baby on a quilt in the angled sunbeams coming through the long western windows. "Sit down, Miss Fremont," he said, drawing the rocking chair toward the colorful pad and placing himself on the floor alongside the newly christened Justin. "We have business to discuss."

Lacey placed a slender hand along the back of the chair and nervously regarded the man stretched out beside the baby. "I—Can't it wait?" she asked hesitantly, catching her lower lip between her teeth when he raised a probing gaze to hers, forcing her to confess, "I cannot seem to find my copy of our agreement."

"You what?" he queried in an aggressive tone. Then, with a threatening growl, "This farce has gone on long enough, don't you think?"

Lacey was unable to suppress the frightened gasp that filled her lungs, then said in a display of false bravado, "I suppose you think I don't know the terms of our contract."

"On the contrary," he responded. "I'm certain you *do* know them." The baby was crawling toward a sunbeam dancing on the bare floor. Helverton drew Justin back onto the quilt. "Would you mind refreshing *my* memory?"

"I . . . I don't know what you mean," Lacey stammered.

"All I want to know is: how many more children are you going to adopt in my name?" he demanded, adding, "Without my consent or my knowledge? Don't you know I can withdraw

241

my support at any time?"

As if a ton of bricks had settled on her heart, Lacey realized the awful truth. He wished to be rid of her and her troublesome brood. But if he dissolved their contract, he would be abandoning the children to orphanages and workhouses. Better for them if she left them in his care. The law only recognized his authority.

Wondering what kind of mother she'd be to abandon her children to a father who didn't care for them, she lowered herself in the chair and said, "I have always gotten Mr. Whitcomb's assurance that you approved of my rescues," in a quiet, resigned voice that grew stronger and more convicted as she went on. "If you don't want me to take in any more, I will not. . . . How can you be so heartless, my lord? Baby would have grown up in Fleet Prison did I not care. Or," the distasteful words caught in her throat, but she forced herself to say them, "he would have died there."

"Still, you cannot save every unfortunate child in England," Helverton said, dangling his chain with its fobs and seals just out of Justin's reach so that the baby squealed and reached insistently for it. Finally, letting the baby have its will, the marquess handed the lot over and grimaced as the child chewed and dribbled on the jewelry. "You would bankrupt both of us."

"I know that, my lord," Lacey said, clasping her hands together and leaning forward urgently. "But if I thought about those I cannot help, I would never sleep. This way, I can save a little of England, and they can, perhaps, save a little more."

He chuckled cynically. "At the expense of your reputation, ma'am? Do you know what the World has been saying about you?"

"I try not to attend gossip, my lord," Lacey replied in a sickened voice. "If I did, I might not take the chance for another child."

"Spoken as a true mother," Helverton said in an ironic tone that perplexed her. "Still, your children have no hope of mixing in society, even if they were, as gossips would have it, your children by several titled gentlemen. And you know none of them will deny the charge."

Shocked by the depravity that had victimized her, she sat

upright, asking, "Have you denied the liaison?"

"In my case, it is deemed a matter of protesting too much," he said, retrieving his chain from the now sleeping infant's grip. Drying the fobs and seals on his dangling neckcloth without once looking at Lacey, he added with a resigned chuckle, "They claim you have cuckolded me."

Wondering whatever could have possessed her to rely for support on a man who would find such a suggestion amusing, she demanded, "How can you laugh, my lord?" He seemed to care nothing for others, but only to enjoy life on his terms. How could she have been so fooled in him?

"What else am I to do?" he queried in an intense tone that frightened her against the cushion of the rocking chair. He held her there with a piercing stare as he enlightened her. "It is a regrettable fact of life in the *ton;* wives are expected to take lovers; even mistresses display an appalling lack of fidelity toward their protectors. And mothers abandon their own children to strangers."

"Not I," she vowed.

"Even you," he retorted.

Of a sudden, she decided he deserved the wife he had chosen, one who would betray him with other lovers and forget her own children for the lure of flattery. That he was allying himself to such a woman as could make him hate all women drove Lacey to defend herself. "Did I abandon Kate or Paul to the measles or force you to walk Cassie through her bouts of colic?"

"You never told me they had been sick," he said in a tight, conscience-stricken tone.

Lacey leaned forward until she stared at him nose to nose. "Because you insisted you didn't wish to know about such childish complaints. I've raised these children alone, my lord."

"By choice," he added as if he thought she was rebuking him for negligence. "Have you ever regretted not marrying?"

"I'll not grieve what I've never known. Besides, what man would have me, tainted as I am by scandal?"

He sniffed as if her declaration smelled like day-old fish, then said, "You might have considered how your own family would feel to be reared among the sons and daughters of har-

243

lots and thieves."

He might as well have slapped her as insult her children. Arising in righteous anger from the chair, she looked at him sprawled negligently on her—*his* nursery floor, and said, "*These* children are my family, my lord. They will never have to turn a trick or pick a pocket; I've seen to that." She stood over him, feeling as if he were a snake she should grind under her heel and wanting to hurt him as badly as he had hurt her. Taking a steadying breath, she proclaimed, "They don't need you, Lord Helverton. And you may tell your anxious bride-to-be that I don't want you."

"No?" he demanded, springing to his feet and crossing the room in quick strides that sent Lacey scurrying toward the door like a rabbit trying to evade capture by a fox.

He barred her escape by closing the nursery door and spinning her around to face him. She came up hard against his length and gasped, staring up at him with wide, frightened eyes. "Let me go," she said when he gripped both her arms as if he owned her.

He ignored her command but glared at her with a feral light in his pale eyes that made her desperate to get away. Fearfully she twisted in his grasp, finally succeeding in breaking his iron grip. She whirled out of reach, determined not to be this roué's amorous victim.

He, it seemed, was just as determined to have her. His hand snaked out to grab her. She skidded to a halt inches from his splayed fingers. But as she evaded his grasp once more, a corner of the quilt on which Justin was napping shifted under her feet. She was going to fall. Frantically, she twisted, reaching for her pursuer to keep from injuring her baby.

Then, suddenly, she was caught in a powerful embrace and crushed against the hard length of the marquess.

Her own arms caught between them so that she could not fight him off, she cried out, hoping the noise would awaken the baby. But warm, well-fed, and dry, Justin was still limply asleep on the quilt. Collapsing in defeat against her tormentor's frame, Lacey felt as if the infant had betrayed her.

Helverton seemed fully aware that the baby obligingly slept on despite his mother's outcry. His hold on Lacey gentled as if he knew he had won the contest, but it was still inescapable. Nor was she certain she wished to escape his clutches.

His touch was awakening coals that she thought she had long ago banked. Despite her determination to give up love for the sake of her children, a fire seemed to be kindling in her breast, and she had no desire to throw water on the flames. Indeed, she doubted she possessed enough self-control to deny feelings that, once released, were rushing over her like a wildfire.

And that was more frightening than being unable to flee.

Worldly wisdom told her she ought to be furious with him. Her heart argued that anger would only destroy the link with her only ally, even one who laughed at her.

Regardless of her independent declaration, she knew she needed the marquess's good will. Without it, she would lose her children. They, not her outraged reputation, must be her only concern. She must do everything she could to safeguard these boys and girls she had rescued from prison or chimney masters or procuresses. She would even allow rumor to become truth.

The surprising revelation compelled her to raise her chin so she might recant her hastily spoken, angry words and offer to become whatever he wanted of her. His gaze probed hers until, self-consciously aware of her tumbling, improper thoughts, she focused on his mouth and moistened her own lips, not knowing that in his jaded world such a coy glance invited a kiss.

He did not refuse the invitation, but did not swoop down on her like a bird of prey either. He closed the distance between their lips by slow degrees, as if waiting for her permission.

Their breath mingled in a warm, sweet mixture of tea and mint that made her want to taste deeply of him. The pounding desire impelled her toward his kiss until she felt she hovered on the brink of a precipice. Frightened, she hid behind the natural protective instinct of a mother as she said, "You'll wake the baby."

A scarce inch from kissing her, Helverton chuckled. "I shall not wake Justin," he declared, "And neither will you," as he settled her in the curve of his arms and covered her lips with his own.

She was twenty-four and could claim to have been kissed before. But this bold caress reminded her forcefully that her two other romantic experiences had really only been shy pecks on the cheek.

His gentle, searching, melting kiss evaporated all fear, dissolved all resistance. Her eyes fluttered closed. Her lips fell half open. He moved his mouth over hers and molded her pliant curves to his unyielding frame until she could not even support her own weight but had to rely on his strength, which seemed more than sufficient to keep them upright.

As she yielded to his overshadowing embrace, her arms slid free of their confinement between their straining bodies. Instinctively, when they each took gasping breaths, she clung to him. Her fingers tangling in the thick, black hair curling at the nape of his neck, she sighed rapturously, compelling in sibilant surrender a closer embrace and a deeper kiss.

He seemed to understand perfectly what she wanted. His arms tightened possessively around her, molding her hips to his in a circular motion to prove he was as deeply affected by her as she claimed not to be by him.

His tongue darting into the moist recesses of her mouth teased a response from her. Desire tugged on her heartstrings, arousing an unfamiliar, yet intimate thrum deep within her that set her ashiver with longing. Then, just as Lacey's lungs felt as if they were going to burst, Helverton breathed a long exhalation. Trembling in his arms, she raised shining eyes to his and wondered, *Why does he not kiss me again?*

He regarded her with a look that seemed satisfied and more than a little amused. Hurt by his silent, smug mockery, she leaned a cheek against the solid support of his chest and compelled herself to take slow, steadying breaths that would stop her world from spinning. Such a wanton loss of control was dangerous in the game of hearts.

"So," he said at last, his indulgent utterance fluttering the strands of auburn hair that had escaped the bonds of hairpins in their embrace. Despite the lightness of his tone, he longed to bury his fingers in the fiery mass and compel her to raise her lips to his once more. No one had ever kissed him back so

246

innocently, yet so willingly, or made him so forget himself as to kiss her uninvited and in anger. Certainly the Honorable Edwina had never allowed him such liberties. After tasting the delights of Miss Fremont's lips, he was positive he did not wish to make free with Miss Carstairs. All he wanted was Lacey.

But voicing such a sentiment was dangerous. She could turn it against him the way his mother had. Recalling his parent's treachery and the little-boy fear that had hardened into a cold lump of contempt for all women, he forced himself to chuckle as if he found their embrace amusing, then teased her, "You don't want me?"

Hearing his mirthless laughter, she felt the heat of a mortified blush warm her cheeks. "I don't know," she replied as the humiliating suspicion possessed her that he must think she was guilty of receiving other gentlemen's favors behind his back. But it was not true. She had never known any man, had not even known what desire was. Now she knew: she wanted only him.

For six years he had been her champion, standing in as father to her children, offering unquestioned support when the rest of the World whispered poisonous slanders. He had been her knight in shining armor ever since he came to Ghillie's rescue. And like the knights of old, his chivalrous devotion to her cause had been pure. But all that had changed.

How could she tell him that with one kiss he had awakened her to desire. One kiss, and she was thoroughly lost in passion's spell. Feeling that such an admission must surely mark her as a woman of easy virtue, she breathed another confused, "I don't know."

He was not prepared for the violence of feeling her confession aroused. It assailed him like a knife to the heart. It was all too new, too painful, too easy to believe the worst of the gossip and discount her fierce maternal instincts.

If she were like other ladies of the *ton*, his charming mother in particular, she would eventually tire of the fetters of motherhood and leave her demanding brood for the excitement and glitter of Town life. He had to protect the children from her fickle, uncertain devotion.

"That is not what I expected to hear," he mused.

247

His uncertain avowal was not what the long-denied romantic in Lacey's soul wished to hear. What she wanted was a fervent declaration of love, an offer of commitment.

None was forthcoming, but he did not release her. Though she was disappointed not to hear an impassioned proposal from his lips, Lacey could do nothing but remain within the circle of his arms.

She felt safe, protected, cherished for the first time in her life. The unfamiliar sensations amazed her. Wanting to hold onto them as long as possible, she snuggled against his soft linen shirt, warm and fragrant with his characteristic essence of leather, starch, and sweet grass. She could feel the rapid thud of his heartbeat returning to a slower, more regular pace, and the deep rumble of another chuckle vibrating within his chest.

She raised a questioning gaze to him. He was grinning down at her in a way that made her want to throw caution to the winds and kiss him again.

But he did not give her the opportunity. He reached forth and touched her lips, then said as if enjoying a private joke, "If gossip is to be believed, you must kiss every man you do not want in that obliging manner."

Lacey gasped in outrage. With no male relative to challenge such slings in the time-honored manner, she had endured too many insults without defending herself. But she was done ignoring slanders. Angrily she raised her foot and stamped her heel on his instep.

Surprised by the inadequate assault, Helverton released his hold on her. But instead of complaining about the abuse of his Hessians, he started to laugh.

How dared he mock her?

Lacey was not going to let this insult go by unchallenged either. Humiliated by years of innuendo and cruel snubs for which he alone was responsible, she slapped him.

The blow stung her palm and left a red print on his cheek, but he scarcely flinched. The contact brought tears to Lacey's eyes. Staring watery daggers at him, she clutched her bruised hand and forced herself not to cry in pain or fury. She had never struck another person and now felt as if she were sinking

248

through the floor in humiliation.

He was looking thunderously at her, as if he would like either to return her challenge or force her once more to his will. Determined not to yield to his domination in any way, Lacey stiffened her spine and said, "Don't think you can insult me again."

"I wouldn't dream of it, ma'am," he said in what looked like an attempt to straighten the grin on his face. Rubbing his abused jaw, he added, "Your aim both times was deadly. I'd not chance you're as good a shot as you are with your fives."

"Perhaps I *ought* to take up shooting," she said warily.

"I'll spread it about Town that you have," Helverton said, grinning. "It might be the one bit of gossip that could stifle poisoned tongues."

He was being so amiable, she felt almost in charity with him again. However, he sunk himself when he added, "That should give the gossips something to chew on."

Breathing a frustrated sigh, she said, "Wouldn't be the first time they've taken me with tea."

He raised an eyebrow and occupied himself in straightening the lay of his coat and placement of his cuffs in an offhand manner that did not prepare her for his query, "Am I to believe I'm your first?"

She clenched her fist against the sheer insensitivity of men and clamped her lips together. Counting to ten to control the urge to do more violence to his person, she said in a menacing voice, "I wouldn't give you that power, my lord."

"A direct hit," he said, bowing. "Never underestimate your adversary."

"Is that what we are?" she enquired. "Adversaries?"

He shrugged. "I believe we must be."

Lacey had the sickening feeling that he deemed their embrace worthless, as nothing more than relief from natural instincts. Doubtless he would make of it an amusing tale to entertain friends at White's.

Realizing that of course their embrace could mean nothing but what the marquess intended, she picked up the baby and lay him in his crib, taking longer in smoothing the blanket than usual to compose her features into a serene mask to conceal the truth: that she did want him and that he wanted her.

The kiss had proven that to her, if not to him. It seemed to explain why he had accepted the responsibility for children he had no earthly interest in. And it explained why he was so adamant about discharging his responsibility now.

Faced with marriage to a socially acceptable woman, he could not risk associating with her.

When she reminded herself of his impending wedding, she was able to control her desire. Someone else's husband-to-be had kissed her as if he had meant it.

Given his rakish tendencies, Lacey thought she ought to be glad he was marrying another. But how could she be glad he would hold another woman, kiss another woman, love and have babies with that woman when *she* loved him.

Didn't he see that? Didn't he care?

It didn't hurt that he cared nothing for her; no one except her parents had ever shown the slightest concern for anything but her fortune. And the marquess was wealthy enough not to care a fig for that.

But he seemed to care nothing for the children. And for that she could not forgive him.

Turning to face him, she drew a shaking breath and said, "I know this is your house my lord, and I have no right to command you to leave. But as the children and I have nowhere else to go, would you mind?"

His confident mask seemed to slip before he glowered at her as if he meant to tell her he'd be the master in his own home. She began to feel surging through her veins the hope that he would say just that, take her in his arms again, and kiss her in the masterful way he had just exerted, but his stiff reply quelled that absurd longing. Bowing, he said, "Your servant, ma'am," then strode toward the door when he turned and said, "But count on this; I shall return. And we shall have our day of reckoning."

Reeling under a host of conflicting emotions—anger, desire, and a stinging humiliation that his kiss should have aroused her to such a state—Lacey remained in the nursery, listening to the echo of Lord Helverton's steps recede down the stairway. The booted rhythm seemed to reiterate his promised, "I shall return," but his parting declaration left her fearing that eventuality.

A "day of reckoning" he had called it.

The way he said it elicited uneasy thoughts of the Day of Wrath. Judgment Day.

Though she told herself she had done nothing worthy of the marquess's wrath, Lacey could not suppress fears that he meant her to pay for his good will. What that price might be, she could only guess, but the conjecture excited a fluttering pulse and fearful tremblings that left her weak and vulnerable.

Not even a determined occupation with her children in the weeks that followed could keep her fears at bay for long. Instead she would send the children outside, allowing her to make a desperate attempt to organize the house against the event the marquess should send them packing.

During one of these panicked flights in which every treasure and keepsake in the salon must be cleaned and catalogued, she was dismayed to hear the sounds of several vehicles coming down the long driveway toward Woods Hole. Setting down the framed picture she had been dusting—one Ghillie had done shortly after his adoption, she flew to the window over the pedimented front doors and peered outside.

To her horror, a cavalcade of two plain coaches, several wagons, and animals in train were making their way toward the house. It looked as if he had brought an army of workers to restore Woods Hole to its former glory. If that were true, he obviously meant to evict them immediately.

Accompanying the wagons, Lord Helverton was riding a roan stallion which pranced arrogantly around the heavy vehicles as if flaunting its high-blooded heritage before the stolid draft animals. The rider also seemed in high spirits, as if looking forward to the changes he was planning for his estate. More likely, Lacey thought in her pique, he was looking forward to the peace and quiet they would leave him after their departure.

Lured by the approach of what must have looked to them like a circus, her children, excepting Cassie and Justin, burst

251

out of the entrance and clustered excitedly around the marquess's knees. Lacey heard their excited questions and Helverton's stern rejoinder to "Have a care for Paladin's hooves," and thought bitterly that he might have expressed his concern in a kinder fashion. But the children backed away, all except Gordie, who grasped the animal's bridle and began gentling the high-spirited creature without a care to his own safety.

Helverton reined in to bark orders at the drivers, then dismounted and turned to survey the broad expanse of his childhood home. He turned his face upward to sweep a critical glance over the upper stories.

Lacey did not draw back, for the sight of his upturned face excited a desperate longing in her breast. She wanted him to see her watching for him. But if he saw her from her vantage point in the window, he gave no sign, only turned aside, giving his mount's reins to the hands of a groom who appeared miraculously from the stables, before striding into the great hall.

Wiping her hands down her skirt, Lacey fought the dizzying premonition that he meant to move them out lock, stock, and barrel to begin immediate renovations for his bride. Her fears and an unreasoning outrage that he had given them no warning, no time, no opportunity to find other lodgings blinded her to the procession which, followed by the stampede of laughing children, was lumbering toward the stables.

Anxiety and anger combined to send her directly to the marquess to plead against immediate removal; however, she disciplined the impulse to challenge him. She was not composed enough to initiate any discussion with him. Besides, she would know how my lord Helverton had decided to dispose of her household when he called for her. Until then, she had to do something to occupy her mind and keep it from dwelling on her fears.

Or her traitorous desires.

She ought to return her keepsakes to the table from which they had been removed for dusting, and. . . . Turning back to finish the chore, she caught a glimpse of herself in the mantel mirror. Her auburn hair was crushed beneath its dusty cap, her face smutty with dust, and her hands, although fragrant with lemon oil, were grimy and had left long, black smudges on the ivory-colored muslin skirt she was wearing. Horrified by her appearance, she hurried to her chamber to scrub the dust from her face and hands, smooth her hair, and change into a fresh frock.

Cleanliness and a change of clothes restoring her confidence to its more customary balance, Lacey returned to the salon where the housemaid was replacing the last of her treasures. "Thank you, Mattie," Lacey said, taking up a tambour and setting several stitches to settle her nerves. "Has Lord Helverton asked to see me?"

"No, miss," replied the maid. "His lordship is outside, playing with the children."

"Playing with the ch—" Immediately Lacey dropped the needlework on her worktable and bounded toward the door. "Where are they?"

"Outside, miss," Mattie said helpfully. "By the stables. Did you know he brought his own servants—"

But Lacey did not wish to hear any more. Scurrying outside after taking time to don a bonnet and draw a paisley shawl around her shoulders to ward off the cool spring air, Lacey found the marquess surrounded by children watching a groom harness a pony to a cart. "There's your mother," he said, lifting Katelin and Missie into the box and handing the reins to Gordie, who jumped up beside them. "Show her how well you drive."

Urging his dappled gray pony into motion, Gordie tooled the brightly colored cart around the cobbled yard. Missie and Katelin clung to the rails, squealing, "Go faster, go faster!" while the wind of their flight tumbled their blond curls about their shoulders and turned their cheeks pink. The equipage rumbled past Lacey with inches to spare and tore down the graveled drive.

Lacey watched and prayed that her son would not turn them over, then turned a frightened look upon the marquess. He was strapping another gray pony to another colorful cart in which sat Ernie and his shadow, Paul. Goaded by fear into taking hold of the pony's bridle as Helverton handed Ernie the reins, she cried, "My Lord, they've never—"

"Then they'd better learn," he said, muttering a few low-voiced tips on controlling high-blooded cattle into the ten-year-old's eager ear, and then commanding, "Paul must drive back. Agreed?"

"Yes, sir!" Ernie said, waiting until Lacey removed her hand from the pony to cluck it forward. The docile creature took off at a sedate clip, then broke into a good-natured trot when the boy slapped its rump with the ends of the reins.

Ignoring her, Helverton lifted Cassie into another cart to which was hitched a panting St. Bernard. "Oh, no, my lord," Lacey protested, possessing herself desperately of his arm. "Surely you don't mean to let her drive?"

"Of course not, Miss Fremont," he replied, giving a pair of useless reins into the little girl's hands. Jerking them up and down, Cassie crowed, "Git up, Dog."

Possessing himself of a sturdy leash, Helverton urged the great dog forward. "Go fast, Dog," Cassie cried.

Pulling back on the lead, Helverton said, "Heel, Hannibal.

"Walk with me, Miss Fremont," he invited, offering his arm and a smile to quell Lacey's frowning anxiety. "Assure yourself I mean no harm to . . . our children."

Taken aback by his hesitation, Lacey placed her hand on his arm and fell into step beside him. "I do not know what you mean to do about the children," she said as they moved down a row of the apple orchard. The white blossoms spreading overhead enveloped them in a fragrant cloud. "I can only hope you have their best interests at heart."

"Ah, I do," Helverton assured her, ducking his head to avoid a low-hanging branch. "I want them to like me."

"Like you?" Lacey parroted. "But why?"

Chuckling, he cast a sideways glance at her. Lacey was not at all easy under his appraising scrutiny, but she returned his glance with what she hoped was an even gaze as he said, "I believe it is customary for one's offspring to like their parents."

She could not restrain an answering giggle. "Oh," she remarked merrily. "And did you like your parents?"

Immediately she regretted her teasing query.

His smile dropped from his lips, leaving them tensely disposed. "No, Miss Fremont," he said. "I did not. But lest you chide me for not honoring them, allow me to say they did not particularly court my good opinion."

"My own parents were very strict," she confessed in an attempt to identify with his pain. "But I do not hold it against them. They loved me."

"How fortunate you were," he said in bitter tones. "My lord father and lady mother abandoned me to the care of a ruthless tutor here while they pursued separate lives in Town. They did not care whether Bramble beat me or starved me, only that we left them alone."

Lacey felt a rush of pity for the lonely, frightened boy Helverton had been and realized he was still carrying around the bitterness and hurt of a little boy who couldn't understand why he was in exile. "I'm sorry," she said.

Her gaze was darkly sincere and made him feel as if the weight of his past was suddenly bearing down on him. Shrugging his shoulders, he said, "You needn't be. I am my own man now, and if I choose to present these children with tokens of my esteem, who can stop me?"

"No one, my lord," she confessed. "Only, what will they do when you tire of indulging them?"

Ignoring her query, he said, "I saw Whitcomb while I was in Town."

Fear that he had found a way to extricate himself from his vow to protect the children made her heart hammer against her ribs, but she took a calming breath and enquired, "Was he able to free you from this sad coil?"

"He offered some sage advice," Helverton said with a narrow-eyed look that was anything but reassuring. "I came back with every intention of following it."

Lacey was possessed of the uncomfortable sensation that he was stalking her, waiting for the right moment to call her to account. Or for the right moment to seduce her.

If that was his plan, she had no defense against it. She felt strangely drawn to him, as if Fate had chosen him out of every gentleman in London to champion her orphans and protect her. That he had taken his time in showing any interest in either pursuit signified nothing, she told herself sternly when

255

a foolish doubt reminded her that protection in this day and age was of two kinds — honorable and dishonorable.

He had already requested the honor of protecting Edwina Carstairs in marriage. Was he going to take advantage of the gossip that condemned her to the only form left?

As she was possessed by these disturbing thoughts, they came to the end of the orchard, where a grounds man was piling fallen limbs. Seeing his master, the man doffed his cap and bobbed his head in respectful welcome.

"Bob Pruitt, isn't it?" Helverton said, eliciting a broad smile from his employee. "It's been a long time."

Bobbing his head once more, Pruitt said, "Welcome back to Woods Hole, my lord. You've been away too long."

"Thank you," Helverton said without commenting on his plans.

Though he had grown up here, Woods Hole had never felt like home. He had always thought of the place as an institution, devoid of heart or joy. It was the reason he had let it to Miss Fremont and her orphans.

To his surprise, he had discovered on his only visit that she had transformed it into a home he was unwilling to leave. But that only distracted him from his purpose — extricating himself from Edwina's clutches and finding favor with Lacey. And he could achieve neither purpose under the watchful gaze of an innocent child.

Handing the lead into Pruitt's hands, Helverton asked him to take the cart back to the stable and hand Cassie to the nursery maid he had engaged.

Uneasily Lacey watched them go, Pruitt leaning on his rake and talking to Cassie who was still cheerfully flapping the ribbons against the box. When they had gone, she removed her hand from the marquess's arm and said, "I don't know what you're about, Lord Helverton. Bringing such extravagant toys to —"

"Children for whom I'm responsible?" he said, reclaiming her arm and leading her more deeply into the orchard.

Turning a suspicious look upon him, she said, "What else did you bring in your bag of tricks?"

"Magic," he said in a husky, provocative voice that drew her

256

against her will into the depths of his heavy-lidded stare. His broad grin was playing havoc with her pulse and making it so difficult to draw a deep breath that she felt as if she were drowning.

"Magic?" she queried breathlessly. She felt as if she were under a spell, but he had no need to resort to tricks to enchant her; all it took was a look and a smile. And a kiss.

Perhaps that was what had fueled the gossips. Had they seen how drawn she was to him?

But how could they? She and the marquess had no social ties; their relationship was based solely on their interest in the children. It was simply that tattlemongers saw something that was not there.

That was the power of gossip after all, to make something out of nothing. *Like magic,* said a mocking inner voice that shocked her out of her romantic confusion.

Turning away from his provoking grin, she filled her lungs with the sweet perfumed air enveloping them and said with a tone of firm conviction, "Nonsense. There is no such thing as magic."

Helverton raised a dubious eyebrow and said, "As you will, Miss Fremont. Only the children do not share your cynical view of life. I hope you will allow me to—"

"Shatter their illusions, my lord? Certainly I will do no such thing."

"But you will shatter mine," he said repressively. He raised a hand to crush a twig full of blossoms. "One would think you wished one to go away."

"Your presence here cannot help but fan the gossips' tongues," Lacey replied.

He made her feel guilty for voicing such an unladylike opinion when he said, "You wound me, ma'am. And you deprive the children."

"I have given them everything they nee—"

"Except ponies and carts," he replied. Smiling enticingly, he added, "And magic."

"Lies," she retorted, adding in righteous indignation, "I have lavished my time, my love upon them. What, excepting pony carts, have I denied them?"

257

"A father," he replied.

"You mean a figurehead? No, my lord, they don't need a guardian who'll pop into their lives to indulge them with extravagant gifts whenever his wife allows him to exercise his charitable nature, and then pop out when he tires of their childish demands."

"Is that what you think I mean to do?"

"What else? You've shown no interest in the children since your initial burst of conscience six years ago."

"And every Christmas since."

"Yes, more presents," she chided in a resentful tone.

"I did enjoy buying them," he said defensively.

"Too bad you couldn't have taken the time to watch the children unwrap them," she snapped, turning back toward the stable. "You sent enough toys for an army, yet you didn't even know how many we—I was caring for. They couldn't use half of them."

"So what did you do with the rest?" he demanded, following her step for step.

Feeling for the first time as if she had done the wrong thing, she confessed, "I delivered them to the tenants' children. In your name," she added lamely. "Because you couldn't come down."

He caught her hand before they were in sight of the stables to stay her escape. Drawing her into the shadow of a tree, he wrapped a gentle arm around her waist, saying in an irresistible voice, "I am here now."

Her heart thrummed with a fearful delight as he pulled her into a possessive embrace. But she was angry and suppressed the thrill with a pouting frown and said, "Yes, you have returned for our day of reckoning."

"You will have it so," he replied, settling her more comfortably against his length and drawing off her bonnet with his free hand. Lacey tried to cling to its strings to no avail. Off it came. He tossed it away. As it went flying into the boughs, he declared, "I am calling your bluff, Miss Fremont."

Struggling to free herself from his insinuating embrace, she grasped his shoulders and leaned away from him.

That, she realized immediately, was a mistake. The uncomfortable posture pressed his hips against hers and left her in no doubt as to his interest in her. Shocked by the intense longing the intimate pressure incited, she ceased the futile struggle, stammering, "I . . . don't know what you mean."

"Don't you?" he enquired. He was caressing her back in enticing circles that drained her of the will to resist. "I rather think you must stop playing the game according to your rules."

Caught in the spell of his silvery gaze, Lacey couldn't think straight. She didn't have the strength to maintain a rigid posture but became pliant, so that although she was clinging to his shoulders, he had to support her weight in his arms.

As if sensing her vulnerability, he lowered his voice until it became a feral growl that made her shiver. "Don't play the coy young thing with me, Miss Fremont. An innocent doesn't kiss the way you last kissed me or cling in such a dependent fashion." He grinned slowly, lazily, looking to Lacey for all the world like a wolf licking his chops in anticipation of a kill.

But she was mesmerized by his transparent stare and could not help being drawn into his trap.

"I rather like your wanton response," he confessed, dropping his gaze to the lips she was moistening in apprehension. "But we will play without the subsequent hysterics this time. I shall show you a far better outlet for your passionate nature."

Before she could protest her innocence or wriggle free of his confining grasp, he swooped a kiss upon her parted lips.

Stunned into a breathless, vertiginous response, she could not even summon the strength to fight his will, but twisted her fingers in his windblown locks and clung to him with a desperation born of fear and a traitorous longing.

His consuming kiss drained her of any will of her own, left her only an aching need for him. It fueled a hunger that increased every moment she tasted him, imbued her with a power to fight back, to demand of him the same craving that impelled her. She was caught in a whirling maelstrom of feeling, and she wanted him to relinquish his command over the riotous rush of sensation with which he was seducing her. But though he pressed her, molded her to his form, drew from her every particle of resistance and displayed every evidence of desire himself, he seemed determined to keep a rigid control over his emotions.

Sobbing, she was plunged into a second kiss that devoured her plea for mercy, her appeal for affection. He wanted her, and he did not care who knew it or saw her shame, and she could not help wanting him.

God help her, she had never wanted any man until he demanded her to want him. Now, he was all she wanted.

"Oh, Char," she intoned when they broke for a gasping breath. He turned, pressing her back against the rough bark of the leaning apple tree, leaning his weight upon her, as if he meant to make of them one person.

A shower of fragrant blossoms rained down on them, recalling her to their surroundings. Frightened, pushing against his chest, covering her bruised lips with shaking fingers, she cried, "Oh, my lord, have pity."

Their rapid, rasping breaths pressing her against the hard wood of their improvised bed made her wonder if he meant to suffocate her rather than let her go.

"Pity, Lacey?" he enquired, still leaning over her menacingly. "No, there is nothing so pallid in my feelings for you. I want you."

Stroking a gentle hand across his dark brow as if soothing away a fever, she confessed, "And I, you," to the accompaniment of a heated blush that stained her cheeks a becoming pink. "But we are not alone."

He released her wide-eyed gaze to sweep a cursory glance around the walled orchard. Pruitt had the foresight to close the gate, barring any possibility of interruption. Indicating as much, he said, "We are utterly private, ma'am. And since you are willing. . . ." He lowered his mouth to taste of her once more.

Turning her head aside, she importuned, "Please, my lord, do not take me like this. I beg you will have a care for the children."

"The children are occupied," he said, pressing kisses on the cords of her throat. "And the gate is closed."

"Gates mean nothing to them," she whispered, closing her eyes against the rapturous pressure of his lips against her throbbing pulse. Steeling herself against his insistent onslaught, she said, "They would think you were hurting me."

"I will not hurt you," he vowed, cupping her chin in one hand to compel her gently to look at him. She closed her eyes in denial when he said, "I want you to face the truth. We belong together."

She rejoiced at his confession, then, recalling one unequivocal hindrance in the path of their love, steeled herself against soaring hopes. "But you are engaged," she murmured, shivering when he dropped two kisses on her eyelids. "Promised to another woman."

"A mere formality," he protested. Swaying, she clung to a branch, while he retrieved her discarded bonnet and his fallen hat. "It has nothing to do with us."

His nonchalant attitude toward inviolate commitments sank her hopes like a stone in a well. "Doesn't it?" she queried in a dull voice.

"No," he replied, giving the bonnet into Lacey's unfeeling hand. "You place too much worth on the match."

Looking at him for a long moment in weary disappointment, she began to pick her way between the rows of trees, murmuring, "And you, too little."

"There's where you're wrong, my dear," he said, placing his curly-brimmed beaver at a jaunty attitude that made him appear to mock everything she believed. His insouciance infuriated her. "I know exactly what my engagement is worth, and I'm willing to pay Edwina's price."

"Most gentlemen are willing," she remarked as she fumbled with the latch securing the gate. To her fury, it would not open, and she added between clenched teeth, "To get what a lady considers beyond price."

Laughing, Helverton covered Lacey's fingers, staying her frantic efforts. "You have too little faith, Miss Fremont. When she understands my need, Edwina will accept my offer."

Lacey jerked her fingers free of his restraining grip. Turning to face him, she raised her chin defiantly and said, "So you think she will turn her head the other way while you satisfy your needs with—"

"You?" he queried on a note of amusement.

261

Lacey wanted to stamp her foot in exasperation. He made dalliance sound romantic; her reluctance, foolish.

"Yes, you are everything I need," he said in a voice that irresistibly beckoned her. "Everything I want."

He was saying everything she had always wanted to hear, but he was saying it for all the wrong reasons. He only wanted her in his arms, in his bed. For her it was too much to ask and not enough to give.

"My price is too dear," she snapped, throwing open the gate at last. "Go back to Miss Carstairs. She will make you the perfect wife." Marching through the gate before he detected the tears that stung her eyes, she stiffened her back against the sardonic laughter that rumbled toward her like thunder warning of a coming storm.

But as the spring wore into summer, it seemed more to have been an empty threat. When he was not riding about his estate with his agent and the children were not cloistered with the big-boned, good-natured tutor he had engaged or in the care of the gentle nursery maid who inexorably took Lacey's place in the nursery, the marquess himself entertained the children.

He took them fishing, taught Gordie to handle his own pair of high-blooded cattle, flirted with Kate and Missie, then gently taught them not to flaunt their charms like Haymarket wares, played knight and dragon with Paul and Ernie, allowing them finally to vanquish him, cherished Cassie, and dandled Justin on his knee.

Even her aunts were drawn to him like ants to a lump of sugar. But if he was warm-hearted with the children and respectful of her aunts, he was only polite to her. And not once in two months did he approach her, in either anger or desire.

Lacey feared he was deliberately shutting her out of the games and tea parties from which bursts of high-pitched laughter mingled delightfully with the dear echoes of his baritone voice.

Walking into the library to find another book of poetry to occupy time grown heavy on her hands after the long months of exclusion, she encountered a merry gathering that immediately grew suspiciously hushed. Faced with an unmistakable

262

resistance to her presence, she darted a distressed look at Helverton, who had the grace to flush before he turned a conspiratorial wink toward Gordie.

The boy smirked a silent reply.

Halting on the threshold, she said in a shaking voice, "I hope I'm not interrupting anything."

Stretching, Helverton smiled enigmatically and enquired, "Is there something you need?"

"A book," she confessed, self-consciously walking toward a low bookshelf, knowing that his silver eyes stalked her every step, seemed to bore into her soul, tear from her the truth of her need.

She needed no book; she needed the children. More than that, she needed him.

Halfway toward her stated purpose, she halted and whirled on the intimate family circle. Sitting cross-legged on the red leather settee, cradling Justin and Cassie on his knees, Helverton was smiling amusement and glowing with pride in his adopted offspring. Katelin and Missie sat adoringly at his feet with Paul and Ernie guarding either side of him. Cookie and Nonnie, who were seated in opposing armchairs, turned back to their contented stitching. Gordie, who had turned a probing gaze toward her as if searching her heart, closed the circle as he returned his attention to his guardian.

Lacey's heart slammed into a painful rhythm as she realized the children had completely accepted the marquess, looked to him for approval, for security, for affection. Even Justin, who usually fussed himself into a restless sleep had once again fallen peacefully asleep in Helverton's arms.

It was what she had wanted for them, a father to love them, care for them, but she hadn't counted on being forsaken in the exchange.

"If you like, I can put Justin down for his nap," she offered hesitantly.

Removing his piercing gaze from her strained countenance, Helverton regarded the baby lolling trustingly in his nonchalant grasp. "Don't trouble yourself," he said with a lazy smile lighting his gaze. "If he gets restless, we'll stretch him out here. Right, crew?"

The children, and even her aunts, chimed as one in their various voices and styles, "Right, Papa," or "As you say, my lord."

Lacey clasped her hands together to keep from snatching her baby from him. He had left her no one to need her, no one for her to hold. At the same time, he had awakened a burning need in her and left it in possession of her soul.

Unable to fight such tactics, she resigned herself to them, saying, "Suit yourself, my lord. I'll just get my book."

When she had selected the volume, she disposed herself in a chair near the window and began to stare at the blurring pages.

After a few minutes, Helverton enquired, "Do you have enough light?"

Startled out of her unseeing daze, Lacey raised shining eyes from the page, but did not dare peer over her shoulder. "Yes, thank you. How good of you to ask."

"Not at all," he said, his voice tinged with amusement. "Only you have been staring at the same page for the last ten minutes. Would you like to sit with us?"

Hastily drying her damp eyes, she sprang from the cushion and moved toward the circle, offering a hesitant, "Only if I'm not intruding."

"Certainly not," he replied, drawing her forward with his mesmerizing gaze. "We were making plans that concern us all."

Anxiety made her hesitate. Plans that concern us all. Did they also include her? But his gaze was so magnetic, she suppressed her doubts and hastened toward the settee.

Flinging her arms possessively around her guardian's neck, Cassie stared at her, blurting out, "Go 'way, Mama. We don't need you now."

Haltingly Lacey mumbled, "I see that you don't," then stumbled out of the book room.

When she stood shaking in the hall, unregarded by the army of Helverton's servants, all who had taken it upon themselves to satisfy every one of her children's needs, it occurred to her that she was not only not needed here, she was no longer wanted.

With a jolt of understanding that made her feel as if she had been struck by lightning, she realized why the marquess wanted the children to like him. So they would not need her anymore, not want her anymore.

So she would leave.

Hurrying outdoors to a secluded corner of the garden, lest someone see the tears that were spilling down her cheeks, she did not hear anyone following until her arm was gripped in an iron fist. "Let me go," she cried as her tormentor drew her into the shadows of a boxwood hedge maze. "Cassie was right, none of you need me; I see that now."

"Cassie did not mean it the way you heard it," he argued.

"Yes, she meant what you will not say," she countered, twisting to free herself from his iron grip.

"We all of us do need you, Lacey," he said, encompassing the sides of her face with both his hands to compel her to look at him. "Me, most of all."

Tears tracking down her cheeks as if not hearing, she repeated, "Please, my lord; let me go. I won't stand in your way with the children. By law they are yours. Only let me go."

"Where will you go?" he demanded, searching her stricken face with a penetrating stare that made her feel as if she were shrinking, becoming a part of him.

"Anywhere you say," she said in desperation. Attempting to avoid his probing look, she felt he was squeezing her head between his hands. Finally, unable to bear the piercing stare any longer, she dropped her gaze and mumbled, "I don't know."

Gently, yet inexorably, he raised her chin and covered her lips with his.

The kiss was as tender as the breath of summer sighing around them, but Lacey felt as if she were tumbling head over heels down a rough hill. To keep her feet, she clung to him as if he were her life, and when he broke off to look at her with a curious half smile twisting his dear, handsome face, she released her breath on a sob.

"Tell me you can leave me," he said, his gaze sparking a challenge she could not meet.

Closing her eyes, she said, "I must. There is nothing for me here but heartache."

He longed to show her just how wrong she was but satisfied himself with another searching kiss that had her again depending on him. "If you leave, you will break my heart," he said against her lips. "If you stay, everything in my power to bestow is yours."

"Except your name, my lord," she said in a low voice that was scarcely loud enough for him to hear, especially in light of the screeching clamor that had erupted at the mouth of the maze.

The pinched, soprano tones drove him to clasp Lacey in a possessive, inescapable embrace that held her beside him until the intruder found them as he wanted her to.

"Ah, Miss Fremont, making free with my betrothed," Edwina said in aerial tones. Casting an impatient look over her elegantly clad shoulder, she called out, "Here they are, Jules." She waited until the puffing, overdressed gentleman leaning negligently on his cane drew to a halt at her side and wiped his brow. "Will you call him out now?"

"I'll do no such thing, dear Edwina," Jules said, pocketing his yellow and black-striped handkerchief. Stretching forth a white hand, he introduced himself. "Jules Rudland. Sorry to intrude, my lord."

"That makes two of us," Helverton said, ignoring Rudland's hand but taking in the proprietary manner in which his betrothed was holding onto the man's canary yellow left arm. "I take it Edwina expects you to rid her of an unwanted *parti*."

"No use beating round the bush," Jules puffed. "Can't oblige her by killing you, my lord. Good swordsman, bad leg. Terrible shot."

Lacey felt the cold fingers of fear clutch her heart as the overdressed fop confessed his injury and lack of skill with dueling pistols. She was afraid Helverton would kill him and be forced to flee the country. What would she do then? What would the children do?

Clinging to him, willing him to restrain the deadly virile instinct to accept any challenge to one's honor, she pressed her shaking form against his unyielding frame.

The marquess felt a smile creep up one corner of his mouth as Lacey crushed her soft curves against him, and in an unconcerned tone he hazarded a guess. "Am I to believe you wish me to bow out so you might pursue Edwina yourself?"

"You'll not get off that easily, Helverton," Edwina interjected, staring daggers at Lacey. "That woman has dragged my name through mud this spring; I doubt I'll ever recover. It is a wonder Jules could even speak to me."

"A wonder," Helverton agreed, eying her decorative escort in a calculating manner, then piercing his inconstant betrothed with his gaze. "If I am not to oblige you by dying, Edwina, how are you to be rid of me? Do you want me to cry off?"

"Then I'd have to call you out for insulting the woman I love," Jules said. "Won't do it."

"Thank you," Helverton said.

Lacey shivered in relief that the man she loved was not to kill a man or die himself in a duel and then stared at Helverton in wonder. She loved him. The realization struck her dumb.

Thinking she was taking a chill, the marquess led everyone back to the empty book room, rang for tea, and poured out two glasses of brandy. While Lacey numbly poured tea for Edwina and herself, the marquess went on, "So it's to be an unhappy match for us, Edwina?"

With an uncertain smile for Rudland, she said, "I'm not sure I want to marry you now."

"No?" Helverton enquired suspiciously. "What's the catch to our freedom?"

"I'm sure you will agree a monetary settlement to end our engagement is not too much to ask for . . . discretion."

Helverton bristled. "You mean pay for your silence?"

Edwina had the grace to blush. Confirmed in his suspicions, the marquess said, "Were you to spread any more oil on those flames, Edwina, I would have to seek satisfaction from your cowardly suitor. Isn't the left leg your bad one, Rudland?"

Immediately the fop collapsed on the settee beside Edwina. "Simple way out. Pay her bride price." Rudland was examining his impeccable manicure in a manner that seemed to convey his unconcern in the matter. But Lacey saw his black eyes glitter avariciously and knew he was no innocent bystander. "So you see, old man," he was saying, "you hold the key to wedded bliss." Passing a cavalier look over Lacey before settling on the marquess, he added sneeringly, "For those of us so inclined, that is."

His snide reminder recalled Lacey forcibly to the fact that Helverton had never spoken of marriage, only of wanting her. And he had not even confessed that weakness before his betrothed and her escort. Doubt suddenly made her feel very small and insignificant and frightened.

Taking the teacup from her shaking fingers, Helverton engulfed them in his warm hand. "Heard you were dipped pretty badly, Rudland. I'm not sure Edwina's bride price will cover your debt and set you up in style."

" 'Twill be enough to guarantee three people's happiness, old man," Rudland said in a tone that had a brittle edge to it. "I come into my inheritance when I marry, but Edwina's *père* wouldn't smile on the match."

Having taken off her ice blue kid gloves to drink her tea, Edwina was fidgeting with them. Of a sudden, Helverton growled, "What did you do with your engagement ring, Edwina?"

"Pawned it," she said, stretching out her fingers as if she just realized the ring was missing. "Rundell and Bridges, if you're concerned I did not get what it was worth." Opening her reticule, she drew out a ticket. "Jules and I needed the money." She cast a worried glance at her sweating escort and said, "You can buy this if you want."

"Scotland?" Helverton guessed and was confirmed in the couple's guilty silence. "Sorry, my dear," he said, pocketing the slip of paper before she could snatch it away, "you ridded yourself of a piece of jewelry that was not yours to sell. Family heirloom."

Edwina erupted in tears.

Lacey was inclined to think them tears of frustration rather than grief, but she expressed her best wishes on the match.

"You would think so," Edwina said cattily. "It leaves the field open to you."

"I rather think it leaves Lord Helverton free to marry anyone he likes," Lacey responded carefully in the awkward silence that followed.

"Well, the cat's out of the bag now," Rudland said, engulfing her hand in his beefy one. "Had to marry her, old man. Knew you wouldn't take the fall for our indiscretion since you were engaged in your own."

Helverton was possessed of a crushing rage. Rudland's leering supposition had caused Lacey to flinch as if he had flayed her with a whip.

Given his own troubles, Rudland had no right to cast aspersions against the woman he loved. But controlling his surging instincts to protect her against all opposition, Helverton said, "Right you are, old man. I would not marry a woman who used that goad." Glaring barely controlled fury at his former betrothed he said, "You must have panicked when I inconveniently left Town. How fortunate for you that Mr. Rudland agreed to do the honorable thing."

"You beast," Edwina snarled. "Jules married me for love, not out of a perverse obligation."

"No accounting for love," Helverton muttered in an amused tone as he considered his and Lacey's entwined fingers. It was time to break with the Honorable Edwina Carstairs and follow where his heart led.

Sweeping a neutral gaze toward the couple seated defensively together on the settee, he said, "I wish you joy in each other, Mr. and Mrs. Rudland. But you will receive no blood money from me to soften your father's disapproval, Edwina."

"No?" Edwina enquired, turning her malevolent eye on Lacey. "Society can be so cruel, Miss Fremont, but then you know that. What they will say when they learn how you alienated Charlton from me so that the rift compelled me to marry against my parent's wishes, I can only imagine."

Lacey felt the marquess tense at her side as if he meant to leap into the fray himself. But this was a battle she could wage herself. Gently she said, "I'm sure we share the same concern, ma'am."

"Oh?" Edwina enquired in an unconcerned tone. "And what might that be, Miss Fremont?"

"Why, to spare our families the evil effect of twisted truths,"

Lacey replied in that same gentle voice.

Edwina bristled. "Are you threatening me?"

Before Lacey could answer, Helverton interjected, "I heard no threat voiced except yours. Do not think you can shake my faith by smearing Lacey with slander; she is the only innocent party among us."

"But she is an unwed mother!" Edwina whined, as if forgetting that she herself would have been tarred by the same brush had Jules not been willing to do the honorable thing.

"All adopted, Mrs. Rudland," Helverton snapped back without further comment on Edwina's increasing state. Drawing Lacey to her feet and enfolding her in a protective embrace, he pressed home his defense in a rush of words that drove their unwanted visitors from the settee and toward the hall. "You may tell Society, madam," he said, propelling Edwina and Jules toward the front door by his determined pursuit, "that Lacey now has a devoted champion who means to defend her against all attacks. And Jules, you might remind gentlemen who claim to have intimately known my betrothed that I am a crack shot."

"You would defend Edwina's honor?" Jules blurted out stupidly.

"That distinction belongs to you," the marquess said. Bestowing a look of infinite tenderness on Lacey, he said in tones of breathless wonder, "I was speaking of Miss Fremont. She was about to make me the happiest of men when you interrupted us."

Lacey's gasp was drowned by Edwina's screeching protest, "But you were engaged to me!"

"I believe you removed that bar when you eloped with Rudland," Helverton reminded her as a footman ushered the couple outside and into their carriage.

Lacey met his adoring gaze with a faltering look. "Congratulations, my lord," she said. "You have won your freedom."

"Yes," he said, "And now we are free to marry."

"Marry?" Lacey breathed incredulously, her heart pounding in fearful anticipation. "But what will your family say?"

"Our children will be delighted," he said, dropping a teasing kiss on the tip of her uptilted nose. "They have been pressing me for the last month to make you my wife." Two more kisses followed immediately on either eyelid.

"But why?" she asked in an attempt to control the astonishing sensations his distracting kisses were producing in her breast.

Ignoring the bustle of servants, Helverton crushed her to him, tumbling her hair and tangling his fingers possessively in it. "One's children's parents ought to be married," he said before devouring her lips in an exhausting kiss that left her clinging to him.

Looking at him in a dazed manner that admitted that she wanted to be kissed again, she murmured, "That never stood in our way of adopting children before."

"Having seen my parents' miserable union," he confessed, "I considered we were better friends without making vows. But you have changed my mind. About marriage and about children. Our ready-made family needs us together, and I want children of my own," he added, obliging her by dropping another lingering kiss on her lips.

The tenderly proffered, penetrating caress moved her more than if he had forced himself upon her lips. Shaking, she clung to him, drawing warmth and an indefinable reassurance from his gentle persuasion.

But after the initial shock of their bodies flying together settled into a burning need to merge into one form, Helverton went rigid and held her almost fearfully, as if she were a piece of fragile china that must be protected against rough handling.

Breathing hard, they stared at one another across a seemingly unbridgeable chasm. Lacey, seeking to close the distance between them, raised a hand to smooth the tousled lock of hair that fell boyishly across his brow.

He flinched and sucked in a tortured breath as if she had struck him again.

"Oh, please my lord," she cried, wrenching her hand away, "I did not know you disliked my touch so much."

He caught her fingers in a warm grip and withdrew to a more private place in the shadows of the great staircase, then placed her hand alongside his face.

271

Chuckling deep in his throat, he confessed, "I crave your touch, Lacey. But I fear it."

"You?" she enquired in disbelief. She stared wide-eyed at him, trying to make sense of his confession. "But you are so much stronger than I," she whispered. "What can I possibly do to hurt you?"

"Refuse me," he said, inhaling the sweet violet scent of her. Rushing on before she could laugh at his sensibility, he declared, "I never knew how much a man could love a woman until I began to love you. Lacey . . ."

Capturing his face in shaking hands, she pressed a fervent kiss on his lips in a silent confession of her own feelings.

Every heartbeat cried, "I love you." He was her life's blood, the air she breathed. He was her life. "Oh, Char," she breathed after his tongue had plundered the tingling recesses of her own mouth. "I love you. What are we to do?"

"There is only one thing to be done, my dear. You have to marry me."

Lacey felt her heart plunge to the bottom of her stomach as she cried out, "Have to . . . ? It is too bad of you to feel we *must* marry. I have no wish to torment you."

He took pains to gentle her by soothing his hands along her spine, saying, "You cannot help doing so, my heart, if you keep pressing against me in that delightfully inspiring way." Grinning, he added, "But if you refuse, you will condemn me to a monk's life and deny our children their father."

Stunned into silence by his declaration, she stared unsteadily at him as she considered his threat. Then, deciding he could never abandon them, she said, "Surely not, my lord."

"You may count on it," he replied in a fervent tone that increased her fears. Piercing her with an intense stare, he said, "Whitcomb told me he had written into that wretched document only two ways to dissolve our association—death, or to find either party unfit for the charge of bringing up children in a wholesome environment. Said he did it to protect the children."

"Were you hoping I would bring such charges against you?" she whispered in pained confusion. "How could I? Why, my lord, would I believe rumors against you? You have been like a knight leading a charge all these years."

"Don't say that," he ground out guiltily. Tearing his gaze from her, he confessed urgently, "I first came here with the most despicable motives — to seduce you and prove you unsuited for motherhood."

"That I will never believe," Lacey vowed. "You scarcely touched me all summer."

"That self-denial alone ought to prove my good intentions," he said fiercely. His pale eyes glowed dark in the dim light as he said, "Lacey, I love you. But if you refuse me again, I'll have to leave. I simply cannot keep my hands off you. Marry me or say goodbye."

Her heart pounding in her throat in fear that she might drive him away, Lacey whispered, "Stay with me, Char. I will marry you. As soon as we decently can."

He placed a piece of parchment in her hand. "Special license," he said when she stared in confusion at it. "We can be married as soon as the vicar arrives. That's decent enough."

Then he whirled her into the hallway in a giddy waltz that drew an applauding audience.

Laughing, she turned her startled face toward the gleeful assemblage peering over the banister. Lacey lovingly took in her children's bright, happy faces and her aunts' rosy embarrassment. "My lord," she breathed, covering her own warm cheeks with the license as the world spun around her, "How long have you been planning this?"

His first reaction was to kiss her so thoroughly her toes curled. Their ready-made family raising a ringing hurrah to the rafters, he grinned passionately and said, "From the beginning, Lacey, my dear. From the very beginning."

A Mischievous Matchmaker

The stench in Mrs. Pratt's small cottage was nothing short of fearsome.

Grateful she had never been the swooning sort, Elnora Prescott gazed from the besmeared and fly-flecked window across the rolling green Devon fields, deliberately blocking everything else from her mind as she desperately sought to summon the image of Dulcie's errant lover.

She had met him once but, to own the truth, she had paid little attention to the unprepossessing young man at the time. How could she have possibly foreseen the dreadful series of misfortunes that lay in store for Dulcie?

To the best of her recollection, he had brown hair and brown eyes but even of that she was uncertain. She greatly feared she would fail to recognize the scoundrel even in the unlikely event he should walk into the room at this very moment.

Though she had never actually set foot in a place quite this noxious, her many years devoted to looking after the unfortunates in her father's parish had done much to prepare her for the dirt, the disorder, and the foul smells inside Mrs. Pratt's cottage. No one she had met during those years, however, had quite prepared her for Mrs. Pratt herself. Questioning the woman had been a well-nigh hopeless task.

She turned away from the window, determined to make one more effort to wring an ounce of sense from Mrs. Pratt's babble. Otherwise what could she do but choose the girl baby she believed to be the right one? But what if her choice proved wrong?

To Elnora's surprise, there was now someone with Mrs. Pratt, a handsome dark-haired gentleman who had evidently walked in through the open door while her back was turned. Could he possibly be Dulcie's betrayer spurred here by a guilty conscience? No, for if she had met this particular gentleman before, she had not the slightest doubt she would have remembered him.

Elnora remained where she was, watching and listening.

"Good God, woman, this plaguesome place stinks worse than the Augean stables." The elegantly dressed gentleman grimaced in disgust.

"I does me best, sir," Mrs. Pratt insisted. A plump, graying woman in her middle years, she wore a gown as filthy as the rooms she lived in. "Little 'uns can be a great trial."

"Nonsense!" the stranger snapped, waving his hand dismissively. "Properly cared for, children are no problem at all. Come now, tell me the names of these three."

Elnora suppressed a smile as she anticipated the answer, having asked that very question not more than ten minutes before.

"And how should I be knowing that, sir?" Mrs. Pratt succeeded in combining indignation with humility. "Those as what leaves 'em here often as not don't leave nothing else. 'Tis a lucky day the poor wee tykes come to me with so much as a stitch of clothes on their backs."

The man regarded her with baleful disbelief. "Surely you inquire as to a child's name when you take it in."

"No, sir. Never. Them as don't want 'em, don't want no names made known if you see what I mean."

He scowled. "Very well, then, which of these," he nodded at the three approximately year-old babies penned in a corner of the room, "are females?"

"Why, all of them, sir. They all come to me in the same week, the three of 'em. Calls 'em One, Two, Three, I does, after the way they come."

"Who brought each child?"

Elnora shook her head. She had already been through this with Mrs. Pratt. He was unlikely to learn anything more than she had about this grievous muddle, and she had learned nothing at all.

"Floyd," said Mrs. Pratt, "a man what knows I take in babies. Floyd gets 'em from here and there, but he ain't around for ye to talk to. 'Twouldn't be no use if he was. Kinda simple, Floyd is."

The stranger gave her one last scathing look, then turned to stare down at the three babies. When he did, Elnora, threading her way carefully between the piles of rubbish on the floor, walked toward him.

She had already examined the little girls and had found them so shockingly begrimed it had been impossible even to determine the actual color of their hair. One had blue eyes, another brown, and the third the most beautiful green eyes Elnora had ever seen.

Though not completely certain—she had never set eyes on Dulcie's baby—she thought the green-eyed child must be the right girl since, after all, Dulcie had green eyes. Not the clear bright shade of the baby's, Dulcie's were more hazel, actually, but green nonetheless.

Just as she opened her mouth to make the gentleman aware of her presence, he spoke without turning around.

"I want the child with the green eyes."

"No!" Elnora cried.

The man whirled to stare at her.

"That girl is my friend's baby," Elnora said. "I came here for her, and I intend to take her with me."

"No, you shall not." He spoke coldly. "I have decided on the child with the green eyes. Just who are you and where did you come from?" he demanded.

"My name is Miss Elnora Prescott and I arrived here before you."

He nodded frostily. "Lord Kendrick," he said, introducing himself.

She succeeded in making her brief nod even icier than his. "Since I made my decision first, my lord, the child is clearly mine," she told him.

"You are wrong, madam. Do you claim to recognize the child as belonging to"—here he paused, looking her up and down in an insolent manner that infuriated her—"your friend?"

Did he mean to imply she was lying about having a friend? Suggesting the child might be hers? How dare he! Elnora trembled with rage. Despite her effort to remain calm, her voice rose. "I admit being unable to positively identify the girl, but my friend has green eyes."

"And so does the person whose child I came to retrieve."

Elnora, vexed beyond endurance, drew herself up. Lord or no lord, he had no right to Dulcie's daughter. "In other words you fail to recognize the child."

The green-eyed baby began to whimper, and the other two immediately joined in, quickly working their way into full-throated bawling.

"You succeeded in upsetting them," Elnora accused. "I trust that satisfies you."

"How have I upset them? Am *I* shrieking?"

"I do not shriek!" she cried above the din. "I have never shrieked in my life."

"I suggest we settle this awkward situation elsewhere since I find the stench in this miserable cottage unendurable." Without allowing her time to answer yea or nay, he stalked across the room, limping slightly, pausing when he reached the door.

She marched across the room, through the door, and into the yard. The day had darkened, and it had begun to sprinkle, a chill April rain, and she saw that the driver of her rented rig had moved his carriage to the dubious shelter of an oak. Lord Kendrick's traveling chaise waited a short distance down the lane.

"Shall we?" He gestured toward the chaise.

Since her alternative was to stand conversing in the rain, she gave a curt nod.

After a few words to his coachman, Lord Kendrick assisted her inside. Shut in the dark interior of the chaise with him seated across from her proved to be far more intimate than she had expected. Annoyed as she was with him, she could scarcely help but be aware that he was not only an exceedingly good-looking man but that his nearness affected her in a strange way. Why, her heart was positively pounding!

Frowning, she realized with a pang how unaccustomed she was to being in the company of men. At twenty-three, the first bloom of her youth lay far behind her, and she had come to accept, albeit reluctantly, that she was well along the quiet, shaded, and often melancholy path leading to spinsterhood.

"If resolving this confusion, this mare's nest, is merely a question of money," he said once she was settled, "you will find me prepared—"

She raised her chin and held up an imperious hand. "Do I appear to you to be the sort of person to accept money in place of a child?"

"Pray make an attempt to be rational, Miss—Prescott, is it?"

"I care neither for your manner nor your insults, Lord Kendrick. I came to this—this baby farm to rescue my friend's daughter, and I mean to do precisely that."

"Baby farm?" He seemed bemused. "Is that what they call these beastly places? An appalling concept and certainly a miserable habitat for the babies."

Slightly mollified, since she agreed with him, she said, "My heart aches for those three little girls."

"Obviously something must be done. A felicitous solution for two of them would be for us to choose different children."

"A splendid idea. If you would choose baby two or baby three, our problem would be solved."

"I made my choice, as you are well aware. I warn you, Miss Prescott, I have the reputation of being a man who rarely if ever changes his mind once I arrive at a decision."

When his gaze again roamed over her, making her uncomfortable, she forced herself to sit still so as not to give him the satisfaction of recognizing her unease. "I have never considered inflexibility a trait to admire," she told him. "After all, you admit to never having seen the child you came to rescue."

"That fact has nothing whatsoever to do with the matter. After carefully studying the children, I harbor not the slightest doubt concerning which of the three is the right girl."

"But neither do I, and we both selected the same girl. I warn you I have no intention of backing down."

His dark eyes fastened on her blue ones, deliberately trapping her gaze for a long moment, disconcerting her further.

"I should have expected trouble when I first saw your stubborn chin," he said.

The shape of her chin was no concern of his! "I realize a lord such as yourself has more influence than I do," she told him, "and so you may quite likely prevail over me in dealing with Mrs. Pratt. But you, Lord Kendrick, would be making a dire mistake. I happen to be well-nigh positive that that child is not whoever you believe she is."

"And you would be justified beyond a shadow of a doubt in taking her?"

Elnora bit her lip, recalling the many times her minister father had warned her that falsehoods, even small fibs, were sins. "I believe I chose the right girl," she said slowly, "but I must admit there is an ever so slight possibility I might be mistaken."

"As I might be," he confessed. With a sigh, he said, "We seem to have reached an impasse."

A tapping on the chaise door gave them both a start. When Lord Kendrick opened the door, Elnora saw Mrs. Pratt, a shawl over her head and shoulders, standing in the rain.

"Me lord, miss," she said ingratiatingly, " 'tis sorry I am to be bothering ye, but there be one way to settle the matter. Ye can take all three of the babes off me hands. Won't cost ye much more than taking the one."

Flabbergasted, Lord Kendrick stared at Elnora and she stared back at him. All three? Having seen the misery the babies lived in, she wished she could save all of them, but it was impossible since she had neither the wherewithal nor the facilities for doing so. On the other hand, surely Lord Kendrick must have both. He could certainly see to it that the other two little girls found homes where they would be raised decently.

Since he seemed to be waiting for her opinion, she gave him a slight, hopeful nod. His eyebrows shot up and then he turned back to Mrs. Pratt.

"Please be kind enough to wait in your cottage," he ordered, "while Miss Prescott and I discuss your suggestion."

"One other thing," Mrs. Pratt said. "I'm certain Floyd wouldn't mind having a go at cleaning that stable of yours."

"Stable? What stable?"

"That aging stable that's so filthy. Floyd's a dab hand at mucking out manure."

Lord Kendrick shook his head. "Sorry," he said, "that particular stable was thoroughly cleaned some time ago."

"Never hurts a body to ask," Mrs. Pratt said before hurrying off through the rain.

"You *must* realize," Elnora said once the carriage door was closed, "we have a duty to remove those three girls from this ghastly place. Heaven only knows what might befall them here. If I had the funds to provide for them, I would be more than happy to, but unfortunately my circumstances are much too modest to allow for such a—"

"Then you should be quite willing to listen to my suggestion."

She looked at him guardedly.

"Though we find ourselves at sixes and sevens," he said, "as to whether or not the girl with the green eyes is yours—I do beg your pardon, your friend's—we both agree it would be absolutely criminal to allow Mrs. Pratt to keep any of the children."

She nodded.

"It seems only fair," he said, "that if I assume the care of

281

all three, you should offer to assist me. First of all in coping with the children on the journey to my home at Seacliff Hall in Cornwall. My plans definitely did not include returning with three tiny children. The rest of your, ah, duties can be discussed after our arrival. And you have no occasion to look at me askance, for my maiden aunt resides there with me."

That was all very well, but why did he persist in gazing at her so intently? She wore a drab dark green traveling dress, a matching spencer, and a far from modish bonnet; she had never considered herself to be a beauty, even when dressed in her finest clothes. His words were innocuous enough, but she sensed a dark and hidden meaning lurking beneath the surface.

"While I understand why you would need my help on the journey," she said primly, hoping she showed nothing of her increasing disquiet, "I fail to see what else you might expect of me."

His slight smile did nothing to reassure her. "I prefer to wait until a more auspicious occasion to outline my plans. When that time comes, Miss Prescott, I expect to find you willing enough to give me what I want."

Elnora and Lord Kendrick sat side by side in the chaise watching the three girls sleeping serenely on the seat opposite them, the babies lulled by the rhythm of the horses' hooves, the soft tattoo of the rain, and the gentle swaying of the coach. For a considerable time, preoccupied with their thoughts, they were both silent.

Lord Kendrick faced a moral dilemma, albeit, to his mind, a rather trivial one. When, after deciding to take all three babies with them to Seacliff Hall, he had walked to Miss Prescott's rented rig to order the driver to transfer her belongings to his chaise, he had chanced to notice an open letter on the seat. The scrawled word "baby" caught his eye, and he had, despite a few misgivings about the propriety of his action, scanned the brief note.

And quickly discovered, in contradiction to his half-formed suspicion, that Miss Prescott actually had a friend named Dulcie — Dulcie had, in fact, penned the letter — who implored Elnora to rescue her baby girl.

Hence his dilemma: Should he reveal his discovery to Miss Prescott and apologize for his mistaken assumption when by so doing he would be forced to admit he had secretly read her private correspondence?

Since apologies had never come easily to him, he decided to say nothing, reasoning that in any event he had made no accusations, having merely hinted in a most general and discreet way at an impropriety on her part. In the future, his words and actions would demonstrate his new-found respect for her virtue.

This lightly taken decision was to have unexpected and unfortunate consequences . . .

While Lord Kendrick was thus pondering how to resolve his dilemma, Elnora's anger was mounting as she recalled each and every one of his not-so-subtle aspersions on her character. Evidently he refused to take her word that the baby was Dulcie's; for some reason he wanted to believe she was the mother.

How dare he think such a thing!

Perhaps, she told herself, he entertained this abominable suspicion because of his own character and his own dubious proclivities. She was forced to admit she considered him fascinating; other women, less susceptible than she, must have found him equally appealing. Combine his attractiveness with the debauched ways of the *ton* where he undoubtedly spent most of his time — tales of pleasure-seeking rakes and their bits of muslin had spread to every nook and cranny of the realm — and the truth became clear.

The baby Lord Kendrick sought was most certainly his own, a by-blow from some romantic indiscretion. How natural, then, for him to suspect another, in this instance herself, of committing a folly so akin to his own.

As she reached this unpleasant conclusion, Elnora edged away from him until she sat in the far corner of the chaise, determined to remain aloof while enduring as best she could this journey with him to Seacliff Hall. She pictured what the Cornwall home of a man of his depraved character must be like, imagining a brooding fortresslike mansion of dark stone perched high on a cliff overlooking an angry sea whose waves crashed against a rocky shore.

She shuddered involuntarily at the thought of the ghastly secrets that the house, from its dank dungeons to its crenellated towers, must be privy to. But she refused to let him intimidate her. Though she would be forced to tolerate his presence until she rescued and returned Dulcie's child, she would, by word and deed, show him she considered his profligate ways to be abhorrent to her.

Lord Kendrick broke the silence with the first foray of his campaign to ingratiate himself with her. "How clever of you, Miss Prescott," he said, "to have me cut the carriage robe into three pieces to create blankets for the babies."

When she said nothing in reply to his praise, he made a second attempt to melt her iciness. "And how farsighted of you," he said, "to think of stopping in the village to purchase other necessities for them, including milk and bread to feed the babies if they should awaken. I expect they will, however, sleep for the entire journey to Seacliff Hall. As you heard me tell Mrs. Pratt, with a bit of thought and careful preparation, babies are easily cared for."

When she still said nothing in reply, he glanced in her direction and found her staring straight ahead, her face impassive. By God, he told himself, she did have a stubborn chin. Though he would hesitate to call her pretty — handsome, perhaps, with her chestnut hair and blue eyes — she possessed a spirit and a determination that appealed to him. As he grew older — he had turned twenty-nine only the month before — and especially since his return to England from fighting on the Continent under Wellington, he had grown ever more wearied of the fluttering coquettishness of the young ladies of the *ton*.

Praise had failed to soften her, but surely, he thought, there must be some subject that would engage her interest, that would give him an opening to pierce her armor. He tried once more, this time being deliberately outrageous: "Can you hazard a guess as to what crossed my mind when you endorsed Mrs. Pratt's suggestion that we take all three babies?" he asked. Without expecting or waiting for an answer, he said, "I recalled shopping for a waistcoat last winter at Swan & Edgar's when, unable to decide which of three I preferred, I told the clerk to send them all."

"Babies are not waistcoats," she said indignantly.

"Certainly not!" He quickly tried to take advantage of her spark of interest. "In the first place, babies have names while waistcoats do not. I, for one, consider it a botheration having to refer to these little girls as Miss One, Miss Two, and Miss Three; therefore I propose we assign them more appropriate names. I suggest we call them Mary, Maud, and Millicent."

Elnora shook her head. "I have no decided preference for the other two, but as for my baby"—she paused, surprised at her mistake in referring to Dulcie's child as hers—"for my friend's baby, the one with the green eyes, I intend to call her Faith."

He shrugged. "An excellent suggestion," he told her, "though by consenting to the name I do not agree that the baby belongs to your friend rather than mine. If she is to be Faith, numbers Two and Three shall perforce be Hope and Charity."

"Just so. Faith, Hope, and Charity, these three."

Elnora heard herself stuttering the last few words as the chaise left the smooth road and began jouncing across ruts and in and out of holes. One of the babies began to whimper.

"Hope has started to cry," Lord Kendrick told her. "Perhaps if you fed her some of the bread and milk?"

Elnora lifted the blue-eyed girl onto her lap and handed her a chunk of bread which Hope immediately began to gnaw on.

"Good, she's stopped crying," Lord Kendrick said, then frowned when the brown-eyed girl began to wail. "Now Charity has begun crying," he said. (An unnecessary observation, she thought). "I suggest you put Hope down on the seat while you feed Charity," he added. "Notice, if you will, how Faith shows her more amiable disposition by continuing to sleep peacefully."

"Will you hold Hope while I feed Charity?" she asked.

"I must decline, for I know nothing about the correct method of holding babies. Ah, now their screams have awakened Faith. Here, let me pick her up and quiet her."

"You should nestle the child, Lord Kendrick, not shake her like that."

He scowled at Elnora. "She obviously must be hungry; be so kind as to pass Charity to me while you feed Faith."

She willingly exchanged babies with him.

"Do all babies squirm like this?" he demanded. "How in the name of heaven can I be expected to hold her?"

"Place her against your shoulder and pat her on the back."

"Like this? Ah, she *is* becoming quieter. Charity evidently appreciates a man's firm touch."

Elnora gasped. "Hope is about to fall from the seat; catch her quickly! Hold her in your other arm while I finish feeding Faith."

"Why does Hope try to crawl away from me, Miss Prescott?"

"Perhaps her woman's instinct has warned her to be wary of you, Lord Kendrick."

He glanced at Elnora with a look of questioning puzzlement, but all he said was, "There, I have her. Now both of them are out of harm's way."

"Please hold Faith again while I give the last of the milk to Hope."

They juggled the babies back and forth until all three had been fed bread and milk.

"Capital," he said. "At last each and every one of them is quiet. At least for the present. Miss Prescott, I perceive a general principle emerging from the midst of this chaos: a husband and wife should never permit themselves to be outnumbered by their children."

She winced as she felt a sudden pang. He had said "a

husband and wife," and for a moment she had imagined herself married with a dear child much like Faith. Almost immediately the unlikelihood of that ever happening swept over her, making her draw in her breath as she experienced a stab of regret.

"Are you all right, Miss Prescott?" he asked. "You appear distressed."

Although surprised he had noticed her anguish, she kept a note of asperity in her voice when she answered. "Quite all right, my lord," she said. After a pause, she went on. "I admit to being somewhat astonished that you arrived at Mrs. Pratt's without a nursemaid for the baby you expected to find."

"I deny being a complete fool, Miss Prescott. The young woman I engaged fell ill at the last moment, and I decided not to delay my search for my—that is, for this child. I never expected to be coerced into taking three."

Though she found it impossible to imagine this arrogant man being coerced into anything, Elnora held back her tart rejoinder.

They rode in silence with two of the babies in his arms and one in hers. The coachman's whip cracked, and the chaise gathered speed as it rumbled over a relatively even roadway. All at once they were subjected to a particularly violent jarring.

"Oh my God," he exclaimed.

"You should caution your man to drive slower on these frightful Cornwall roads," she told him.

"Dash it all, the jolting of the coach is nothing. Look here at the shoulder of my coat."

"Evidently you spent too long walking in the rain."

"I assure you, Miss Prescott, that my coat was completely dry not more than two minutes ago. Moreover, I feel a dampness in other places that the rain had nothing to do with."

"I believe you were the one, Lord Kendrick, who stated that with proper planning the care of babies was a simple task. Could it be you were living in a fool's paradise? Obvi-

287

ously you failed to notice I placed a cloth on my shoulder as well as on my lap."

"You were the one who suggested bringing all three babies with us. I recall that most clearly." He blinked, grimacing. "Do you smell something?" he asked. "From which one does that indescribable stench emanate? Perhaps both? You must change their whatever-you-call-thems at once."

All three babies began to wail.

"Good God!" he exclaimed.

"Raising your voice will only make them cry louder. I intend to change them as quickly as I can."

"How unfortunate they lack the ability to talk, to tell us what they want rather than communicating by means of this infernal howling. I should think they'd know how to speak by this age. Are they slow-witted?"

"Merely too young. Lord Kendrick, do stop her! Faith is trying to open the carriage door!"

"Damnation. No, Miss Faith, none of that. There, I have her in hand." He sat uneasily on the edge of the seat gingerly holding a squalling baby under each arm. "I understand why people have children," he said. "It represents the triumph of passion over prudence. Why they *want* children in the first instance is completely beyond my comprehension. It must be the triumph of blind optimism over experience."

"Children are wonderful. Adorable. Look at the three of them, so sweet and so helpless, all of them needing someone to look after them."

"Obviously we view the matter rather differently. To me it seems that Wellington could have defeated Napoleon merely by strewing small children in his path and allowing the Emperor the opportunity to attempt to rescue them. Such a tactic would have ended the war sooner while saving many, including myself, considerable pain."

She recalled his slight limp. "Were you with Wellington?" she asked.

"I happened to serve under the Iron Duke in Spain and at Waterloo."

As she changed the second baby, she nodded, impressed despite herself.

"I recall that after I received my wound," he said, "the surgeon offered me a swig of brandy before he proceeded to remove the bullet. Perhaps a few drops would be the prescription that would calm our charges."

He handed the last of the weeping children to her. When all three were dry and clean, their wailing faded to whimpers and stopped altogether when she began to softly sing a lullaby.

The babies were soon asleep.

"They do appear harmless," he admitted. "When sleeping."

"Not only harmless, beautiful."

"Speaking of brandy reminds me—" Lord Kendrick reached beneath the seat and brought forth a wicker hamper. Unhooking and opening the lid, he rummaged inside and then held up a bottle of amber wine.

"Shall we have a sip of madeira?" he asked her. Bringing two tumblers from the hamper, he placed them on the seat between them. "If you would be so kind as to hold the glasses steady—I must remember to speak to Squire Jamison about the upkeep of this blasted road."

She hesitated and then held the glasses while he poured the wine. He raised his glass, and after again hesitating, she did the same. To refuse would be churlish, she decided; after all, a few sips would do her no harm.

"To amity between us," he proposed as a toast. "To no longer being at daggers' points."

"To Faith, Hope, and Charity," she said.

As they sipped the wine, Elnora felt the coach veer to the right. Looking from the window, she saw that the rain had stopped, and low above the horizon, the late afternoon sun shone between pink-tinged clouds. The road ahead of them curved into a grove of trees; beyond the trees the rays of the setting sun glinted from the windows of a house.

"At long last," he said with a sigh. "I bid you welcome, Miss Prescott, to Seacliff Hall."

Elnora Prescott received two surprises on her arrival at Seacliff Hall.

The first was the Hall itself.

When their chaise emerged from the trees and the Hall rose before her, she was reminded of a child's simple drawing of a house—she saw a rectangular block with a short sloping roof and a red-brick chimney at each end. Instead of the fortress-like towers she had expected, there were four small turrets, one at each corner. The three-story Hall, built of variegated gray stone, was certainly imposing, but she had to admit it would best be described as charming rather than forbidding.

Beyond the house and below the cliffs which had inspired its name, the gray sea stretched into the banks of fog hovering offshore to the north and west. A lone fishing boat sailed toward the shore escorted by swooping seagulls.

Her second surprise came when they entered the Hall. Mrs. Allison, the housekeeper, and all the other servants welcomed Lord Kendrick's return with expressions of delight. Not only did they exclaim over the three babies, they greeted the master of the Hall with an undisguised warmth.

Elnora had always believed that one of the best measures of a gentleman's character was how his servants perceived him. They saw him at his best and at his worst; they were the victims or the beneficiaries of his moods; they became privy to many of his secrets. Since she had only recently formed a decidedly poor opinion of Lord Kendrick, their obviously sincere smiles served to confuse her.

Of course, she told herself, a man might display one face in Town and another in the country. He could be a rake in London and an amiable gentleman in Cornwall. While possible, was this likely? she wondered. She admitted she wanted to think well of him, wanted him to be the benevolent employer his servants appeared to consider him. But only, she assured herself, because she desired to think the best of Lord Kendrick just as she did of everyone, not because she had become favorably disposed toward him.

During the sumptuous dinner in the great hall with Lady Adelaide Mathias, his aunt, sitting to his right and Elnora to his left, Lord Kendrick went out of his way to be charming and ingratiating. So much so that her suspicions concerning his motives surfaced once again.

"May I show you the estate in the morning?" he asked. "You do ride?"

She had the perfect excuse to refuse. "I fear I failed to pack a riding habit in my portmanteau."

"We can surely find something appropriate, my dear," Lady Adelaide put in.

To refuse such kindness would be churlish. Besides, she had never visited this part of Cornwall before. And, Elnora admitted reluctantly, the thought of riding with Lord Kendrick stirred something within her, a something she identified as a desire to learn more about his divided character. It was curiosity, she assured herself, nothing more.

So, against her better judgment, she appeared in the doorway of the drawing room after breakfast the next morning wearing the dark green riding habit that Miss Mathias had produced, a costume that fit her reasonably well. Lord Kendrick looked somewhat startled as he hurried across the room to greet her. Though he was still dressed in black, she saw he had exchanged the finery of Town for a simpler country style without losing a whit of his natural elegance.

"Before we ride, pray come with me," he said, leading her up the stairs and along a hallway to a room at the rear of the house. Opening the door, he stood aside and said, "Behold."

The three babies, shiningly clean and attired in white wool dresses, were playing on the rug under the watchful eye of a nursemaid. Faith immediately abandoned a pile of blocks and crawled toward them when they entered, pulling herself onto her feet by holding onto Elnora's skirt. Hope and Charity followed her.

After being introduced to the nursemaid Kate, and Tillie, a young girl from the village, Elnora knelt, hugging each of the little girls in turn before helping them pile wooden block upon wooden block to build a zigzag tower that Faith, to the delight of the other babies as well as Lord Kendrick, quickly sent crashing to the floor.

A short while later, as she and Lord Kendrick walked from the house to the stable, Elnora said, "Last night I wrote to my friend and told her how I came to be in Cornwall. I asked her to describe her baby."

"And you expect her to reply saying her daughter is none other than green-eyed Faith?"

She gave him a suspicious glance, but his face was impassive. Was he accusing her and Dulcie of conspiring against him?

"Yes, I do expect something of the sort," she said.

He scowled. "You will discover you are wrong. However, I have no desire for us to be at sixes and sevens on such a glorious day. This morning the children are exactly what you called them yesterday, beautiful, and even the weather has taken a decided turn for the better."

She looked up at the clear blue sky as she felt the summerlike breeze caress her face. The day *was* delightful. Since Lord Kendrick obviously wanted a truce, and since she was naturally peace-loving, she was more than willing to agree to one.

They rode away from the house with the sun at their backs, Lord Kendrick astride a blood bay gelding, Elnora on a gray mare. Though they followed the shoreline, they were forced to ride a considerable distance inland because of gorges gouged in the cliffs as though by the strokes of a mythical sword. She heard the surf rumbling on the rocks below, saw the mist hanging like a gray shroud over the ocean, and savored the tang of the sea.

When they slowed their horses to a walk, he said, "That riding habit becomes you."

"Thank you," she told him.

"My sister Violet left it at the Hall when she ran off to marry an Irish officer. Against my father's wishes."

While she was wondering if she should inquire about what had happened to his sister, he sighed.

292

"Poor Violet. She had green eyes, you know, much like Faith's. Unfortunately I was away when she left home and so was unable to take her side. Our mother had died some years before." He spoke slowly and hesitantly, as though each word caused him pain. "I might not have approved of this Lt. Seamus O'Neal, but I would never have turned my back on my sister."

"The baby you sought at Mrs. Pratt's was your sister's?" Elnora wondered if she could believe him.

He nodded. "O'Neal was posted to Egypt not long after the birth and then Violet took ill with a fever and died. Alone. I wrote to O'Neal after I returned home, after the deaths of my sister and father, but I never received an answer. The man might well be dead himself."

She said nothing, sharing his anguish, and they rode on without speaking. A rabbit scurried across their path, giving her a start, seagulls cried out from above the cliffs, and ahead of them she saw long wisps of white, shimmering in the sun as mist was borne in from the sea.

When they reached a fork in the path, Lord Kendrick reined to the right and they rode toward the sound of the sea along the edge of a gorge, stopping atop a barren promontory high above a pebbled beach. He pointed to the far side of the gorge, and through the mist that came and went in restless swirls, she saw the dark stone ruins of an ancient battlement.

"Nothing more remains of the castle of Tintagel," he told her.

"Tintagel." The name reverberated in her mind. "I remember hearing a legend about Tintagel when I was a child."

"A legend? Here in Cornwall we prefer to believe it all actually happened more than a thousand years ago, that this ruin was the Duke of Cornwall's castle where he lived happily with his wife Igerne until the great chieftain Uther Pendragon fell passionately in love with her."

"As I recall, a sorcerer cast a spell to bring Igerne and Pendragon together."

293

"Not exactly. According to the story, a magician aided Pendragon by having him appear to Igerne in the form of her husband and so allowed her to accept him without guilt."

She glanced at him, wondering if his words carried a hidden meaning, some reference to herself and his unwarranted suspicions about her and the baby. No, she decided, he meant only to relate the ancient story.

"And the son born to Uther Pendragon and Igerne," she said, "came to rule the land as King Arthur."

"Precisely. Below us, where the sea has formed a hollow in the rocks, is the magician's cave, Merlin's cave. The Knights of the Round Table, the sword Excalibur, the kingdom of Camelot, and the search for the Holy Grail all had their beginnings here in the mists of Tintagel."

Watching Lord Kendrick as he looked first at the ruins and then across the white-capped sea, his dark brown eyes narrowed against the steady breeze, his black hair ruffled, she could imagine him as one of those ancient Britons who had fought first against the invading Romans and then the Saxons, or as a knight wearing a lady's favor as he jousted or a warrior crossing a drawbridge as he rode into the unknown in search of adventure.

The wind off the sea strengthened, sending shreds and tatters of white whirling about them, the mist becoming thicker until she could no longer see the castle ruins. Lord Kendrick turned and, swinging his horse away from the sea, led her back the way they had come.

"No matter whether King Arthur lived or is purely mythical," he said, "I still believe there's something magical about this land of Cornwall. If Arthur returns to save England in her hour of greatest need, and there are those who are certain he will, I fully expect him to appear here at Tintagel."

She smiled as his romantic notion struck a chord in herself, making her recall long-forgotten daydreams from her childhood when she still believed in the existence of knights who rescued maidens, still believed that someday, somehow she would be roused from her prosaic life by a prince's kiss.

When they left Tintagel, she thought he was leading her back to Seacliff Hall, but after several minutes he swung his mount farther inland, and they followed a track to the crest of a low hill and down the other side into a woods.

"The last time I rode this way," he told her, "must have been more than ten years ago."

The track they were on became overgrown and then disappeared entirely, forcing them to proceed at a walk through the dense growth. They came to a rippling stream and followed it until at last she saw sunlight ahead of them and after a few minutes they emerged from the trees into a glade of new-green grass.

Lord Kendrick dismounted and led the two horses along the stream to a fallen tree where he stopped and reached up for her. She slid from the saddle, and he caught her, holding her for a long moment with his hands gripping her waist. Her breath caught: no man had ever caused such an inexplicable quiver of excitement to course through her.

He lowered her to the ground and when he failed to release her, she glanced up at him and, reading surprise in his eyes, wondered if he had been touched by a feeling akin to hers. Quickly dropping his hands, he turned away to sit on a fallen tree; she sat at his side.

"This was my favorite spot when I was a young boy," he said. "A place where other boys and I played knights and dragons or where I came to be by myself to read or to do nothing at all except perhaps to dream."

She smiled as his words brought back memories of her own childhood. "When I was a girl," she said, "we lived in a village on the River Dart. There was an abandoned scow beached on the shore, and I loved to climb aboard her and sit watching the boats sail down the river, wondering where they were bound, imagining myself on larger ships on my way to Singapore or Bombay, to Egypt or Jamaica."

He smiled at her. "I always wanted to spend a night on top of the pyramids, to swim the Hellespont, to visit the Parthenon."

"When I listened to my father read the Bible to us on

Sunday evenings, I imagined myself exploring the Holy Land. Even though I realized the farthest I would probably ever travel from our home in Devon would be to London."

He drew in a deep breath, and when she looked at him, she saw that his eyes were closed. "On the same day I received my wound," he said, "my best friend was killed. We were riding side by side when the bullet hit him. After my regiment returned to England from Waterloo, most of my companions would laugh and make light of their experiences when asked about the war. I understood why they had to, but I could never bring myself to do that."

"You must have hated the fighting."

"No, not true. I both hated it and loved it. I abhorred the senselessness of the killing, yet I was drawn to the excitement of battle and enjoyed the camaraderie we shared. When I returned to London, the interests of the *ton*, fashion and gambling and so forth, seemed trivial to me. Which, I suppose, is why I came back to Seacliff Hall."

"Are you happy here?" she asked.

"For the most part. I found peace, I appreciate the quiet of the country, and yet, from time to time, Cornwall seems a lonely place."

She nodded, thinking again of her own childhood, and to her surprise she found herself telling him of her life in the parsonage, the joy of growing up in a happy home with a loving mother and father, of her mother's untimely death and her father's eventual remarriage.

"Helen is quite young, almost as young as myself," she told him, "and one might think, as I thought, that we would have a great deal in common, but quite the opposite turned out to be the case. For a while after Mama passed on, I was mistress of the parsonage, now Helen is; for a while I was first in my father's affections, now, as is only right and proper, he must cleave to his wife."

"So you, too, are lonely at times," he said. "I wonder whether, if we could see into their hearts and minds, most people are."

"You must take me for a complainer. To own the truth, I

296

fail to understand why I said what I did. My life, for the most part, has been a perfectly happy one."

"As has mine." He stood and reached down, taking her hand and helping her to her feet. He kept holding her hand, and for an instant she thought he meant to draw her to him to comfort her. Even the notion that he meant to kiss her darted through her mind.

He did neither. Instead, he released her hand and turned abruptly away. She felt an unexpected stab of disappointment.

As they rode back to Seacliff Hall, she was surprised by a rising tide of anger directed not at Lord Kendrick but at herself. How could she have become so bemused, how could she be so presumptuous as to suppose that this man, a lord who could pick and choose among all the titled, fetching young ladies of the *ton*, could be seriously interested in her?

The notion was preposterous, the dream of an addled miss, of the slip of a girl she once had been rather than of the mature woman she had grown to be. The enchanted air of Cornwall, she told herself, must have encouraged these romantic daydreams to creep unbidden into her mind.

Just as a child on a swing will soar high into the sky only to plummet earthward once more, so her thoughts turned, perversely, from extravagant hope to abysmal fear, and what she had seen tinged by a rosy hue now appeared dark and foreboding.

Somehow Lord Kendrick had discovered a flaw in her — wasn't he, a man of the world, experienced in these matters? — and shamelessly exploited it with the intention of leaving her vulnerable to whatever scheme he had in mind. She shuddered in apprehension.

No matter what he might propose, no matter how deviously he might present his plan and no matter how innocent it might appear, he would find her on her guard.

As the three little girls played on the sloping lawn beside the hedge bordering the garden, the midmorning sun tinged the fair hair of Hope and Charity with golden gleams and revealed unexpected glints of auburn in Faith's darker tresses. Faith, with a charming unselfishness, held out her hand to Hope, offering her something, while young Tillie played peek-a-boo with Charity.

Faith was a most lovable child, Elnora thought as she watched from the side terrace. Footfalls on the stone flags warned of someone approaching, and the quick leap of her heart, as much as her sidelong glance, told her who it was. Last night at dinner he had asked her to call him by his first name. Though she still hesitated to say it aloud, she now savored his name in her mind, smiling slightly. Wade. Wade Mathias, third Earl of Kendrick.

After three weeks of being in one another's company, it was probably true they were well enough acquainted to use less formal terms of address than "Miss Prescott" and "Lord Kendrick." Loath though she was to admit it, hearing her given name on his tongue thrilled her. When he called her Elnora, the lingering way he said the word—dare she call it the affectionate way?—made her feel both attractive and desirable. Only her fear that she was allowing him to become too familiar tainted her pleasure.

Her smile disappeared abruptly as she realized exactly what Faith was handing to Hope—red berries plucked from the nearby hedge. "No!" she cried, rushing down the terrace steps and across the lawn. "No, Faith! No, Hope! Stop!"

Tillie turned toward her in startled alarm. Hurrying past the girl, Elnora flung herself onto her knees beside Hope, grasped the hand the child was bringing to her open mouth, and took away the berries Hope obviously intended to eat.

Hope burst into tears.

Elnora turned to Tillie. "Make certain she has no berries in her mouth," she ordered.

Picking up Faith, Elnora uncurled the child's fingers, removed more of the berries, and flung them into the hedge. The corners of Faith's mouth turned down and her lower lip trembled.

Elnora cuddled her soothingly, watching Wade stride

across the lawn to lift Charity into his arms and examine her hands and face. He nodded reassuringly just as Tillie, in a relieved though frightened voice, announced that Hope hadn't eaten any of the berries.

"I'm that sorry, milord," she added with a quaver in her voice. "I never thought about them berries being so close and all. Be they poison?"

"I'm not certain," he said. "Luckily, no harm was done, but to be safe move the blanket and the babies away from temptation and be more careful in the future. If there's anything for Faith to get into, she will. That child is mischief personified."

After the blanket was shifted far from the hedge and the other two girls were once again settled onto it with their toys, Elnora started to place Faith next to them. Faith, having a different notion, clung to her.

"Da!" she cried, refusing to be left. "Da!"

The word brought Elnora back to her own childhood, for it was the name she had once called her father. Without thinking, she said, "No, not Da. This is Da." She pointed to Wade, then blushed crimson when she realized what she had said.

Faith held out her arms to Wade. "Da!" she crowed triumphantly.

Grinning, he took her from Elnora's arms. With a nod toward her, he said to Faith, "Mama."

Faith, paying no attention, patted his face. "Da, Da," she crooned.

Reaching into his pocket, he brought forth a somewhat dented silver teething ring and offered it to Faith. She grasped it in her left hand, eyed it with interest, then brought the ring to her mouth. While she was distracted by her new toy, he placed her on the blanket.

"Shall we steal away?" he murmured to Elnora.

They walked beneath an arbor of climbing roses to the gazebo at the bottom of the lawn. The day was clear and sunny, the rumble of the sea beneath the cliffs muted.

"I wonder," he said after they were seated, "if I should ask

Tillie to take Kate's place when she leaves." The nursemaid had recently announced plans to marry and had given a month's notice.

"She does seem very young. As we witnessed only a few minutes ago."

"If it hadn't been for you—"

Savoring his praise yet feeling uncomfortable, she changed the subject. "Was that your teething ring you gave to Faith?" she asked.

He shook his head. "It was her mother's. Violet's."

Faith's mother, indeed! Elnora opened her mouth to protest, then paused, recalling him telling her that his sister had been appropriately named since she had always been a quiet, unassertive young woman. "As a child," she asked, "was your sister as mischievous as Faith?"

He studied his hands for a long moment. "In truth, no. I was the incorrigible Mathias offspring, not Violet. Which is why I was so astounded when I heard she found the courage to defy our father to marry this O'Neal chap." He looked sharply at her. "What about your friend Dulcie? As I recall, you mentioned you two more or less grew up together. Did she possess Faith's gumption?"

Elnora bit her lip. "Dulcie has always been rather timid. Whenever the two of us landed in trouble, I fear I was the ringleader."

He nodded as though his suspicions had been confirmed. "Have you noticed how bright Faith is? I believe her to be much more advanced than the other two girls."

"Yes, I agree."

"Three weeks have gone by," he said, "since you wrote to your friend, and still you have no word from her."

Did he believe Dulcie was a mere figment of her imagination? An attempt to deceive him? "I find the lack of news difficult to understand," she admitted. "Every day I expect a letter from Dulcie, and every day my hopes are dashed."

He shook his head, knowingly she thought, as if to tell her he no more believed her story about a friend now than he had the month before at Mrs. Pratt's. He clearly thought

300

she had gone there seeking her own child, born out of wed-lock.

With an effort, she controlled her outrage. "I do wish Dulcie would write," she said as calmly as she could. "I realize three weeks is a long time for me to impose on your hospitality."

He gave her a searching look. "I have an idea that might solve the problem," he said. "The notion occurred to me shortly after we met, but I felt we should know one another better before suggesting it. I think the time has come for me to put any feelings of possible impropriety aside and speak directly."

She folded her arms, waiting, distressed about what she feared he meant to suggest.

"I have a proposition to make to you," he said.

His words recalled their conversation on the day they rescued the babies. No matter how objectionable his proposal might be, she intended to hear him out, to give him the opportunity to reveal his true nature. How, she wondered, could she ever have thought such a devious man to be fascinating? He was obviously someone accustomed to using his charm to entice the unsuspecting.

"I admit to observing you closely since the day I met you at the infamous Mrs. Pratt's," he began. "My conclusion is that you like Cornwall and enjoy staying at Seacliff Hall. And I believe nothing I have done has given you cause to complain about me or my behavior. Am I correct?"

"I have no cause to complain," she said stiffly. "Until now, at least."

"Capital, since my notion is to ask you to consider remaining here at the Hall permanently. By so doing you would give me great pleasure, and you would, I hope, receive certain benefits in return."

She reddened. A few minutes before she had been overjoyed watching him playing with the children and seeing how sincerely interested he was in them and their welfare. During the last three weeks he had showed her respect if not affection. Now his words had turned her joy to pain. Had

301

he no compunction whatever about asking her to be his mistress? How little he must think of her to put her into this awkward situation!

"Surely," she protested, "Lady Adelaide would object to any such arrangement."

"Adelaide?" He sounded genuinely surprised. "I have no reason to think so. With all respect to my aunt, this matter concerns my affairs, not hers, so she would never oppose me."

He frowned. "It occurs to me," he said, "that you might think your rather limited experience would prove an insurmountable handicap. Nothing could be further from the truth; in my opinion, a woman with experience might have a hardness, an inflexibility, while someone such as yourself would be more willing to try new approaches. At the very least you could have a go at it and then cry off if you found the arrangement failed to please you."

Had he no sense of shame? She opened her mouth to speak but, her every feeling offended, she failed to find words to express her outrage.

"I would be the first to admit," he went on serenely, "that you might find your position here rather difficult at first in a social sense, rather betwixt and between, but the passage of time has a way of taking care of most things, and I expect it would in this case. Women in general and yourself in particular possess a certain innate capacity for love and affection, more so than we men, and I give you my word I will be the last to demand you fulfill all of the normal requirements during your first weeks or months at the Hall. There are those in Town who might dispute me, but I believe you will find me to be a patient man."

Still unable to speak, she shook her head vigorously.

Wade raised his hand. "Admit the truth," he said. "Since you first arrived in Cornwall, have you ever observed me being other than agreeable even when provoked? I think not. At the very least, I must seem rather inoffensive to you and, after all, nothing more than that is necessary."

"I believe I should leave before you say more."

When she started to rise, he gripped her wrist, stopping her. "You should refrain," he said, "from making a hasty decision you might well come to regret."

"I really have no desire to hear another word on the subject, Lord Kendrick."

He frowned at her use of his title. "Pray hear me out, Elnora," he said, "since I can think of several more reasons why you should change your mind and accept my offer."

"Please let me go," she said with anger threading her voice.

"Not before you listen to me." He proceeded to speak rapidly as if afraid she might break free and flee from the gazebo before he was able to finish. "I spend a certain amount of time in London during the Season," he said, "and so, if you think me as distasteful as you indicate, I can promise to be absent from Seacliff Hall now and again."

She closed her eyes and slowly shook her head back and forth.

"I could arrange for you to have quite limited duties in the beginning," he suggested, "then gradually increase the time allotted as you grew more knowledgeable and more comfortable with your role. I could also arrange convenient free days for you, Wednesdays for shopping and Sundays for church, for instance. And I think I can confidently promise there will be no more babies."

She gasped. Had he lost all sense of propriety? Not only suggesting church attendance but mentioning a limit on the number of babies.

"Every unmarried young woman should consider having a profession," he persisted. "Perhaps if you enjoy what I have to offer you, and I have every hope and expectation you will after you become accustomed to the routine, this could be yours. And if you ever grew weary with the country life at Seacliff Hall, I would be more than happy to give you a glowing reference. I could even personally recommend you to some of my good friends in Town."

Completely undone by his callousness, she pulled her hand from his and jumped to her feet. When he, too, started to rise, she put her hands on his chest and pushed him, hard, and he fell back onto the bench.

He blinked in surprise. "Believe me, I never meant to upset you. If you can, try to consider the matter from my point of view. Think how much better for me it would be if you were to remain here permanently. Then I would never again have to depend on the services of a hit-or-miss succession of girls from the village."

Choking back a sob, she turned from him and fled without answering. At the foot of the gazebo steps, she swung around to face him with tears in her eyes. "You may consider yourself at liberty to employ the services of all the village girls you want," she said. "And I hope you and they rot in hell together. Which you most assuredly will." She turned away from him and ran across the lawn to the house.

"Elnora!" he called after her. "Wait!"

When she ignored him, he stood and stared after her, shaking his head in bewilderment. "Damnation," he muttered to himself. "Never will I understand women. Why on earth would she get into such a high dudgeon over an offer to remain at the Hall to help care for the babies?"

Still shaking his head, he walked slowly toward the house as he reviewed in his mind everything he had said in an attempt to determine whether he had committed a faux pas of some sort. All at once he stopped and struck his forehead with his palm.

"Oh my God!" he cried. "What have I done?"

Wade overtook the sobbing Elnora outside the door to her bedchamber where he immediately confessed to having found and read Dulcie's letter asking her to help find her baby, apologizing profusely for this gross impropriety, and then explained he had been offering to employ her at Seacliff Hall to oversee the care of Faith, Hope, and Charity after Kate left to be married.

Brightening perceptibly, Elnora stifled her sobs.

Somewhat encouraged, he ventured to take her hand

while he told her again how much he regretted reading Dulcie's letter, sighing with relief when she accepted his apology. He never mentioned nor even alluded to her misinterpretation of his offer of employment although he was by now well aware she had suspected, nay, been certain, he had been asking her to remain at Seacliff Hall as his mistress.

Elnora also avoided referring to what she had viewed as his most indelicate proposal. She was well aware that Wade knew what she had thought, and she also knew he knew that she knew he knew it. Even with all this excessive knowing, they both deemed it wise to leave the truth unspoken, for they rightly believed that words, once uttered, often become as enduring as if carved in stone while mere thoughts were more apt to be written in the sand on the beach, ready to be washed away by the next high tide.

As he was about to leave her, he said, "Pray consider my offer of a position at Seacliff Hall. If not for my sake, for the children's."

Watching him walk away, Elnora sighed, realizing her feelings for him had undergone a sea change as soon as her doubts about his intentions had been dispelled. Just as the prodigal son was welcomed home with a feast of celebration while his righteous brother watched in dismay, just as the reformed rake's return to the congregation is greeted with hosannas of joy while the diligent worshiper who never left is unhonored and unsung, so Wade rose in her esteem to a higher level than he would have attained if she had never suspected him of reprehensible conduct.

Even as she came to see him in this new light, she recognized the impossibility of remaining indefinitely at Seacliff Hall. Here she was neither fish nor fowl. As much as she had come to love the babies, Faith in particular, she was afraid to stay. Not from any fear of Wade's intentions—he had totally exonerated himself in her eyes—but from a fear of the consequences of her own feelings.

Much later that evening, his last words to her before she left the drawing room to retire to her chamber were, "I hope and trust you reconsider."

"I fear I cannot," she murmured and was touched by his look of disappointment.

She lay awake for what seemed an eternity after the long clock in the hall chimed twelve—even the comforting rumble of the surf failed to soothe her—tossing and turning as she sought to come to terms with the realization that she loved Wade Mathias. Hers was an impossible love, she was well aware of that, a hopeless, unrequited love, but love nonetheless. All she could do to lessen her present pain and the possibility of even greater heartbreak to come was to leave Seacliff Hall just as soon as Dulcie's child was returned to its mother.

Shortly after reaching this decision, she fell into a sleep troubled by dreams of ships adrift in storms being buffeted by raging seas, dreams of loss and desolation. The memory of those dreams still had the power to overset her when, the next morning, she and Lady Adelaide sat with their embroidery in the drawing room.

The clatter of a carriage at the front of the Hall caused her to look up from a runner adorned with red and blue knights and their ladies. After a few minutes she heard voices in the hall. The drawing-room door was then thrown open, and Wade strode in followed by a blond curly-haired young man, meticulously garbed in the black of mourning, who crossed the room with the hint of a cock-of-the-walk swagger.

"Aunt Adelaide, Elnora," Wade said, "may I present Lt. Seamus O'Neal."

"No longer lieutenant," O'Neal said. "Now 'tis plain and simple Mr. Seamus O'Neal, recently arrived on these fair shores from the land of the pharaohs by way of the Emerald Isle."

He greeted the two ladies in turn, holding both Elnora's hand and her gaze a trifle longer than necessary. Elnora could imagine a shy and timid girl, as Wade had described his sister, being swept off her feet by this handsome man with a rogue's glint in his blue eyes.

When she glanced at Wade, she found him glowering at her. Almost, she thought with a prickling of pleasure, as if he were jealous. She was quite taken with the notion that he might be.

"Mr. O'Neal," Wade said, "has come seeking his young daughter."

O'Neal nodded. "I was directed to Seacliff Hall by the avaricious Mrs. Pratt after several coins of the realm found their way from my purse into hers."

Wade led them up the stairs to the nursery where Kate and Tillie were feeding the three girls. "Mr. O'Neal is able to identify his daughter," he told Elnora, "by a small birthmark on her left shoulder."

" 'Tis a wee crimson mark," O'Neal added, "most befittingly shaped like an Irish shamrock, or so I always described it to my dear departed Violet." When he mentioned his wife's name, he removed a rather large handkerchief from his pocket and dabbed at his eyes.

Hearing of the birthmark, Elnora gave an inaudible sigh of relief since she had seen the mark not on Faith but on Hope, the baby whose eyes were as blue as Seamus O'Neal's.

To Elnora's surprise, Wade said, "Perhaps this is your daughter," nodding toward Charity rather than Faith. Why would he, after insisting for all these weeks that Faith must surely be his sister's child, now suggest differently to Seamus O'Neal?

"No?" Wade said after both of Charity's shoulders were shown to be unblemished. "Perhaps, then, this is the one." Again he ignored Faith.

"Aye," O'Neal said when Hope's birthmark was uncovered, "she's the sweet bairn who's never once been out of my thoughts all these many months." He picked up his daughter, gave her a toss in the air and caught her. Elnora was pleased to hear the baby crow with delight.

"We call her Hope," she told him.

"Her baptismal name is Katherine Anne Mary O'Neal," he said, "though under the circumstances I do believe 'tis

307

Katherine Anne Mary Violet O'Neal I'll be calling her. In memory of her dear departed mother."

When Elnora saw him glance in the direction of his pocket, she thought he would once more reach for his handkerchief but, with both hands occupied cradling the baby, he did not.

Despite Wade's repeated invitation, Seamus O'Neal declined to remain at Seacliff Hall. " 'Tis home to the land of my forefathers I must be journeying," he told them. "My mother, God bless her soul, will care for wee Katherine while I pursue my fortune." He lowered his voice. "I have wonderful prospects," he confided.

After watching his carriage disappear into the woods, Wade said to Elnora, "Perhaps he intends to join a troupe of traveling players. His bombast and posturings might enthrall audiences in some of the smaller Irish villages."

"I thought him quite charming."

Wade gave her a frowning look.

"And he did return to England for his daughter as soon as he was able to," she pointed out.

"Before he left he reminded me several times that Katherine Anne Mary et cetera is my niece and expressed the fervent hope I would not forget the fact. I assured him she would be remembered." Wade thrust his arms out as though pushing his way through a thicket. "Would you object," he asked, "if I opened the window to dispel the overpowering scent of his pomade?"

She shook her head—the scent *was* rather strong—but in the end he left the window closed. "I was mistaken about Faith," he admitted. "She may be your friend's child after all."

"I intend to write to Dulcie again without delay. I admit that she does, on occasion, behave like a flibbertigibbet, but I fail to understand why she never answered my letter."

As she was leaving the room, he said, "Elnora," and when she turned he went on, "O'Neal seemed taken with you, though perhaps he behaves thus with all young women. Did you truly find him charming?"

308

She hesitated and then, with a slight smile, said, "No."

A short while later as she sat writing at the desk in her bedchamber, she heard hoofbeats at the rear of the house. Going to the window, she looked down and saw Wade galloping away from the Hall along the track at the top of the cliffs, horse and rider a dark silhouette against the gray offshore mist. She remained at the window until he disappeared from her view.

Her letter to Dulcie was posted in the village that very evening but was never received nor answered because on the following day an ebullient Dulcie, as petite and pert as she had been before her illness, arrived at Seacliff Hall accompanied by—

"Mr. Richard Blanding." Dulcie made the announcement with pride as she introduced him to Wade and Elnora in the drawing room. "My husband since Thursday last."

Richard smiled and bowed, but before he could speak Dulcie said, "Dear Elnora, I fully intended to write but, lord a mercy, by the time your letter arrived so had Richard, and we had so much on our plates what with the posting of the banns and all the preparations for the wedding that I had not a moment to spare, and then in a twinkling it was too late since we were already on our way to you." She glanced at Wade. "Lord Kendrick," she said, "I do find Seacliff Hall dreadfully imposing."

She leaned toward Elnora and whispered, "Richard journeyed thousands of miles from Canada to ask me to marry him, never even knowing about the baby." She paused. "Elnora, do you like my new bonnet?" she asked. "I bought it last week in Frankel's, the new shop on Picadilly near Fortnum and Mason. It was ghastly dear."

Elnora, overjoyed to learn of her friend's marriage, said, "You must be very happy. And I do think the bonnet becomes you."

Dulcie nodded. "Richard and I are traveling posthaste to Southampton from whence we sail for Quebec. Richard positively flourished in Canada catching those little animals—beavers?—the ones they make the hats from, and so we intend to live there for ever and ever, don't we, Richard?"

Her husband started to answer, but before he could, Dulcie asked, "Are you quite certain the baby is mine?"

Elnora frowned. She'd been surprised and disappointed when her friend had failed to ask after the baby when she first arrived. Now Dulcie almost seemed to want to deny the child's existence. "We believe one of them is," Elnora told her, explaining why there were only two babies rather than the three she had mentioned in her earlier letter.

Wade escorted them up the stairs to the nursery where Faith and Charity were asleep in their cribs. Richard Blanding waited by the door while Dulcie hesitated and then gave Elnora a turn by walking slowly to the nearest crib and staring down at Faith.

Elnora bit her lip. *No, not Faith,* she thought, blinking in surprise when she realized that she hoped Dulcie would recognize the other baby as hers. And this after she had insisted that Faith *was* Dulcie's child because they both had green eyes! She had the feeling, admittedly irrational, that Faith belonged to her, not to Dulcie.

Suddenly she recalled how Wade had attempted to steer Seamus O'Neal away from Faith the day before. Was it possible he harbored the same possessive feelings about Faith that she did?

When Dulcie shook her head, turning away from Faith's crib, Elnora sighed with relief. Dulcie looked into the second crib and immediately nodded. "This is Elizabeth, I'd know her anywhere," she cried exultantly, lifting the baby from the crib and cuddling her. "This is Elizabeth, my dearest little love." Charity—now Elizabeth—blinked awake and smiled sleepily at her mother.

Elnora smiled as well, realizing her fears were unfounded, since she recognized the love clearly evident on Dulcie's face.

"I was so afraid," Dulcie said, "afraid I wouldn't find my baby here after all, and so I suppose I tried to postpone this moment." She shook her head. "How foolish of me, but then you know, dear Elnora, how prone I am to being foolish at times. Richard, do come and see our darling baby."

Acting as one, Wade and Elnora looked down at the sleeping Faith. She was neither Violet's child, Elnora thought, nor Dulcie's. The baby had no mother, no father, no one in the world . . .

Later, while she and Wade were alone for a few moments before dinner—Dulcie and her husband were staying at Seacliff Hall until the following day—Wade said, "Seamus O'Neal and now your friend Dulcie and her mute mate seem to have resolved part of our maddening mull, the identity of two of the three babies, only to leave us with another."

Elnora nodded. "What will become of Faith? When she talked to me upstairs, Dulcie seemed on the point of offering to take both of the babies, but I discouraged her."

He raised his eyebrows slightly. "I would have done the same," he admitted.

At the sound of Dulcie's voice in the hall, he hurried on to say, "After giving our quandary considerable thought, I have a suggestion as to how you and I might solve the dilemma."

"And that is?"

He looked decidedly uncomfortable. "You may find my notion unsettling," he said, "so I intend to wait until after Mr. and Mrs. Blanding leave before I tell you."

The next afternoon, following many tearful embraces and amid the fluttering of handkerchiefs, Dulcie, her husband, and their newfound daughter left Seacliff Hall in a hired chaise on their way to Southampton and the Canadian wilderness. Elnora felt sadness at her friend's departure as well as a touch of envy; Dulcie had evidently found both love and happiness.

As soon as the carriage was out of sight, Wade offered her his arm, and she walked with him to the arbor where they sat side by side beneath the season's first blooms of the

311

sweet-scented red roses.

Wade drew forth his watch, appeared to study what the hands revealed—the time, he remarked, lacked twenty minutes of three—then returned the watch to his pocket. He proceeded to adjust the knot of his cravat, which required no adjusting, and then straightened his waistcoat, which needed no straightening.

"The wind off the sea is rising," he said. "The weather seems to be changing."

She nodded, glancing at the mist starting to billow above the cliffs.

"I expect," he said, "that Dulcie and her husband will both be doting parents."

"I agree." She was surprised by his evident unease. What was there in this peaceful garden to perturb a man who had faced Napoleon's cavalry and cannons?

He drew in a deep breath and, taking her hand in his, said, "Do you recall sitting with me in the gazebo a few days ago and my asking whether you were content living here at the Hall?"

She nodded. How could she forget?

"I believe you admitted you had been happy." He paused at the sound of a voice calling faintly from a distance. When the call wasn't repeated, he went on. "Both Aunt Adelaide and myself have observed how genuinely fond you are of Faith. In truth, 'fond' is too mild a word. I should have said we know how much you love the little girl. As all of us do."

"Who could help loving her? Faith may be mischievous, but she's also amiable, quick-witted, charming, and adorable. She's all anyone could ever wish for in a daughter."

"I concur wholeheartedly." He bit his lip, frowned, started to speak, stopped, started once more. "In the last three days," he said, "the nature of the quandary concerning the children has changed considerably."

Again she nodded. Since two of the babies—she still thought of them as Hope and Charity rather than Katherine and Elizabeth—had been reunited with their parents, only the question of Faith's future remained

312

unresolved.

"I admit I was sorely perplexed," Wade said, "so yesterday I rode for what seemed like hours along the cliffs to Tintagel and beyond to give me time to think the matter through. I did and, happily, I reached a satisfying conclusion."

Without a doubt, she told herself, he intended to offer her employment at Seacliff Hall overseeing the care of Faith. Was it possible he believed she had declined his previous overtures because the notion of caring for three babies had overwhelmed her? She could never own to the truth, no matter how much she longed to stay with Faith, would never admit to Wade that she was much too fond of him to risk accepting his offer.

"There is only one perfect solution, and I beseech you to give it the most careful thought," Wade said. "There is only one course of action that will assure Faith's happiness, as well as mine and yours as well, and that is for you, Elnora, to agree to become my wife. Will you? Will you marry me, Elnora?"

She stared at him, dumbstruck. She had secretly dreamed of this moment, of Wade Mathias, Earl of Kendrick, offering for her hand. And now, when she least expected it, he had. With pain in her heart, she realized she must reject him, must refuse what she wanted more than anything in the world.

"As I understand what you said, you want me to marry you for the sake of the child." She drew her hand from his.

He frowned. "As I just now explained—"

"I heard your explanation. You find yourself in a dilemma, and I represent the most convenient way to solve it." Her voice trembled with anger and disappointment, "By marrying me you gain a devoted mother for Faith. You have no doubt my answer will be yes because you happen to be a lord while my father is naught but a clergyman."

Before she finished, he began shaking his head. "No, no, no," he protested. "I don't give a tinker's damn what I am or what your father is. I asked for your hand in marriage, clumsily perhaps, not your father's."

313

She sprang to her feet and stood looking down at him, her eyes glistening with tears. "You ask me to be your wife, but did you speak of love, even of tenderness? No. Do you truly care about me? Me, Elnora Prescott, not Miss Prescott the nursemaid, nanny, governess, or whatever but me, Elnora? No, you do not. You care about yourself, want to make life easier for yourself, more comfortable. You see a way to acquire a companion for the time you happen to be in residence here in the country."

"You misunderstand." He rose, reaching for her hand, but she backed away; he stepped to her, and she turned and ran toward the house, sobbing.

"Elnora!"

His shout only made her run faster. Soon she heard his footfalls thudding on the grass behind her, and she glanced over her shoulder. And almost knocked down Tillie who was rushing toward her.

"Miss Prescott!" the young girl cried. " 'Tis Faith, she's gone."

"Faith?" It took a few moments before Elnora could sort out what Tillie was telling her.

"Where is she?" Wade demanded from behind her.

"She were right there with me playing as sweet as you please," Tillie said, her words coming in a frightened rush as she fought back tears, "and then she wasn't. She was gone in the twinkling of an eye, and I called to her and called to her, and she never answered, so I come for you and Miss Prescott."

Wade grasped her arms. "Where did you see her last?"

"I glanced away to watch the carriage drive off and only took my eyes off her for a second, and she was gone."

"Where, Tillie, where?" Wade demanded.

"Not near them berries, I was ever so careful about that; she was next to the privet hedge."

"The cliff!" Both Elnora and Wade gasped the words at the same time. The cliff edge was less than a quarter of a mile from the other side of the privet hedge.

"We have no time to lose," Wade told them. "Tillie, you

search on this side of the hedge, in the garden, and around the gazebo. Elnora, come with me." He led her to the privet hedge, pushed his way through and then held the branches aside for her as wisps of fog drifting toward them from the direction of the sea dampened her face. "You go that way," he told her, pointing to their right, "while I look in the other direction."

She nodded and set off, calling Faith's name. There was no answer; the only sound was the frightening crash of the surf. Faith couldn't have wandered far, she assured herself, the child had barely learned to walk. How long, she wondered with a tingle of apprehension, had Tillie searched for her before seeking help?

Elnora followed the hedge for a hundred feet without seeing a sign of Faith, so she veered to her left intending to circle back to her starting place. As she walked across the grass, the breeze sent probing tendrils of mist undulating toward her as though a monster from the deep was seeking to coil its tentacles around her and draw her to its lair beneath the sea.

"Faith!" She paused, waiting for an answer but heard nothing over the sound of the waves except Wade and Tillie calling the baby's name.

As she hurried on, the fog thickened. Looking about her she saw only the chimneys of Seacliff Hall protruding above the white shroud of the mist. She called Faith's name again and again; there was no answer.

The fog whirled on all sides of her, enveloping her. She stopped and turned in a full circle, seeking some familiar landmark to guide her back to Wade, but everywhere she looked she saw only the white mist. Even the sun had disappeared. Hesitating only a moment, she stepped forward cautiously, attempting to keep the sound of the surf to her right, all the while calling Faith's name.

She stumbled and fell. While pushing herself to her feet, she found that the ground was rocky, unlike the grassy turf near the hedge. She could see nothing except the enclosing fog; the surf seemed to pound on all sides of her, so even if

315

she called to Faith, she doubted whether the child would be able to hear her.

Above the roar and crash of the waves, she thought she heard a man's voice. Wade? She called his name, again heard the voice, and hastened toward the sound. A figure loomed out of the fog ahead of her, and she ran forward.

Wade caught her in his arms. "Thank God you're safe," he said, "you were almost at the edge of the cliff. If anything had happened to you . . ." He paused, his brown eyes speaking of concern for her and more, much more, making her realize how mistaken she had been, how much he did care for her.

He drew her to him, and when her arms went around his neck, he kissed her, a long and tender kiss. "I love you, Elnora," he whispered, his lips moving against hers. "I think I have from the first day I met you. I know I will until the last day of my life."

"And I love you," she murmured. As he enfolded her in his arms and kissed her fervently, she felt she would die of happiness.

When finally she drew back a little, she asked, "Faith? Have you found her?"

"No," he said, "and we must." Taking her hand, he led her confidently through the mist. After a few minutes the sky around them brightened and then they were out of the fog and into the sunlight with the hedge a few feet in front of them.

"Lord Kendrick!" Tillie ran to them holding Faith in her arms. "She was in the gazebo all the time," she said. "I never thought she could climb them steps. I'm terrible sorry. Please, sir, give me one last chance. I swear I'll never take me eyes off her again."

Elnora, blinking back tears of joy, took the baby, pressing her close, kissing her again and again while Wade enclosed them both in his arms. As though to celebrate Faith's safe return, the bell in the village church began to chime the hour.

Six weeks later the same bell pealed once more, sending

its joyous message across the countryside. Latecomers who had found themselves unable to enter the crowded church clustered around the entrance, shading their eyes from the bright June sun. Suddenly the doors were flung open, and the bride and groom walked from the church to stand side by side at the top of the steps.

A murmur of approval rose from the onlookers as they turned to each other to remark that never had they seen a more handsome couple than Lord Kendrick and his bride. He wore a blue waistcoat, she a white silk gown with a lace-trimmed chemisette at the low neckline. Tiers of ruffles decorated both the bodice and the hem of her long flared skirt. Her mother's white Belgian lace wedding veil was fastened to a coronet of white rosebuds.

"Kiss your bride, milord," someone called.

Wade smiled at Elnora. "They think I need an excuse to kiss you again," he murmured, taking her in his arms. "Little do they know the truth, that I'll never tire of kissing you."

The kiss was greeted by loud huzzahs.

As they walked arm in arm down the steps and along the path toward their waiting landau, a commotion at the church door made them stop and turn.

Faith toddled from the church to the top of the steps, sat down with her feet straight in front of her, then bumped her way step by step to the path. She stood and ran to them.

Elnora held out her arms.

"Mama," Faith cried, "Mama, Mama, Mama."

Elnora lifted her from the ground and hugged her. "Yes," she said, "and your mama loves you dearly."

Faith glanced at Wade. "Da," she said, pointing a chubby finger at him. Wade took her into his arms, kissing her cheek.

"Shall we let her come with us?" Elnora whispered.

Wade nodded, smiling, and they walked to the landau where he shifted the baby to his other arm before handing his wife into the carriage and then joining her.

A vicar from Somerset, stopping to watch the scene out-

317

side the church, raised his eyebrows. "I consider that to be highly irregular," he said to a villager standing next to him, "but I suppose it's better late than never."

Which could easily be the moral of this story, but is not.

The villager, well aware of the facts of the matter but, being by nature rather perverse, chose not to enlighten the stranger, merely remarked, "All's well that ends well."

While certainly appropriate, neither is this the moral of the story.

At that moment a young, overwrought girl ran from the church and frantically pushed her way through the crowd of well-wishers to the door of the landau. "Do you have Faith?" she cried as the carriage started off.

Wade leaned from the window. "Yes, Tillie," he told her, "we do."

Tillie sighed with relief, stepped back, and, taking a handkerchief from her pocket, waved goodbye to the departing couple.

The Somerset vicar nodded. "How wonderful," he said, smiling benignly on one and all. "As I have told my congregation time and time again, faith makes all things possible."

And that is the moral of the story.